PRINCE

PRINCE

IB MICHAEL

TRANSLATED BY BARBARA HAVELAND

PICADOR USA

FARRAR, STRAUS AND GIROUX

NEW YORK

Picador® is a U.S. registered trademark and is used by Farrar, Straus and Giroux under license from Pan Books Limited.

For information on Picador USA Reading Group Guides, as well as ordering, please contact the Trade Marketing department at St. Martin's Press.
Phone: 1-800-221-7945 extension 763
Fax: 212-677-7456
E-mail: trademarketing@stmartins.com

Grateful acknowledgment is made for permission to reprint "Autumn" by Rainer Maria Rilke, from The Book of Images, translation © 1991 by Edward Snow. Reprinted by permission of Farrar, Straus and Giroux.

Designed by Jonathan D. Lippincott

Library of Congress Cataloging-in-Publication Data

Michael, Ib.
    [Prins. English]
    Prince / Ib Michael ; translated by Barbara Haveland.
        p. cm.
    ISBN 0-312-27325-8
    I. Haveland, Barbara.   II. Title.
  PT8176.23.I5P7513   1999
  839.8'1374—dc21   99-32515

First published in Denmark under the title Prins by Gyldendal, Copenhagen

First published in the United States by Farrar, Straus and Giroux

First Picador USA Edition: April 2001

10 9 8 7 6 5 4 3 2 1

To my soul's companion

CONTENTS

PRINCE

IN WHICH
THE SHIP COMES
TO LIGHT

It begins in mist. Far up on the top of the world, where no one sees, the ice splits with a crack that rings out over white fjords. The sea shows blue between the floes; the night that has lasted half the year, with the sun lying below the horizon, is over. The ice rim creaks and groans, fissure chases fissure as a mountain of glass—the size of the palace of fairy tale, with turrets and crenellations and windows long hidden by the snow—breaks off and puts out to sea in howling winds.

The long day has returned.

It rocks on seas running south, is tossed by storms that wash its sides smooth once more while its turrets taper into awls and drip under a sun that climbs the heavens, a little higher with each day.

The palace rests on a foundation of aquamarine shadows. As the heat gains a hold, the ice grows brittle. The water starts to undermine it, outside and in; small lacunae appear, drop by drip it is whittled away. In certain lights it resembles a cathedral with stained-glass windows, round and tall, as the ice forms prisms and breaks up the light. Or it twirls gently in the current to reveal a mosque with onion domes.

Everything floats and the sun wheels in its course. The rifts slice right through; with an echo of the fjord which, after more than half a century's slumber, set the iceberg free, it too calves. A shape comes to light at the heart of it, a darker pattern reminiscent of tattered cobwebs in the palace halls.

Relentlessly the erosion continues. The salt of the sea, days of sunlight, the steadily rising temperature. Like fairy-tale palaces, this one is in fact porous; ever so slowly, as it nears human habitation, it is trickling away of its own accord. But the structure at its heart still stands, the cobwebs hanging now from spars; the palace has altered shape and no turrets now reach skywards.

By the time it leaves the Arctic Ocean and the North Atlantic winds take over, it has become a shadow of itself, a crystal formation, all sharp edges.

These are the next to go. From cathedral to village church, from palace to ruin, the transformation progresses into more rounded contours. The iceberg bobs on the waves like a message in a bottle from wastelands where men and dogs perish. Within the confines of the glass the image is starting to develop. It looks like a ship with a hundred masts.

Ninety-seven of these disappear; they were but reflections in crystal, refractions of the light, particles and impurities within the fabric. But three remain, and three are enough for a ship. A wooden craft with broken masts that have collapsed onto the deck to lie there in a welter of savagely ripped sails and ropes from the rigging.

Still it lies behind glass, but the glass runs with moisture, eaten away to a thinner pane with each day that passes. Details become visible.

The ship appears to have been caught in a gale. The galley

has been smashed to pieces, the cabin lies shattered beneath the spanker, the blades of oars stick out here, there, and everywhere from lifeboats that no living soul had time to launch. Spars and cleats have come adrift, davits have been twisted out of shape, and ventilator cowlings crushed beneath the shrouds.

There are no dead to be seen. Only the shambles they left behind them.

Under the hatches, emptiness and ivory hold sway; in the hold a coffin lies lashed to the foot of the mast. I hear the hooting of a ship in the fog, wake, stretch, and give a great yawn in these cramped quarters so reminiscent of a bunk. We are approaching a foreign coastline. One by one, foghorn answers foghorn.

IN WHICH
TIME BEGINS

I see a boy. Hard to say how old he is, I'm no expert on children; but he is at the age when the wonder is great and the grief, when something breaks, devastating. The beach is fraught with wind and the world cuts right through him as he comes tearing around the bend, all dog roses, sandy track, and farmsteads, and suddenly finds himself, out of breath, by the sea. It is the best bend in the world and he flies around it with his arms spread into wings.

Farther on, beyond the cliff that rears up, crowned by windblown tufts of sedge and lyme grass, stands the lighthouse. The lighthouse at the end of the world. A delft-blue cap is all that can be seen, sticking up above the cliff side with its drifting sands and foxes' lairs; spy holes in the whitewashed tower and glass all the way around carry the light across white nights in which birds never cease to sing, while the day hovers and grows thin on the horizon.

The sea holds him transfixed. It knocks the feet from under him, whether it is stretching glassy calm as far as the eye can see or thundering against cliff faces and stone dikes that shatter its teeth. A sea that devours sailors and crushes their spirits like eggshells. He can hear it—even when he is asleep in his berth with the timbered walls and the window that lets in the white sky. Distant thunder murmurs when he puts his ear to the wall. He lives in a conch of a house, and the windowsill is spread with his collection of seashells and pebbles.

Nor do I know what place this is, though I have—in my time—seen many like it. A fishing village, with boats on the beach, stones, rollers, and a winch for hauling the boats out of the water. The winch is turned by a fishing stake that has been washed ashore, scoured white, and saturated with saltwater that lends its weight to the wood. It takes one man to brace his chest against the stake, another to keep the dinghy on an even keel as it runs up onto the rollers. Fishing nets are hung out to dry and when the sun hits the live-boxes the airholes shine like silver coins.

Summer clothes have changed since my day; lacy flounces flap about the legs of the women, who wear flat bonnets of straw, with streamers of ribbon fluttering from them. The gentlemen sport walking sticks and waistcoats on the beach, watch chains draped from their pockets across their stomachs. They wear light-colored suits on summer evenings.

It is the boy who has dreamed me up: a secret playmate, the sort born when children play too long under the full moon. He carries on long conversations with me when we are alone. The boy is alone a lot. We are alike, we two. He has furnished me with a fearless name, whiskers, and a ring in one ear. I have been to every corner of the globe and stand tall in the world of men, a head higher than most. Above all, I am always there when he needs me.

He is a summer boarder. At a guest house called Sea View, which nestles in the front row of dunes running down to the sea. He sleeps in the attic, in the gabled room above the servants' quarters. It is a linen room and otherwise bare. Here he has his bunk bed. Above him the bunks are piled high with quilts. Below him the chamber pot. For the rest there are cupboards and chests of drawers, sheets, comforter covers, and neatly folded tea towels. And tucked between them, bags of naphthalene crystals. The rough floorboards are strewn with little lumps of plaster that crunch when he steps on them. The dust does not bother him—not as long as it is dancing in the sunbeams that stream through the attic window.

Sea View is yellow-washed, thatched with sun-ripened straw, and hedged about with brier roses. One wing has been given over to guest rooms. There are bluebells on the wallpaper, a marble top to the washstand, and a mirror with a shelf. At the top of the mirror, the frame curves into a gilded Greek vase; in the washbasin float sprigs of lavender that are changed every morning and fill the room with their pungent scent.

The main building houses the dining room with a white grand piano at one end, the kitchen and pantry, and, in an adjoining room, the captain's saloon. The hall is dominated by a large Venetian mirror, hallstand, and bureau. The bureau is painted with bunches of violets and red ribbons, the hallstand hung with the guests' summer hats. Clothes brushes are laid out on the glass shelf in front of the mirror, a shoehorn hangs down at the side, and the floor is taken up by bootjack, umbrella stand, and overshoes.

Above the captain's saloon, overlooking the sea, is an open veranda of wood, its boards creosoted. On sunny days the balustrade bubbles and fills the air with the scent of resin. Throughout the summer season, deck chairs are put out and each evening before sunset the cushions have to be taken in. On gray days we have the veranda to ourselves. We sit in the bare deck chairs, study our feet, and tell each other stories.

I can see right inside his head when he talks, as if his skull were made of glass—green glass, like the balls the fishermen use for their nets. He has a ship there, a frigate from the days when steam and sail took turns. You can tell by the tall funnel positioned between the masts. The bowsprit rears up, along with jib, foresail, and flying jib. When he gets excited, the rigging blazes with Saint Elmo's fire and bluish sparks encircle it.

I tell him of the harbor in Surabaya, where the boats have eyes painted on their bows so that they look like sea monsters, and the streets are full of boys his age running around pulling rickshaws. He can roll a name like the Sunda Strait around his tongue for hours without tiring of it, reel off the volcanoes of Indonesia, round Tafel Hoek in the dark, and come ashore on coastlines where the great turtles have buried their eggs in the sand.

On Komodo he puts his ear to giant lizards that could eat a man whole; he accompanies me to a street circus in Shanghai, where coolies with naked, sun-wizened torsos swallow live snakes and send them shooting out of their mouths again on tongues of flame, stroking their limbs with lit torches all the while. We eat meat on skewers, dipping it in bowls of *satay*, and fiery chili peppers burn holes in our throats and turn us, too, into fire-eaters.

He sees a monkey chained to a platform the size of a bird feeder and frets over the rattle wrung from the chain by each restless movement. When he goes to feed it a banana, something unknown in his world, it bites his hand and he throws down the fruit in fright. Out of reach of the monkey. The expression in its eyes makes us laugh, and the boy sucks at his wound and feels the first touch of wonder at a pain that is mingled with delight, though it springs from the same source.

He is with me in Zanzibar, where the clove tree scents the whole island when it blooms. Where the blacks shout

"Jambo!" and old men with ash-white curls clamber about in the tops of palm trees, nimble as monkeys, collecting coconuts. Where I was set on a throne made out of the jawbone of a sperm whale and given one of its vertebrae for a footstool. Where I dived in the realm of the dolphins and the school's chief female reared up onto her tail fin, opened her bill, and sent a stream of sounds warbling through the water at me like the singing of sirens. I reached out my arm and her nose nudged my finger. At that moment a spark leapt from God to Adam, I rose up and became a man unlike any other. That was before I fell, Malte, and my light went up in flames. Then they called me the very Devil himself and mistook my endeavors.

He nods and yawns heavily, soon he will slip away from me, and when the turmoil of his dreams overtakes him I see the ship light up behind his eyelids and take on a bluish cast. I am alone with my echo, watching over his slumber until the dawn.

There are nights when he suddenly sits up in bed, swings his legs out over the edge of the bunk, and tags along behind, feet shuffling mechanically across the floor. The boy walks in his sleep. One night he walks through the French windows, which some guest has forgotten to close, out to where the garden runs into sand and lyme grass, and on down to the beach by way of the roses' winding path.

I follow him at a suitable distance. He is dangerously close to the breakers, one with the darkness in his blue-striped pajamas, the ship alone rocking with its ghostly light over the waves. With eyes that see nothing, he gazes out to sea—until the lighthouse flashes and the small figure on the beach gives a start. In the instant, that same sensation strikes at me, like spindrift on skin, and I dart forward and grab his hand.

There is saltwater on the boy's eyelashes, he is awake now and afraid of the darkness he has just passed through. I lead him back along the path to the house. Grateful, he turns his face up to mine, breathes easily only after I have him back under the eiderdown and tuck it in well at his sides. Everyone has the right to an angel, I whisper from my point in space. His eyes close. In the morning, when he wakes, he will have no memory of his nocturnal foray. It will merge with his dreams.

He spends his days on the sands. The strong light on the beach makes his head reel. His body is gypsy-brown, his trunks wet from rolling around in the shallows. He builds, gathers pebbles and shells, breaches the moat wall, and lets the water run into channels he has dug with his fingers. He finds sticks and fits them with pennants of seaweed. He catches crabs and pops them into jelly jars, feeds them beach fleas, and tips them out as the day is drawing to a close. Or else he lays starfish in the bottom of the jar and holds them up to the sky. Slowly he turns in a circle, leaving a wreath of sunflower petals in the sand with the soles of his feet, puts his eye to the bottom, and uses the jelly jar as a stargazer. Dissolved in light, he watches the galaxies whirling through space.

He takes his meals with the adults in the guest-house dining room. Three times daily, young Oda, the housemaid, strikes the gong with a padded hammer and calls the guests to table. Minding his manners, but with his thoughts as far away as any spaceship, he forgets half their questions and the rest he answers so vaguely that they leave him to his own devices and pick up the threads of a conversation that has no beginning and no end. It summons up faces that talk and listen by turns, serves no other purpose.

When new people arrive at the guest house, it is not unknown for the widow Swan to come bustling out from the kitchens to greet them. Then she will put her arm around him and introduce him to the new arrivals. "This is Malte, my summer boy!" she says, and squashes his nose flat against her apron pocket. She smells of pastry and margarine. Sometimes he gets flour on his cheeks and clothes and has to be brushed off.

Mrs. Swan inherited the guest house from her late husband. She makes berry custards, rose-hip jam, fish terrines, soup, and roasts. Serves up bowls of curds and cream for breakfast, bakes rye bread and reuses the crumbs, which she mixes with brown sugar and sprinkles over the curds, over the yellow skin that makes his stomach turn. His standard approach is to bury it in the sugary crumbs, then shut his eyes and puncture the skin with his spoon.

As long as he keeps his eyes shut, it slips down all right. Under the skin, the curds are white and glistening. The spoon is the icebreaker and his lips supply the sound effects as the floes are plowed up.

If the sun is shining in a clear blue sky he spends the rest of the day chasing the orb of the sun, and when the light has baked him blue and the surf tossed him about, he heads for the opening in the cliff to find shade and feel goosebumps on his skin again.

He has found a fox's lair with cubs in it, and he brings them leftovers from the dinner table: chicken bones garnished with paper frills, heel ends of ham, the rind turned to caramel in the mesh in which it was bound. He can hear the cubs down there in the darkness, yapping and whining as they poke their noses into these tasty morsels, growling and snapping at one another's fur.

He walks home along the cliff top, balancing at the rim, where the soil has crumbled away and ruffs of grass jut out precariously into space. Far below, the silt churns. Pebbles and gravel plummet into the depths. You hear no splash, only the distant sigh of the sea, and from up here the foam does not look real. He walks along with his tongue stuck in the corner of his mouth; then he stops, slowly raises one leg and both arms, and teeters—deliberately—on the edge of the world. Just as he is about to fall, the roar of the wind swells in his ear. He does not know why, but he carries the seeds of that fall in his belly.

IN WHICH
IT RAINS

Rainy days we while away in the captain's saloon. Not that Sigurd Swan was ever a sea captain during his time on this earth, but he was a great admirer of seafaring folk and fitted out the parlor with the big tiled corner stove, with brass lamps, compass roses, and a barometer. When the guest-house business picked up, chesterfield sofas were introduced and capacious armchairs, a sextant on the windowsill, and ashtrays in the shape of ship's wheels with mahogany rims in which a woodcarver had etched the words *Sea View*, flanked by two pennants.

The desk has stood just so ever since his day—nothing new has been added. The jar for shag tobacco and the pipe stand are in place, like the roll of blotting paper, the inkwell with the hinged lid and the double *S* of his initials engraved in the silver. The *Ss* make the lid look like that of a saltcellar.

The desk pad is edged with gilt leather, the drawers are reinforced with iron struts and fitted with locks; tucked away behind the right-hand door is a safe. This is where Mrs. Swan does her accounts, sticking bills on a steel spike and writing out new ones. She does the dusting herself, and each time she comes to the model of a tall ship in the middle of the bookcase, she stops for a word or two with her husband. Her tone is chatty, her talk full of doings great and small—mostly the latter. Occasionally, he gets the sharp edge of her tongue. When things are threatening to get the best of her, that is.

Sigurd Swan has grown so small since he died. He sits there all curled up in the fo'c'sle when his wife flies off the handle and gives him an earful. At other times he stands on the bridge wearing a white cap; with the megaphone to his lips he issues directions to his crew in a race that is run halfway around the globe, from Ceylon to London Bridge. The ship is a model of one of those tea clippers for which the century was famed.

We sit amid the books in the saloon, though we never take them off the shelves. Outside, the rain rattles against the windowpanes, and when there's a wind, it seeps in and forms little puddles around the potted plants.

Malte is a good listener; it takes no time to transport him to the rain forest, where we set out from Iquitos—jewel of the Amazon—on the deck of a paddle steamer crowded with swaying hammocks and black-eyed natives. I have a pistol at my belt and a knife down the side of my boot, because all hell breaks loose when the blood starts to boil.

The boy loves the part where the paddles have stopped turning and the steamer is drifting with the current, deeper into the jungle, while everyone is silent, casting fearful glances toward the riverbank. The river is wide as the ocean at this point, the opposite bank far out of eyeshot.

The treetops echo with the screeching of birds; through the green shadows move figures clad in earthen hues. Hair and faces are smeared with a red paste made from legumes mixed with resin. Over their shoulders they carry long blowpipes, with a quiverful of arrows apiece, the shafts tipped with a wisp of cotton and the heads dipped in a poison black as tar. Silently they follow our progress from their secret paths through the forest, paths indistinguishable from the tracks of wild animals. But they do nothing. They keep an eye on us, they do not interfere. The world through which we are traveling is not theirs.

We are caught by the current. Faster and faster it runs after the first swirl, and we spin on our own keel as we surge toward the falls farther downstream, and the riverboat captain and his men sweat oil in their efforts to restart the engine. It is clear to crew and passengers alike that we will be smashed to pieces on the rocks if they don't succeed. The riverbank flashes past our eyes like a kaleidoscope, inducing nausea and dizziness.

Down comes the rain, ropes of rain that cause the river to rise. By now the waters around us are in total ferment. Then all at once everything is swathed in cloud. There is no thunder to be heard, but bolt after bolt of lightning rents the horizon from end to end, and to judge by the other passengers, their prayers and screams, the Flood itself must have opened the sluice gates. I dig my nails into the rail, tight-lipped and with eyes lashed to slits by the tropical downpour. It came on so suddenly that I am still gasping for breath.

At one point it strikes me that we have stopped spinning. Indeed, it feels as if a sure hand has seized hold of the keel and is steering us through the waters at a steady clip. Gradually it dawns on us that we are over the falls, the seething rocks have disappeared, that's how much the river has risen. Above the rocks, the whirlpools are visible, but they have lost their bite and no longer present any threat to the steamer.

I loosen my grip on the rail. We still have no engine power, no smoke signals issue from the funnel, and the paddle wheels are not turning. In the wheelhouse I can see the captain spreading his arms as he turns to his enormous stoker.

Hands gripping the wheel, he indicates that he has lost control—or, rather, the boat is steering itself. One by one the terror-stricken passengers raise their eyes from their prayers and rosaries and, crossing themselves one last time, get to their feet. The storm has abated but we are sailing on a different river. We have crossed the falls into another world . . .

Malte sighs. He knows what is coming.

We sail on for days and days, holding a steady course, carried along by the current's own magic. The river is still rising. All around us now is a Garden of Eden, with long-tailed parrots swooping over the treetops and the shifting yellow and black of the jaguar glimpsed between the trunks. There are companies of monkeys and herds of animals; tapir and deer graze in meadows and clearings, while wild boar root up the earth.

Amazingly, we watch them through trees up to their crowns in water. We see lily pads that could take the weight of a man, and tropical flowers open before our eye to display hues and stamens that no living soul would believe. Beetles big as a hand fly to and fro, bearing the outline of a death's-head on their backs; at night these airborne skulls glow green. Creepers run along branches decked with red and yellow scales, cushions of moss fill spots through which the sky used to peek, parasitic plants ooze forth and by the next day are hanging in garlands and falling in curtains of gothic impenetrability over the forest.

From our hammocks, hour by hour, day after day, we witness the transformation. We live on bananas from the hold, coconuts, rice, and manioc. Like everyone else on board, I am seized by a mood akin to intoxication. Unicorns might appear between the trees at any minute, at dusk the air is filled with white clouds of mist that wrap a veil around the steamer. At night we are guided over the hushed silvering of the river by will-o'-the-wisps. That vessel which once coughed cinders out of its funnel and spattered everything with mud from its paddles bobs now like a swan on the surface of the water.

The banks close in, meeting over our heads to form a tunnel. We round a point and the stream branches out into arms and tributaries; on we drift beneath the leafy canopy of creepers, heading into the heart of the primeval forest, where only legend has gone before us.

We no longer dream of moldering temples or gold and treasure. We dream of the unknown, of things beyond our imagining. One day we wake to find that the water level is starting to fall again. Before us, the arm of the river widens and, rocking on waves that are now flowing more swiftly, we bear down on the bend up ahead. The haze lifts off the water in white rainbows; beyond that the eye cannot see.

We glide into the bend and out into another light. What a sight! We flock to the port side and the paddle steamer—named after a saint, I have forgotten which—lists under our collective weight. An ethereal piping—imagine the sound of songbirds under water—falls on our ears, filters all the way through to the body's pleasure centers and makes the bones thrill to the sirens' song. A pair of long-nosed dolphins have been left stranded on the branches of the trees when the river dropped. Like fabulous storks, they clack their beaks.

It is then that we see the Indians for the first time. They are working their way up the trees, carrying nets woven from willows; they look as if they mean to free these large songbirds that live underwater—and in the tales they tell their children. Some of the passengers think they are doing it for the meat, but then why would they need the nets? And from the sea I know that no decent human being will eat a dolphin. There is an age-old pact, the origins of which we have forgotten.

The current wheels us around and we leave this scene behind. The banks have receded into the distance once more, we are out in the middle of the channel. We are still surrounded on all sides by water, but the natives are sniffing the air and exchanging glances. What now? In the distance, a bustle of activity, a thrum that has nothing to do with the forest. This is where the sailor in me climbs aloft to look ahead. For the first time in the voyage I am struck dumb.

Ahead, the river reflects a broad, many-branched delta. A town has come into view: huts perched on stilts in the marshy landscape, with dugout canoes moored to the stilts. Then white houses, supernaturally white; nonetheless, this is Iquitos, the place from which we set out! I recognize the cathedral with its bell tower, and even as I do so, I hear the men shouting from the deck and the wheelhouse.

We are simply sailing into the town from the other side, more upriver. The current has led us in circles. There is an hour to go until sundown, at which time we will tie up at the quayside from where our journey began. Perhaps it will begin all over again tomorrow, perhaps none of it ever happened. What, then, is time? And who are we, returning in an altered light? Have we any way of knowing, when the bells ring for sunset and we have reached a point in the stream that we have passed before?

I just ask, Malte. You do not need to answer.

The boy looks away. His eyes search the shelf containing the English tobacco tins and stop, as so often before, at the silhouette of the Indian. Outside, the rain pours down, lyme grass and rosebushes are drowned in cloud. On the dunes the sand has turned gray. It looks as if the rain will go on all day. Buried in armchair and sofa, we let our minds wander as we study our socks. Malte puts his feet up. Before very long, he is taking his afternoon nap, and I lay the crocheted throw over him. When the ship lights up and the skin of his face begins to glow, I know that he has found the answers to questions he will not recall when he awakes.

4

IN WHICH
A SAILOR IS
WASHED ASHORE

The days pass. There comes a morning when the fox's lair lies deserted and only the smell remains. The boy tries to shine a light inside. He strikes match after match but burns his fingers before he can make anything out. It is strange underground, the air is damp and catches in the throat. The darkness stretches out, filled with all the things his eye cannot see. His nostrils contract and his pupils expand.

Bird skulls with beaks, the wings' collection of bony shafts, skulls and corpses complete with hair and brown nails. His fingers run up against something, a rusty clamp in the loam.

The boy shudders. Feels gravel running down inside his collar as he pulls his head back. He rubs his fingers on the grass to wipe off the gunk, jumps up, and all but keels over again as everything goes black—echo of the darkness that will not loosen its hold on the nape of his neck. He feels steeped in the stupefying stench of burial mounds; the earth has chambers in which white coffins lie tier upon tier with only the gravestone sticking up as a seamark.

He takes the path up to the lighthouse. Brushes his shirt and trousers to get rid of the sour reek, his breath coming in gasps. He bends down to pick up a stick and swipes at the lyme grass; a breeze runs over the crest of the hill and had he my eyes he would see a chorus of spirits wafting outward with the fans of grass. He calms down as he nears the lighthouse, stops at the garden gate overrun with briers. Hangs back a bit before lifting the latch and letting himself in. The lighthouse keeper has become the one friend among the living in whom he confides. He throws back his head and calls up to the tower.

Shortly he hears the stairs creak, a pause at the door handle.

"Is that you, Malte?"

The boy nods. The pause is prolonged before the door opens and the lighthouse keeper appears in his fisherman's sweater and smock, chewing on his stubby pipe. He regards Malte with eyes that crinkle at the corners, puffs out smoke rings.

"Why didn't you answer?"

Malte does not think about such things. The words just stay inside him while he nods. Afterwards he thinks he has said them. Olesen, the lighthouse keeper, strokes his goatee and steps aside, a giant in wooden shoes, to allow Malte to squeeze past. The clogs on his feet clatter all the way up the spiral staircase inside the tower. He and the boy do the rounds, inspecting the big reflector as they go. Malte is allowed to wash the night's harvest of insects off the lantern windows. Then they have tea and cookies in the lighthouse keeper's sitting room; they talk about the old days, when the people on Wrecker's Hill lit fires for ships, causing them to run aground on the sharp rocks of the reef.

Shipwrecked sailors were dispatched with boat hooks and clubs, the ships plundered. The men's bodies were hidden on the cliffs and when the moon is full you can hear them wailing before they leave the ground and show themselves over the waves in the shape of sea mist. A mist that can be hard to tell apart from the fog and that—should it creep over one's threshold—brings sickness and bad luck to the house before the next new moon. So people said back then; the keeper thinks it is all a load of hogwash: sleet is sleet and the garden gate bangs; the dead rest in their graves and it would take more than a smattering of mist to drive him off the deep end.

The boy nods again and thinks his own thoughts. There it is again, that mirror which splits him in two. Olesen must surely imagine that he is agreeing with him, but in actual fact Malte's repeated nodding is bound up with the images he has carried away with him from the fox's lair, where the skull of a Portuguese sailor and a sheared-off boat hook speak the same language. The lighthouse keeper has set down his pipe and turned to munching on cookies that he first dunks in his tea. Malte does the same. It feels good, even if Malte has all his own teeth. The sugar crystals go all slick at the edges, the vanilla rings turn soft and mushy, and the crunch does not come until almost to the hole at the center. Malte swallows; cookies make his fear of ghosts taste sweet.

"Well, Malte, and what have you been up to?"

The boy splutters a mouthful of tea back into his cup. He chokes on the answer; with us, silence is what counts, but in the lighthouse keeper's sitting room words rule. Malte says nothing of the den, tells instead about his morning round of the farms to collect eggs and vegetables.

"Can I see the ship?"

It is a standard ritual, the question with which Malte cuts short each and every one of his breathless accounts. The keeper clatters over to the shelf and takes down the ship. He built it himself, inside a bottle that is blue and sealed with wax. You can see the cliff and the lighthouse, a little jetty running out

into the water, and the cottage in which they are sitting. The
sea is of painted putty and the sky behind the ship suggested by
a few white brush strokes. Those are the clouds. The rest of the
space is taken up by the ship. A full-rigger, with windlass and
rope ladders of sewing thread radiating down from the mast
like a spider's web.

The lighthouse keeper shows him a brush, the hairs bent at
an angle to enable him to paint inside the bottle. Then together
they step out to the workshop, where Olesen has a ship on the
stocks. He glues the funnel and the paddles onto the body, then
feeds it through the neck of the bottle and, pulling ingeniously
on the strings, raises the rigging. The ship is made of balsa-
wood, freshly painted, and it smells of glue. Malte's face
glows; the ship looks exactly like the riverboat from the delta
of his dreams.

The bottle is potbellied; bubbles caught in the glass distort
the details and make the waves rise and fall when he squints.
Affixed to the front of the funnel is a real steam whistle, and a
figurehead in the form of a mermaid has been positioned beneath the bowsprit. Malte devours it all with famished eyes; he
watches how the keeper inserts the cork and trims it with a
sheath knife, working it around the bottle neck with his thumb.
He lifts a stick of sealing wax, heats it over the tinder flame until it starts to bubble. Three sizzling globules drip onto the cork.
Finally, the keeper takes a block of wood and presses down on
the seal as it hardens.

He winks at Malte, keeping his weight on the block a while
longer. Then he removes it. Malte leans forward to take a look;
he gives a little cry. An *M* has appeared in the red wax. The
keeper holds the ship out to him.

"It's yours," he says, and lights his pipe. "If you want it,
that is!"

This last comes burbling out of his mouth amid clouds of

smoke. His eyes narrow into slits as he says it. Malte is dumb-
struck. He takes hold of the ship from the bottom, weighs it between his hands. He shuts his eyes and opens them again. The
steamer lies bathed in reflections behind the curved glass walls;
gingerly he balances it on the palms of his hands and starts
to form sounds as he rocks the ship back and forth. First a
spluttering, then a stuttering works its way over his lips to
end as "Thank you." He has ground his toes deep into the
sawdust.

Malte races home with a shining egg in his arms, the clouds
scudding beneath his feet. He charges through the dunes and I
do not dare to think what will happen if he should fall now and
crack the shell. But, old salt that I am, I know that the harder
one runs at luck, the better it holds. That is how I earned my
wings.

We land in the deck chairs at the same moment—he in his
and I in mine. We have the sea view to ourselves; no one else
wants it, for the wind has turned and is blowing the clouds inland. It is warm. Thunder is brewing and the swallows swoop
low, but the air is balmy.

He shows me the ship in the bottle and straightway has to
be told that this is how it looked, exactly like this, the paddle
steamer that drifted about in the heart of the Amazon, steered
by a naiad. Wisely, I keep to myself the memory of what an old
tub it was.

We do not talk about the clouds; we watch them form with
the same eyes and they turn to smoke in our brains, as the wind
drives them on. They are shaped by the rays of light into
clamshells in the sky. The sun is hidden by cloud, the horizon
merges with the sea, and the line that divides our world is

erased by pearl-gray mist. Out of the mist a glowing orb materializes. The day is drawing to a close.

Suddenly it is evening. The last hour swoops past on swallow's wings and the fields stretch away behind Sea View, waving with corn and poppies. A rumble sounds from the seaward side. The row of fishing stakes now runs all the way out to the skyline, where the light is fading to a more somber spectrum. The flat calm amplifies the sound of the thunder rolling in with the clouds, but there are no flashes of lightning, only an oppressive feeling around the chest. The same pressure that has smoothed out the breakers and grounded the insects in their flight.

The air is cool after the heat of the day. The boy senses my presence but not my unease. After all, I know what is coming; he is simply waiting for the first flash of lightning so he can count the seconds till the thunderclap. Sight and sound part the waters; emanating from the same source, each is subject to its own delay. I introduced him to this marvel early one morning when the fishermen were hammering in the fishing stakes. He saw the blow strike in utter silence, then the sound follow like an echo of his vision.

Foreknowledge is founded on the same principles—all time is but an echo of something that has already taken place. So with the light—it is like the waves on the ocean. The individual particles go nowhere; in other words, light has no speed. It is nothing but the echo effect of one primary cause! For such as me, the universe—with its star clusters, spiral nebulae, and distances measured in light-years—is no bigger than the head of a pin. But you might as well know now, Malte, it's not something that can ever bring you joy.

Nonetheless, you seem to know how to feel joy, where others feel sorrow. Your ship could fall apart: one day the bottle might be shattered and the genie flown. Then you could call yourself Sinbad the Sailor and set yourself to figuring out how the egg of eternity will be broken.

The boy nods. He is not listening. And before the thunder breaks, the gong has called him down to the dinner table. I am left alone with the seething of my thoughts; then at long last the clouds break open and drench them in rain. There is no need to count, for the thunder crashes directly above the guest house and settles with a chirr in the glass panes of the veranda door just as the flash lights it.

I have leapt to my feet and pace back and forth, sweeping the length of the balustrade like a restless hound, while lightning bolt unleashes lightning bolt from the sky and illumines the countryside in stark chiaroscuro. I see the bolts strike the water, I gaze out to sea in the direction of what is to come. There is a whiff of burnt sulfur in the air. The boy has asked to be excused and is tucked up in bed when the storm passes over, fading to an ever more distant rumble.

The clouds part. Full moon. Like opening the oyster and finding the sun transformed into a pearl of cool light. It is blowing hard out there, riffles run toward the shore. And while the boy tosses restlessly in his bunk, talking in his sleep and kicking off his eiderdown, his ship sits on the windowsill among shells and stones and draws moonbeams to it. I prepare myself for the long night ahead.

The dog watch has begun.

Hours have passed and my shadow hunches over the balustrade; from the veranda I peer out into the night. A good lookout, that's the sailor's first commandment, as my old friend the captain always said. The wind grazes my forehead and slips in under my brows with cooling breath. When the lighthouse beam sweeps across the silken sheet of the sea I catch the first glimpse. Far out on the open sea, where the riffles have swollen into billows that rush to shore, the coffin heaves into sight. It could be taken for a capsized dinghy, floating bottom-up. The lid arches, reflections striking off the varnished surface, and mirrors the stars in the heavens as the front end dips and rides in on the wave.

The coffin, black-seeming under the silver plating of the reflections, heels over in the swell. The water has seeped in, making it list. With each nudge of the waves it drifts toward land, with every sweep of the lighthouse beam drawing a hairbreadth closer to the shore. It grows in magnitude, shutting out all else—so long have I known that it was on its way.

The details are only visible in snatches, when the lighthouse beam illuminates the mahogany casket as it floats, pitching at an angle. A cross has been carved in high relief on the lid. When the groundswell washes over the cross, it grows sinuous in form, resembling a sea monster risen from the deep. In his bunk the boy has started up; he sits bolt upright in the narrow confines of the room and listens in the dark.

With a rasp the coffin runs aground. It snags on the first reef, bobs over stones, clamshells, and bladder wrack. The tide is out; the shore lies exposed, dotted with rock pools, and the earth has many moons tonight, all mirrored in the pools. When the boy appears at the veranda door, his hair disheveled by nightmare, I stroke his brow until his eyes droop shut once more. I lead him through the darkened rooms, turn on a nightlight in his bunk, and help him up the ladder.

Before I leave, I look about me for a toy animal or something like that to wrap his arms around—in the end it is the pillow that he hugs to the point of oblivion while his breathing wavers. One minute it is coming in long, guttural wheezes, then it kicks in again to the accompaniment of small twitches and flailing feet. I stay with him until he settles down.

Good Lord, it is no more than a respite, but then so is all sleep. Until the last.

The veranda door rattles in the blast. He has forgotten to shut it behind him. The stairs creak as I steal down and out into the front garden. I linger by the gate; if anyone were to see me, they would be bound to think I was a ghost. But no one else is out walking in the night. I turn onto the path leading down to the churchyard and disappear into the chapel.

Day breaks over the church down.

The boy is up with the first crow of the cock, and out the door like a gust of wind. He has built himself a kite out of flower canes and the paper from the butter crock. The bows for the tail are made of pages from the newspaper, and the gardener has given him a reel of string. He races through the dunes with the sand drifting at his heels, trying to launch it. The kite crashes to the ground, scaring a seagull, which flies up from a fish skeleton, the head as yet intact, and wheels lazily through the air that the boy has reached out to with his flimsy construction. He tries again and the kite flaps in his face. Seagull cries sound far above his head—high and full of wonder.

Then suddenly he has it. The beating turns to a high-strung whoosh, the line arcs over the hilltops and the kite climbs. Malte follows it, holding his breath as it plunges into the sky. It dwindles to the size of a licorice lozenge, and still he has some string on his reel. He almost begins to feel anxious, it is flying so high; the tail makes sounds he can no longer hear. The kite is a piece of himself sailing up there, dizzyingly high above the lyme grass.

He high-steps it, head thrown back to follow the kite's flight. What if it scratches the sky's seagull porcelain; he bites his lip to stop from laughing, wrinkles his brow, and shoos away the thought. The line gives a tug, a headlong tug that drags him with it. The kite is making for the sea and Malte stumbles after it. The paper, shiny with grease from the crock, sends long flashes down over his head.

All at once the line goes slack and the kite dives. He tries to run, reeling in the string as he goes. It has made him ring with delight, it must not fall now. As soon as he feels resistance, he regains control. Step by step, tongue between his teeth, he walks it away from the beach, the kite starting to turn figure eights.

Again it dips perilously low, the tail snapping and the cross of flower canes showing bright through the paper. Intent, he grapples with the line. At the last minute he manages to check its dive into that watery element which mirrors the sky in films of blue.

Which is why he does not see what he bumps into, and when he does notice it, he lets go of the kite and watches it flap about in fright before it comes crashing down. The tide has lifted the coffin off the reef and up onto the shore. It looks like a shipwreck, one side buried in the sand. Openmouthed in disbelief, he takes in the brass handles and the gaping lid. He stands on tiptoe to peek over the side, he cannot help himself. The coffin is full of water. A wreath of wild flowers floats to the surface, covering the man's face.

5

IN WHICH
THE SAILOR
DANCES A JIG

Malte pulls his nose back. The caustic fumes from the open casket make him wince; he hears a shout and whirls around. But there is no one there; the cry is but an echo of his own. Once it has escaped him, he is left feeling hollow and jangling inside; tears sting his eyes and he tries to swallow. The scent of putrid flower water drifts upward. Level with his lips, the air starts to fill out. He tries again but is still unable to swallow. He walks backward, one step as if in a trance, the next landing in a puddle. He stands there, rooted to the spot, as the water creeps up around his ankles.

A wave running onto the shore strikes the coffin. The wreck sinks a few inches more in the backwash, lists ominously to the boy's side, and disgorges some of its contents. Sounds come from the wood; the nails creak like strings being tightened with a tuning key. The hole in which he is standing sucks at his feet. He struggles to free himself from the quicksand, everything starts to slide, the sky reels above his head, riven by seagull cries, and beyond the surf the fishing stakes heave and strain frantically. He pulls himself free, leaving one shoe stuck in the hole.

Malte bolts. He hates adults who dunk him underwater, jumping up and down first with a one and a two and a three . . . Worst of all are the ones who put a hand on his head and force him to stay under to a count of ten. That really makes him blow his top; he kicks and punches and tears at their bathing suits when he shoots back up from the cold terror below. It is this same fury that propels him now. In stocking feet and squelching shoe he careers through the meadow thistles with never a thought for their flaming barbs. The wind is in his teeth as he runs up against it.

Panting for breath, he reaches the light. It is out now, having flashed all night, and the lighthouse keeper has turned in. Malte limps the last bit of the way past the pump, where the yard is bumpy with cobblestones. He opens the door of the cottage and finds his way to Olesen's cubbyhole with its pallet and chamber pot.

The keeper's snores fill the room. He has gone to bed in his fisherman's sweater and smock; his cap hangs from its hook and his clogs gape beneath the bed. The eiderdown smells of breakwaters; it is stained with tar from his pipe, which lies at hand by the headboard, along with an oilcloth tobacco pouch and a box of matches. Light and watery reflections flood through the windowpane. Small as Malte is, he feels as if he has landed in a live-box.

Gently he pokes the slumbering man. "Mr. Olesen . . ."

The lighthouse keeper jumps at his touch; grunting like a walrus, the bulky figure rolls over in the bed. The keeper is used to being roused. The first thing he does is to reach for his pipe. He swings his legs over the side, gropes with toes clad in woollen socks for his clogs. Having got his pipe lit and puffed out the first clouds of smoke, he scratches behind his ear with the tip of the brier stem.

"Well, what's up, boy? Anyone would think the devil was on your tail."

Malte is breathless. Breathless and exhausted. His chest rises and falls as he struggles to get the words out. But he is no longer afraid. He brightens up, as the big man's presence shunts the fear down a side track. There is a czar in the room, and Malte is courier to the czar.

He tells him about the beached coffin. Behind the stuttered words, his story takes shape, and grumbling in his throat, the lighthouse keeper digests it. He hears Malte out, although there is a glint of skepticism in the corner of his eye.

"Come on!"

Malte tugs at his sleeve, pulling him out into the yard and over to the tower. They climb aloft and out onto the gallery and Malte leans over the balustrade and points down to the shoreline, way over on the other side of the cliff. Rust flakes off the balustrade and sifts into space. The keeper's eyes narrow as he makes out the stranded shape through the shimmer. From the lighthouse the coffin looks like a piece of doll's house furniture.

"Well, I'll be darned," he puffs. He gives Malte one of those looks that make a boy stand tall. And from that moment Malte is no longer on the run. He is the boy who found a body washed up on the shore.

Together they make their way down the path, Malte taking two steps for every one of the lighthouse keeper's long strides through the gravel. At the wharf Olesen stops to hail some fishermen who have been out tending their nets and are unloading their catch.

The boy approaches the coffin for the second time, now in the company of six burly men. Another man has joined them at the crossroads leading up to the church: the parson in his dressing gown, going down for his morning dip. He listens gravely as Malte pours out the news of his discovery. The boy's mood has done a complete turnaround. As if by magic, his nightmare has been transformed into men's business and Malte is their witness. Out on the water floats his kite, a summer kite with line and reel, but he pays no attention.

The first thing the parson does when the group reaches the coffin is to cross himself. Then he closes the coffin lid, face averted. The fishermen bow their heads and doff their woolly hats, the lighthouse keeper fiddles with his cap, and Malte executes a sort of salute. All are filled with awe. At the water's edge, the pebbles swirl in soft rushes.

Unsure what to do, the fishermen adopt the same expression as the parson. He looks at the lighthouse keeper, who responds with a shrug.

At length the parson clears his throat. "Let us carry the coffin ashore."

He appends a "Peace be with you" that betrays his disquiet.

They split up, three to each side of the coffin, spit on their hands before bending down and grasping the handles. They straighten up, red in the face, not having moved the coffin an inch: the dead man weighs the earth. Again Malte is the one to enlighten them.

"It's full of water," he mutters. First so softly that no one hears, then so loud that he, too, jumps: *"It's full of water!"*

Just then the handle, the brass of which is coated with slime, slips out of the lighthouse keeper's grasp. The other men loosen their grip on the casket as if they have burned their fingers on it.

The keeper swears like a trooper—to the parson's horror and the fishermen's silent amusement. He looks as though he is bending over to rinse his hands, but he comes up again holding a large rock. Purposefully he steps up to the front end of the coffin and deals it a hefty blow.

A sharp crack—as of something striking the lid of a grand piano—the mahogany box splits open, and a cascade of flowers comes pouring out with the swill. An appalling stench wafts across the beach. The stench of putrefied clams, rotting sea-weed, and fish carcasses. Malte holds his nose, but the glint in his eyes gives him away.

Olesen chucks the rock over his left shoulder.

"Now," he says, spitting on his palms again, "up with the bugger." This time he positions himself at the head, digs his fingers down into the hole, and hooks them under the coffin. Malte can see his massive arms straining. The others heave as before; the handles hold, and with a plop the men free their burden from the suction that has been holding it down.

The coffin lifts into the air. As the end tips forward, something falls to the ground with a tinkle, followed by a skittering sound from inside the casket. The body's feet burst through the shattered wood, bare and blue-tinged, then the lower half of his leg glides into view. One trouser leg has snagged on a nail. The leg is covered in long, black hair and the toenails have sprouted into horny claws.

Malte cannot hold back the scream. Misunderstanding, the parson releases his hold and hurries over to comfort him. In fact, the boy is over the moon. The superstitious fishermen behave as if the dead man had kicked out at them. They, too, have let go of the handles and have left the coffin to go its own way. The lighthouse keeper alone is still holding his end, and laughter shakes his large frame as he supports the coffin on his belly. It is the most glorious summer morning any boy could wish for.

Once started, Olesen cannot stop. Every time the parson shushes him, his guffaws redouble and the coffin bounces about on his stomach. The vibration runs right down into the sailor's legs. He dances a jig for fishermen and parson, with Malte as his stooge and the lighthouse keeper as puppet master. Only when the widow Swan ascends the brow of the dune and stands there, hands on hips, does the company quiet down.

"What in the world is going on here?"

The parson bathes in the nude, summer and winter. He lifts his arms in the gesture with which, in church, he accompanies the benediction. His dressing gown falls open, revealing a tanned belly complete with appendage that prompts Mrs. Swan to look the other way.

She calls out again, an edge to her voice this time: "Malte, come here!"

He did not show up for breakfast at the guest house. It is Sunday, and this is the first time he has not presented himself at the table when the gong has sounded. They have been looking everywhere for him: in the shed, the pantry, and the laundry room with its big copper kettle. Upstairs and down, under the stairs, in storerooms and attics, where cobwebs hang in dusty clumps. There is no end to a boy's hiding places, which add rooms to the house too fast for the imagination to keep up.

He makes his way toward her, dragging his feet. No one turns his back on one of Mrs. Swan's meals and gets away with it. And all the while he is just about twisting his head off its stalk, turning around again and again to watch the group of men, who are addressing the matter in hand with renewed gravity. They have hefted the coffin again, the lighthouse keeper now leading the way, fingers latched under the base like a professional's, his ample behind holding the body in place. The parson, suddenly superfluous, trots anxiously alongside, hand on the lid.

The men reach the crossroads and Malte has to forgo what comes next. He sneaks a last look at the coffin, bobbing up and down like a ship between the dunes. Malte himself is standing in a hollow and now he starts to walk across the sand, which slides back and away under his feet. He leans forward from the waist and slogs on while the sun shimmers in waves in the sky.

"Malte! Where's your shoe?"

He gazes at his sock in confusion. She scolds him, hauls him by the ear onto the path, then sends him on ahead with a smack on the backside. The rosebushes are overgrown with briers that catch on their clothes. Mrs. Swan is dressed in her Sunday best, with poke bonnet and flower basket. Her starched white apron is mainly for show.

At the guest house, some curds and cream have been put out for him, and he'd better eat it up. He is on pins and needles until the bowl has been scraped down to the last traces of melted sugar and rye-bread crumbs.

"All done," he says, gulping. "Thank you, that was delicious."

Mrs. Swan is mollified. She has stayed in the dining room to straighten it up for the next meal. On Sundays, everything is done backwards. They eat a hot meal in the middle of the day and in the evening there are platters of cold cuts and bread rolls fresh from the oven, ale porridge, and elderflower heads fried in pancake batter.

She hums as she arranges flowers from the basket in vases, changes the decorative cloth on the white piano. She runs her fingers over the music stand with its carved angels and harps. Malte loves it when it is just the two of them in the dining room. The floor smells of lye and the light falls over his feet in lacy patterns. She airs the room, making the curtains billow. Then she crosses to the glass cabinet, takes out the candy dish, and lets Malte help himself.

"Poor little one," she says, giving him a hug. Malte sighs and sinks against her bosom. The starch of her apron cools his cheeks and makes it Sunday all over. He could just stay there with his eyes closed, purring the hours away in that rosy darkness with no thought for anything else. She strokes his hair and lets him lie there a while longer, before tipping him out of the chair.

"There, there, Malte, enough of this cupboard love. Off you go and play."

His mood swings like the steps in a sailor's hornpipe. One minute he is trembling and has a lump in his throat, the next minute everything is sunny again and he is running out the door, ready to outstrip his need with fresh adventures.

He heads for the fateful spot. Arrives there to find the sand still bears traces of the coffin. With a shudder he recognizes the prints of the stranded body's feet, bare and flat and ending in the indent of the tip of the toenail. They stand out clearly amid those of clogs, rubber boots, and the parson's slippers. He plays detective. Using a blade of lyme grass, he proceeds to measure the dead man's feet.

When he tires of this, he starts digging in search of his shoe. The water has drained away, the clods of sand he digs up harden in his hand. He is up to his elbows in mud by the time he comes on his shoe. Mrs. Swan has sent him out in his bare feet, so he is no better off than before. Malte, the half boy, the boy forced to hobble to the ends of the earth with no shoes on his feet. Little Karen from the fairy tale, her feet were actually better off, even though it was sad that she would never be able to stop dancing. It's confusing. After all, dancing is something you do when you are happy, and girls love red shoes.

Water is trickling back into the hole. He takes hold of the back of the heel and pulls for all he is worth. The shoe comes clear and he falls over backwards. He has to take a breath before sitting down cross-legged, tipping his shoe upside-down and emptying it. Everything is quiet around him: the rush of waves and pebbles, bird cries, and the empty sough of the sky. The beach stretches out on all sides with not a soul to be seen.

He sniffs the damp leather, but there is no comfort to be had there, only a resurgence of the stench from the coffin. He mimics the lighthouse keeper's action and chucks the shoe over his

shoulder. But before he has time to come to himself, he hears
the shoe hit something with a crack. He crawls over to it on all
fours. The shoe has landed on glass. He pushes the shoe aside
and brushes away the sand. It is a photograph in a silver frame.

Suddenly he remembers that something fell out of the coffin
just before the seaman's feet came sliding out to stop the show.
In an instant it comes to him.

He picks up the photograph. The portrait has been cropped
into an oval. It is of a girl. She has a round face and eyes almost
hidden by the curve of her cheeks. Her hair is drawn into a bun
on top of her head. But it is her skin that is strangest. It gleams
with a luster he has never seen on any living being and it looks
dark as shoe polish.

There is something written in the bottom corner in faded
sepia ink. The words slant across the cardboard in flourishes
and curlicues. He turns the picture over. There is a tab at the
back that folds out so that the picture can stand on a bureau.
The edges of the frame are pasted down. The back is damp and
moldy, but the water has not penetrated behind the glass. He
tests the glue with his finger; it feels gummy, the backing has
come loose.

He is hot on the trail. He stands up and tucks the photograph under his shirt; the silver frame scratches his stomach.
He takes a final look around; adults never notice anything, they
are too busy talking. He locates the spot where the coffin's
front end has left a V imprinted in the sand. Positioning himself
next to it, he surveys the beach.

One can almost hear his eyes ticking in his head as the seconds pass. Before the minute is up, he has another bite. This
time he races down to the water's edge to rescue a sodden cap
that is sloshing back and forth on the waves.

It is a sea captain's cap, with anchor and gold braid. He
hugs it to himself, getting his shirt wet. He can barely walk

with all the weighty things threatening to slip down the leg of his shorts.

He leaves his shoe lying in the sand. Glass and frame are cold against his stomach. And as he clutches the picture, Malte finds his stride. He returns to the most secret of all hiding places, where he can be alone with his newfound treasures.

The following day, just past noon, the bells suddenly start to peal out over the church down, slowly, somberly, like a funeral knell. They ring out over the fishing village and slowly the congregation gathers at the main door, where the sexton is waiting to usher them into the nave of the church. They are in their Sunday best; the most weather-beaten of the men bristle in their wing collars, chins jutting from their jackets in a discomfort that raises red blotches on throat and cheeks.

Olesen wears a battered derby and frock coat. He has the look of a man with a mission; the parson must have given him a talking-to, the way he stands there looking chastened, surrounded by fishermen chafing at their collars and shifting restlessly from one foot to the other. The wives gather in gossipy huddles, avidly probing the rumor concerning the dead sailor, which has spread—first from house to house, then beyond the bounds of the parish and all the way to the nearest seaport. Distinguished visitors from the town are expected.

What they get are a customs official and his assistant, who arrive last of all. They apologize for the absence of the mayor, who has gone fishing with the privy councillor—such matters do have to be attended to. The sexton nods understandingly. In fact, it does not really matter that much; so long as they see some uniforms, the congregation will be happy. He throws open the doors of the church.

Malte, freshly washed and scrubbed, clutches Mrs. Swan's hand. The skin under his fingernails still smarts from the clippers and orange stick; he is wearing borrowed shoes that pinch, and his hair has been slicked into a pancake on his head. Just before he disappears into the church, he glances toward the chapel. The door is open. He sees a bier, and above the bier the great guardian angel beaming through a cloud of doves and the lance heads. I wink at him. No more than a single golden glint; on such a day as this there is room for no more.

Inside, the organ roars. For the first few steps along the aisle carpeting, Malte is still looking over his shoulder and being dragged along by Mrs. Swan. With a tug at his arm, she calls him back to earth, and for a moment Malte goes blank. Then he is present and correct. Deep within his eyes he looks like someone who has just woken up.

The organ rings out. The final chord careens around the lofty chamber and draws Malte's gaze to the altar. He gives a start. Up there sits another coffin, white and decked with fresh flowers. There is a dreamlike congruence about this reprise; it is a feeling he knows from nightmares, in which everything alters in seconds. Yet all that has happened is that the battered mahogany casket has been replaced by a new white one, the old one being in such a terrible state—not to mention the deep-sea reek from its insides! So his common sense tells Malte.

The coffin is open. Malte has never been to a funeral, but intuitively he knows that this is not how things are usually done.

Behind the coffin stands the parson in his cassock and fluted collar. He raises his arms. Malte smothers a giggle and sneaks a peek at the Swan. It is the same gesture as the parson made on the beach, when his dressing gown fell open, exposing him.

The congregation bunch up; sounds of shuffling feet and of throats being cleared are heard during the prayer, which is silent, with heads bowed and bared. Everyone remains standing. The church pews are empty. This is no normal church service; it is an interment. The older members of the congregation have been through it before, when a body has washed up onshore and there has been no next of kin to put a name to the face.

"Let us call down God's blessing on the departed."

After a speech in which the parson first alludes to death with a line from a song—no one knows the day until the sun goes down—then goes on to dwell at length on the lot of seafaring folk, the congregation divides into two groups, men and women: the men to the sword side, the women to the left. Malte is the exception, he stays with Mrs. Swan. Slowly the two lines move up the aisle, the men's first, filing past the coffin. No one recognizes the stranded sailor, and this they convey to the parson by a shake of the head. He scrutinizes every one of those filing past.

Malte comes last and has to stand on tiptoe. Step by step, he has swung between terror and expectancy. Now he lifts onto the balls of his feet, rendered weightless by his delight in the combination of the two.

The dead sailor lies open to his view. The hands are folded on the chest; he nestles in the white satin of the coffin like a statue borne up on ice flowers. There is a stillness under the bows of the eyelids such as Malte has never seen before.

The boy gasps. The blank face has been painted, the hair glossed with pomade. No discoloration of the skin, no, there is no color at all beneath the makeup. The living take their color from the blood, he realizes that now. But he has never seen a finer-looking man. His hair is black, the whiskers follow the line of his jaw. Over the chest his jacket arches into gleaming anchor buttons.

Malte steps down from the dais. He takes his place in the line, tight up against Mrs. Swan's skirts.

The parson lowers the coffin lid.

As he does so, the doors fly open.

"Stop!" comes the cry from the foot of the nave, where an ancient figure has appeared. She raises her stick above her head and brandishes it at the parson. It is the old woman from Crow Towers, and a ripple of unease runs through clergy and congregation as she wobbles up the aisle, tap-tapping with her stick.

6

IN WHICH
CROW TOWERS
TAKES FORM

Crow Towers lies far out among the dunes. It takes its name from its towers of glass and red-painted timbers. From what was originally a summerhouse, the towers have sprouted as outcrops and offshoots. At the very top, the panes of glass have been arranged in prism shapes that send beams of light flashing across the countryside when the sun is low on the horizon. To the front of the building lies a jetty, though all that is left are the wooden pilings, two rows of worm-eaten stumps running out over the second reef, where the water is deep. The jetty planks collapsed a lifetime ago. On the beach lies the carcass of a dinghy; boards and ribs yawn apart where the copper nails have fallen out.

The main house is only inches from the dike, so buried in boxthorn and brier roses that both stinging tendrils and itchy seeds assail anyone who attempts to invade its territory. What is unique about Crow Towers is that it was acquired and then expanded with the proceeds from amber. The man who purchased what was then a modest summerhouse died many years ago. He was an amber collector, exceptionally well favored by fortune, who had come to the area—flat broke, foreign, and free as a bird—combed the beach, and found his sea gold among mounds of washed-up seaweed. Good fortune paired with nimble fingers: exquisite brooches and necklaces found favor with the ladies and built him a flourishing business.

He wound up with his own mercantile house in the city, ships in the harbor that sailed far and wide and came home from foreign parts with holds full of fan coral, narwhal tusks, and turtle shells, all of which were fashioned in his workshops into true works of art. While transforming its fruit, he still stayed true to the ocean from which his wealth derived. From walrus tusks he created creatures with long heads and slanting eyes. He claimed that the creatures knocked on the ivory from within; he was merely the man who applied the knife to let them out. It was when he acquired the nickname the Amber King that he began to expand the summerhouse into a castle.

The Amber King had become a shipowner. From the drawing-room beams he hung a Greenland kayak, brought home by one of his captains. Complete with paddle, hunting bladders, harpoon heads of bone, and fishing lines. The frame was built of driftwood. A fingernail run over the skin produced a noise like that of a shaman's drum. For all he cared, they could keep the pyramids of Egypt, the steam engine, and the telegraph: that kayak of hide and bone was the finest thing ever to come from the hand of man.

He spent his summers puttering with his treasures and his growing collections. In one of the towers of the castle, it is said, there are glass cases holding pieces in which insects have been embedded for millions of years. It is also said that he once found a chunk containing the wings of an elf and a perfect miniature skeleton. The wings were transparent as a fly's, iridescent blue, and bigger than those of any living insect; the skeleton was quite humanoid, with a skull, rib cage, and verte-brae—filigree work more exquisite than any goldsmith on earth could produce.

Another tower is devoted to shells and all the things that can be garnered from the shores of the world. A third is given over to butterflies in glass cabinets where the dust on their wings lasts forever and the colors never fade. The fourth tower belongs to the wind and has stood empty since his death. He married and was divorced, a ne'er-do-well son took to the sea; for his own part, he never traveled, but he did adopt a child from Greenland, where icebergs sail the fjords and the great whales swim.

She became the pride of his collection and his sole com-panion. He spent his retirement at Crow Towers, which his adopted daughter inherited upon his death. By that time, peo-ple had wearied of the beauty that had held him in thrall throughout his life, and the Amber King's realm had crumbled to sand in the hourglass.

But all this happened so long ago that no one has any mem-ory of it. The old woman at Crow Towers never goes out among people. She sets her nets and eats the fish she catches, smokes them in an earthen oven and tends her garden while she chews on the remnants of a fortune that once was. For long spells at a time she has been thought to be dead, but anyone go-ing near the house at night will see a kerosene lamp burning in the window, shedding its light over the rise of the dunes. Ru-mor has it that the old crone is a witch. The Amber King's daughter is the oldest member of the parish and has never set foot inside the church.

And so a thrill runs through the congregation when she stomps up to the parson and demands, in a croak, that the coffin be opened. Flustered, the parson complies with her wish before she can raise her stick again. Malte has never seen such a crinkled face: her eyes are no more than two long slits in a maze of lines, her hair is wispy and white and the skin of her throat and hands is brown and leathery. She looks like a weather-beaten scarecrow.

A breathless hush has fallen over the church. The hinges creak as the lid swings back, and the parson stands aside to allow her to view the deceased. She leans over the coffin, rummages in her apron pocket, then places a rosary on his breast. She strokes the wax of the cheeks, stands for some time murmuring something that sounds like an incantation in a foreign tongue. When she turns back to face the congregation, the furrows in her face are moist.

She looks down the length of the church, eyes unseeing. She is standing underneath the ship, where it hangs suspended on its chain from the ceiling. Light washes the walls white and reflects off the gold crosses on the hymnals. No one says a word.

At length the parson steps up and takes her hands. "Aviaja, do you know the deceased?"

She bites down on her gums, responds with a shake of the head. He asks again, this time a little louder. She tightens her lips, full of mute emotion. He asks a third time and with this the ritual is observed and he releases her hands. Afterwards it is hard to say how her gesture should be construed, and there are those who believe that she nodded the last time the question was uttered over her head.

The parson is left in a state of uncertainty. He closes the coffin, this time with a bang that signals to the congregation that there will be no encores.

As she braces her stick against the floor, preparing to wobble off again, the parish clerk sidles out to keep her, the customs official at his side. The old woman blinks in alarm at the sight of a uniform. She shuffles from foot to foot, with the look of someone who is about to be sick. It is the parson who intervenes. With a forbidding glance at his flock, he steps up, lends her his arm, and assists her down the aisle and out the door. The set of his shoulders makes it plain that no one is going to run the gauntlet in his church.

The old woman from Crow Towers disappears over the crest of the hill. The sound of her stick and her shuffling feet hangs in the air long afterwards.

The parson turns to the congregation. "Let us bury our dead."

The burial rites are performed in the churchyard; soil is sprinkled on the casket once it has been lowered into the grave. Malte marvels at the toy shovel and the tray of sand; he is standing right in front, leaning over the edge, not wanting to miss anything. With one last shiver he notes that the water has seeped up from the ground and crept halfway up the sides of the grave. Earth is shoveled over the coffin. When the church bells start to toll, he feels he is dangling by his neck from the bell rope.

The world reels this way and that beneath his feet and he cannot catch his breath. Mrs. Swan pulls him away.

In the parsonage office the paperwork is completed in the presence of the customs official and his assistant. Olesen—with the face of an undertaker beneath his derby—tells of finding the body on the shore, and the parson says his piece as acting coroner. The deceased evinces no signs of swelling and few patches of discoloration. He cannot have been in the water all that long. He is a relatively young man—they would reckon somewhere between twenty-five and thirty, maybe older. But death knows no age and transforms a child into an old man in an instant.

The body is surprisingly well preserved, the face and brow smooth, with a withering of the cheeks such that the blood might only just have left them. The official and his assistant have carried out a thorough examination in the chapel. He is dressed in the uniform of a naval officer, but with nothing that might reveal his name, nationality, or date of birth. His cap is missing; it is normally placed next to the corpse. Otherwise, there are no clues in the mahogany casket to the original burial, and it is assumed that this must have taken place at sea.

The examination of the body does, it is true, reveal a deep lesion at the back of the head; it has to be presumed that the coffin has taken a few knocks along the way. They witness the death certificate. The customs official nods to his assistant and sweeps up the papers. Both on the death certificate and in the parish register it will say *Unknown*. But then, what else are you when you are dead?

The case is closed.

The following Sunday, Malte is back at the churchyard again, this time with Miss Oda. The summer days sing, there are flocks of birds in the cornfield, and dragonflies bumble right out of the blue and hit you on the nose. It is Oda's day off; she has dispensed with her apron and cape but kept on her black housemaid's dress. On their way here they have picked flowers. Oda lays a posy on her mother's grave and sniffles. She is all pink and white, a scattering of freckles over her nose, a child's plump cheeks, and a blossoming bosom. Her cloche hat makes her look like a grownup.

Malte tugs at her arm. He wants to see the sailor's grave. She protests, but the boy pulls her along. A person might be scared of Mrs. Swan, but not of Oda; from her turned-up nose down, she is molded out of freshly churned butter. And smells like it, too. Between freckles the skin is milk-white; she has only to show her face in the kitchen for the cat to start purring. When they are alone together, Malte harasses her until she is quite out of breath.

A stone has been erected over the grave. The soil still looks fresh and there are no flowers, only a single wreath. Malte puts down his posy. He has picked daisies and poppies. He stands with his hands clasped over his stomach and his head to one side. He is not happy, you can tell by his mouth. Suddenly he runs across to one of the other graves, grabs an empty flower holder.

And before Oda can say a word, the holder has found a new home. The grave seems less bare with Malte's posy in its conical vase. Oda hops from foot to foot and keeps looking over her shoulder. The churchyard is deserted except for the gravedigger's black cat. Malte is miles away.

This time it is Oda who tugs at him. "Come on! Or are you going to stand here all day?"

Malte ignores her. A cuneiform legend has been engraved on the stone; he stares at the letters, which are painted gold.

"What does it say, Oda?"

She is taken aback. "Can't you read?"

Malte scrapes at the gravel with the toes of his shoes. "Uh-uh."

There is an odd little crease on Oda's forehead, at the point where her eyebrows meet. It always appears when there is something she does not understand.

"But you go to school, don't you?"

"Yes."

It would have been easier for Oda if he had said no, since no further explanation is forthcoming. His reply stops her and the wait spins out with the birdsong between the graves. Malte's face has grown pinched. Heavens! She does as she is asked and reads him what is written on the stone. He nods, points to the gold lettering on the ribbon hanging from the wreath.

"That part that's all squiggly, like pretzels—what does that say?"

Oda cannot help but smile. It really does look like the baker's gold pretzel sign, the capitals especially. She spells it out:

"In Loving Memory . . ."

Malte is none the wiser. "Yes, but who's it from?"

"There's no knowing," says Oda. "It doesn't say."

She looks quite distressed at the thought of having to decipher the inscription. She attended school from seven until thirteen. After that, she went into service. To be honest, it was all a lot of mumbo jumbo to her—something you hear in church. It doesn't make any sense. After confirmation classes, it was all forgotten; blithely she sings along to the hymns each Sunday when the angel of light passes in all its glory through the choir.

But Malte says nothing. The bloodhound in him has bayed, and a real detective has to put two and two together. Not that *that* makes much sense either; this is something he has long since got used to. Half of what he hears is gibberish, the other half he makes up himself. He sets pictures to it. Two by two he takes the pieces of a jigsaw puzzle and puts them together, filling in the gaps.

The church bells have stopped ringing by the time Oda takes hold of him. "Come on, Malte. We're going to be late!"

Halfway through the service he shuts his eyes and calls up the image of the gravestone and the words engraved in it. It looks so fine:

BENEATH THIS STONE

* LIES *

AN UNKNOWN SEAMAN

He knows it by heart, shapes it silently with his lips. Malte does not understand. Unknown? But he has seen the name tag inside the captain's cap, it's just that he can't read the letters. Maybe it was wrong of him to hold on to those treasures. Suddenly he is overwhelmed by all the guilt the church is designed to hold, with its figure of the bleeding Christ.

He feels drained and weak, wriggles about on the pew until he lights on a nailhead sticking out of the wood. He tilts his body and shifts his weight onto one buttock. The nail digs in, and in the midst of the pain he finds a blissful moment when everything is at peace. He spares a thought for Jesus, understands all at once the look on the Saviour's face as he hangs on his cross.

By the time the service is over, he has ripped a hole in the seat of his trousers. Oda gives him a shake. It is a shamefaced Malte who stands waiting at the foot of the pulpit.

"Reverend, sir . . ."

"What is it, Malte?"

He blurts it out. "I've got a cap, it's the captain's . . ."

The parson is the picture of benevolence as he pats him on the head. "Good for you, Malte, I'm sure it's quite splendid. Now you can play at being a real sailor, eh?"

"It was in the coffin . . ."

"Watch what you're saying, Malte!"

The parson pinches his cheek. It does not hurt a bit, it is just a playful tweak and he has rustled up a smile, as if recalling his own boyhood.

Just then the chairman of the parish council comes over. The men shake hands.

"Reverend, I have something to show you. But it is for your eyes only."

He gives Malte one of those looks that can call the congregation to order. It leaves the boy barely able to stand upright.

"Say hello to Malte, our summer boarder."

The parish clerk confines himself to a nod. Malte responds in kind, dumb and chastened, his feet taking root in the church floorboards. Of this man, who wears a waistcoat with fob watch and chain, he can see only the paunch.

The parson maintains his benign air to the last. With a little tap on the shoulder he dismisses the boy. "You run on home and play, Malte. I'm sure you have plenty to do."

Oda is waiting outside on the churchyard path. "Where have you been, Malte? It's always the same with you, keeping people waiting. And then you just stand there gaping, so anyone would think your feet were glued to the spot."

"I can find my own way home!" Malte is in a sulk.

Oda tosses her head, more of a child than she thinks. "And that's just what you're going to do. I'm not going to waste my afternoon off on such a sourpuss."

He is left to run home alone. All the way back, he has a picture in his mind of the parson and the parish clerk sitting and nodding under a huge pair of eyes that peer down from the heavens. Those same eyes that have been seeking him, playing I-spy with him and making the clouds blaze gold at the edges.

He finds his treasures, puts them in a box that he lines with cotton, then buries them in the back garden. He hides in the den. Deep in the darkness he crouches beneath the sighing of the tall poplar trees, rocking back and forth, arms hugging two scraped knees. Not until the gong sounds for dinner does he emerge, strangely earthy and red-eyed.

7

IN WHICH
A STRANGER
MOVES IN

The clouds come rolling in, enveloping the lighthouse and building into a gray-hued landscape over the cliff. Sailboats scud around the point. In those spots where the cloud layer is thinnest, rays of light play down in shining colonnades. At the apex of the dome, swirls of vapor form, a hatch opens, and the blue luster of the heavens peeps through.

I had gone to rest among the stars. High above, I let my light burn with a colorless sparkle. Up here, the wave of time has flattened out, white dwarves hold sway amid gravitational pits around which the light spirals, is sucked down, and grows dark. I do not belong to any higher order; we have been called demons, the undead, devils, and the damned. Or angels, guardian spirits, and messengers of the gods.

Truth is a sliding scale. To us there is no difference between evil and good. We constitute a rungless hierarchy, barren, incapable as we are of undoing the patterns of Creation. We hurl no force's flaming swords, have no need of wings; we rise above pain in weightless wonder.

We are not the guardians of the living; the living guard themselves—we represent absence and absence nurses no thought of revenge. We are phantoms, no longer moved by the flesh; we see and hear with the echoes of senses that once were. We have been reproduced in marble and endowed with bloodcurdling names, likened to the death birds of the soul, alternately torn apart and patched up with piety to stand as monuments to other dead.

I was lying dormant when I heard someone call. Who, if she screamed, would still know my name? I charged through the gap in the clouds, spun in the midst of my gliding descent, and became the earth's guest in the sunset. No one sees it—a faint glint bouncing off the water, that's all.

As the boy gathers himself to send a stone skimming across the waves.

For a moment he is dazzled and shades his eyes; then he looks about him, that same wonder, and forgets the stone in his hand. There is dirt on his clothes, damp leaves are caught in his hair, and down his cheeks run dried streaks.

The stone is split across, black beneath the white layer of silica. I dart inside it, fill a flint with awareness. He is on the point of throwing when he takes another look at me. A wrinkle has appeared on his brow; he weighs me in the palm of his hand. Then he changes his mind. Even he does not know why he slips me into his pocket.

I snuggle down in the darkness, until he takes me out and talks at great length to a stone. I do not recognize him, it was not he who called, and among the stars our memory is short. The flint shard rests on his palm like an open eye.

It is now or never. I say it without blinking: a moment's distraction—and a hundred years will have fallen away. Eternal vigil is the coin with which I buy time, which is to say, with sleeplessness and nights that are far too long. But haven't we already met? I know I have seen him before, though I have forgotten where.

I have also forgotten his name. It is embarrassing, I know—one ought to be able to remember one's characters. If he hurls me away from him now, the thread between us will be broken. And I can go back to my penance among the dwarves, sit there and stew in my own juice, more and more weighed down by gravity, and grow sad and solitary as the other stars.

The boy tosses me into the air, throwing me in an arc from hand to hand, higher and higher each time, as he clenches his teeth and stares at a brightly lit window. I shut my eyes, preparing myself for the cloud of glass that will burst from the hole in the big bang out of which all things are born. At this moment, I cannot imagine anything worse than to land on a dinner table around which people sit and chat for all the world as if the continuing expansion of the universe had gone right over their heads.

But before the boy can throw, the window bursts open and the housemaid sings out over the garden gate: "Maa-lte! Dinner!"

Saved by the gong. He spits on me, rubs me once with his finger before shoving me back in his pocket. We present ourselves at the dinner table, hair slicked down and with clean nails and scrubbed cheeks, so not a soul can see that we've been crying.

A new guest has arrived. Elegantly attired in a cream-colored summer suit with collar and tie and pearl buttons. He is a foreigner, speaks with a heavy accent; Monsieur Charles, the others call him. His skin is golden. A set of coal-black whiskers sweep down to meet his narrow mustache, skirt his jawline and form an arch over the narrowly shaven upper lip. His hair is worn longer than is customary and falls into raven wings from the center part.

He is the youngest man in the company and he weaves his way from guest to guest like a cat slinking around the leg of a chair. One has only to look at Oda, who is even more pink and white than usual. She watches him out of the corner of her eye, steals glances at him, curtsies when she hands him a plate, and blushes furiously every time his muscovado-brown eyes linger on her bosom a moment longer than they should.

He lowers his eyelashes and juts out his chin when he talks. His words roll out, pinched by the narrow-bridged nose; he conducts himself in the manner of another world. He says "thank you" and "allow me," "good evening" and "my pleasure," but when he wants to have a proper conversation he switches to French and one has to keep up as best one can. His expression is alert and attentive and he seems to understand everything.

He has moved in, bringing with him a whole procession of trunks. They are lined up in the hall, reinforced with wood and fitted with sturdy clasps. They are covered with labels from every corner of the globe: steam-driven liners with tall funnels, the White Star Line, which carried him across the seas. Others show the palm trees of the Far East and houses with gable ends like nothing Malte has ever seen, address labels inscribed with swooping letters reminiscent of Aladdin's lamp, calligraphed characters and chunky script—all plastered on top of one another in layers.

The door to the hall stands open and Malte cannot take his eyes off the trunks. He can see them from his chair. In his mind he opens each trunk in turn; every single one pulls a peep show out of the darkness, a concertina for the eyes. Continents rise up, opening into vistas, fold by fold. Or else he sees shrunken heads, spears, and knives with jagged blades poking out from curly-toed slippers, fezzes, and loose-fitting robes. He just manages to catch a glimpse of a quiver full of poisoned arrows and a tin of tobacco that would lend wings to the soul, before the cabinet slams shut once more and all the perfumes fade away. Malte is in Paradise, and verily I say unto you, before the week is out, Oda will have joined him there.

I could happily have lived without the sight, but Malte stood up, went over to him, and showed the guest his stone. And before he hoisted the boy onto his lap he assured himself of a housemaid's blush. A child of God, a bride of Saint Lucia who lifted a candle to the mirror in the dark of winter in hopes of glimpsing the shade of a man. The candlelight played over her cheeks; out of the mist in the mirror a shape emerged and fell in a veil over her shoulders. She was dressed in white, crowned with myrtle; through the winter days he grew into a dream and with the spring's first anemones he came, dressed in white as she.

The promise of Twelfth Night has been fulfilled. There he sits at the table, large as life, playing with a stone, the links at his cuffs fashioned into golden dice. Oda is captivated. She feels the room spin beneath the chandelier. She fights for breath, digs her nails into the palm of her hand, forgets the time, and serves from the wrong side. The bell in Mrs. Swan's kitchen never stops ringing; Oda spills the jug of lemonade and quinces when she goes to fill his glass.

Eventually, the gentleman pushes back his chair and gets to his feet. By then Malte has long been out of the picture. Monsieur Charles wishes them all good night, bows to the ladies. He has his trunks taken upstairs—to a room with a sea view. Oda follows him through the door with her eyes. When she is clearing his place at the table, she notices the stone. She picks it up, kneads its rough edges as she makes a silent wish. Then it is allowed to slip into her apron pocket.

The first night he scratches at her door, she lies rigid under the eiderdown and does not answer. The following day, after she has cleared the table and tidied up the kitchen, she is in the hall, polishing the mirror, when he appears behind her. His image in the looking glass bears such a striking resemblance to the one in her daydream that her hand is left hovering in midair and a little gasp escapes her. He bows and says he is sorry if he has startled her.

The purl of his accent makes her head swim. He does no more than brush her with one wing before pulling back. When his hand touches hers, a thrill runs through her from top to toe, and that night she lies awake, listening in the darkness. Gnaws at her knuckles and longs fervently for him to break the door down. But not a floorboard creaks. He lets the silence speak for him.

Around daybreak she falls asleep, exhausted, having squeezed a pillow between her legs. When the cocks crow, she jumps up, bed straw in her hair. Someone was knocking. She pulls open the door; there stands Malte, gagging and panic-stricken. There is sleep in his eyes, grit from the dreamy rambles of the night in which he tends my stars like a little prince.

He has got out of bed in the gray of dawn, his mouth gummy from thirst. He pads down the stairs in his pajamas. On the marble shelf in front of the mirror sits a bottle full of what looks like milk. Still half asleep, he picks it up and puts it to his mouth. He does not scream until his tongue starts to bubble and the blistering spreads to his lips.

He has drunk from the bottle of mirror polish. With its flip top and spring clip, it looks just like a lemonade bottle, but the minute the ammonia starts to bite, he spews it out over the mirror. Aghast, Oda recognizes the liquid that froths from the corners of his mouth.

She does not stop to think. His heels drum against her knees as she grabs him around the waist, tips him forward, forces his mouth open with a finger, and gets him to vomit. He is sent flying into the bathroom, where she washes out his mouth and makes him gargle over and over. To show him what to do, she looks in the mirror and throws her own head back. She bursts out laughing and her anger is forgotten before he is sent out to play.

When she goes to make his bed, her mood turns sour again. He has wet the bed. The whole bunk will have to be stripped.

It is late in the morning and she is busy hanging out sheets in the back garden, where the breeze is less blustery. The first thing she is aware of is the scent, a whiff of southern cologne, then he appears in the lane behind the willow hedge. Complete with hat and cane and white spats. Such a gentleman! Swanning about in the middle of the day like a real dandy. Oda clenches the clothespin between her teeth.

He sees her and stops, hesitates for a second, then makes his way through the hedge.

A hat is raised across the clothesline. *"Bonjour, mam'selle!"*

Oda responds with a toss of her head, stands on tiptoe to pin the corner of a sheet. It flaps away from her and falls to the ground. With a cry she snatches the clothespin from her mouth, bends down to gather up the sheet. He beats her to it, swift as a polecat. With a neat sleight of hand he has picked up the sheet and plucked the pin from her hand. The wind billows the washing and she stands there gaping.

She can sense him behind her, his breath brushing her ear. She is breathless, her heart aflutter. The birdsong is drowned out by the sighing of the trees. Something falls from the sky and settles on her hip. She is struck dumb and stands with her eyes closed as the warmth of his hand penetrates the fabric.

He advances with a little chassé. She feels something press-

ing against the back of her dress. At first, she thinks it must be
his walking stick. Then she manages to free herself and whirls
around, a slap of the face ready to hand. She lowers her arm
when his face meets hers.

He is the picture of innocence; it *was* his walking stick. He
had it wedged between his knees when he bent down to come
to her aid.

Oda is embarrassed. She does not know what to say to him,
and if she could put into words the feelings that have welled up
in her, it would come out as gibberish. And she has no idea
what to do with her hands. She bends over the basketful of
comforter covers.

"Allow me to assist you, mam'selle."

Together they hang the wash. Their fingers work their way
along the clothesline and their eyes meet. She walks the tight-
rope with him, oblivious to all else. Dimples have appeared in
her checks; she is bathed in a rosy glow. She dares to rap his
fingers when he drops a clothespin on the lawn. They comb the
grass for it and their fingers touch. A surge of electricity runs
through Oda.

She feels faint when they get back to their feet, brush off
knees and skirts. Something inside her has melted. The last
shred of resistance has gone. In silence they finish with the
wash. Oda nods, sure in her mind; it is their hearts and souls
that they are pinning on the line.

The clothesline is full. He takes her hand and holds it while
the moisture from his kiss evaporates. He places his other hand
over his heart.

"You cast a spell over my days, mam'selle. *Je suis enchanté.*
Permit me . . ."

He delves into his waistcoat pocket, produces a velvet box
held between two fingers. The flick of a fingernail undoes the
catch and flips up the lid. Oda leans forward to see.

"I do not want you to have any doubts as to my intentions. Think it over, please. My heart longs for your answer."

Oda blushes and pales by turns. On two cradles in the velvet sit a pair of wedding rings. She stutters and stammers; her dull everyday words cannot match his silver tongue. Bewildered, she squirms under the gaze that lingers on her.

"Oh, good heavens!" she exclaims. She turns on her heel and rushes into the pantry. The kettle has boiled over. Soapsuds are spilling out, popping on the cement floor. He hears her poking at the firewood. A smoldering log falls hissing into the lake of suds. He snaps the lid shut, fiddles absentmindedly with the catch before slipping the box back into his waistcoat pocket.

Beads of sweat form beneath his mustache and he mops his brow with a handkerchief. Then he drops his gaze to the toes of his shoes, disturbed by a thought.

He wrinkles his nose at the trail of slime left on his spats by a slug. He knocks the creature off with his cane, positions the brass tip directly over the tiny head and crushes it.

Murmuring contentedly under his breath, he continues his stroll.

All that week I lie in her apron pocket. Malte I see only at mealtimes. He'll have to fend for himself. At the moment I am here only to feel desire reaching out in waves, day after day, toward my lattice of flint molecules. I could compare it to a spell on Cassiopeia, but I am really too old for that sort of game. I have been lying dormant for too long. May I never again have to writhe on that thorn in the flesh that makes me forget everything else.

Easier said than done when one spends twelve out of every twenty-four hours bumping against a bodice, stupefied by a scent that wafts like freshly churned butter in a sailor's nostrils. For the other twelve I hang over the back of a chair, and in the middle of the night I have to put up with her moaning and clenching the pillow convulsively. Desire has its phantom aches and pains and this I endure, like other souls who are older than their time. It is like the fires of hell: one minute absence, the next red-hot coals. As in the early days of matter on this earth. In the end the rock is bound to crack.

He is a master of the art of wooing. Sends her billets-doux containing little verses. He has copied them by hand from the Song of Solomon with many a flourish and curlicue, and he enlists the boy into service as messenger. Oda giggles to herself over his pretzel scribbles. He sends her little bottles of scent, showers her with looks as well as caresses, and she, housemaid that she is, feels like a queen. He is also careful to allow discreet lulls in his courtship, which only serve to increase her longing.

No one realizes what he is up to. He plays the piano to entertain the other guests. So as to prompt cries of wonder and admiration. Chopin at a gallop that makes other renderings seem as pedestrian as the ticktock of the metronome. He moves in time to his own tempo rubato, rocking back and forth on the three-legged stool, emitting little sounds, quite carried away.

He sends her a look. Oda is standing in the back, listening. She clasps her hands over the pocket of her apron, recognizing the sounds. They are the same as those she stifles with her eiderdown in the darkness of her maid's room.

Only after everyone else has retired for the night does some devil possess him and she has to defend herself with all her might, hands and knees, and lips averted.

In no time, he has become the center of the company. A position he has listened his way to, letting others do the talking. After dinner, the guests gather in the captain's saloon. Amid the books in their tooled bindings on the shelves they tell their stories, the great and the small. He is the soul of attentiveness. On those rare occasions when he touches on events in his own life, the ladies draw closer. "Monsieur Charles" is a name adopted solely for the sake of convenience; his real name, when he utters it, is all fire and fury. Afterwards, no one can remember it.

He comes from a family of land barons in far-off Peru, carries fancy handkerchiefs embroidered with their coat of arms. He never says as much, but behind his back it is whispered that he is of noble blood. There is some hint of a family tragedy, and he lowers those dark eyelashes. The sudden look of sorrow on his face moves Oda deeply.

It is all part of the slow seduction that leads to the windblown pinnacles of passion.

They meet in the back garden, behind the woodshed, beside the spring in the nearby forest, where the country lane leaves the fields behind. In the cool shade of the trees she drinks in his first kiss and her skin crinkles with goose bumps. The first time she feels his hand on her lap she doubles up, weeping. She pulls herself free and runs off into the trees, and he catches her for a laughing reprise. No more than a token this time, replacing breathlessness with lightness. From there on, they are in a world of their own. She rests her head on his shoulder, closes her eyes, and allows herself to be led through the birdsong.

Before he retires to the room with a view, he renews his vows to her. They shall live on a country estate worked by Indian peons. In the midst of rubber and cacao plantations. She will have servants, carriages, and parasols. Oda sings like an angel; he has heard her in church. He will have an opera house built on the banks of the river, where cities in the New World are springing up like mushrooms and the rubber is off-loaded in bales that bring wealth for everyone. She was born to stand on a stage, he can see that, and Oda feels the earth giving way beneath her feet. When the nightingale from the willow hedge meets the trees of the rain forest, its song will take wing and soar over regions where it has never before been heard.

She does not understand the half of it, but the sound of adventure is in itself blissful. She has never heard of tarantulas but she approaches this creeping thing so timidly that he laughs aloud. There were serpents, mam'selle, in the Garden of Eden!

That afternoon, Oda catches the boy with a frog. She brushes the dirt off his cheek and chucks him under the chin, bursting with excitement. She confides in Malte, who has brought her the love letters. She makes him swear not to tell and he crosses his heart and hopes to die. Then she fumbles in her apron pocket and shows him the red gold.

She has said yes; their engagement is her heart's secret. She will wear his ring on the day that Mrs. Swan gives her consent and the parson blesses their union. He has already informed his family; they are expecting a telegram from distant parts.

Malte stands openmouthed. He has other things on his mind, but she has made him her accomplice. He snuggles up in her lap, filled with a craving for love that springs from something other than hers. She strokes his hair and rocks him in the leafy shade dappled with sunlight.

Softly the light filters through her apron. Something occurs to her: when she was searching for the ring, her fingers came upon a stone. She pulls out the flint, hands it to Malte.

"Isn't this your lucky stone? Thanks for letting me borrow it!"

Malte slips it into his pocket.

8

IN WHICH
MALTE RIDES
THE WIND

It is rumored that the old woman from Crow Towers has started going out among people. Not only that, but she stops them and speaks in tongues. They say she has lost her reason and that she is hagridden by the past. The ferment in her head seethes as she confuses figures from days gone by with those who stand before her. For a few moments, it is the Amber King, then her first love, dead these many years. In her delirium, she talks to the dead; it is a ghastly business, if one crosses her path. The horny nails dig in and then there is no shrugging her off.

Sad, the way age takes its toll on the last years of the living. The doctor has been sent for. The parson is against it, but there seems to be no way around it. She is disturbing the peace of the parish. A place has been made ready for her in the county asylum. And besides, unless something is done, she is going to end up dying in her own filth, you just have to ask Mrs. Swan, who keeps the poor soul going with whatever the guests send back to the kitchen.

Most of this goes over Malte's head. He has enough to think about with his own visions. Feverish nights have turned his bed into a sweatbox; the eiderdown has to be taken off and aired on the clothesline every day. He has been told to stay indoors: the mumps! The shades have been drawn in the captain's saloon, the daylight shut out by blinds. He lies on the sofa, wrapped in a blanket. He leafs restlessly through the books, looking for pictures between the spindly-legged characters. He struggles to get them to march in step, he can recite the alphabet by heart and in the right order, but those spindly legs refuse to renounce their mute state and form into words. Malte does not know it, but the gaps in his schooling are far too great.

One book in particular he returns to again and again. The illustrations make a mystery of it; some sort of mechanical steel fish rises out of the sea and attacks ships, the captain can sail underwater and play on an organ in the belly of the steel fish while outside, fish glide past in the bluish light from the round portholes. This vessel surfaces before the mouth of a lofty cave ringed by foaming breakers; powerful beams of light shoot out from it and a dinghy full of men is making toward it. In Malte's mind, the beams of light play back and forth and dance over the walls of the cave.

Malte has never seen anything like it. If reading is what it takes to learn about such wonders, then, suddenly, it cannot happen quickly enough. But he struggles in vain.

As long as I am sprinkling stardust on him, it does not matter, and he needs no script other than that of my thoughts. But I have gone into exile. Imprisoned behind the lattice of molecules, I cultivate the fossil. My brain is of no more use than that of a petrified sea urchin. Occasionally I glimpse particles of light in the darkness, sparks and electrical discharges. All the rest is mumps. I am enjoying myself at the dawn of time, a time when one can get away with being mindless and feel the peace which that brings—until the first carbon chains start to link up, creating Jacob's ladders out of rock pools.

On the other hand, as long as Malte is convalescing we are excused from church, although there is something special lined up for today, a concert featuring hymns from all the festivals in the church calendar. Monsieur Charles has been allowed to take over from the organist, and Oda is leading the choir. He has secretly started teaching her to read music, an advantage she deserves to have. And he, for that matter. Her voice strikes higher and truer; she thinks of the symbols as clothespins to be pegged onto the line, as swallows milling about in black tail-coats. She turns the air to crystal with her soprano. "I saw a rosebud springing" has been set an octave higher than usual and Oda's intonation sweeps everyone along with it. She has become the very essence of the song.

The members of the congregation are entranced; they sing with all their hearts, each and every one with a purified voice. And never has the organ sounded like this. It brings tears to the eyes, like the frost on New Year's morning, when he breathes the pipes full of resonance. In him the music has found its wizard: the church grows bigger and the organ looks like a grotto of ice where the light plays in shafts over the curtains of icicles.

With a bow of the head he brings the concert to an end, once the notes of the last hymn have died away. No one dares to clap. Hymn books are closed, people get quietly to their feet and file out. Without speaking and not breaking the solemnity, they go their separate ways.

Afterwards, he has his hour of dalliance with Oda; deep in the forest they have found a nest for themselves and lined it with corn sheaves. Here they drop down, with the birds singing high above them. Once Oda gets going there is no holding her back. Never has she seen such a sweet little starling. She cups it in her hands, feels its tiny heart beating. Petal by petal, with perfect pitch, he plucks his nymph. And only when any hope of a replay is out of the question do they run and frolic, pounding the woodpiles with sticks and stones in a concert that no one hears.

Meanwhile, the doctor is on his way out to Sea View. The hills echo with the backfiring of a gasoline engine, puffs of smoke billow from the exhaust and thin out behind it into white wisps. Malte—who was born on the night when a new century was ignited—must think he has awakened prematurely to the fireworks that will herald the new millennium.

The doctor's car is the first in the parish. He drives up in a pillar of steam from the Hammel's engine. Mrs. Swan has asked him to look in at the guest house before continuing on to Crow Towers and his last house call of the day. All the details have been discussed beforehand and it is he who will be responsible for the old woman's fate from now on. He has the admission papers all ready in his bag. His footsteps crunch briskly over the gravel on the garden path as he walks up to the house.

Malte has let the book fall onto his coverlet, but he is lost in its pictures. A prolonged hiss filters into the dim room. He dives off the sofa and over to the window shade, which flies up to disclose a monster sitting out on the road, enveloped in clouds of dust. A new fever burns in his veins. The automobile stands gleaming out there where the illustrator's imagination leaves off. Forgotten are the pictures in which he has so recently been engrossed.

The doctor comes into the saloon, accompanied by Mrs. Swan. "I see this young gentleman has taken the first steps on the road to recovery."

He is a young man, bearded and clad in a windowpane-checked jacket. He is also wearing a leather helmet and goggles; these accoutrements alone make him a hero in Malte's eyes, and the boy throws back his shoulders. Automatically he starts tucking his pajama top into his trousers. He does not know where to put himself and he manages to trip over a rug on his way back to the sofa. The doctor has set his bag down on the tiled tabletop with its pictures of Dutch sailing ships and windmills.

"Up you go! Now, my boy, what do they call you?"

"Malte!" interjects Mrs. Swan, and this time he is embarrassed at never answering quickly enough. A man in flying goggles deserves a smart salute, not dithering. Malte jumps to obey, throws himself onto the sofa, and opens wide.

The doctor pulls off his driving gear. He is ruddy-cheeked beneath his beard; a rim of dust encircles his eyes like a mask. Before opening his bag and taking out his instruments, he grins at Malte and winks.

He takes a look at Malte's throat, catching the light with a mirror on his forehead. He asks Malte to unbutton his pajama top, puts a stethoscope to his chest. Malte has to cough. He manages a feeble burst. Then he has his temperature taken, and the doctor folds up his stethoscope and wraps the wooden spatula in a napkin.

"Hansen," he says, holding out his hand.

Again Malte is too slow. For a moment he has the impression that the hand has shot out from some dimension where the rest of the man remains invisible.

"Shake hands with the doctor!" The Swan, in a flurry of tut-tutting. That boy . . .

Instead, the doctor puts his hand on Malte's shoulder. "There's nothing wrong with you, my friend. You don't even have a temperature."

He sounds relieved. He strides over to the other window,

flicks up the blind, opens the window, and sets it ajar, waving air in as he does so. The stuffy atmosphere in the room begins to dissipate.

He picks up his leather helmet and tucks his ears in before pushing the goggles up onto his brow. He has the air of a man primed for combat when he turns to Mrs. Swan.

"Light and air, that's the best medicine for a boy his age."

She doesn't answer. Mrs. Swan belongs to a century in which sickness means darkened rooms, bedstraw, heavy eiderdowns, and bitter potions.

He snaps shut his doctor's bag. Malte has already swung his legs off the sofa and is poised to jump to his feet. "Can I get up?"

Dr. Hansen pauses in the doorway. He considers Malte for a moment. Then his pale eyes are all smiles. "You get dressed, and I'll take you for a spin."

Malte's sun lights up; he hops to the floor and over to the chair on which his clothes lie neatly folded. He struggles with his shirt and Mrs. Swan's protests, but everything falls into place as he buckles his belt and declares himself ready, loud and clear.

"But he's my summer boy. I'm responsible for him, Dr. Hansen."

"Don't you worry. I'll get him back to you in one piece, I promise you, ma'am."

Malte pictures himself torn limb from limb by wheels and driveshafts, picked clean by crows and jackdaws on Wreckers' Hill. He shivers.

They disappear through the French windows, leaving the landlady shaking her head.

When they reach the car, Malte stands back in awe. It looks like a high-wheeled gig. Dr. Hansen gives him a leg up onto the passenger seat, walks around to the front, and starts the engine with the crank handle. Eventually the car is jumping by itself. He climbs aboard.

Before they drive off, he tucks a traveling rug over Malte's knees and ties a scarf around his mouth. "Shut your eyes if it gets too dusty. Watch out for flying stones!"

He releases the brake. "Hold on tight!"

He pulls down his goggles and grabs the steering wheel, which is set horizontally on a brass column. The engine noise erupts into backfiring as he pushes in the throttle. They are off and running. Malte teeters on the verge of ecstacy. He digs his nails into the seat under him. A little later, when they have picked up speed and the surrounding countryside has been reduced to a blur, he feels the force of the wind puffing him up until he all but lifts off. With a string of firecrackers on their tail, they tear across the hills. The sedge on the grassy ridge in the middle of the road is no longer visible, disappearing beneath them in a rippling banner of green.

The road winds this way and that; they drive through a stand of mountain pines. Suddenly they are trundling over a carpet of pine needles, islands of moss and sand scattered beneath the boughs. The tree trunks are stubby and stunted, a wilderness of twigs and pinecones stretches out to either side of the path. From his lofty perch, Malte feels as if they are flying across a forest, the treetops forming mazes down below. Until he is caught by a branch, a smack on the brow that draws blood. Malte ducks too late.

The car bounces over a stone. He is jolted out of his seat and after that he hangs on tight to Dr. Hansen's arm. The doctor shouts something and grins broadly beneath the goggles. A shower of gravel flies into the air, sent up by the wheels as the car swerves into a clearing. They catch their first glimpse of the turrets of Crow Towers.

On the last part of the way through the dunes they roll

along at a more sedate pace, not wanting to scare the old woman's sheep. The sea appears once more, the water sparkling around the truncated jetty. But it is wilder here; the shore lies deserted as far as the eye can see. They draw up alongside the boxthorn hedge. The car shudders a couple of times before coming to a standstill, the firecrackers giving off a few last sparks. Dr. Hansen hops off and helps Malte down.

The doctor is in as much of a hurry as any fireman. Malte realizes that the engine needs to be stopped now. The doctor reaches in under the tailgate for a can. He takes a rag and wraps it around his hand before starting to unscrew the radiator cap. Up shoots a geyser of boiling water. He empties the contents of the can over the geyser to quench it, and the metal sputters and hisses. Gradually the automobile stops steaming and is still. Only then does Malte breathe. On Dr. Hansen's side the whole operation has been conducted in silence.

An unnatural quiet descends upon the place. But it is a long while before the swooshing in Malte's ears subsides.

The doctor puts an arm around Malte's shoulders and pulls him close. "Well, Malte? Did you like that?"

"Did I!" is all Malte says, the full force of his exhilaration directed upwards.

This time Dr. Hansen leaves his helmet and goggles on the seat before lifting out his bag. They lie there, sunk in on themselves, like a head with all the air let out. The goggle lenses have a silvery sheen; a piece of sky is reflected in one, a heavily distorted fir tree in the other.

The garden gate has been overwhelmed by the shrubbery; briers climb all over, wrought iron and hedge inextricably entangled. The doctor makes no attempt to open it; he looks around for a back way. A thought occurs to him, and he runs back to the car and returns carrying the can.

He hands it to Malte. "Find the well," he says, "and fill that up. We may need it on the drive home."

Together they walk around to the back of the main building, by a path densely pearled with goat droppings. Malte carries the empty can. From the dune comes the sound of bleating. A tremulous note. He thinks it is something calling him and looks around, searching for the creature. His eye falls on a row of posts; he stops and inhales deeply, nostrils flaring. They are hung with row upon row of fluttering white salted oblongs, fish, split open down the back. The dried flounder look like the bows he ties to the string of his kite.

There is also a frame with an animal hide stretched across it. For a moment, he thinks it is a sheep, but sheepskins are not patterned, nor do they glisten in the sunlight. Besides, the skin is oval in shape, with no corners for the legs. It is stretched taut as a drum and he is filled with wonder over this, the second fabulous creature of the day.

Dr. Hansen is calling him. He is lagging behind.

They round the corner of the stable and find themselves in a patio. At one time it was enclosed and wild vines climbed over it. Now all that is left is a rickety framework. They stand quite still, detect no sign of a living soul. A checkered pattern of shadows falls over them. Cobwebs hang from the window-panes of the building before them, cobwebs and cracked glass that make its towers seem blind.

With all its offshoots and outcrops, it is impossible to get a clear picture of the house. The towers are smaller than he had imagined and look as though they have sprouted from the corner bay windows in a sudden spurt.

Dr. Hansen clears his throat. He has seen the pump. "You fill up that can. I'll find our patient."

With a creak he opens the door onto the darkness and is swallowed up by it. The minute Malte is left alone, the creepy feeling washes over him again. He struggles with the pump handle, putting all his weight on it. It is rusted solid and will not budge. He gives up and sits down on the edge. When he knocks on the lid, it sounds hollow. A rank smell rises from the well and the planks of the lid are green with mold. All at once, there it is again, that sponginess in his throat, as if he were about to cry. A shudder runs through him; did he hear a moan from the stable? He jumps to his feet and runs after the doctor.

When he first steps inside the house, he cannot see a thing. And everything is far too quiet as he waits for his eyes to get used to the dark. Doors ajar and mysterious empty rooms. A pair of narwhal tusks curving up in the hall. He opens the door of a bedroom. At first he thinks the bedspreads must be cro-cheted, but then he sees that moths have been at them. Softly he closes the door again, risks calling out, but no one answers. The doctor has vanished, leaving behind him some open doors and nothing else. He fights the panic that wells up inside him, tries to keep a clear head.

He passes between the narwhal tusks and finds himself in the parlor. He can make out a stuffed monkey among seabirds, and glass jars containing snaky forms bleached by alcohol. All the chairs are covered with a thick layer of dust; the dining table has sagged at the knees, and above it the kayak dangles from one strap. The skin is dry as a mummy's; the ivory knob is aimed straight at him. He pictures a giant, a cannibal pointing a thighbone at him. He is going to end up in the big black caul-dron. The manhole in the kayak engulfs him.

Just then he hears footsteps on the floor above. He does not know whether to be relieved or terrified. Again he calls out to the doctor but receives no reply. Taking his courage in both hands, he steps out into the hall. He listens at the stairwell for some time before he starts to climb, step by step. He has been listening for the sound of the walking stick that would betray the old woman's halting gait.

Face alert, he reaches the landing on the next floor. There

are two doors before him. One leads to the tower. Both are ajar. The turret stairway is dark, the room bright. In the ray of light, he can barely discern the back of a rocking chair. He is not sure; perhaps this was what creaked so high above his head. He steels himself and pushes the door open.

Malte screams.

9

IN WHICH
MISTER DEATH VISITS
HIS BLUE-EYED BOY

Three things trigger his scream. One is the cat's fur, like a burst of static as the cat streaks out between his ankles. He catches the glint of a pair of greenish-yellow eyes as it passes. The second is the bundle in the rocking chair; a granny shawl cowls the head. The third is the shout that collides in midair with his scream.

"Damn it all, Malte, you scared the living daylights out of me!"

The cowl has slipped down onto the doctor's shoulder; he is on his feet now, and the rocking chair gives one more swing as he walks across to the window and pushes it wide open. The light mingles with air that has been trapped inside for a lifetime.

"Dr. Hansen," says Malte, "I couldn't find you."

"The patient has gone underground. What do we do now?"

The doctor strokes his beard, fiddles with the hasp. It comes off in a shower of moldering wood, and the window starts to bang. Malte thinks for a moment, before drawing himself to attention.

"I think I heard a noise coming from the barn."

"From the stable? Well, I suppose she must have livestock."

"It sounded like someone moaning. Like . . ."

"Like a ghost, Malte? Do you believe in ghosts?"

"No," the boy lies. "Not as long as . . ."

"You're with me, right? That's one hell of an effect we doctors have on people. *I* believe in ghosts. Life's more fun that way—it's the same with my car."

The doctor stays by the window a moment longer, deep in thought, before tearing himself away. "In the barn, you said?"

Malte nods.

They walk out onto the landing. A crystal chandelier suspended from the ceiling tinkles in the draft from the open door. Malte is entranced.

The doctor pauses by the banister. "Coming?"

"Yes," says Malte, lying for the second time. Of two minds, and eyeing Dr. Hansen uncertainly. Suddenly he is more afraid of the sick woman than of ghosts; he remembers her gnarled finger in the church, the witch in the gingerbread house.

The doctor makes things easier for him. He has been rummaging in his bag and now comes up with a carbide lamp. He gives it a shake and lights it.

"Here, Malte. Now you can go exploring on your own. This place is better than the fun house at the fair. I'll call you when I'm done."

He gives him a thumbs-up and heads down the stairs. Malte climbs up into the tower. The dust no longer bothers him; he walks straight through cobwebs and they look almost funny in the glow of the lamp. Turn for turn he gains on the past. The spiral stairway opens out into a hexagonal room in which darkness has settled in windowpanes all around.

He shines the light on the walls. Vestiges of wallpaper, ripped by the claws of incarcerated tigers—Malte puts his courage to the test—a splotch of blood that will never wash off. Rub as one might. It is the stain from a swatted mosquito that has been there long, forgotten by time.

The light falls on glass cases reminiscent of the desks in a schoolroom. They are ranged against the walls, between the windows. Three in number. The cases are on legs. Their lids slope down from the high back edges, and under each lid's frame is a keyhole. He tries to open one of the cases but it is locked. He rubs at the glass; the side of his hand comes away black and powdery-feeling. He shines the light down into the case. Sees lumps of amber, cat's-eyes gleaming beneath the glass. He runs the beam down the woodworks. And finds a key hanging there. Malte is on fire with excitement.

He tries the key in the first case. With trembling fingers he gets it to turn. Tongue between his teeth, lest the key snap.

Gently he pries the lid open; nothing special there—shells and stones such as he has collected himself. He manages to remove the key and tries the next case. Butterflies caught on pins. The ones with death's-heads on their backs are the best, the white-and-yellow ones he recognizes from the garden. He saves the largest case for last.

The charge from the amber has spread to his fingers. His hand shakes a little before he pulls himself together and swings the lid open. There they lie, brown and golden. Some the size of pigeon's eggs, others mere slivers worn smooth by strand and stone, still others like teardrops. All of them unworked. There are milky surfaces in which the sand has scored its stipple pattern, deeper, golden chambers in which an insect can be made out. Malte lets the light play over them.

He gropes around inside the case, where they lie in a jumble. They chink beneath his fingers, feeling neither like glass nor like stone. He is conscious of revulsion and attraction, each piece exerting its own pull. The largest lies like a child's hand in his. He weighs it and finds it wonderfully light. When he shines the light over it, he spies a black flake shaped like a sea horse. The beam of light creates a shining cloud around it.

All of a sudden, Malte's heart stands still. It is an elf! The tiniest of little people, with four wings, the curve of a spine, and, at the very top, the airborne seed of a skull. The wings are attached to the shoulder blades and irradiated by thready patterns that give them the look of leaves.

Once he has it in his hand, he cannot let it go. He rubs the piece of amber against his shirt, feels the spark leap to his finger, and his heart beats again. He must have this treasure for his own. He glances around the room before pocketing it. Then he stands for a moment in front of the case, digs into his pocket again, and leaves the stone in its place.

That suits me fine; I switch to amber. At long last, I am out and whirring freely. The size of a dragonfly, I deliver myself up to the winds of the pine forest. The air rushes around me, sticky with scent. Resin runs from the tree trunks in great globs. Malte is millions of years farther up the line and the earth is still in its infancy. Swaddled in bracken and pinewoods, cycads and marshland. Everything is stupefyingly hot and damp; the dark humus is busy laying the groundwork. Plants spring up; in the course of one day they gain in height and spread palmy crowns over the night. Under the shield fern in the forest eternal, twilight reigns.

Lady fern, ostrich fern, staghorn fern—names that lie tucked away within the shapes of the leaves, waiting to be brought to fruition through chaos. Strange to be so small in a world where everything is free to grow unchecked.

Giant cicadas sing in the trees; just before sunrise and just after the sun has gone down, they work themselves into a frenzy of frequencies that could blow apart a skull such as mine. This time is taboo; we pass it in the seclusion of the hive. *Because . . . because* we are so smart. We have special cells, padded with wax, in which to live through the first and last minutes of the day.

I am out collecting honey for my brothers. Tiny people that we are, we have tools for the purpose. A straw for the calyx, a stamen used as a riser pipe, fed down into the cup of nectar. That is all we need. We fill our bellies and regurgitate into the cells surrounding our queen; the cells are built up in blocks and tiers, and a humming fills the hive.

I fly out through the opening at the top of the hive, where the walls are made of masticated pulp. We fertilize the queen, touch one another only for pleasure, and the females are our worker bees.

I fly home with my honey sac bulging.

My flight creates a pattern along the route between the outside and home. When we dance I reenact the pattern of my flight, to help my brothers find the shortest way back to the same nectar source. Our wings enable us to hover in the air while we drain the cup dry. Other species have to make do with two and will, in the dance of time, evolve into hummingbirds.

The drone elf is our leader. He alone wears a Phrygian cap, through which poke the tufts of his ears. He is my lover, and I say this with pride, for he taught me the art of flying. We describe Catherine wheels in the sunlight, giving off sparks as we dart after each other. At night we make the vaults of the hive luminous with our lovemaking.

We fly over the swamp, play at hunting each other, dive and brush a couple of fern leaves in passing. The long neck that cranes up is far too slow and we leave it snapping at thin air. We are crossing the water when he gets caught in a web. Summoned by the alarm thread, its eight-legged proprietor emerges. I dodge all eight, and the hairy beast stops, waggles its front legs inanely. Then I swoop down into the center and pull my mate free. He loses his balance and topples backwards out of the spinner's net as I sob with laughter. He looks like an acrobat miming a fall.

But my laughter is left suspended in midair. We are too small to produce an echo. And while he is still struggling on the surface, buoyed up by an invisible film, he swirls slowly out into the current. I dive out of my air space to give him a hand—just in time to see a shadow come leaping up. Lobe fins flap and the mouth opens wide. The sea monster snaps its jaws shut and he writhes as he breathes his last. There is no time for farewells before he is gone. A trickle of green slime closes over the water.

His cap is all I manage to save. Nuzzle it long against the iridescent brushes on my stomach, ride the thermals, and climb toward the sun. We are born, we die—and are born again, as the wheel of love comes around again for others. But without his love I will not last one day. Heartbroken I fly from that spot. With the death of the drone elf I will become the new prince. I think of the queen, who soon must be fertilized; obese and omnipotent she wallows in her cell.

She who was but one slave among all the other females until we singled her out and started stuffing her with that food which is our best-kept secret and which has been likened to the ambrosia of the gods. The council of elders guards the secret. The royal jelly has a tremendously rejuvenating effect, though not exactly a beautifying one—at least not in the quantities our queen consumes. She cannot even stand up, just lies there all day while the elders feed her with what, for the rest of us, would spell eternal youth and beauty.

I know what awaits me and my stomach turns at the thought. My semen will be soaked up by the myriads of eggs that she carries behind those moist membranes of hers. And no sooner will I have penetrated her than the penis will break off at the base and seal off her passageway. *My* penis. I don't know who thought that one up, but apparently it is supposed to safeguard her genetic makeup. As for me, I will die soon afterwards with a burning pain in my underbelly.

Better, then, to go the way of the kamikaze. I toss aside the cap, choose the wind of the gods, and fling myself out of the thermal on which I have been wheeling. The sun is at its zenith. On the other bank of the swamp stands a giant fir tree. Everything seems so insubstantial when seen from above; I save a little of this bird's-eye view for future generations on this earth.

I fold my wings together and go into a nose dive. Wind tears at my ear tufts, water is stung from my eyes. My blood is ice-cool, my brain explodes into a fiery flower and sheds its seed on the way down, as the giant fir grows in my line of sight. In the center of the trunk, the bark has flaked off and a stream of resin bubbles forth. I aim for the largest lump. Allow for some leeway, keep my tongue between my teeth and my arms tight against my sides.

My speed, over the last stage of my approach, is meteoric. In comparison, the landing is soft; one twitch in a glutinous bubble and I hang there, stuck fast and faced with the prospect of eternity encased within a golden chamber. The thought crosses my mind that our greatest old graybeards have likened this state to that of bliss itself.

As the sun sears the lump to burning slag against my skin, I die. Yet another elf succumbs to the fury of primeval times.

"**M**alte!"

The doctor's shout rings out from the courtyard below; a discus of distant echoes cuts off his connection in the tower. What was that? He found a treasure and the treasure lent him wings. Now he is back to fumbling at pockets that fill up all too fast. He closes the lid of the glass case, forgetting the key in the lock. The steps of the spiral stairway wind him back to the world from which he came and he just makes it into the brightness of midday, to stand there blinking while the flame of the carbide lamp turns white.

Dr. Hansen brushes straw from his jacket. He smells like a veterinarian now, of stables and animal droppings.

"Ah, there you are! Did you find anything?"

Malte shakes his head, tongue-tied once again. Dr. Hansen takes the lamp out of his hand, extinguishes it, and puts it in his bag. There is sweat on his brow and his hair is plastered around his ears in dark curls.

"You were right about our patient. She's there . . ." He points to the barn.

Malte brightens again. "Is she going back with us to get put in the loony bin?"

"That won't be necessary," the doctor replies dryly. "She's dead."

"But I heard . . ."

"She slipped through my fingers, Malte."

He pinches the bridge of his nose between his thumb and forefinger, lowers his head. When he raises it again, there is compassion in his eyes.

"I found her in the barn, curled up among her beasts, covered in muck. It's a terrible thing to be so old. She was rambling. When our brains grow senile, the whole house of cards comes tumbling down."

His face looks suddenly vulnerable; he does not relish the thought himself. He shrugs off the chill creeping down his spine. Hunts in his bag and brings out a death certificate. Malte lends his back for him to write on. Aviaja Bertelsen. Date of birth: Unknown. Cause of death: Convulsions resulting in heart failure.

This done, he waves the ink dry.

Malte cranes his neck to see. "What does it say?"

The doctor stares at him, dumbfounded. "Can't you read?"

"I know the alphabet . . ."

"Well, we'll have to do something about that—a boy your age!"

The doctor mulls this over in silence, then changes his tack. "Did you fill that can? We have to get going. I'll start up the old crate."

He lifts the empty can off the well cover, waving aside Malte's apologies. "It doesn't matter. We can fill it at the guest house. We'd better be on our way."

He strides ahead, suddenly in a great hurry, and Malte has to keep up as best he can. The chill has spread, and a biting sea fog is settling around them.

When they get to the car, the doctor helps Malte up the two high steps to his seat, setting a hand on his rear to punt him aloft. Then he bends over the crank handle; his back muscles tense beneath his jacket as he turns it once without its catching. He tries again. The engine does not respond. Finally, he puffs mightily and straightens up, placing his hands at the small of his back and stretching.

"What a mess! Hand me my bag, will you?"

Malte hands him his doctor's bag.

"No, not that one. The one next to it, with my tools."

He spends ages tinkering with it. Screw caps and nuts are lifted out and arranged on a cloth he has spread on the grass. Malte follows his every move from up in the seat. The doctor sticks his tongue in the corner of his mouth—exactly like him. He would love to have been the one to hand him his instruments, but Dr. Hansen is perfectly capable of doing everything himself. He blows nozzles clear with ballooning cheeks, wipes the filter with a bit of cotton. There are smudges of oil on his cheeks and a blob of axle grease has stuck to his beard. At long last he puts the whole thing back together and starts all over again with the crank handle.

With as little success. The engine is dead.

Its owner raises his arms to the heavens. "Damn it!"

Malte laughs. High in the sky, a hawk is circling. Slicing and slicing across its own axis.

Apart from that, the world stands still around them. Rolling waves and rushing shingle, seagull cries farther out, and sand drifting across the beach. Until a whinny comes from the dune, followed by hoofbeats. This time it is the doctor who blanches and cries out. He looks around in confusion, takes a step forward to shield Malte.

The old crone comes walking toward them, large as life. A shawl frays about her; the gray mane stands on end and her apron is dripping with dung. Her eyes smolder in their slits like coals. Behind her she drags the nag, halting slightly; she throws up a withered arm and shakes the hand gripping the bridle. The doctor looks as if the grave has just opened up before him.

Malte curls up and buries his head in his crossed arms.

When he looks up again, the pony has been harnessed to the front of the car and stands nodding its head under its long mane and tossing its muzzle. Then, before the doctor can do anything, the old woman steps up and hooks a claw into the boy's thigh. The specter digs in her nails and holds him transfixed on the threshold of pain.

"He's the one!" she hisses, her old carcass quivering. The second time, it is said with a strange calmness, almost like a revelation.

"He's the one!"

Malte swoons and falls forward.

IN WHICH
THE FORESTS SING

Malte comes to with the ground under his cheek and the smell of ammonia in his nostrils. He jackknifes into a sitting position with a sneeze that blows his head clear. The doctor has one hand at his back to support him and a brown pharmacist's bottle in the other. The boy's head wobbles, a trail óf saliva has trickled from the corner of his mouth. His eyelids feel like a doll's, flickering open and closed as his head bobs up and down.

Between grass and sky the world comes back into focus. A wheel spins before his eyes and only once the spokes have converged on the hub and come to a halt is he lucid and the giddiness gone.

Malte puts a hand to his forehead, where a lump has risen. He hit the headlight bracket when he fell off the box. Dr. Hansen considers him carefully and with a touch of concern. But no sooner has Malte regained his sight than his eyes start rolling again and flicking from side to side. He runs a hand down over his thigh, recalling her grip on his flesh.

"Is she gone?"

"Easy, Malte, it's all taken care of. Let's just get you back onto your feet."

The doctor helps him, one hand under his arm. Malte comes upright and props himself against the front fender, which serves as footrest for both driver and passenger. The pony, calm now in its harness, whinnies reassuringly. Having let go of the boy, Dr. Hansen strokes its flank, his hand leaving glossy bands in the coat. It has been a long time since anyone groomed this pony.

"That was some fright you had there. And me, too, I can tell you."

"But Doctor, you said she was dead!"

"I thought she was. I was a bit too hasty. So now you know, Malte, doctors can make mistakes. You might say the old lady got her second wind . . . Romeo made the same mistake."

You can see it in his face. Malte is still trying to make sense of these last words, when the doctor goes on. "Haven't you ever heard of suspended animation? Romeo thought his sweetheart was dead and so he killed himself. When she woke from her deathlike sleep and saw her beloved . . ."

But the boy breaks in. He is not interested in hearing about sweethearts right now. "What's suspended animation?"

"One of the great mysteries of medical science, Malte. Dead people have been known to wake up in the funeral parlor. In some places, a bell is tied to the toe or hand, just in case. At the very worst, a person may even be buried."

"But what happens if they wake up?"

"What happens? Oh, I don't think you should be worrying about that. We'd better see about getting you home."

"But do they ring the bell down in the coffin?"

This is too much for the doctor. "Okay, let's forget about it now."

"Sometimes, when I'm in the graveyard with Oda, I can hear a ringing under the ground. Like sleigh bells."

"That's probably the sheep. Now, that's enough, Malte!"

"If a dead person touches you, do you die too?"

"Malte, use your head. A cold is contagious, whooping cough and measles."

"And German measles!"

"German measles, yes, if you haven't already had them."

He takes hold of the boy by his belt.

"Up you go. We have to get going."

Before climbing up himself, he roots about in his doctor's bag, produces the death certificate, and tears it up. Then he starts muttering to himself, groping in the bag for the committal papers. He pulls them out, rips them in half, bundles the pieces together, and rips them across again. The scraps flutter to the ground. He dusts off his palms and mumbles something to the boy. He could just as easily have been speaking to someone else.

"Everyone has the right to a life. Good heavens, she doesn't have that long to go and I see no reason to blight her last days with a lot of hocus-pocus and cold showers, in a home where no living soul can get a moment's peace for all the fussing of doctors and nurses who can't do anything for them, anyway. She's better off back there among her animals."

Malte nods. Adopts what he considers a sage expression. "Where is she?"

"In her bed, Malte. I changed her as you would a baby and gave her something to help her sleep. I'll call again this evening and we'll take it from there!"

"Can I come?"

The doctor does not answer. He climbs up next to Malte and flicks the reins. The car moves off as he gathers the reins in one hand and steers with the other. Soon they are trundling along the lane, hips jiggling. The girth straps have been tied to the axles and he glances over the side to check that they are holding. Then he continues.

"I couldn't believe my eyes when she wandered up with this beast in tow. You would think somebody had tightened a screw in her head and switched on the light . . ."

And as the doctor drones on, the shadows creep up over their knees. They have gotten as far as the forest. Malte is allowed to try on the leather helmet and the goggles, which fall down about his neck even as darkness descends over the bridge of his nose. The inside of the helmet has an acrid aroma that Malte savors, breathing deep. He makes engine noises in his throat. He and the doctor bump shoulders.

He lifts the helmet for a peek, to find they are driving through fields. The homeward road has no end. It immerses itself in details that swept past in a blur on the way out. He sees a fox among the wheat, with a white snout and slightly narrowed eyes. It follows their progress for some time, head up, the tip of its snout vibrating like a compass needle. It is one of the fox cubs from the den—suddenly he is sure of it—and it is already a young fox while he is still a boy. Strange to be able to recognize a fox—time runs away so fast with puppies and kittens that it is impossible to keep up.

"Hi, fox," he says. It nods, out there among the wheat, and vanishes. One quick flick and it is gone. Dr. Hansen turns to him.

"What do they call you besides Malte?"

"Alexander," he answers promptly. "Malte Alexander!"

The doctor does a double take.

"Is that your father? Alexander?"

"I don't have a father. I made it up myself!"

Malte sits and stews, silent and defiant. Then he picks up the thread once more.

"I made the whole thing up, all by myself," he announces proudly.

The doctor does not quiz him. "That's a fine name," is all he says, "a real warrior's name. You're not to be fooled with, are you, Malte? How old are you?"

"Twelve."

"Well, you've got no fear, I'll say that."

The boy preens himself up there. Two heads nod above the wheat and meet in a smile. The pony is given a touch of the rein and breaks into a trot that fairly eats up the miles. Dr. Hansen has an idea. He brings the car to a halt. "Would you like to get up and ride?"

Malte nods, more than a little impressed at his own daring. The doctor gives him a leg up, checks that he has a good grip on the girth, then climbs back and gets the car moving with a click of the tongue. Soon they are loping along once more. Malte bounces up and down on the pony's back; the motion jars his stomach and takes his breath away if he comes down wrong. He bumps about, high off the ground, and over the last stretch the courier to the czar stretches out in a gallop that sends clouds of dust flying up in his wake. Malte flings his arms around the pony's neck and feels the stiff bristles of its mane against his cheek.

He arrives at the guest house gasping for breath. All the wind has been knocked out of him. The doctor reins in their rig. "Phew," he says, and wipes the sweat from his brow, "a mug of beer would go down well now."

The boy jumps down unaided. Pats the pony's chest; its flanks are heaving like a bellows and its coat ripples, mottled and glistening with moisture. He is proud as an Indian brave after his first ride. The hedge and garden gate come into focus just as a hansom cab drives up from the opposite direction and pulls in alongside them.

The pony whinnies and the hansom horse answers with a snort. New arrivals at the guest house.

It is the pharmacist from town. In one hand he carries a suitcase; a small girl clings to his jacket sleeve. The doctor lets out a whistle of surprise.

"It's you . . . !"

"It's me, indeed!" replies the pharmacist and they shake hands. The two men immediately fall deep into conversation, and the girl with the violet eyes and the delicate skin tugs at the sleeve several times without anyone's paying attention. Malte is mystified: her lips are moving, all right, but no sound comes out.

The afternoon is still young. The little party installs itself around the table in the garden. The doctor calls through the open window and presently Oda appears, bringing beer and lemonade and biscuits on a tray. Malte and the girl tuck in, both their hands coming down at the same time on the last biscuit. Malte wins, because he is bigger. She has to make do with the corner she has clenched in her fist. Not one word has passed between them.

Meanwhile, the doctor is giving a report of the day's house call at Crow Towers, winding up with one more ally. Old Aviaja ought to be allowed to stay where she is, even if it does mean a few more visits. The parson is on their side, the rest of the parish—with the chief elder at their head and Mrs. Swan as backup—are against, and so be it.

But they are the specialists. They clink mugs in a toast.

"Oh, by the way," says the doctor, wiping the foam from his beard, "have you met Malte, my assistant?"

He winks at the little girl, who is sitting sulking under the bow on her bonnet. He leans over and whispers something in the pharmacist's ear. The man with the gold-rimmed spectacles—they are kept in place by a clip over the bridge of his nose

and a cord running down into his waistcoat pocket—nods once
or twice before the doctor is done whispering.

Then: "That's fine by me," he says, "if the boy wants to."

He nods pleasantly at Malte. A little reticently. The pharmacist is tall and his name is Oak. A smooth bald spot about the
size of a coin sits in the middle of his circlet of hair. He clears
his throat.

"Say hello to Ida."

Malte takes Ida's hand and squeezes it until the biscuit
crumbs trickle out. The pressure turns Ida's face red.

"Ida is dumb," the pharmacist says. With his kindly manner, he holds the boy's gaze, until Malte grows embarrassed and
releases her hand.

"I'm very sorry," he says politely and ignores the pink
tongue that curls out of her mouth, adding insult to injury. He
roots about in his pocket and comes up with a crumpled scrap.
A picture of an angel on a cloud.

He smooths it and holds it out to Ida, who snatches it from
his hand and runs off with it down the garden, to where her little figure is dappled by the leafy shade. The ringlets beneath her
bonnet are bleached white by summer. Malte watches her carefully.

Dumb.

He contemplates this in silence. It is the things one never
manages to say that carry the most weight. Ida must have a
swarm of bees shut up inside her head. He feels a hand on his
head, hears the pharmacist high up among the treetops and the
birdsong.

"You could read with us. For a couple of hours a day, if you
like. Ida is learning to write, so we could kill two birds with
one stone. There's nothing wrong with her hearing, you just
have to look at her. You'd be welcome to join us for lessons. Dr.
Hansen told me . . ."

Malte is quick to nod. He does not want to hear any more. He dashes off after Ida.

"Yes, please, I'd like that."

Is what he does not manage to say.

Classes are held in the morning, right after breakfast. The light falls into the room in rectangular shafts and the pharmacist begins each lesson by taking a book from the shelf and reading aloud. His long arms pluck books from the topmost shelf. He clips his spectacles firmly over his nose—they have a tendency to fall off when he reaches up for a book. He reads standing up. When he slams the book shut once more, the dust dances in the sunbeams.

All the while, Malte contemplates—with greater and greater detachment—the empty space in the bookcase. As long as the book is lying open in the pharmacist's hand, the words flow off its pages, rising and falling. A little dancer twirls into view on the pharmacist's tongue; darning needles talk and sound exactly like Mrs. Swan. Paper boats sail down the gutter, a waterlogged rag ball, huge dogs, and soldiers with tinderboxes and hearts of tin.

The pharmacist glides over the pages, but he never stops to show them a picture. The greatest miracle of all is the muteness that finds a voice and, in a second, is transformed into pictures. Back in its place on the shelf, the book falls silent once more and the gap is filled.

Other times, he leafs through a book, explains how the pages are made from wood. Open the book and you can hear the forests singing. Malte will never forget it; little Ida hangs on the pharmacist's every word and shapes the sounds with her lips.

They gather around the tile-topped table with exercise

books, colored pencils, and erasers. Ida sits on cushions, her eyes darting from one speaking face to the other, though she has no way of answering back. The image of the muteness that prevails in the world of letters. She draws the alphabet, with signs that fill the whole page.

This makes it easier for Malte. They can color the vowels blue, red, and yellow—as they sound to them. The consonants are black—they are the tree trunks in the forest. Only the foliage changes color, but the foliage is the sound and the tone and the whole song. The pharmacist explains, and Ida transcribes into sign language with an eagerness that is contagious. He picks one line—"My lass is as bright as amber"—opens the door to the dining room, and plays a chord on the piano. He sings the individual notes out loud. On its own the long *a* of *amber* is brown, but taken together with the short *a* of *lass* and the *i* of *bright* it becomes both golden and transparent.

Once he has established the connection between character and sound and made the move from word to picture, the spindly legs start to link up, forming first into rock pools, then into clusters and chains of continuous action. Malte is reading. He has been walking around with the notes to this music for a long time.

Afterwards he plays with Ida in the garden. He shows her his secret place in the willow hedge. The heart of her face latches onto his every move, listening more intently than anyone with the power of speech. People who can talk are so preoccupied with their own sounds and hear only themselves. Ida listens to the song inside Malte. Together they get lost in the forest; they leave a trail of breadcrumbs that the birds peck at, they find their way to the cave and the gingerbread house. He tells her about the witch who made the flesh on his bone shrivel up; he sends up kites for her and climbs trees to bring them down. Ida claps her hands. He rolls up his sleeves and trouser legs and shows her scars from tumbles he has taken. When she has to have her nap, he is permitted to read aloud to her.

The first book that Malte reads from beginning to end, he shares with her. It is *Twenty Thousand Leagues under the Sea.* Now and again he stops to explain something he only half understands himself. Because when Ida listens, everything is made whole. They forget all about the nap and set off to explore the world that the earth conceals beneath its ocean. Malte has a ship that can dive.

Carefully he breaks the seal on the bottle. In Olesen's workshop he borrows some tweezers, pulls off the masts and paddles, paints the hull blue, and furnishes it with portholes.

He paints the sky like an underwater scene with dancing light beams and fish. Ida watches with bated breath and the lighthouse keeper murmurs in the background as the stick of sealing wax starts to bubble and the taper flickers in the boy's hand. Malte turns his brush around and inscribes an *I* in the seal before it can harden. When he is finished, the ship changes hands. He presents the bottle to Ida without a sound.

One day he shows her the elf. Ida cups the lump in her hand; after she has held it for a time, she starts flapping her arms and making it fly through the air. She pursues a butterfly that hides its insect body under its admiral's cloak, lands on a leaf, and bores down into the flower. Then she opens her mouth and holds her tongue steady in the center.

"E . . . e . . ."

It comes out in long, breathy gasps. Malte is thunderstruck, stopped dead in his tracks. For a split second, there on the lawn, he stands transfixed, then he whirls about and races for the dining room. The pharmacist is in the middle of his soup and drops his spoon when Malte cries, "Ida's talking!"

Oak jumps to his feet, the corner of his napkin still tucked in at his collar, and runs out after Malte. The boy gets there first, intent on ensuring the safety of the treasure on which no adult eye has rested. Because he knows: the tension would drain out of the amber and the elf turn back into a dragonfly. Ida struggles to hold onto the lump when he takes it out of her hand and slips it into his pocket. The pharmacist is making his way across the lawn with his great long strides, squashing a mosquito on the way. He mops his throat with the napkin. But by the time he gets to her, her mouth has set and she is once more as silent as a fish in an aquarium. He bends toward her, the coin is level with Malte's face, ruddy in the evening sunlight.

"Is this true, little Ida? Tell Papa . . ."

She presses her lips together, sets the ringlets swinging about her cheeks with an emphatic shake of her head. But her eyes give her away. They are shining, magnified by a film that could burst at any moment and cause those chubby cheeks to run with tears. The pharmacist does not notice; he sees only her sadness. He tips back his circlet of hair and looks Malte in the eye.

"We must not rush things," he says in a voice so serious that the boy nods blankly and bites his tongue.

So it is with us. We keep our miracles close to our chest. We cannot interfere in the course of events, anyway. To everything there is a season. The living have nothing but that, and soon the story will be played out.

Snip, snap, snout.

The following day, Ida writes him a note, sliding it across the table to him in the middle of the lesson. "I want to see the elf," it says in colored letters. He tucks the note under his exercise book. It is a piece of evidence he cannot use without betraying his secret. The pharmacist almost catches them with a glint from his gold-rimmed glasses. He harrumphs from the armchair. Then he turns back to his book and continues reading in silence while Ida fills the page with letters that spell "ape" and leapfrog along the lines.

Once alone, Malte folds the slip of paper and hides it inside his stamp album. Monsieur Charles has given him some stamps that make the King of Belgium pale into insignificance. There are parrots, jungles, and boa constrictors. He sorts one page at a time, arranging them by size. He loses himself in thought over a furry animal with powerful claws and a tubular snout. Then he sighs and slides the stamp into position, down where the ink turns grayish under the opaque strip of paper.

His blood itches like ants. Malte is restless. It is raining outside; the attic window is all streaked and you cannot look out it without being caught by a raindrop. The willow hedge and the lane have taken on the same gray hue as the stamps in their sleeve. He experiments for a while with getting the lump of amber to float in the washbowl. It looks wonderful, like a golden mountain on the water. He leaves it to paddle its own canoe.

Malte sighs again. He wishes he had a steam engine; then he would fire it up over the spirit lamp and make the flywheel pound. He would sound the whistle by tugging on a little chain, be the stoker on a luxury liner—as big as the one he has seen on Monsieur Charles's trunk—or travel across the desert on a special train as the pyramids disappear in a cloud of black smoke and the coaches are attacked by Bedouins waving scimitars burnished by the sun.

But he has no steam engine. Steam engines are for the children of the rich. Malte gazes forlornly out the window, elbows on the sill and chin resting on his hands. Suddenly two figures come into view down by the hedge. Rain sweeps across them, blurring their contours, but it is Oda—in Mrs. Swan's cloak—

and Monsieur Charles in a top hat, a traveling cape slung over
his shoulders. They embrace, looking all at once like two tadpoles, standing there in the rain, joined in a kiss. Malte looks
away in disgust.

He hears the rumble of coach wheels. He sees the roof of a
hansom, hears the sound of a puddle being sent in all directions
and a snort as the horse is reined in. The tadpoles pull apart;
Monsieur Charles removes his hat and ducks in under the roof.
The tails of his coat are the last to disappear; the slam of the
door is drowned out by the shower of rain that batters the attic
bargeboards. He waves his hat out the window, then Oda is
alone, giving herself a shake as the hansom moves off. She
stands there until the mist has completely obliterated them.

She lifts her face to Malte's window with unseeing eyes.
Raindrops glisten on her cheeks. She drops her head and walks
off slowly between the willows—paying no attention to the
puddles, her feet merely threading their way. When he opens
the window and leans out to the waist he can see Mrs. Swan's
cloak swirling over the dune, heading down to the sea, where it
lies hidden in banks of fog.

Water runs down the back of his neck and he pulls his head
in.

That same afternoon there is a fearful to-do at the guest
house. The room with the sea view has been turned upside
down, Monsieur Charles's bags slung out into the corridor. The
gardener has pried them open with a crowbar to find them
cavernously empty, apart from a few bundles of newspapers
packed inside to give them some weight.

Mrs. Swan waves a bill under Oda's nose; Oda sobs and as-
sures her that he will be back before the week is out—he has
promised her. On his word of honor. He has gone to town
to pick up a telegram that they have both been anxiously
awaiting.

The landlady bristles in her starched collar.

"So that's the way it is," she says, purse-lipped. She turns her back and descends the stairs with ponderous tread. Closes the door of her office and sticks her columns of figures on their spike. Soon the model sailing ship is being knocked about; spittle flies over the rigging with the spume from a storm that has long been brewing.

From behind the closed door comes the sound of something crashing to the floor. Oda jumps. She is still standing on the stairs, from where she has heard the commotion in the captain's saloon. She clutches at the banister and sinks down onto the landing, puts a hand to her stomach, and feels a spasm ripple beneath her apron.

IN WHICH
ODA PUTS HER FAITH
TO THE TEST

Oda danced through the summer night, flying high on fairy dust. Now the fairy mound has sunk underground and the day returned to throw cold water over her. She has morning sickness and hot flashes, aches with longing in her sleep and, during waking hours, holds uncertainty at bay with buckets of lye. She polishes the silver in the drawers, attacks the slats of the lampshades with a cotton swab, changes the lining paper on the pantry shelves.

All week it rains, every free moment she has sees her out on the road listening for the coach wheels that will bring her beloved back. Earth and sky run into one, everything drips and splashes. A raindrop strikes her on the forehead and with a shudder the ripples spread through her from top to toe. She has got Mrs. Swan off her back by confessing right after the ruckus in the saloon.

She shows her the ring: for over a month they have been sweethearts, their engagement was to have been announced this coming Sunday. He has gone to town to pick up the telegram giving them his family's blessing.

He will be back. There is Alpha and Omega in everything
she says. Until he returns, she will cover his debts—Mrs. Swan
can dock her wages for the bill he has left outstanding. In the
first month alone, he has got through as much as Oda earns in
a year, and she is prepared to pay back every penny. Money is
not the issue here. Mrs. Swan is mollified.

Sunday does not bring his return, and the next week Oda
leaves in the hands of the Christ Child. She prays as she did
when her mother lay dying, pouring her heart and soul into fer-
vent faith and hope. She seeks solace in the Bible she received
as a confirmation present, reads the letter to the Corinthians
over and over again: "Love suffereth long, and is kind; love en-
vieth not; love vaunteth not itself, is not puffed up; doth not
behave itself unseemly, seeketh not her own, is not easily pro-
voked, thinketh no evil; rejoiceth not in iniquity, but rejoiceth
in the truth; beareth all things, believeth all things, endureth all
things." Then she can carry on for a little while longer. The
telegram has been delayed, he has taken lodgings in town,
where he waits for the day when he can honor his vow. To her
he is no longer Monsieur Charles but Santos—the name he con-
fided to her with little love bites to her ear. She bears this mark
of their coupling with pride.

She denies doubt entry with an obstinacy new to her. Don't
think she doesn't notice the spitefulness of her fellow parish-
ioners, her girlfriends' tittering in the choir, and those young
pups who squeeze up against her with an impudence they
would never have dared before. Oda and her nigger, that is
what they call them behind her back; set a beggar on horseback
and he'll ride to the devil—likely she thought she was going to
wind up singing at the Paris Opera and driving in a carriage
like a fine lady. Well, she made her bed, and now she can lie in
it.

The child in Oda's face disappears with the villagers' whispering. Their voices rustle in the corners like fallen leaves, but when she turns to confront them she meets only their virtuousness.

Oda holds out; between dreaming and waking she has seen him. Lying in a feverish stupor in his lodgings, the top buttons of his shirt undone, he tosses and turns on the bed and speaks her name in a voice full of longing. She lights candles for him in her room, dries the roses that accompanied his proposal, and hangs them over her bed. She ties his love letters in a bundle with string and lays them in a box.

She rubs the ring to call back her Aladdin. If she goes without eating prunes for one whole day, he is sure to show up the next. In the choir she raises her voice to the threshold of pain, and afterwards, when the members of the congregation have gone their separate ways, she gets down on her knees and prays, and the chill of the church floor works its way into her bones. She feels Malte's fingers slipping up inside her sleeve, gives him a hug. Then they pray together until the sexton clears his throat loudly from down in the nave, rattles his keys, and sees them out.

From the residents of Sea View she receives sympathy in the form of looks that are laced with a dash of hemlock. Oh yes, he was a nobleman—a real swell! I must say, they kept it very quiet. Frankly, Mrs. Münster, I had no idea what was going on. And he looked so nice. It makes the blood run cold. Poor girl. And so young. Then the hemlock: Well, now she'll have to take what's coming to her, poor thing, but she really should have stopped to think before it was too late.

The gentlemen are more interested in the *Titanic*, which has gone down in a blaze of glory, with banner headlines in the *Illustrated Times*. It's already old news, the pages have yellowed in the May sunshine, but that way the ladies can talk all they like.

Oda holds her head high, polishes the lamps, and ignores the women's cackling. One day she finds that her ring has gone green; the metal has lost its sheen and might almost be taken for brass. Horrified, she shines it, rubbing and rubbing at the green spot until the blood flows. But the flow of blood for which she is waiting does not come. She is several weeks overdue, bone-tired when she leans against the ironing board, suddenly short of breath, and feels the tense weight of her breasts.

When she goes to put the bed linen away, she feels faint. She buries her nose in the naphthalene bags, in lieu of smelling salts. Afterwards she pushes Malte away when he comes up and thrusts his album at her.

"When Monsieur Charles comes back with the letter, can I have the stamp?"

Her skin crawls at the thought of the images her lover has sown.

"His name's Santos. And he's not coming back!" she hears herself hiss, then claps her hand over her mouth. She needs to cool her brow. She dips a washcloth in the basin and happens to touch the chunk of amber.

"What's all this mess?"

She does not wait for an answer. Empties the basin out the window and sends the dribble of pee from the chamber pot after it. The boy is caught between tears and rage as he sees his treasure disappear in a stream of amber yellow.

She has forgotten that she made him her confidant—his blind faith in the man was as great as her own. Until this moment, Malte has been her standard-bearer and her accomplice. She has seen his eyes burn with a fierce light in the church when she prays, and afterwards he prays for Ida. But the child's faith makes a mockery of her own; what does a little boy like him know about love?

Malte lashes out at her, scratching and kicking, and she is forced to back out the door, struggling to defend herself.

Her fretting increases; once faith turns to doubt there is nothing left to her. All her rituals are exhausted. She has run out of prayers, is up to her elbows in dishwater. Her hands are red and chapped from the suds. She throws up over the pile of clean dishes and has to start all over again. She washes the debris of her fairy tale down the drain and sees the bubbles burst on the sea-gull porcelain. The drain gives off a rancid smell; in the background Mrs. Swan watches in silence as Oda gets the fire going in the wood stove.

A little later, Malte appears at the kitchen door, one hand on the latch. He stares tight-lipped at Oda's back before lifting the latch and opening the door.

"Where are you off to, Malte?" snaps Mrs. Swan.

"Out."

"Oh no, you don't! Get up those stairs and scrub your nails and wash your hands. It won't be long until we eat. That's all we need, for you to go playing in puddles now."

The bad weather shows no sign of letting up. The sand retains its iron-gray color, the waves wash over the beach, and the streets of the fishing village are deserted. No one ventures out; after dinner, everyone stays put. Malte is the only one to cast a glance now and then toward the French windows. He is playing a game with Ida. He holds up a card with a picture on it and says the word out loud. Ida imitates him, shaping each word with tongue and lips. You can see the cards building into hurdles inside her mouth and she has to start the word over again.

The pharmacist is having a talk with the doctor, who has just returned from yet another house call to Crow Towers. They are discussing not the old woman, however—it looks as if she is going to pull through—but the doctor's new car. His Hammel has given up the ghost and gone back to being a horse-drawn cart; the fishmonger has taken over the old crate. He has stripped it of all its devilish workings and fitted it with a shaft. When he drives to the fish market in town, he piles his live-boxes on the back seat.

Hansen has got himself a new Model T Ford: four-cyclinder engine, nineteen horsepower—nineteen, my friend! And one can just picture it, with the whole team of whinnying stallions harnessed to it. The enclosed body, standing out there in the rain, speaks for itself.

"Starts every time," the doctor says and knocks on the underside of the table.

They order rum punch from the kitchen.

The minute Oda gets off work, she sneaks out. A cold wind is blowing. She stands on the shore and watches her cloud castles in the air turn to water. It is a moonlit night, the heavens are on the hunt and freshen her eyes into slits. She kicks off her shoes, bundles up her skirts. She dips a foot in the water; the wave draws back and sucks at her, the cold numbing her toes. Suddenly she is filled with longing. For cold all over, for insensibility and watery sleep. To let her whole body be carried away and harden into ice.

A merciful death, the fishermen call it. But Oda shies away from the dark suggestion of the water; the moonlight casts curious signs that bob on the surface. She steps back. The next wave rolls in higher and washes over her shins; she all but loses her footing. Panicking, she runs up the side of the dune. She tears at the lyme grass until her hands bleed, screams his name with the wind and the sand full in her face. She knocks the breath out of her belly, pounding on the lump growing in there, which before too long will have gills and bulging fish eyes.

She waits until the lights are out in the guest house and everyone has gone to bed. Then, drenched to the skin, she finds her way back in the darkness, up to her room, teeth chattering. No one sees her except the fox with the white snout. She spends the rest of the night quaking under the heavy eiderdown, while the fox—a thief in a fur mask—roots about under the attic window, takes a lump of something between its jaws, gnaws at it, and streaks across the backyard with it, beneath the sighing poplars.

Malte is out searching at the crack of dawn. The rolled-up bottoms of his pajama trousers are soaked; he crawls about on all fours, squinting up at the window to judge which way it may have fallen. The soil in the bed of peonies squelches under his knees as he sniffs his way, all but burying his nose in the earth. Two sniffs and he raises his head to consider. Every smell is stupefyingly powerful this time of day.

At the root of a clump of nettles he is suddenly certain. A sharp tang: his own dribble of pee. Damn it, the nettles grow so close together. He snaps off the stalks, trying to avoid being stung by the leaves but only succeeding in brushing a cluster of them across his cheek. He rubs his skin to dull the burning, runs out of steam, then dives head and shoulders into the clump.

The nugget of amber is gone. A dull sense of despair takes possession of him, even as he goes on searching. He knows, but still he keeps at it. Frantically, circling farther and farther from the center of probability.

In the end, he sweeps the bed clear and peony petals swirl about his ears like falling stars. The elf has flown, he can hear it fluttering in the air, see the iridescence of its wings soaring over

Sea View, taking a turn over the water before returning to the forests, hatched from its golden egg.

A resounding smack on the ear checks his flight.

"What are you up to now?"

Mrs. Swan yanks his ear, which is still burning from the blow it has been dealt. She is touchy about her flower beds. Now she is out with her basket to pick flowers to brighten up the breakfast table. Malte is sent to his room for the rest of the morning. He broods over the loss of the chunk of amber—now Ida will never learn to talk. She made some noises in her throat yesterday evening, after their game of picture cards. He is convinced she is trying to say his name.

"Mmmm . . ." is what comes out, dredged up as if from the pit of her stomach. She lacks only the vowel sounds that need to be tied on like balloons to send the word floating into the air. The elf could have made it happen; now the day lies in ruins.

Down in the saloon, Ida has her lessons alone. She is told that Malte has been naughty and she hastens to look chastened. But it isn't the same without Malte: Ida's mind wanders, she picks bits off her eraser and swivels her head around when the maid comes in with linden tea on a tray.

The pharmacist notes Oda's pallor, her dull, glazed look and heavy eyes. All in a day's work for him. He is just about to inquire as to her health when she curtsies to him. Her actions are those of an automaton. She twines her fingers in her apron and does not look him in the eye when she speaks, in a voice that is barely audible.

"Mrs. Swan would like to know, sir, if the pharmacist would be so kind as to bring some rat poison back from town."

"Rat poison?"

"Yes, sir. We've got bats in the belfry . . . I mean, rats in the pantry," she hastens to correct herself. What *is* she saying!

"Tell her I'll be glad to. What about naphthalene crystals—or maybe you have enough to last the year?"

"Yes, thank you," says Oda. It is she who sews the bags.

"Does that mean that you would like some more? Or do you have plenty?"

"No, thanks," says Oda, now thoroughly confused. "I mean, yes, we have all we need."

"Fine, Oda. I'll be sure and remember it."

"The rat poison, that is," Oda blurts out. The pharmacist laughs out loud at her consternation.

"My, but we're confused today. Tell me, is anything the matter?"

"No," breathes Oda and fixes her eye on a point outside the room, in the hall, where she has caught sight of a cobweb. Soon afterwards she is busy with the feather duster and the pharmacist perseveres with Ida's writing exercises. The girl gouges great furrows in the paper; *Don't want to* is all she manages to write before the pencil point breaks. They get no further that day.

"Do you miss Malte?" he asks, very softly, as he is stacking the exercise books on the tiled tabletop. Ida stands nodding like a doll in the middle of the room, and once she starts she cannot stop.

Upstairs, a black cloud has descended over Malte. Nobody likes him—why was he brought into the world at all, it seems to get along just fine without him. He's only in the way, an odd sock. A boy who plays with girls—what could be worse? More than once he goes over and tugs at the door, but the key has been turned on the outside. Mrs. Swan has locked him in.

He attempts to start reading his book over again from the beginning, but it's boring by now—Captain Nemo is nothing but a dead duck in a floating tin can. As it happens, the pharmacist has promised him another book by the same author;

Malte couldn't care less about the author, as long as there is more about Captain Nemo. He has not gotten it yet, of course.

He can hear the doctor tramping down the stairs; a minute later the Model T starts up. And Malte was not even offered a ride. He sits down to do a drawing of Crow Towers, pencils in figure threes for the birds in the sky but has some trouble with the towers themselves. He draws the witch with hair sticking out all over and gives her stick snake eyes. Instead of rose hips on the bushes he paints flames, and by the end the whole house is ablaze, when he crosses out his drawing with angry slashes of the pencil.

He has an idea. He opens the bureau drawer, pulls out the bedsheets, ties the corners together, and opens the window. He fastens the end sheet securely and drops the rest out. The rope reaches to the flower bed with plenty to spare. Then he clambers out. He is still in his pajamas; they could be his striped convict's uniform. He steals through the willow hedge and out onto the lane. The main thing now is not to be spotted.

He makes it, unseen, into the forest. Here a bank slopes down to where the railroad track runs past. He puts his ear to the rail and hears it singing way down the line where the tracks converge.

Late in the afternoon the clouds disperse and the sheets can be seen gleaming a long way off. The gardener coming past does not know what to make of them. He mentions them to Mrs. Swan, who wastes no time running upstairs and unlocking the door. The boy is gone. She comes to a decision: enough is enough. This is the last summer she is going to take in a boarder for nothing. It's high time his mother, that gadabout, did her bit. If, that is, they can find her at all. Of course, she is in the big city at this time of year, when all the fine gentlemen flock to the promenade.

Mrs. Swan snorts.

When Malte still has not turned up by supper, she sends for the village constable. He spends the last hour of the day asking around in the neighborhood, but no one has seen a runaway boy in pajamas. He decides to wait to send out a search party until the next day, when they can get tracking dogs from town. His own old Trusty can neither smell nor hear; it's pathetic, but he hasn't the heart to do away with the creature.

IN WHICH
THE ACTS OF LOVE
BEAR FRUIT

Hell—or simply the lot of the hermit? Every night that damn fox's whelp comes and gnaws at my casing; I am a well-chewed knucklebone. The noise is insufferable and the glint of those gigantic canines above my head is downright terrifying as it bites its way through my shell and I feel the primeval skeleton shrink. It thinks there is something in there that it *has* to get at. So whatever is going on inside that sharp and canted brain, it cannot be all that stupid.

And on those odd occasions when it takes a break from its incessant gnashing, it bats me with its paw and makes me blaze with a glint of its amber-yellow irises.

In the end I submit. A rap on the snout, a faint flicker between the eyes, and I slice through the Y-shaped fork of its forehead, turn a somersault, and land in a fold of the brain.

It is soft and spongy in there, pink and warm. Blood-warm. Oh, sweet rowanberries! I had almost forgotten what that meant. Blood-warm all day long. Hunger and desire and the flash of pain when it pricks itself on a thorn or steps on the em-

bers from the gardener's bonfire in the backyard. The vulnera-
bility, the knowledge that everything will come to an end
should the blood supply be cut off for only a few moments. The
drifting of will-o'-the-wisps, the profusion of scents, the exhilaration. The first night I go on a rampage in a chicken run, bite
the throats of those I cannot eat.

I lap up as much of the blood as I can. The rest can rot for
all I care, I am used to the stench. And when the meat has fallen
off the bones, I will have a store of pictures to brighten up my
den in the dead of winter as my sides cave in once more. That
nice boy who brings me heel ends of ham has given me a taste
for men's food. They are greater predators than I, using fire to
tenderize chicken. So rapacious is their appetite that they cannot wait for the meat to fall off the bones by itself. I admire
their bloodthirstiness. Men kill at the slightest excuse, making
mass graves out of one another. Who knows, maybe those are
their winter stores.

He senses—wily customer that he is—that as long as he has
me nothing can harm him. He dares things no fox has dared to
do in a long time. He skulks in the pantry, sprawled under the
bottom shelf, until the people have gone out. Then he takes a
flying leap at the ham hanging from its string. Wanton fox, he
humps it as if it were a vixen's hindquarters, feels the urge to
eat give way to another, stronger urge, dictated by the season.
Then he moves on to the jars of jam and honey. And damned if
he doesn't open the door by himself and sneak out before anyone suspects a thing. He jumps at the latch, but it is the weight
of my mind that bears down on the lever.

He finds time to snap the head off a rat before he leaves the
pantry. The blood tastes bitter after the jam, and he spits the
mangled rodent out, smart fox; to cover his tracks he sweeps
first the body, then the head out of the pantry with a swipe of
his paw. Only when he has done this does he nudge the door

open with his nose. He spends the rest of the day roaming field and forest in search of a mate.

Malte pricks up his ears. A train is coming. He walks out onto the tracks and stands facing toward that infernal wailing—he waits until the sleepers are rooted, vibrating, to the soles of his feet, then jumps out of the way at the last minute. The rush of wind from the locomotive's cowcatcher whips at his cheeks. He clambers up the bank and heads deeper into the forest. Corridors of light run between the trees. When hunger makes itself felt, he pitches into a thicket of blackberries.

He finds a stick and whittles it to a point with a sharp rock. If only he had his trouser pockets handy, a length of twine and this stick would have been transformed into a bow. Now he will have to make do with cutting and thrusting. He practices on the burdock leaves, whacking the stalks to a pulp.

The deep hush of the forest unnerves him. He stays off the paths, cutting instead across clearings, along hedges and ditches. The grain is being harvested. He splits open an ear and crushes the seed inside. The husk is barbed; inside the wheat is sweet and floury. He finds himself wondering why anyone bothers to bake bread. He stands for some time scanning a stream for fish, spies a few, but each time he plunges in his stick, the fish is somewhere else. He cannot get anywhere near the white scuts of the roe deer glimpsed between the tree trunks and the hare's spring is triggered the second he shifts his weight onto his front foot.

He watches the sun set over the fields. The light is golden and dusty, with none of the shining film that spreads across the sea. He is no longer hungry, there is no one to yell at him to come and eat. He sits on a rock, has put down his stick. He rests his head on his hands, sick at heart and a little forlorn.

Anything is an option, apart from home—when night falls he will have to find shelter of some sort and he is not prepared to take on the apparitions of the dark alone.

Then he sees the fox, tensed in the hedgerow. In the light of the setting sun its snout glows red, but it's him, all right—the only fox he knows. There is no mistaking that alert stance or the bushy tail waving gently now on the edge of the forest. He calls softly to it, thinks he sees it wag its brush. He no longer feels so alone. He is bound to be able to find a barn where he can curl up in the hay for the night. He is in his pajamas already.

The fox is still standing there. Malte gets up from the rock smoothly, making no sudden moves. He starts walking, looking back over his shoulder several times, with that same smooth action. The fox is following him. Now he feels absolutely confident. He follows a trail of steaming manure that has not yet settled into cow pats. The hedgerow curves around a bend . . .

A red barn gleams, the ridge of a farmhouse roof can be seen low on the horizon.

Never has the boy taken up more space than when his place at the dinner table stands empty. The mood at the guest house is bleak. The village constable's report has done nothing to lighten it; both the pharmacist and the doctor are against mounting a search party with the tracking dogs the next day. In their opinion, something ought to be done now, and they set off into the night armed with torches. Mrs. Münster comforts the Swan and agrees with all her outpourings. She has connections in the capital and first thing tomorrow morning she will go down to the post office and dispatch an urgent telegram, in an effort to locate Malte's mother.

Ida is inconsolable. She understands far too much; it piles

up in her little head and can find no way out again. A bed has been made up for her on the sofa, so that she can fall asleep to the sound of the grown-ups as they keep their vigil. Lights have been placed in the windows, to burn through the night. Oda has long been no more than a shadow of her old self; she slides along the walls. There is not a cobweb in the whole of Sea View, even though it is high season. That's the only good thing to be said for the present situation.

On top of the piano lies a book parcel that the pharmacist has forgotten.

Late at night, the two men return. They have beech leaves in their hair and their gaiters are soaked. Their hands are sticky with resin from the pine cones and their knees caked with mud. They have combed every inch of the darkness on all fours. No trace of Malte. They have inquired at all the farms and drawn a blank there, too. They sit in the empty dining room, open the door onto Ida's soft, throaty gurgling. Dr. Hansen knows the kitchen like the back of his hand; he fetches the bottle and sets it on the table. They discuss the whole business, keeping their voices low. Malte is a strange boy, at once too trusting and far too hard to reach. Someone is going to have to get to the root of the problem.

They doze off in their chairs, exhausted and aching in every limb.

Come morning they have other things to think about. Oda has been found in her room in convulsions. The eiderdown is covered with pinkish froth. She has taken rat poison. On her bedside table is a note:

Love suffereth nothing, and is hateful; love flaunteth itself and is grasping, seeketh only its own, rejoiceth in the slightest iniquity. Believeth naught, endureth naught, and craveth all. Love is a lie.

The pharmacist is surprised by the biblical syntax. By the time they carry Oda out to the doctor's car, to drive her to the hospital to have her stomach pumped, she is already blue, caught in the clutches of unconsciousness. In the back, the pharmacist first makes some attempt at artificial respiration, then turns to pounding on her heart while the doctor drives with one hand and, with the other, tries to show him what to do. As the car bumps off down Beach Road, he keeps looking back over his shoulder, yelling above the racket of the engine and the flying pebbles:

"Come on, Oak, the *palms* of the hands! Thump hard, damn it! Better a broken rib than a heart that won't beat!"

IN WHICH
MALTE MAKES
A FRIEND

Malte wakes to the buzzing of flies. The reek from the
dunghill outside filters through the barn door. He has slept fit-
fully, awakening suddenly and listening in the dark. And with
every rustle, he has thought: It's the fox! Then he has dropped
off again, exhausted by all the walking he has done.

He sits bolt upright on the bale of hay, yawns, and picks
wisps of straw off his pajama top.

There is a milk churn in the barn. He goes over and lifts the
lid but loses his appetite when the stench hits his nostrils. The
light falls on a wagon propped up on blocks, on a rusty plow-
share. The wagon is covered with pigeon droppings, the seat
ripped and the stuffing sticking out. A bird has built a nest in
the driver's box, but the nest has been abandoned. Malte can
see the shells of the hatched eggs lying in a bed of down. A
strange quiet seems to hang over abandoned bird's nests.

He listens for a long time at the barn door before venturing
out. He drinks in the first rays of sunshine, soaking up the
warmth and leaning back against the siding with his eyes half
shut. There is a tarred rock by the entrance and cart tracks run

across the fields. He follows them, treading warily at first, then striding out. He has seen hunters in these parts and he thinks of the platforms they build in the trees. He wouldn't mind holing up on one of those for the day. He does not think beyond that.

It is quite a way from the barn to the farmstead; he has to cross an open stretch of land. Gradually the ridge of the roof shows above the rise, growing into farmhouse and outbuildings. Behind the house, the forests sing. Beyond the forests lies the town and it, too, is a possibility. In the town, delivery boys scoot about on their bikes with their baskets in front. He has done a bit of that himself, making extra rounds for the grocer's shop in the days before Christmas. This thought comforts him: he will get by, of that he is sure, and you can live just fine on stale pastries. As a matter of fact, that's all you need.

Malte whistles. The day stretches before him and he gets the urge to swing his arms. He swings his arms. The cart track has reverted to a road, with a grassy ridge running down the middle. There are circles around the sun, and it dances before his eyes, quite far up the sky by now.

He steals past one of the outbuildings, sticking close to a whitewashed wall edged with tar. He can hear the cattle inside fretting at their halters. It won't be long, he figures, before they're put out to graze, so he'll have to watch out. A horse neighs—imagine if he had his own horse and could ride over hill and dale exactly as he pleased. Malte the fearless horseman. No one would be able to rest easy in their beds.

He runs right into the farmer's arms. Malte may well have been moving stealthily enough, but he had forgotten to watch where he was going. The wall of the outbuilding has ended without his noticing. His eyes travel from the cleats of a pair of clogs, past the forks of suspender buttons, over an undershirt, to come to rest, startled, on the farmer's bristly face. He feels a hand on the collar of his pajama top.

"Ah'll be danged if we ain't got another un here."

These words are addressed to the hired hand, a lumpish character in rubber boots. The farmhand has a swarthy individual by the scruff of the neck; the tramp's clothes are in tatters. When he tries to tear himself free, his arm is twisted up his back, his face falls forward, and Malte gives a cry.

The beard has grown, covering the chin with blue-black shadow, the cheeks look shrunken, and one eye has been closed by a blow from a fist, but the boy is in no doubt.

It is Monsieur Charles.

A groan issues from within the farmhand's iron grip. Malte has found a friend in need.

"This un here was sneakin' 'bout the chicken run . . ." The farmhand shakes his fist at Malte. "And he kin have another of these if he don't watch out."

"What did I tell ya," says the farmer, "ketch one, an' fore you know it you're up to your eyes in 'em. Stick together like peas in a pod, they do."

"Hold on a minute," says the hand, squinting at Malte. "It's that kid the constable was askin' 'bout yestiday. The one that done run off in nuthin' but his nightshirt . . ."

"You ain't so dumb at that, Hans. You keep an eye on this un an' ah'll send for the authorities."

The farmer releases Malte and dusts off his hands as if he has been handling something that the cat dragged in. He has already started to walk away when there comes a snarl from the bushes. A russet pelt shoots out—the fox is off, jumping up and biting the fist holding the tramp. The farmhand swears roundly and loosens his grip, and as he is sucking at his wound the two miscreants take to their heels and sprint as fast as they can across the field. The farmer tries to give chase, but the pork belly wobbles under his braces and he is soon gasping for breath.

The two tramps disappear into the thicket. He spits after

them and turns back. The farmhand is standing in the yard, staring at the bite and going green about the gills at the thought of all the devilishness that seethes in such things.

He hears a low growl.

"Blasted fox," he mutters. "I'll be damned if it's goin' to git away with that!"

And having uttered this oath, he disappears into the out-building. He reemerges carrying a shotgun. Peering into the thistles, he catches it in midstride, fires both barrels, sees fur and leaves go flying.

But the fox is unhurt. It gives a little bound and dashes off, tail down, after the others. The farmhand rummages in his pocket for more bullets, but before he has a chance to reload, the fox has vanished from view. He stares like a man possessed at the spot where he last saw it. He doesn't get it. He is an ace shot; he could have sworn he had it bang in his sights.

The two runaways have come to a halt in a clearing in the forest. Each stands, panting, his back against a tree. With his one eye swollen shut, Monsieur Charles grins at Malte, who makes a face and struggles to catch his breath. Neither has wind enough to talk. Monsieur Charles winces and cups his hand over his eye, which is starting to throb.

In any case, Malte has no idea what to say. He does not know what to make of his new companion. They stay where they are for a while longer, until their breathing has calmed down. Eventually the man finds his voice, and the explanation that follows is both long and garbled, coming out in spurts and degenerating at times into pure gibberish when he resorts to words that Malte does not understand.

Malte nods once he has grasped the gist of it. Monsieur

Charles—or Santos, as he is known to his friends and as he insists on being called from that day forward—was riding high until he got to the post office in town. From that moment on everything went wrong. The post office people had refused to hand over the telegram to a Latin whose papers were not in order. "I use another name, is easier for you!" he protested. He took a room at the local inn. He was expecting money, but when the money arrived they would not give it to him. For the same reason as before.

Since this meant that he could not pay the bill for his room, he landed in jail, where he was given so many beatings that he could not think straight. No one believed his story. In the end they got tired of feeding him. It had been only three days since they released him, with a policeman to escort him onto a ship waiting in the harbor.

Having seen another side of Malte's country, he had only one thought in mind. To get away! He managed to escape and since then he had been wandering in a daze, with nothing to eat or drink.

Malte listens gravely. He does not really know what to think. Monsieur Charles was a fine gentleman—Santos is another kettle of fish. Only the shirt remains, a pair of breeches, and boots that have not seen a dab of polish in many a day. The boy comes to a decision and starts to walk away.

"Where are we going?"

"Home," says Malte firmly, "home to Oda!"

It looks as if Santos winces again. "Not like this, I not show myself like this."

"Home!" says Malte, dragging him along.

They take a roundabout way through the forest. Malte does not need bread crumbs, he has been here before and he recognizes the clearing off on the horizon. That clearing represents the sea, but they still have a long way to go.

The sun is at its height when they hear the baying of hounds. In the same heartbeat they freeze. They part some branches: down in the hollow they see a couple of men in uniform with their dogs; the hounds have picked up the scent, tongues lolling, they strain at the leash, sending the men stumbling after. Beneath the stubble of his beard, Santos is white; he lays a hand on Malte's arm.

"Not take me . . ."

Malte nods and shushes him. In fact, he does not know what to do. But the game is catching. For him this is cops and robbers, for Santos it is deadly earnest. The dogs are on the right track; they are making straight for them.

Malte turns his head. There is a rustling under a hazel bush; they catch sight of a back flecked by leafy shadows. The fox bounds away, running straight under the noses of the dogs. A red-furred spark that draws their attention and confuses the scent. The hounds give chase, the police officers yell at them and yank on their leashes, scold them and promise that they'll soon show them how to behave.

Meanwhile, Malte and Santos make themselves invisible. Very gently they let the branches fall back.

"It's the fox," whispers the boy, "I knew he was following us! He's my friend."

Santos regards him with a newfound sparkle in the black eyes.

"*Eres un indio, Maldito, un indio!*"

Malte needs no translation. Someone has just stuck a feather in his headband. Silence has returned to the forest, the baying of the dogs recedes into the distance.

It is late afternoon. They have been walking in the shade of the oak trees, the blue glint of the sea is visible between the tree trunks. Suddenly they come on the wheat sheaves with which Oda and Santos built their lovenest. A sunbeam breaks through

the treetops and falls on Santos. He puts his hands to his head.
The music they shared, echoes of a marimba. All at once the
memory is fresh. He rests an elbow on the woodpile, hides his
eyes. Malte hears the stifled sounds he makes. Now he is certain of it, he likes Santos better than Monsieur Charles.

They turn into the lane, continuing until Sea View comes in
sight. Malte slows his pace and Santos tries vainly to hide behind a narrow pair of boyish shoulders.

A pall hangs over the guest house. The mournful expressions
and dark clothes speak for themselves. A bit of crocheting is
going on in a quiet corner, and afternoon tea is being taken
with decorum, cups are set down with care. They wait for news
from the hospital—neither the doctor nor Oak has returned.
Little Ida sits on Mrs. Swan's lap and sniffs. Her nose is wiped
and she sniffs again.

The usual roles have been reversed; the guests have made
their own tea and set the things out themselves. The plates of
cookies lie untouched. Outside, the sun is shining once more,
but someone has considered it appropriate to draw the curtains. The parson is sent for and turns up wearing his cassock.
He moves about the room, speaking quietly to each of them.
May the Lord have mercy on us in this our hour of need. God
moves in mysterious ways, his wonders to perform. All those
present respond as if he were the personification of Fate itself.

Eyes are closed, hands are clasped in laps, but no one is
openly praying.

Mrs. Münster is the first to notice the sound of an automobile approaching. Her crocheting needle stops in midair and the
mat on which she is working falls to her knee. The faint thrum
swells, turning into the roar of an engine as it rounds the bend,

leaves Beach Road, and draws closer. The sound of rubber tires on gravel and the screech of brakes that follows are still so unfamiliar to most of them that they all give a start. They are half out of their seats when the doctor and Oak enter the room.

Ida jumps off Mrs. Swan's lap and runs to her father.

There are far too many voices, all vying for answers. Dr. Hansen raises a hand to still them. "Easy now! It's too early to say for sure, but Oda is alive. She's unconscious, but she is alive. We are fighting to bring her back. She has had her stomach pumped. From a clinical point of view she was, in fact, dead for a couple of minutes, and I'm afraid she may slip away from us again. If she survives, there is no telling what sort of life she will have. Her mind may have been affected, her brain . . ."

He spares them the rest, wrenching himself free of faces that are anxious to know more than he can tell them, and winds up by saying, "There you have it." He turns to the parson. "Does my honorable colleague have anything to add?"

The parson declines. He is too wise a man willingly to lay himself open to ridicule by atheists.

With a glance at Oak, who has wrapped the whole of his lanky form around Ida, the doctor speaks again: "I'm sorry we don't have better news for you. Now, what about Malte? Has he turned up yet?"

"That," sighs Mrs. Swan sanctimoniously, "is in the hands of the powers that be." And she smooths her apron, which is freshly starched and spotless. She throws him a defiant look, makes as if to stand up, thinks better of it, and stays seated; the kitchen can wait. But heaven cannot. The parson walks over and places a hand on her shoulder. The doctor is bristling like a fighting cock.

"I'm sure that both Oda and Malte are in the very best of hands. I think we should bury the hatchet. What is the point of all our petty bickering when death is knocking at our door?"

As the parson speaks, he pulls a book in a black binding out from the folds of his cassock. This he now opens, having cleared his throat: "I have a text here which seems to suit the occasion . . ."

He fits his spectacles over the bridge of his nose. The doctor looks ready to explode.

The parson reads slowly and deliberately, pausing dramatically after the title:

AUTUMN

The leaves are falling, falling as if from far off,
as if in the heavens distant gardens withered;
they fall with gestures that say "no."

And in the nights the heavy earth falls
from all the stars into aloneness.

We are all falling. This hand is falling.
And look at the others; it is in them all.

And yet there is One who holds this falling
with infinite softness in his hands.

By the time he is finished reading, silence fills every corner. When the poem is done, an angel passes through the room. He shuts the book and looks straight ahead, not directing his gaze at anyone in particular.

"Rainer Maria Rilke," he says.

The pharmacist nods, the doctor is abashed. He goes over and squeezes the parson's arm.

"Thank you," is all he says.

There is a knock at the door. A hesitant little knock that makes everyone jump.

"Come in," says Mrs. Swan, getting to her feet. And this time she remains standing as the door swings open, making way for the figures who stand on the threshold, the one with a hangdog air about him, the other a feigned jauntiness.

Malte makes a beeline for Mrs. Swan's skirts. She raises her arm, ready to strike him, but Dr. Hansen leaps forward and grabs hold of it.

"Now, now—this patient is under my care."

Malte grins up at him gratefully. He has just been spared the sort of blow that can make the gray matter slosh around inside.

"We understand your relief, Mrs. Swan. You do not need to express it physically."

She calms down, stroking the boy's hair as he burrows his head in her apron and mutters a "sorry" that only she can hear. Then she turns to the door to thank the officer who has brought the boy back.

She receives a fresh shock when—after a long moment—she recognizes Monsieur Charles.

Here is something to set the whole room buzzing. Suddenly Malte is the center of attention; first he has to tell Santos's story, then plead the man's case, both of which he does excellently. Mrs. Swan is flabbergasted: they could never get the boy to say a thing, and now the words are pouring out of him. They hop back and forth in time and space, but the picture they paint is clear enough.

Santos is met with skepticism. The odd murmur of outright disapproval is heard. No one has forgotten his predecessor.

When Malte and he hear Oda's story, each reacts in his own way.

Malte seizes up completely, turns his face to the wall, and closes his ears to the man's sobs. He kicks at the wainscoting

and has to be taken from the room. This time it is the doctor
who does it, pinning Malte's arms to his sides. He talks sooth-
ingly to him, gets him settled on the chaise longue. Then Ida
takes over; as long as she is nearby, the boy will not do anything violent. But the split he feels flickers in his eyes and he is
shaking like a leaf under the blanket.

Santos has sunk to the floor; he is on his knees, huddled
over the crucifix he wears on a chain around his neck. His
prayers rise and fall rhythmically; Santa Maria is the name that
is repeated most often. It recurs like the theme in a rondo that
is forever chasing its own tail. There are those in the room
who, in their sheer indignation, do not see his remorse.

Four people manage to keep their heads. The parson, the
doctor, and the pharmacist confer around the smoking table.
Mrs. Swan has taken herself off to the kitchen—some sustenance is called for, otherwise everything is going to go to hell in
a handbasket.

By the time the table is set, Malte has fallen asleep. Dinner is
eaten in silence. Afterwards, the doctor gets to his feet and
makes a brief report to the assembled company. He and Oak
have considered the matter from every angle and have come to
the following conclusion regarding the man now calling himself
Santos:

Personal differences are of no account. Each of them may
think what he or she likes. Oda's recovery is all that matters. If
they can rekindle the spark of life and restore to her the man to
whom she has bound herself heart and soul—preferably restore
him in the romantic image to which she clings even now, in her
comatose state—then both heaven and the truth can wait. He is
banking all his medical expertise on this hope. Medicine is
nothing if the patient does not want to live. The main thing
now is to get Oda back.

His suggestion takes nerve. It gives rise to protest and then to silence as the idea begins to sink in. Santos will have to be spruced up again, to look like the man he once was. Not only that, but he will have to be supplied with the long-awaited telegram from his family, so that their engagement can be announced.

Mrs. Swan shakes her head and slams the serving window shut. Santos hovers, motionless, over a plate that has been scraped right down to the china. He stares at the doctor in disbelief, trying to figure out how he has done it: can they really pull such a rabbit out of the hat? His dark eyes are wary. He is ready to duck the minute the blow falls.

The doctor concludes his report and takes his seat.

His last words on the matter are: "Things are not always as black as they are painted—or as the parson may think!" But his eyes are smiling, and the parson smiles back.

IN WHICH
THE SCENE SHIFTS

Malte wakes up on his sofa. The blanket slips off his shoulders as he sits up and says something no one has heard him say before: "When do we eat? I'm hungry."

The table has been cleared. But Mrs. Swan warms up some food and puts it out for him. Rib roast and rum pudding. Malte hides a great big bone under his shirt. First chance he gets, he puts it out in the backyard, with a big dollop of pudding next to it.

Who says foxes can't have dessert?

Immediately after dinner, the transformation begins. The doctor starts with an ice-pack, which Santos holds to his eye until the swelling begins to subside. Then Mrs. Münster takes her turn with the makeup. Suddenly everyone is eager to play their part in the charade. If Oda is returned to them, she must not suspect that anything is amiss. At any rate, not right away. Monsieur Charles will behave exactly as he used to, playing nocturnes on the piano. They will hire him to give music lessons. Mrs. Swan gets her way on one point: he is being kicked downstairs along with the rest of the help. Dr. Hansen winks at the parson. That should suit the fellow just fine.

Hot water, shaving soap, and shaving brush are brought in. The doctor lathers him up, turns his face this way and that, wields the razor with a practiced hand. The scrape of the blade fills the room as his face gradually reverts to its original appearance. Then it is dabbed with a towel and cologne. Mrs. Münster steps in again and touches up the makeup.

Next comes the costume. Santos is given some of the doctor's clothes; they are a bit too big and too checkered for the little dandy, who is starting to look more and more like a harlequin. And bless my soul if he doesn't start to find fault and demand to have the sleeves altered. Mrs. Münster bites on the sewing needle and does as he asks. A cravat—not the height of fashion, perhaps—provides the finishing touch, and the parson's wife, whose role in such gatherings is not exactly a prominent one, donates a gold pin to hold it in place.

He primps and preens in his borrowed plumage. They all but lose patience with him, seeing him strut back and forth in front of the mirror. Oak sits down at the table and drafts the telegram. He vacillates between German and French but eventually decides on the latter as consistent with the Gallic courtliness displayed by Santos in his previous incarnation. Then it is off to the hospital. The doctor drives Santos. The conspirators are falling over one another in the hallway to wave them off. The pharmacist stays behind; with Malte and her father gone, Ida has been alone all day.

After this burst of action comes the anticlimax. Will the plan work? Who can say—after all, it was devised on doctor's orders. And everyone has their own ideas about that. Again, there is not a lot to do except wait. The parson's wife helps with the dishes. That is only to be expected, but Malte's helping is most unusual. All of a sudden, he is very busy keeping his hostess happy.

With the washing up out of the way, everyone congregates in the parlor once more. Mrs. Münster sits down at the keyboard and entertains them with a serenade. The pharmacist takes a headache powder: she could use some lessons, and like everyone else who is tone-deaf, she gives it all she's got. When the last note—an off-key fifth—has died away, he slaps his forehead, crosses to the piano, and picks up the package lying there.

Malte rips off the paper. It is *The Children of Captain Grant.*

Oda lies motionless on a bed in the hospital. The night light makes her look pale and wan; a large crucifix hangs above the bed. The nurse, a nun from Saint Joseph's Infirmary, sits nodding under the snowy ship of her wimple. She comes to with a start when the front door bangs. She leans over the bed to listen for the almost inaudible breathing, takes Oda's pulse again, just to be on the safe side. The patient is under observation around the clock. She lets go of the bloodless hand and crosses herself. The swathed oval of her face consists of eyes, nose, and mouth. Those features that lend expression to the face evince two things: compassion and deep concern.

The door to the small room opens. On seeing the doctor, Sister Johanne instinctively steps away from the bed. They hold a brief whispered consultation over by the washbasin as Dr. Hansen washes his hands, dons his white coat and head mirror. Then she nods distantly to the distinguished gentleman accompanying him. She notes the fleeting sketch of the fingers with which he acknowledges the cross over the head of the bed.

Hansen switches on the lights in the room, adjusts the angle of the bedside lamp. The pallid hue of Oda's face assumes a bluish cast; not so much as a quiver passes over her eyelids, her lips are parted, her jaw hangs loose. The air flows in and out of her, with the odd pause and a sporadic gurgling in the throat.

The doctor bends over her, lifts an eyelid, and manages to get a ray of light to fall on it with the aid of his head mirror. A shiver runs down Santos's spine when he sees the white eyeball and the upturned pupil. The doctor supports her neck and shoulders, removes the pillow. He lays her down gently. He repeats the procedure and this time he looks up with a certain urgency in his movements. He has caught some pupil reaction. "Sister Johanne," he says, "get some sleep. You look tired. We'll take this watch."

But Sister Johanne draws her lips into a thin line and shakes her head. She works on a different schedule from most people's; hours spent with the sick and dying will be redeemed with yet greater bliss. She permits herself a smile. "If I leave, it will only be to make us a cup of coffee. I could be needed at any minute."

Hansen nods gratefully. Santos is already close to fainting, his pallor rivaling that of the patient. It takes no great stretch of the imagination to picture how he would react were his help suddenly required. Sister Johanne is a nurse with plenty of experience with the dying.

They can hear her busying herself with the kettle and the coffeepot in an adjoining room, the hiss of the gas flame and the short whistle when the water boils. She comes in with a tray and they drink their coffee in silence. They have a long night ahead of them and there is not that much to say. One thing has excited Sister Johanne's curiosity. She turns to the stranger and asks, "Are you Catholic?"

It is the sign of the cross that haunts her.

"Yes, Sister," replies Santos, "in my country everyone is Catholic. Even the Indians."

At this, her face softens. Sister Johanne is neither young nor old—a veiled woman knows no age. She and the doctor discuss Oda's blood pressure, her pulse, her temperature. A coma is a strange thing, there is nothing anyone can do—the absence of consciousness holds time suspended. Such a state can last for hours, days, or months. Everyone near at hand has the feeling of being drawn into that borderland. The patients' brains grow shadowy; do they dream, are they awake, do they hear what is said?

Such are the thoughts that run through the doctor's mind as he observes Oda intently. Though there is nothing to observe, nothing except the stillness of the body. This border also marks the limit of his knowledge. And yet it fascinates him. The weight loss when they die. He glances up into the corner. There is a sense of something suspended in the room that causes first one, then the other of them to clear their throats.

By midmorning Dr. Hansen has nodded off. He feels Sister Johanne's hand on his arm. He gives a start and the birdsong outside the window sounds clearly in his ears. Santos is sitting on the floor, one raised arm flung across the eiderdown. He is sleeping, apparently peacefully.

Sister Johanne whispers, "The patient is moving. Her blood pressure is higher . . . I think she is trying to say something!"

The nurse is standing right next to him. Still holding the cuff and the rubber bulb from the last blood-pressure check. The doctor is instantly wide awake. Oda has shifted position, her arm has come free of the eiderdown, and her head is turned to one side. Her eyelids flutter and her lips move. He leans close.

Her voice reaches him from another world, he catches the words "afternoon off" and "sourpuss." Oda is in the churchyard with Malte, but only I know that.

"She's delirious . . ."

Slowly his amazement turns to exultation.

"I'll be damned if she isn't delirious! Quick, Sister Johanne, wake him up, and find him a bunch of flowers."

"A bunch of flowers? Are you serious?"

Sister Johanne looks almost as if she thinks he is the one who is delirious.

"Where am I going to get flowers? At this time of day?"

"From one of the other beds, goddamit!"

Sister Johanne shakes her head. Not at his language—that she is used to—but because she cannot figure out what he is up to. In God's house, other rules apply, but while she is at work the doctor's word is law. She does as he says. First she rouses Santos, then, with a dip of her starched veil, she sails out, to return carrying a large bouquet of red roses interspersed with a bit of greenery. The doctor is delighted.

"Perfect, Sister, damned if I didn't think you were going to swipe one of the funeral sprays."

"Dr. Hansen!"

This is snapped out so sharply that he ducks his head.

"No offense, Sister. What would I do without you?"

She hides a smile with the back of her hand. Her eyes crease at the corners. Now the doctor has his work cut out for him. But not with his patient. He gets Santos onto his feet, dusts off his jacket, straightens his cravat. The black eye is starting to show through the makeup.

"Sister Johanne, do you use makeup?"

Her face speaks for itself. The doctor turns.

There are definite stirrings from the bed. A blissful sigh escapes Oda's lips. The doctor pushes Santos forward. Digs in his jacket pocket for the telegram, shoves it into Santos's hand, then follows with the bouquet. Santos yawns sleepily.

"Stand up straight, goddamit, and try to look like a man."

Santos pulls himself together. Eventually his pose begins to look convincing and his features fall into their familiar folds. He is the living image of a gentleman paying a hospital visit. Suitably subdued by the gravity of the situation, with a sympathetic look in his eye and just the right note of awkwardness.

The doctor bounds across to the window and throws it open. Fresh air and morning chirping flood the room. Santos receives a final nudge in the small of the back, clears his throat, and holds the roses out toward the sick bed.

He does not get the chance to say a word. Oda opens her eyes.

"Santos," she says, quite clearly and distinctly, "what *have* you done to yourself?"

IN WHICH
THE FOX FLIES
AND THE SPIRIT
SPLITS IN TWO

Is she dreaming or is she awake? When Oda comes home from the hospital, her chest bandaged to hold her broken rib in place, everything has been turned around. Mrs. Swan is at the door to welcome her; with an icy look at Santos, she gives Oda the room with the sea view. All Oda has to do now is get her strength back. Until further notice she has been excused from all household duties, and this from the lips of the Swan herself with a firmness that will not be gainsaid. The residents crowd about her, Mrs. Münster with hugs and gushing, most of the others with more restrained expressions of sympathy. Gone is the derisive pity—replaced by the compassion engendered by the events of the last few days.

Oda feels self-conscious; she stands first on one leg, then the other, but it does no good. Under her freckles she flushes red; she stares at the tips of her shoes, which could do with a polish. She is helped up the stairs to the bed that has been made up for her. Several of the gentlemen offer her an arm, but it is Oak who is granted the honor. The room has been aired, there are fresh flowers in a vase, and the curtains swirl into the room on the breeze.

Oda hovers on the threshold; she cannot bring herself to cross it, stands with her hand over her nose, shakes her curls. It cannot be true, she is only there to change the beds, that is how it is! Usually, she moves around these grand rooms with a timidity that makes her steer clear of the mirrors. She sees the waves rolling under her windows, which are wide open, letting in the sound, clear and surging.

Overcome, she blows her nose into the palm of her hand. Tactfully, Oak guides her over the threshold, then withdraws, closing the door gently behind him.

As soon as Oda is alone amid all this splendor, she goes down on her knees at the foot of the bed and clasps her hands in prayer. Then she throws herself eagerly on the tea tray, crunches on toast with slices of cheese. She spreads rose-hip jelly over the cheese, stirs honey into her tea, and perches for a moment on the edge of the bed, alternately overcome by fits of giggles and waves of emotion. She goes over to the window; down below, Malte is heading off across the beach with yet another kite. He has painted eyes on it and given it a pair of pointed ears. She wonders why.

She gets undressed, rounds her hands over her petticoat. She stands there lost in a dream as Malte launches the kite into the air. Caught by a gust of wind, it swoops backwards so that it is right in front of her window, where it nods at her. Oda sees a Chinese face. Startled, she nods back. For a moment there, it was as real as could be. She yawns and at long last dares to slip under the eiderdown. Soon she is in a deep sleep. Outside the window, a kite tail flutters, from down below floats the distant sound of voices and, not long afterwards, that of the doctor's car driving off.

From Oda's broken rib comes a man. She smiles in her

sleep, sees him with a boy like Malte. Wherever he goes, the boy trots at his heels, in awe of a father who uncovers the treasures of the world for him. A log half-buried in the earth, crawling with wood lice, an anthill that they poke at with a stick. Then she drifts down into a deeper wave, where the pictures from her dream turn to foam in the surf.

When Malte has had enough of playing with kites for that day, he goes in search of Ida. He is haunted by thoughts of the den; he wants to show her how he has fixed up a secret place for himself between the trees in the backyard by weaving the willow branches together. There is a threadbare rug for the ground, and he has managed to scrounge a couple of candles and a kerosene lamp to brighten things up. The reservoir is rusty and there is no wick in the lamp, so he puts a stump of candle in it and leaves the glass propped open when it is lit.

He thinks he might read to her from his new book, which he has tucked into his belt and under his shirt. Captain Grant's children have just been stranded on the island.

Outside the den he stops. Something in the soil has caught his eye; the ground has been dug up, and there is a bitten-off rooster's head lying in it. Ida shrinks back a step or two when he picks the head up and shakes the comb at her. Malte laughs. It's a lot easier to be daring when you have somebody to scare. Then he stiffens at the sight of something else.

It is the lump of amber. Slowly he bends down, brushes the soil off the nugget. At first he is happy, then he bites his bottom lip; it does not look the way it used to. The amber has split right down the middle, and the other half is missing. The bit that is left has grown opaque and there are teeth marks on it. He turns it this way and that; the elf is nowhere to be seen.

Then he has a lump in his throat and once again, close to tears, he is the boy who plays with girls.

Ida watches him with the close attention of the mute. The shifting play of expressions over his face, Malte's dismay—and her own, when she realizes that the elf is gone. When at last his face lights up again, hers lights up with it. Malte has an idea.

"Come on, Ida, let's run up to the lighthouse and borrow Olesen's workshop."

Half an hour later, they are at the lighthouse. Normally he can make it there in half the time, but Ida's legs are shorter and she stops along the way to gawk at the slightest little thing. The wiggling of the inchworm, the flight of a butterfly, and snails that she studiously steps around, her little nose wrinkled in disgust. More than once, Malte almost blows his stack.

Olesen is at the little house containing the generator, a building with no windows and a door that is way too small for him. There is a lightning bolt on the door. Every time Malte sees it his heart skips a beat. Heavy-duty cables run down into the ground and come up again over by the lighthouse.

The keeper is tinkering with a drive belt covered in grease. Machine parts lie scattered all around him, waiting their turn. He is standing outside with the door open. Each time he goes in to fiddle with something, he comes out backwards in a cloud of smoke from his pipe.

"Is that you, Malte? And you've brought your girlfriend. Well, how about that!"

Malte has cockscombs in his cheeks. The keeper squirts at him with the oil can, then sends a gob of spit flying from the corner of his mouth. The stubby pipe is sputtering nicely.

"It's seized up, the old devil. If we don't get it sparking again, I won't be answerable for them ships tonight."

"Can I use the workshop?"

"Feel free, Malte, just so long as you don't break anything."

"Olesen, what's your first name?"

The lighthouse keeper thinks for a moment.

"Promise you won't tell a soul? Cross your heart?"

"Cross my heart!"

He wrings his hands in a rag, smearing the grease. He can barely get it out. "Sirius, my name's Sirius . . ."

"Ida," yells Malte, "his name's Sirius!"

"You little rogue. You just promised . . ."

The keeper takes a swipe at him. Malte ducks, comes up again with a foxy look on his face.

"Well, she can't tell anyone, can she?"

Ida is glowing from all the attention.

They go into the workshop. Malte makes straight for the grindstone revolving on its wheel in the water bath. He drags a box over to enable Ida to reach. Shows her the handle.

"You turn, Ida, and I'll grind. When we've ground it down enough we'll be able to see the elf."

Malte says this in a voice heavy with veiled expectation, while Ida mouths her "mmm" and nods eagerly. At a sign from Malte she starts turning the handle and he puts the amber to the grinding surface, gingerly, as if he might burn himself on the stone. The sound takes hold, one corner is smoothed off. He presses harder, removing the bumps and wrinkles first. Ida is convulsed with silent laughter at the cockeyed look of him twisting and turning the nugget.

Gradually he shapes the nugget into a teardrop. When he holds it up to the light it is still opaque, but when he dips it in the water the outline of the sea horse formed by the skeleton of the elf can still be made out. He buffs the stone with emery cloth and the cloudy coating disappears. Ida follows his every move with mounting excitement.

Last, he rushes around the workshop, hunting for the lump of jeweler's wax that he has seen the lighthouse keeper use on the pieces of coral he fixes inside the bottles to create the illusion of a tropical sea. Jaw set, Malte rubs and rubs.

Abracadabra! There is the elf.

He holds the amber up to Ida, coaxing her with its teardrop shape. If she can say "m," she can say "e"!

The gem sparkles. It is so smooth and delicate, *too* smooth and delicate, and it lacks wings and a head. Where the skull formed a seed there is a clear spot in the amber, a hollow cavity, an empty little bubble. The elf is no longer there to inspirit it. Ida remains mute.

Numbness washes over Malte; the magic is gone, his effort all in vain. He has rubbed and polished and buffed, but there is no genie in this lamp. He stands there, defeat in his hands, his lips drawn into a thin line.

A new idea is taking shape in his head—this is one of those days when Malte cannot afford to give up. He fits the teardrop into the clamp, bores a hole in the top, and glues in one of the eyelets that Olesen uses to secure the rigging. When the glue is dry, he takes a piece of tarred string, pulls it through the eyelet, and ties it with a reef knot. He unscrews the clamp and dangles the gem in front of Ida's eyes, before hanging it about her neck. But she does not want it now; she shakes her head emphatically. And Malte can see for himself. It is far too big for her, hangs right down over her stomach. Malte resigns himself.

By the time they come out of the workshop, the keeper has got the generator reassembled. He is bent double, the seat of his trousers sticking out the narrow doorway as he tugs on the starter cord. The motor coughs but does not catch. The whole effort ends with him staggering backwards onto the grass to sit there with a baffled expression on his face, still clutching the cord. His face is scarlet. Malte puts his hand over his mouth to stop himself from laughing. The lighthouse keeper has to start all over again. Storm clouds are gathering on his brow—this is not the moment to show him the necklace. Malte sticks it in his pocket, mutters a "thanks for letting us use the workshop," and hastens out of there with Ida before the first roll of thunder.

Back at the guest house they are getting ready for the second act.

The curtain goes up when Oda wakes. Mrs. Swan makes frequent trips up the stairs to listen at the door. Santos is sitting in front of the mirror with a dishtowel around his shoulders. He waxes his mustache, trims his whiskers with nail scissors. He parts the raven wings of his hair in the center, sprays the better part of a bottle of toilet water over himself, pumping feverishly on the rubber bulb. He masks the black eye completely with makeup, then lets his arms fall to his sides, shuts his eyes, and takes a deep breath. Shakes his wrists.

The pharmacist helps him into his jacket; they skip the cravat. They do, however, unearth a silver tray for the telegram. After all, Santos has only a walk-on part in this. Once Oda is back on her feet, God knows what is to become of him. Mrs. Swan's manner makes that quite clear.

Mrs. Münster furnishes him with both her own and her husband's wedding rings. This last she has worn on a chain next to her heart ever since her husband's untimely demise. A pox on the man. A year to the day after his bachelor party he was gone, and she has spent the rest of her long life a widow. In the circles in which she moves that is better than being a spinster.

The rings are slipped into Santos's vest pocket. For a moment, the gold is the only genuine article in the room.

A moment later Malte arrives. Ida has stayed behind in the garden with her jump rope. Malte blows in on the draft from the door and flies straight up the stairs, ignoring the cries to stop. He charges into Oda's room and over to the bed. Downstairs the players wait, expressions cued to the ringing of the house bell. The curtain has gone up. There is no turning back.

A last shuffle of the feet, a last clearing of the throat. Then they make their way up to the room, Indian file. The parson fiddles with the black book emblazoned with the cross, holds it close against the folds of his cassock. He is ready to let his face shine upon them, memorizing lines he has always known by heart. His wife remembers a letter opener, which she lays alongside the telegram.

Inside the room, Oda has opened her eyes. The sea view has moved in. She sits up in bed, greets Malte with a smile that still bears the imprint of her dream. Malte dives into his pocket for the amber necklace.

"This is for you, Oda, I made it myself!"

He places the gem around her neck. It fits Oda perfectly. She strokes it and feels the spark leap to her finger. She has a lump in her throat and her cheeks are wet. Reaching out a hand, she pulls his head down onto her shoulder. They are totally immersed in each other when the Indians file in.

Malte is crying, too, but his voice is even. "What if you had died, Oda," he asks. "Who would look after me then?"

Oda clasps him to her bosom.

When the room is full, Santos steps forward, holding the tray. He bends down, kisses Oda lightly on the brow. She waves away the perfumed vapors that hang around him; she cannot help but giggle. Malte has removed himself to the foot of the bed.

Mrs. Münster holds the tray as Santos slits open the telegram. Then he reads it out, a slight roll of his *r*s marring his otherwise melodic French. The pharmacist has put his hands to his head—either his headache has returned or he is having second thoughts. Haltingly, Santos translates, sounding all at once like a schoolboy.

His father, Count Sedano y Leguizano, takes great pleasure in giving his, and thereby the family's, consent to the marriage of his son, Santos Linares Sedano y Leguizano, to Miss Oda Falbe Hansen. He extends his and the family's best wishes. They hope to see the newlyweds at the estate before the end of the year.

Santos shows her the signature. It has to be the most elaborate web of curlicues Oda has ever seen; the document is embellished with a seal bearing an eagle's head.

With the utmost solemnity, Santos now produces the rings. The smaller one he slips onto Oda's finger; the larger just fits his own. The parson makes his face to shine upon them. Their betrothal is thus official. Oda is a bit confused—the rings now have to be removed and put away for the big day in church. He is allowed to kiss her, and this time the kiss lasts longer and causes Oda's thigh to shift beneath the eiderdown. Mrs. Swan snorts.

Reluctantly, the betrothed couple pull apart. Oda drops her head back onto the pillow. Is she dreaming or is she awake? She lies still for a while, not caring one way or the other—as things stand it makes no difference. Then she reaches out and takes her future husband by the hand. Happiness shines from the bottom of her simple soul.

"Santos, I'm so happy. So, *so* happy . . ."

And those cheeks that have been growing plumper with each hour since she awoke are truly glowing.

"We're going to have a little one!"

It is said in a stage whisper, heard by every one of them. Her betrothed turns pale—that is to say, his sunburned skin takes on a grayish cast. Mrs. Münster gasps and the tray falls to the floor with a clatter. Oak groans and props himself up against the wash stand, and the Swan—the Swan rolls her eyes heaven-wards. Now she is stuck with this chicken thief for who knows how long.

Asleep in the fox's den, day by day I note how another part of me is putting out shoots: the seed coat of the brain. Growth is a wonderful thing, sugar cane striving toward the light from the darkness of the earth.

A seed leaf, sending its quiet white flame shooting upwards, conveying sap to the cells and boring its way through the mold. Never was truer word spoken: we aim for the stars, solidifying only once, in the light, into thistle or gingko.

Willpower is our blowtorch.

Within me I feel a life that is 175 million years old and found only in fossil form. But one grows younger as time goes on. It gets easier: when I was an elf, I had several hundred million years weighing me down. In this realm I wish only for the chlorophyll to do its work, for the freshness that prompts leaves to bud and—who knows—may even turn my shoot into a great tree.

When Malte sees me, all will be revealed and he will gain access to treasures he has forgotten. Until then I will carry on, growing slowly and steadily under the ground. No need to be told everything at once.

Then there would be no point in living, would there?

16

IN WHICH
MALTE HAS
A VISITOR

An hour before sunset, the generator kicks in at long last. The lighthouse keeper listens for some time to the cadence of the engine; after all its hacking and coughing, it is running again, chugging away nicely. He closes the door of the whitewashed building and the noise recedes into the hillside. Malte, who has spent the day acting as gofer for Olesen, digging out nuts and bolts for him from his boxes in the workshop, sees the vexation in his eyes turn to relief. Now the ships can round the point once more, guided by the flash of the lighthouse beam, before vanishing into the night.

After a visit to the pantry, where Olesen coats his hands and arms with margarine, then wipes off the oil with a dish towel, they go up to the tower together, into the little watch room where the telegraph sits. Olesen calls it the Marconi room. He hunches over the Morse key and transmits a message; sparks fly from the key's contact switch. Malte picks up a rhythm in the crackling—it flows as easily from the lighthouse keeper's finger as words from his mouth. Malte pounces on the sheet of paper covered with dots and dashes; here are new letters for his hungry brain, but the telegraph apparatus goes far too fast for him to keep up.

On a shelf above it sits a row of ring binders. These are where Olesen files his reports and shipping notices. Across their spines run the years, printed on the type of labels that are stuck on jam jars. It strikes him that on the oldest of them the ink has faded, though the century that died on the very night he came into the world has been captured and held. He marvels at the passage of time.

He glances out the peephole. At the end of the jetty, the dinghy's white paint has turned golden. Outside, the air smolders in the flush of evening and the lighthouse hill rises up out of the landscape. The cormorant stretches its long neck and spreads its wings to dry its feathers. Like a totem it stands on the top of its fishing stake.

Through half-shut eyes the boy has a sense—prompted by a vibration spreading upward from the soles of his feet—of the machine deep inside the earth, the hoist that lowers the sun and raises the shaft of the tower into the sky. He is high as his kite. Olesen has asked him if he would like to help mind the light and Sea View has given him permission to stay the night. It will be up to him to mind his own bedtime.

Supper consists of hunks of rye bread with rolled pork sausage, margarine, soft brown sugar. Malte can taste the oil in his sandwich—the plate has been wiped with the keeper's towel. They have had tea, strong and black with tannin and sweetened with milk and honey. The boy is elated. He has borrowed one of the keeper's old caps; it stays on him only because he has stuffed the crown and the sweatband with rags. A whiff of turpentine wafts about him.

When the lighthouse keeper is finished sending his signals into the gloaming, he gets to his feet and he and Malte step out onto the gallery. They stand with their backs to the lantern housing, stand until the sun is no more than scales floating on the sea. The watch has begun; here the day starts when everyone else's is done.

The keeper gives Malte a nod. They disappear into the lantern housing and Olesen heads straight for the panel with the big porcelain fuses. They are standing on a latticed steel deck. Olesen clicks down contact switches shaped like rockers. A humming fills the room and the mechanism begins to revolve. A light bulb surrounded by huge sheets of pebble glass. And a copper mirror, silvered on the inside—also an integral part of the system. Fascinated, Malte follows the facets, the lenses and prisms of this bug eye designed to concentrate the light into a lance. He hears the contact kick in. Then he shatters into a million bits and pieces.

"Cover your eyes," growls the keeper, a second too late. The light, staggeringly white and faster than thought, slices through Malte from the top of his skull to the tips of his toes. It leaves him with spots before his eyes, and the prisms go on producing figures of ice and fire on his retinas for a long time afterwards. He feels the air snatched from his lips, stumbles back, and covers his face, blinded. Olesen calls him over. Bursting with the patterns of the beam, he backs out onto the gallery, leans up against the rail, and watches the purple supernovas spinning across the landscape. In short flashes and long, the light floods across the sea.

The lighthouse speaks a language not unlike that of the Morse key. Sailors count the flashes and the black seconds between them to determine where they are. Far out on the horizon he can see another light starting to flash, no bigger than a pinhead in the growing darkness. It is coming from Seal Island. Olesen is thrown into massive silhouette. The hand he places on Malte's shoulder still smells of margarine.

"Will you take the first watch while I go below and take forty winks?"

Malte's face shines.

"If the telegraph starts clicking, just call me, hear?"

Malte raises a finger to his cap. The spiral stairway resounds as the lighthouse keeper disappears. Malte straightens his shoulders and gazes out to sea. The mist causes the beam to shoot out above his head like the Milky Way, before being cut off once more. A steamer coming out of the harbor begins to hoot.

As darkness falls, he has the feeling of being transparent. He stands on the bridge of his tall ship and calls forth the stars one by one. Malte counts flashes, because everything is flashing. The spheres up above, the lighthouse beyond, the lanterns between the crests of the waves; and the sea is a huge clock face on which the ship has jerked a bit farther forward for every time the beams strikes it. The steady flashing has a hypnotic effect on him. For the first time in ages he is not afraid of the dark, looking upon it instead as a two-way process. Things come into being in the spaces between.

Inside his head an image arches, a glistening blue-tinged jellyfish with four eyes. A being from another planet has taken control of his thoughts and stitches the stars to his flesh with sparks. He feels it rustling behind him.

"Olesen?" the boy whispers.

But Sirius is fast asleep in his live-box. Malte catches a glimpse of fur and a long tail sweeping down the spiral stairway. He cannot be sure—it might have been the cat, which is every bit as red as the fox, but the night is suddenly full of wings: angels are watching over him.

He steps into the watch room and makes himself comfortable in the lighthouse keeper's wing chair.

From space a signal flows, rhythmic and persistent. The souls of all seafarers are calling and Malte's head rolls from one wing of the chair to the other, the back of his hand tensing on its arm. Malte slumbers in a chair that has been electrically charged; sparks from the apparatus jab at his skull.

All at once he is wide awake. It's the telegraph!

He leaps out of the chair. Something is wrong. The long whir from the tower has died away. He looks up. The light has gone out. Outside, pitch-black night reigns and he closes his eyes, offering a silent prayer. Then he clatters down the spiral stairway to rouse the keeper. Heavy-limbed and bleary-eyed, Olesen tumbles out of the folds of the comforter. He curses his way down into a swirling black hole; sleep has taken him by the scruff of the neck and hurled him into it while the generator was petering out, succumbing to the mechanical fault he worked on all day. His first impulse is to get it started again, but Malte is tugging at his sleeve.

"The telegraph! It's saying something!"

The lighthouse keeper grabs a kerosene lamp and lights the wick, burning his fingers as he slips the glass back into place. Lantern in hand, they race out into the yard and up to the tower. The telegraph, working on backup now, is still tapping out its SOS in the cubbyhole, and the color drains from Olesen's cheeks. He stoops over the key and responds to the call with lightning bursts of his fingers.

The incoming signal changes, the symmetry has been broken, and Olesen starts making notes on a sheet of paper. The string of letters runs together to form a message, giving the ship's name and its position. He wipes his brow with the sleeve of the fisherman's shirt in which he always sleeps. Concentration has settled on his brow. He refers to another table before telegraphing again, this time at a more relaxed tempo. Then he turns to Malte.

"Phew! It was farther out to sea. I've sent a warning to all ships to stay clear of the point. Now all we have to do is get that machine going again. One minute you've got an engine, the next it's nothing but a heap of scrap!" He clasps Malte's wrist, lowers his voice. "D'you know what it means when a ship send out an SOS?" He raps out the signal on the arm of the chair. Answers himself.

"It means 'Save our souls,' a distress call to make a sailor's blood run cold. Thank heaven this one had nothing to do with us and help is on the way. To be responsible for the loss of others—nobody can live with that."

The lighthouse keeper falls silent. Malte has gone stiff, living the fear with every ounce of his being. The ocean spreads wide inside him, with ships going down, drowned faces amid blue lights, flares and life preservers that drift on empty through the days that follow, empty under the blazing sun, while all else has disappeared and only the ship's name, repeated a hundredfold, is left bobbing on the waves.

Olesen sighs. He'll have to see to it again. This time in pitch darkness. He needs some spare parts; what the lighthouse really could do with is a new generator—but there's probably not enough money for that.

"You'll need to stand watch a while longer, Malte. Until I can get that old devil going. Then I'll come up and relieve you."

The boy sits down at the telegraph. Holds his finger poised over the key, shuts his eyes, and dreams that he is leading a rescue operation that ends with a medal being pinned to his breast. Afterwards he makes a speech to the Society for the Aid of Seamen's Widows, and a dark-haired version of Oda comes up to him in raptures and presses an amber gem into his hand.

His finger twitches. Then it twitches again. He has to restrain himself from pressing the Bakelite knob. But he does it anyway, just once, and when the spark leaps, it is with a spine-chilling reminder of the force that can sink vessels vaster than the mind can conceive of.

He jumps in fright. The light is back on. Once more the

tower vibrates under the soles of his feet and the beam plucks at the air as before, splitting the night into sections as the prisms burst with sparks and flashes. Soon Sirius is standing before him, a grin on his oil-smeared lips. He must have wiped his mouth with the dish towel. He looks like a Pierrot, only in blackface.

"Sailor, time to turn in. I'll take the dogwatch."

Malte grins back, more than a little proud at being addressed in this fashion. He does not need the lamp to find his way to Olesen's berth: the light shines so brightly that the cobblestones in the yard show up white in the night. Snug under the quilt, he wrinkles his nose at the powerful aroma of tobacco, fish, and margarine, but the nest is nice and cozy, and he sleeps soundly, in a deluge of dreams.

The next morning Malte is woken to tea and an omelette.

"Okay now, skedaddle," says the lighthouse keeper, "and let somebody else get between the sheets."

The sun is up and the light extinguished. Sirius yawns; his pipe has gone out in his hand. He sits down heavily on the edge of the bed, so that Malte pops up. Quick as a flash he is out of there and has his shoelaces tied, while the keeper snuggles down under the quilt. He has dropped off before Malte can thank him for breakfast. He gulps down the tea, but picks at the omelette, which has been served to him in the pan; he scoops it out with the spoon, avoiding the burnt spots.

He wanders home along the beach. Stops to look at a swan that has been washed ashore. By the look of its wings and plumage, the storm must have torn it apart; the winds on which it was once borne have turned against it, transformed it into a dragon skeleton spread at the boy's feet. The feathers are mat-

ted and spiky from oil. The angry beak has lost its color, the
flesh on the body has dried to the bone. He shrinks from touching it, makes do with poking it with the toe of his shoe. Kicks
some sand over the worst of it and feels better.

Malte pulls himself together, but the sight has triggered the
signal that flowed from the lighthouse out into the night. It
makes him tap his fingertips; it makes the skin on the back of
his neck crawl. He starts to run, brushing along the side of the
hedge, where the first rose hips have turned leathery. He bursts
open the door to Sea View, and trips over a suitcase sitting in
the hallway.

His eyes grow accustomed to the gloom and still he stands
there, gazing at the bag in disbelief. It is his own—or rather his
mother's—battered suitcase, and it is packed, fat and bulging as
on the day he arrived. Malte is suddenly very, very still; some
sentence has been passed in his absence—they are tired of him,
the time has come for him to return to the town and the apart-
ment where eternal twilight holds sway among the lampshade
tassels and shawls. He bites hard on the knuckle of his thumb.

He shuts his eyes and wishes the suitcase gone. It flies off,
and his mother with it, hanging onto the sides; her hat has
come off and her hair streams across her face. She casts horrified glances at the roofs and spires dwindling beneath her in a
giddy whirl as she is sucked into the clouds. He wants to call
out to her, to tell her not to be afraid, but a gust of wind
snatches the words from his lips before they can be uttered. Finally, when she has shrunk to the size of a winged seed and the
clouds have hidden her from view, something falls out of the
sky and lands at Malte's feet. It is her hat.

He looks up. It is almost as if he were upside down in
midair himself, for there it hangs on the hall stand, a harebell
atop the cloak with its brooch and pearl pin. He looks down.
The suitcase is still there, it and no other, bearing the label of an

American liner on which the two of them have never set foot. Malte gulps.

He opens the door of the saloon, just a crack. Stays where he is for a long while, holding it ajar and listening. Coffee cups and saucers rattle, hushed voices talk back and forth, chair legs screech. Over these sounds flutters a laugh that stains his throat red. It is his mother's. She is sitting at one end of the table, being waited on by a man he has never seen before.

He narrows the crack, turning it black. Softly he closes the door again. His first instinct is to take to his heels, but he thinks better of that idea and tiptoes up the stairs, up to the room with the sea view, hoping to find Oda in her sickbed. He barges in, not bothering to knock. She is sitting propped up by pillows and seems quite unperturbed by his appearance. She has the look of someone who is humming. She is knitting something, the needles jut out at the sides. Tiny bootees for a blue romper suit.

"Who packed my bag?"

"Your mother did, Malte. She arrived yesterday evening. We were going to fetch you from the lighthouse, but she said it was better if you stayed there."

"I don't want to go home!"

"Now, now, that's not for you or me to decide."

"Summer isn't over yet."

"But you have to go to school, Malte."

"I don't want to go to school. At school I can't read."

"I thought you would be pleased. Haven't you missed her?"

Malte doesn't answer. He has crossed to the window to stare blankly out to sea. Oda sighs and lowers her knitting.

"It was the mistress who sent for her. Well, you did run away, and everybody was at their wit's end."

"It's all your fault . . ."

"My fault? What's that supposed to mean?"

"You threw the elf away. That was a really rotten thing to do!"

"What *are* you talking about, Malte?"

"There was an elf in my piece of amber. That was what I was looking for when I was sent to my room. And now it's dead. See for yourself, there's a bit of the wing left in the necklace."

"Malte, come here."

He goes over to the bed and she draws him into the hollow of her throat.

"It's the best present I've ever gotten," she whispers.

"Better than the ring?"

"Much better."

Malte is comforted.

"Now, Malte, you go on down to your mother."

He extricates himself from her embrace; her freckles have begun to smell of milk, and the warmth of the bed is making him feel groggy.

"I think the fox has taken it," he announces.

Oda looks as if she is counting on her fingers. Then she brightens up.

"Foxes don't eat elves, foxes steal chickens and ducks and geese if they get the chance . . ." She stops and slaps the eiderdown with her hand. "Oh, Malte, the way you get me going. Now go on down and give her a hug. I'm sure she's eager to see you."

"I don't want to go home."

"But you'll be back next summer."

She smooths the eiderdown tight across her stomach, trying to make it bulge, then she pushes her bottom forward until a decent bump appears. She has a thought, rummages among the things on her bedside table and produces a tiny cap. It has a pointed crown and earflaps.

She dangles it under Malte's nose.

"Next summer the elf will be here; and you can play . . ."

"Only girls play with babies."

"You wait and see, Malte. This baby is going to be something special. And Santos has been an angel ever since he found out. He's so looking forward to it, oohh . . ."

She rolls her head and hunches her shoulders. Just as she does, a spasm crosses her face; the cracked rib has spoken. She places a hand over the bandage. Malte is there like a shot, ready to help her back onto the pillow, and she sinks into it wreathed in smiles and pain.

"You won't leave without saying goodbye, will you?"

"You bet I won't," he says pluckily.

Her hands lie limply on the knitting, her head falls to one side.

"Could you draw the curtains before you go?"

Malte blots out the sea with a tug on the curtain cord. Oda has dozed off. He lingers a while in the room before going out. Then he sets his feet on the stairs, one step at a time; his hand slides down the banister, faltering when it reaches the knob at the very bottom, as though he can go no farther.

Dr. Hansen is in the hallway. He has come to look in on Oda. He hangs up his checkered cap—the headgear that has replaced the flyer's helmet since he has had the Ford's roof over his head—and hefts his doctor's bag.

"Hello, there," he cries, as if nothing were amiss. "How's the patient doing?"

"Fine," says Malte sulkily. He has *just* been up to see her.

"Next stop, Crow Towers. Want to come?"

"My mother's here . . ."

"What?"

Malte says it again, barely loud enough to be heard.

"Oh, that's right . . . See you later, then?"

Malte does not bother to answer. His mother turns up and suddenly nobody understands him. Dr. Hansen makes his way upstairs.

Malte takes a deep breath and walks into the saloon. Hands are clapped together. The sound is almost as loud as the door clicking shut. Then he is up to his nose in fox. Showered in twitters and kisses.

"Oh, Mama has missed you so much!"

He manages to avoid having blood drawn from his cheeks by the pin with the dangly bits that holds the fur closed.

"Mmm, mmm, mmm," she says as she kisses. Malte tears himself free and wipes his top lip. She ruffles his hair. "You're so brown. You look like a little gypsy."

"I don't want to go home," he says, pouting.

She pays no attention, turning instead to the man at her side and introducing him with a little flourish straight off the stage. "Say hello to Ottosen. He's in the comestibles business. He has a shop on the fanciest street in town."

Malte has no idea what comestibles are. But they sound grand. As grand as "bijoux," which is what her previous gentleman friend dealt in, the one with suitcases that flashed and sparkled when opened. Malte shakes hands and says hello with a little bow he learned in dancing school.

The man sitting next to his mother is plump and smooth-skinned, and brilliantine glistens in the thin hair on the top of his head. He has a twirled mustache, curly as a pig's tail, thick lips, and a girth that reduces his mother to a tiny slip of a thing. He calls her "My dear Odette." Malte is startled, not by the name, which he has grown up with, but by the tone of voice, which is thick and cloying and makes him uncomfortable.

His mother has changed her hairdo since he last saw her. She has had a permanent that has made her hair all wavy; he hasn't seen that dress before either, and each time he and she are reunited, the lines around her mouth seem to have grown slightly more strained. Her lips are thin and bloodless, she plasters them with lipstick to hide the fact.

She has no bust to speak of. Her collarbones stand out sharp.

Odette was a child of the Royal Ballet. Her young life was all practice, practice and no childhood. Just when she was about to make her debut in the part for which her training had prepared her, she tore a ligament. From one day to the next, she was out on the street.

Malte never knew his father, Alexander. She swears that when she was young he was the company's finest solo dancer, much sought after by other companies—until the day he disappeared in Russia, never to be heard from again. Malte knows every line of her stories, but he still does not know what to believe. She once showed him a photograph of his father and in that, with all those glittering sequins on his chest, he looked more like a circus performer.

The man in the comestibles business, whose name is Ottosen and whose pate glistens so, leans forward and speaks to him; farther down the table Ida points at him with a fork, and his mother dabs her mouth, leaving bloody seagull's wings on the napkin. Malte is supposed to answer, but he is engulfed in sights that allow no room for hearing.

He has crawled into Ida's muteness; the sequence of pictures is replayed. Still no sound. The comestibles man turns to his mother. The puzzled look of appeal in his eyes sets her hands fumbling with her napkin and she gazes imploringly at her son.

Malte braces himself against the corner of the table. Twists the draped fall of the tablecloth around his wrist and puts all his weight behind the tug. China, cheese-dish lid, and teapot slither into the fold now gaping before him in a minor earthquake; knives and teaspoons dance on the crest of the white wave. The seagull china flies into the air, the marmalade dish and the bread basket following.

"I don't want to go home!"

The boy's voice rings out shrilly above the crash.

17

IN WHICH
A PACT IS SEALED
FOR MALTE'S SOUL

Far out at Crow Towers—in the gloom of the parlor behind the soot-blackened windowpanes—the kayak comes loose from its strap and dives, bone tip first, through the cobwebs and fly husks. With a resounding drumroll from the skin, it comes to rest on the dining table, draped in tendrils of fluff. The line rest has snapped; the bird dart with its spiky barbs is left dangling like a daddy longlegs from the ceiling.

A death's-head monkey peeps from the corner of the room, the hair of the little face gleaming white in the darkness. The bestiary of seabirds, stuffed penguins, and adders in alcohol comes to life, glass eyes shot through with light, as the sun comes swirling out from behind a cloud, sending its rays streaming through the window and raising banners over the rug.

It is but the aftershock of the fall that runs through the room, and the rest follows. With a whir, the pinecone in the grandfather clock runs the length of its chain and drops to the floor of the case; moths, caught in the lamp chimney and dried by the warmth of the sun, disintegrate, paper-thin under the weight of the dust on their wings. Lace cuts loose, the tassel falls from a bellpull, and, with a crack that shoots abruptly from the star out, the commemorative Christmas plate flies apart, leaving only the nail on the wall.

A tremor has run through Crow Towers. A quivering of animal fur, a breath expelled, never to return.

Aviaja is dead.

No one knows, no one except me. It was she who screamed. They will find her in the straw, her face collapsed into mummy-like creases, her mouth puckered into a parson's nose of already receding flesh. She will look a thousand years old, the only living thing about her the filth she leaves behind.

This time neither skin nor bone will break death's seal. The drumbeat of her heart has stopped. She has jumped over the moon, she has jumped through the sun. With flames in her scant and lifeless hair she has shown herself in the night sky, she has crept under the skin, cleansed herself of flesh and blood, and sat, with the eyes of a seal pup, on the lap of the mother of all the oceans.

Here she froze a heart's breath ago. When that and the heat of her body left her, the windows in the barn misted over and the lamb that was licking the salt from her skin trembled from its muzzle to its tail. Aviaja, I have danced to your drum. Who is there now to conjure me into the ground when the urge comes over me yet again and I clench my fist to hammer on the lid?

Aviaja is dead. And I am as alone in space as only other souls can be; no living being can understand, but only in the flesh can we come together and only in the flesh does love make any sense. We do not gather on the Elysian Fields to hail one another with palm branches and hallelujahs, we never meet on the second star to the right. Up here we are as elusive to one another as clouds of gas or stellar nebulae. Whoever we were, we are no longer. Romeo's mistake, therefore, was twofold: he will never find his Juliet on the other side.

I see that now.

The resurrection takes place in the saloon. Malte is caught in a deluge of broken crockery and streaming tea leaves and coffee grounds. Half buried in the snowy folds of the cloth. A moment earlier he was prey to the wrath of an archangel; now he has salt on his shoulder and a deflated look in his eyes. On his cheek are the marks of four plump red sausages, left by the comestibles man.

His mother is weeping, Mrs. Swan is reading him the riot act. Mr. Ottosen stands, back turned, in a window bay, puffing as he tries to light a cigar intended to lay a smoke screen over the furious beating the boy almost had coming to him. There is a tightness in his gut and he is gasping for breath. Ida has run out of the room and the pharmacist has rushed after her.

Malte is still as a statue in his voluminous toga, hearing out the tirade—so it seems—with the dignity of a senator. When Mrs. Swan shakes him, he turns the other cheek, but not a sound escapes his lips. There are neither tears nor defiance in his eyes, only a glassy hardness.

He has removed himself to the uppermost level of his mind, to the jellyfish with eyes in all four corners of the globe and filaments connecting him with the farthest confines of the universe. The rubber plant that adorned the table has exploded into a star of earth around his feet. He is up to his ankles in pottery shards; below the cuff of his shorts his thighs are splotched scarlet, scalded by the water for the tea. But he does not feel a thing. Not even the hand that removes him from the pile of debris he has left on the freshly scrubbed floor.

The floor is swept, the cloth is lifted off his shoulders and knotted into a bundle in which silver spoons and knives rattle around among the butter stains. The corners drip as the cloth is borne out to the kitchen, out to Santos, who is in charge of washing up, with hands that have become wrinkled beyond recognition.

Back in the saloon, Odette has stopped crying and is now running around in circles, trying to be of some use, but—no longer knowing which way to turn—she knocks her heel against an ashtray that was already doomed and sends it flying into the baseboard. Mrs. Münster comes to her aid, helps her onto the piano seat, folds a napkin into a cone, and holds the silver egg with the smelling salts under her nose. Odette leans back to be met by a boom from the depths of the piano.

The same hand that led Malte away from the conflagration guides him to the chaise longue and eases him down onto it. Expertly it spreads salve over his burns. The touch makes his limbs shake, his teeth chatter; the pharmacist tilts the boy's chin upward, tries, in the golden reflection of his pince-nez, to catch the eye that rolls to the side. He is concerned more about the boy's silence than about his anger, snaps his fingers to bring him around.

Malte responds. As if a raindrop had landed on his nose. With surprise—though still with an air of distraction—he takes in the surrounding chaos, rubs his elbow, and looks up at Oak.

"Was I napping?" he asks. "The light went out."

The rest of the morning is taken up with negotiations around the dining table. Negotiations conducted behind closed doors. The comestibles man has pulled out his wallet; the compensation for crockery and china is generous and has put Mrs. Swan in a milder mood. The question now is what is to happen to Malte. The pharmacist has just gone to bat for him.

"Miss Odette," he says, "as far as school is concerned, he would be better off here. He is a help to Ida and he has made tremendous progress. He reads very well now. I don't know whether you are aware of that."

Odette herself never learned to read. After a day's rehearsal she had no energy left for that. She receives this information with a genuine but bittersweet delight. She thinks of all the years her dream was being honed into a perfect machine—until the spring broke and tossed her out into the world with no language except that of the body. There is a quietly rueful edge to her smile.

"My daughter Ida is mute," he continues. "She lost her mother under, well, tragic circumstances. Malte has done more for her than any doctor, both Dr. Hansen and I will vouch for that. There is something between them, and I would not be surprised . . ."

He checks himself. Removes his glasses and rubs them studiously, makes a slight adjustment to the nose clip. When he replaces them, there is a very different note in his voice: "In other words, I am prepared to pay for him to stay on here. I realize that his time as a summer boarder at Sea View is at an end."

He looks at Mrs. Swan, who nods.

"What do you say, Miss Odette? If Malte stays here for the rest of the summer I will take care of his schooling personally."

Odette clears her throat nervously. This wordless appeal to Ottosen elicits no response; it is up to her to do the talking.

"That is most generous of you, I must say, Mr. Oak. He has always been such a difficult child. He has been throwing tantrums like these ever since he was very small. You can never tell what he is thinking. One of these days he's going to get himself into trouble—oh, I *am* sorry, perhaps I shouldn't have said that . . ."

"I have discussed the matter with Dr. Hansen. We will be keeping a close eye on the boy and are quite willing to take responsibility for him for the length of his stay here. His is not a 'case' in any medical sense. I have Hansen's word on that."

Mrs. Swan intervenes. Somewhat grudgingly. "It's only his keep that has to be paid for. I won't take money for the room, it's not used for guests."

Then all at once she is off and running. She turns to the comestibles man.

"We might be able to take care of it with a few supplies. Some smoked meats, a side or two of ham? I'm told you carry a line of canned goods?"

Ottosen is on home ground here. Hard-nosed as a cattle dealer. At last something he understands. "Now you're talking!"

The bargaining gets under way. It develops into a tug-of-war over meat pies and other delicacies that will revolutionize the Sea View kitchen. The two of them are in their element, oblivious to everyone else. They haggle unabashedly. And the more they haggle the more they warm to each other.

"If you want my opinion," she mutters to him behind her hand, "that slap was well deserved."

They huddle over a sheet of paper on which the deal is set down in black and white, the list of items growing longer and longer. At one point Ottosen is heard to exclaim: "The boy doesn't eat *that* much, surely!"

From then on, the pharmacist is out of the picture. When it comes to the hard facts of life, he is as much of a lame duck as all the other humanists, growing uneasy when the talk turns to buying and selling. He looks quite uncomfortable when he turns to Malte's mother and asks: "Is that all right with you then, Miss Odette?"

Odette sighs. "Oh, I suppose so!"

She looks resignedly at Ottosen, who is in the act of appending his signature to the document.

Next door, Malte is doing lessons with Ida. The murmur of the grown-ups' voices reaches them through the closed doors, almost drowned by hemming and hawing and the scraping of chair legs. Ida is sitting at the tiled table, writing, her head to one side, her cheek just above the paper. *Robinson Crusoe* has been taken down from the shelf; Malte pages through it impatiently.

Their writing exercise out of the way, he reads aloud to her, the part where the shipwrecked sailor discovers Friday's footprints in the sand. Malte rattles on, never once getting caught up in the images created by the words; his thoughts are elsewhere. Ida becomes wrapped up in the story anyway, unperturbed by Malte's jabbering.

Malte has been taking stock: in the midst of his fear he secretly rejoices. One tug and a slap around the ear, but then he has also thrown up an obstacle to his mother's latest attachment. As for the rest, he bites his nails. There are some thoughts he does not dare to take to their conclusion.

He jumps up when steps are heard in the hallway and Mrs. Swan's voice rises above everyone else's.

As soon as the ink is dry, Mrs. Swan opens the door and summons Malte. He walks into the saloon with a Sunday-school expression on his face; his heart is thumping and his stomach is in a knot. When he hears that he can stay until the end of the summer, he throws his arms around his mother's neck with such vigor that the white-painted legs of the dining-room chair almost collapse under them.

"My big boy," she murmurs into his flaxen summer crop— "my big, big boy."

A fly hits the window. Suddenly Malte feels like going outside. Mrs. Swan stops him in the doorway; he is caught by a starched apron that blocks his exit.

"Oh no, you don't, my fine friend. We could do with an extra hand in the kitchen. Oda has been doing the work of two. Now *you* two characters will have to do your best to make up for that. And you're going to have your work cut out for you!"

She is thinking of Santos. He has been kept busy, acting as all-around handyman since Oda's return. The house, the garden, the kitchen, all the things the residents never see when the logs are lying, neatly chopped, in the basket on the hearth and the fire is lit before five o'clock tea. And the most amazing thing happens: Malte nods at the logic of this pronouncement and, before hurrying off to the kitchen, he whispers an apology to her that no one else hears.

The washing up goes fairly well. In a way, the boy has taken care of the lion's share of it already. But it is before lunch that they really outdo themselves, washing vegetables and hauling water and wood for the stove—all this amid the boiling and the frying and Mrs. Swan's throwing red-hot iron rings about. Santos sweats buckets and crosses himself whenever he has a free hand; if these are the flames of purgatory, then saints preserve him from the fires of hell.

Over lunch, when the worst of the rush has tailed off into the afternoon lull, they sit under the overhang of the tool-shed roof and peel potatoes for dinner. Santos suddenly feels chilled; his face is tired and drawn. The gardening has ruined his fingernails. The skin below his collar line itches. He has borrowed a wool sweater from the gardener and he scratches at himself every time he drops a potato into the pot, which is the size of a small cauldron.

He has the look of a man doing time as he sits there, suffering the vagaries of the Danish summer. The day is windy, with the occasional shower, and the poplars are sighing. Malte has rolled up his shirtsleeves; it is no worse than that. They sit for some time in silence as the peelings pile up in the bucket. Whenever it is full, Malte runs over and empties it onto the compost heap. All at once, Santos clutches at his stomach and begins to rock back and forth on his stool in pain.

"Go on up to Oda," says Malte. Totally deadpan. For one thing, the pot is almost full. For another, he knows that it will take Santos ages to get himself dressed for his tryst with Oda. As long as the masquerade is being enacted, even Mrs. Swan has no choice but to play along, keeping her mouth shut. There is no going halfway. But for every hour he spends with his betrothed, he is coming to look like a more and more unkempt version of Monsieur Charles.

At long last Malte catches sight of Ida in the garden. He has promised to show her how easy it is to make a parasol like the one Crusoe carries around with him on the island. He salvages the remains of the rubber plant from the compost heap. The minute the last potato has been peeled and the pot lugged inside, the splashes from it cooling the burned patches on his legs, he is off with Ida, down to the hideaway under the poplar trees.

It is Dr. Hansen who brings the news.

The old woman at Crow Towers will no longer be a burden on the parish, now that she has passed into the hands of a higher authority. Irrevocably this time. Her mortal remains have been taken to the hospital in town; when he found her, in the barn as before, a lamb was licking at her throat. He rolled her up in a horse blanket that weighed more than her body, lifted her into the backseat of his car. Rigor mortis had an iron grip on her jaw, the first livid patches had appeared on the back of the hand. Nonetheless, he spent a long time rubbing the withered limbs with alcohol and examined her thoroughly before proceeding—in a room at the hospital—to perform an autopsy. Old age—there is nothing else he can add to the cause of death.

He went to the parsonage to turn over her private papers, among them her last will and testament. And that was that. None of those present had known Aviaja Bertelsen personally. She was an odd, reclusive woman who had shunned the society of the living for as long as anyone could remember.

Even so, everyone is seized by a strange uneasiness. Things are mislaid—spectacles, sewing, sheet music—they all glance around the room, the ticking of the clocks seems too insistent. Heads swivel to look after no one, thoughts turn to a distant relative, a cousin long neglected. The unease settles in their feet; toes are scuffed, ankles wound about chair legs. There is a mental counting on fingers, as if something is missing.

In an attempt to lighten the mood Mrs. Swan brings out the schnapps and pours a round on the house.

Only Odette and her beau are exempt. They come down from their room after an extended afternoon nap. Mr. Ottosen holds the door for her, pulls out her chair, and eases it under the back of her dress as she makes herself comfortable. His coarse manners have turned to a sort of gauche gallantry. He is tripping over himself in his efforts to please her.

Odette is already dressed for dinner; her gloved arm ends in a cigarette holder. She introduces herself to the doctor: "Mr. Oak has said such nice things about you. I'm Malte's mother."

No one goes out of their way, however, to inform the couple

PRINCE   1 7 1

of what has happened. Neither of them has ever heard of the
deceased. They are presented with a glass, so that they can join
in the toast. They are still wrinkling their noses at the bitter
liquor when a door bursts open, letting a gust of wind into the
room, and a black object glides across the parquet floor, leaving
a long trail of dirt behind it.

Mrs. Münster catches her breath. As if that creeping sensation at the back of her neck had finally manifested itself in a vision. It *was* said that the old crone from Crow Towers was in
league with the Evil One himself, and the people of the parish
still recall with a shudder that midsummer's eve when she
showed herself in the shape of the black dog that howled so
heartrendingly beside the midsummer bonfire, while the witch
atop it soared into the air on her fiery broomstick.

The figure has come to a halt in the center of the room. It
takes some time for it to dawn on the company that it is a small
person, a child of ashes, soot, and all manner of other black
stuff. The pharmacist gives a cry.

The child is Ida, dressed up as Friday. A grass skirt bristles
about her waist; she turns a pirouette by the piano, her hands
unfolding like petals: Look at me! Her eyes pierce the soot, un-
naturally bright, they fill her whole face, bursting with glee and
anticipation.

A second figure makes its entrance. In Ida's wake comes
clarification, striding sedately under his parasol of rubber-plant
leaves, wearing a fur cap cut out of an old muff from the stor-
age room. The tableau eases the tension: there is laughter and
clapping. Ida curtsies and acknowledges the applause like a little ballerina. Odette is on her feet, clapping furiously and
shouting, "Bravo!" and "Da capo!" A sudden tug at her heart-
strings works its way into her eyes.

The pharmacist stoops over Dr. Hansen, whispering intently. When the applause has subsided and the gathering has

settled down once more, the doctor goes over to Malte. Punches him lightly on the shoulder, bends down level with his ear.

"I hear they've sold your soul for a hunk of salami and some cheese. What do you say to that, Malte?"

The boy says nothing. He is grinning from ear to ear.

It is a more subdued Robinson who, a little later, serves the cannibals at the dining table. On the menu is rib roast with potatoes and overcooked Brussels sprouts. Being one of the help has certain advantages. You get to eat on your own in the kitchen and you can give the Brussels sprouts a wide berth.

Night drifts over the guest-house buildings behind the dike. The blood-red moon that rose above the poplar trees has shrunk to a bone-white sphere, its glow fading into starlight. There is a ring around it, a force field, the lines of which become visible only at the outermost rainbow-like edge. The moon is full inside its fairy ring, at its height at the midnight hour.

The chirping of grasshoppers cuts through the August night as the creature's bark begins. First it is a faint whine behind the willow hedge, puppyish yaps, then a howling that cleaves the sleep of the living to the marrow. A window flies up.

"Shut up, you damn mutt!"

An object crashes through the leaves and the noise stops. But not for long; soon it starts up again, more insistent than ever. With an echo that shatters glass in the heavens and sets the fetters of lost souls vibrating. The full moon is engulfed in beating wings, as the wedge of gray geese flies across the dike.

IN WHICH
THE WILL IS OPENED

The ceiling of the parson's study is high; from the window he has a view of marsh and meadows where sheep graze against the thin line of the sea. His desk is piled high with books. Volumes in German, Latin, and ancient Greek and Hebrew spiral upwards, towers of Babel from which the bookmarks loll like tongues. With every new title, the piles inch closer to the point when they will come tumbling down.

He is a demon for unearthing quotations, knows exactly where in the piles to come upon them. He sits in the morning light and revels in his island of clutter while, in the rest of the parsonage, strict order reigns. Behind him the forests sing.

He is in the process of going through old Aviaja's papers. Most of them can be weeded out: bank transactions dating as far back as the Amber King's time, deeds to properties that have long since passed into other hands, accounts relating to shipments, cargoes, and deals closed.

There are customs stamps from every imaginable port of call, forms completed on typewriters, with the strokes of the

Danish øs filled in by hand. He comes across a letter from the
Amber King's first wife, hastens to turn the written side face
down—he is not here to pry into private matters. He does,
however, linger for a while over the adoption papers for Aviaja
Bertelsen.

He is looking for her last will and testament. Any specific
wish as to how the funeral should be conducted will, as far as
possible, be respected. He dreads to think what he might find:
the Amber King's daughter was not a Greenlander in name
alone; she was an avowed heathen who would never have anything to do with the Danish Church.

He finds nothing resembling a will. An envelope thus inscribed turns out to be empty, apart from an amulet in the form
of a sealskin pouch. He sits with it in his hand for a long time.
The pouch is held closed by a sliver of bone. He squeezes the
skin between his fingers; there is something inside, a familiar
shape. The sliver of bone is attached to a length of animal
sinew; slipping the bone free, he shakes out the contents of the
pouch. It is a perfectly ordinary wedding ring, solid gold no
less.

He is surprised. Aviaja married? No one in the parish has
ever heard tell of such a thing.

He rolls the ring back and forth across his blotting pad. At
first disappointed, then ashamed. He is the one with the primitive mentality—what did he expect? Nail clippings, viper
venom, and mandrake root? The leering mask of a tupilak to
bring down a curse on one's enemy?

A thought occurs to the parson. He examines the ring under
a magnifying glass.

Again he draws a blank. No inscription, other than the hall-
mark. He leans back in his chair. Sits with his hands clasped,
tapping his index fingers on the bridge of his nose. Shoves the
swivel chair in again, causing the wooden screw to complain.

His eye falls on the paper in which the ring was wrapped. He eases it out of the pouch. It has been folded over and over, but the folds are sharp and crisp. He opens it to find that there is something written on it, smudged and in a hand that slants across the page. He passes the magnifying glass over it.

"Mathilde," he calls out a little later, "could you come and help me make out this scrawl?"

An extraordinary meeting of the parish council has been called. The parson has placed rooms at the members' disposal. Coffee, bread, and home baking have been set out on the table. Aviaja's will is the sole item on the agenda. He has presented the relevant documents and outlined the situation. The queer old lady from Crow Towers has left a more or less untouched fortune, the original principal of which was amassed by the Amber King. No mattresses or pillows stuffed with banknotes, no jam jars buried in the backyard, and no armored safes behind the paintings.

The money is in the bank, where it has been since the Amber King's death. In fact, the fortune has increased enormously over the years, the interest far greater than Aviaja's expenses. Everyone thought that she has desperately poor, that the money had run out—why else would she eke out a living from fishing nets and traps, goat's milk and sheep? Now it turns out that she was richer than all of them, and here's the point: the money is to go to the parish and she has appointed the parson as her executor. There are, however, a number of provisos and it is these that they have to discuss. Aviaja wishes to be cremated and her ashes placed in the grave of the unknown seaman in the churchyard.

The chairman of the parish council drums his fingers on the

table impatiently. He has already got the furnace stoked; if the old hag wants to be cremated, that's fine by him. He doesn't understand why the parson is hesitating. There he sits, equivocating, enthroned at the head of the table behind an open parish register with a binding like that of a statute book.

According to the will, Aviaja had been married, but not according to the parish register. He has made some inquiries at the county registry. No trace there, either, of a certificate of marriage, civil or church. The files have been checked. In other words, it has to be concluded that she died in an unwed state.

"What exactly is the parson getting at?"

It is Mrs. Swan. She is sitting directly opposite the chairman of the parish council and the drumming of his fingers is getting on her nerves.

"We can't just go putting urns in strangers' graves. Now, if he were a close relative, that would be quite a different matter. And besides, there is yet another proviso . . ."

"Oh?"

The parson pauses. Not trying to prolong the agony, but clearly at a loss.

"Aviaja Bertelsen has requested a requiem for the young sailor in the coffin . . . to be performed in our church in conjunction with her funeral."

"So? That can't cost that much, can it?"

The chairman is given a downright reproving look. The parson is no longer floundering in the dark with some unsolved riddle; his voice is sharp. "As our esteemed chairman is perhaps aware, the Danish Church is Protestant. Masses for the souls of the dead are the province of the Catholic Church. There is absolutely no precedent in our liturgy."

"And who decides that?"

"I do! Whatever goes on in my church is my responsibility, thank God, and no one else's. If there is one thing we are not, it is papists."

"Fine, Reverend. What, then, is the problem?"

A pause ensues. And before it can be broken it spreads all the way around the table. Each of them has a right to a dream. And the sum in question is large enough to accommodate all their dreams. Should the terms of the will not be complied with, the legacy will pass to the public trustee. In short, the state.

The parson thinks of the church organ. There is a dreadful wheezing from the pipes, half the stops have given up the ghost, the piccolos sound like a barrel organ turned by a traveling showman, the keys stick, and the works are disintegrating into a mass of reeds and gear wheels that has him baffled. There isn't an organ tuner for miles around who would dare to touch the thing.

He would not mind one of the newer models. With clean lines, gray pipes—all matching—and no gilded cherubs. With one of those newfangled mechanisms instead of the ancient one that drives it now and makes "Nearer My God to Thee" sound like a music-hall ditty.

Mrs. Swan is thinking about the church hall that the parish has never had the money to build. The chairman envisions a tractor depot and a hall for holding their own fish markets. The parson's wife's thoughts are with the poor and the sick; in her spare time she would build shelters where the needy would hold reading circles in the common room and consumptives would embroider altar cloths until such time as they were consumed and—after a cleansing herbal bath—ascended to heaven.

The chairman breaks the silence.

"Aye, it's a lotta money," he says in his island brogue.

And even though they look on him as a mere rough farmer,

his words do not fall on stony ground. There is support from around the table, in the form of mumbled agreement. All at once the parson finds that it is him against them; suddenly it all rests with him. Can he allow such a thing? In his own church? And if it did come around and he decided—just this once—to turn a blind eye to the liturgy, who on earth would they find to perform a requiem in this God-forsaken spot?

His own Mathilde provides the answer. "That Monsieur Charles, as far as I understand, isn't he a Catholic? And something of a musician? I mean, he used to practice with Oda and the rest of the church choir. I remember that Sunday during Trinity—it was heavenly! Remember?"

They all nod. A memory of something bordering on the ecstatic has been called up. The promise of it passes through the room like an "amen," touching all the members of the parish council. A chorale that could take Creation by the scruff of the neck and send it flying down the nave so as to make the hair rise on the back of one's neck, is that not a message from the Most High? Those moments when the soul is uplifted must surely be the closest we come to God in this life. A hymn for the dead sailor, what harm can it do?

Call it a mass or whatever the devil you like, it's only words, thinks the chairman of the parish council, but he holds his peace in the face of the pious. He has some flair for politics, or he wouldn't be sitting where he is. He pulls the gold case from his vest pocket by its chain, flips it open, and snaps it shut again, all with a flick of the wrist, already on his way to his next appointment. Before he rises, he dips an almond crescent in his coffee, munches it, and dabs his lips with the corner of his napkin. A little powdered sugar is left clinging to his mustache.

The parson brings the meeting to a close. "There are certain formalities, and I would in any case like to sleep on this until we meet again on Wednesday. The deceased will be cremated and her remains placed in the chapel of rest until her last wish can be carried out. May it please the Lord!"

He gets up from the head of the table and bids the members of the parish council good day, shaking hands with each of them. Mathilde stands at his side and asks after all the family members, whom he tends to get confused.

The warm summer weather has returned, with the sun shining down on the beach. A party is making its way over the dunes in single file, leaving deep dimples in the sand. At its head walks a gentleman. He is clad in a broad-striped one-piece garment, with a handkerchief knotted at the corners doing service as a sun hat. He blows sweat off the tip of his nose; the sand seems to slide away beneath his feet with every step intended to carry him forward.

In the middle walks a dainty little woman in a bloomer suit, and bringing up the rear a boy, dragging behind him through the sand a parasol, the handle of which is longer than he is. He is trudging across a desert with no oasis in sight, captive of a tribe that totes all its belongings with it. Malte, the boy who rides the wind.

They find a dip in the dunes. Or rather, every time they are about to park themselves in one dip the woman catches sight of another one, where the sun shines even more brightly and enticingly. Eventually they wind up in the first. The man seizes the parasol and wrestles with it, but when the canopy finally unfurls and the catch clicks into place, it sets off a miniature landslide. The gentleman gets sand in his eyes, swears and rubs them until they are bright red. He calls the boy, who has been standing with his back turned, and together they plant the point of the shaft between clumps of lyme grass and seaweed-covered rocks.

In the meantime, the woman has unrolled some straw mats; over this bottom layer she spreads large bath towels from the guest house, sets a basket in the shade. Out of it protrudes the neck of a bottle wrapped in a damp dish towel. Malte doesn't get it; he has been sentenced to a day at the beach. They might just as well have stayed at home.

One good thing: it gets him off kitchen duty.

Odette slathers herself with sun cream. Ottosen has to do her back. He worms his hand so far down that Malte has to look the other way. She stinks to high heaven of fox pee and tallow. Then she lies down in the sun; the shade is reserved for the picnic basket—and Ottosen. He rolls over onto his stomach and tries to maneuver a newspaper in the drifts of sand. The pages flap about and fly away.

His mother half opens one eye: "Malte . . ."

And he's off. It's like running after a kite, and for a moment he is happy.

A moment. Then he has to report back to the dip in the dunes and hand over the obituaries, marked with their stars and crosses. He feels like a dog and his mouth promptly fills with the taste of slippers.

Odette is beginning to melt. She sits up and rummages in her bag, moistens a couple of pieces of cotton with cologne, places them on her eyelids, and eases herself back down into a prone position. She turns her hands palm up and sighs; her skin gives off a bluish shimmer. Ottosen folds his newspaper and flicks a horsefly away from her knee.

Malte runs down to the water's edge. It is one of those rare clear days when the eye is carried for miles on the air. He can just make out the island as a narrow band on the horizon, the one with the lighthouse. Olesen has told him that there are seals out there. He has never seen a real live seal, has found them only in the pages of books. He pictures them, though. All day long they sun themselves on rocks and sand; they have speckled coats and whiskers that bristle impudently.

All of a sudden Ottosen is standing next to him. He has shed the knotted hanky; now he dips a pig's foot in the water, makes a face, and mimes a shudder for Malte's benefit. Then he drops to his knees, digs with his hands in the damp sand, builds a mound, puts a moat around, and runs water into it. He is building a sand castle, giving it cockleshells for windows and sticking a seaweed pennant on top! The massive body roots around at Malte's feet, scrambles about on its hands and knees. The sight makes Malte's blood run cold.

The comestibles man looks up, cocks his head, inviting the boy to join in.

Malte declines. Now he knows what is in store for him. Obviously, steps are being taken to get acquainted—why else would the man put on the jolly-uncle act? Anyway, he has seen him playing croquet with his mother and the pharmacist. He is the type who nudges his balls into position with his foot when he thinks the others are not looking.

Malte wades out a bit. Then he plunges in and starts to swim underwater. If he could, he would not come up again until he came to the seal island. Malte the merman. He sees a pair of chalk-white columns through the shimmering light, legs that end in a giant's feet. The toenails put him in mind of the sailor in the coffin. That was at the beginning of the summer, already a long time ago.

He comes shooting up. Rams the bottom stripe on Ottosen's belly. And before he knows what is happening, the man has grabbed both his hands and is hopping up and down: A-one . . . a-two . . . a-three, he counts. He dunks Malte long before he reaches ten. Malte coughs and sputters and lashes out. He knew it! Gives Ottosen an icy glare and pushes off with a kick that catches the man in the solar plexus. Then he dives underwater again and squirms away, tossing his head.

Ottosen admits defeat. He hops up and down on one foot, waving his arms about to keep his balance, trying to give his lady of choice up there on the beach the impression that he has mastered the art. Suddenly his foot slips into a hole and under he goes. He bobs back to the surface with panic written all over his face. Arms flailing, he goes down a second time. Malte gloats from afar. As soon as Ottosen can get his footing, he slinks back to shore and stands there shivering, drilling in his ear with a finger for water. His attempt to make Malte his sonny lies in ruins, the sand castle has already been washed away.

He retreats to the shade and digs a chicken leg out of the picnic basket. Gets his lips good and greasy. He reaches for the wine bottle to wash it down, picks up the one with the juice, and spits it out all over Odette, who wakes from the deep purple blanket of her sun-baked slumber and proceeds to rub at the blackcurrant stains on her beach dress. The tired lines around her mouth deepen, but when she eventually opens it, it is to say:

"Never mind, Svend Aage, it'll come out in the wash."

He picks out the breast and gobbles it down with spoonfuls of Mrs. Swan's mayonnaise, made from fresh country eggs. He stops in midchew—maybe they ought to try stocking this in the shop. He must remember to talk to Mrs. Swan about it.

"Mother," cries Malte from the water's edge, "I'm just going to run up to the lighthouse to see Olesen."

She raises an arm to call him back. But before she can get the words out, he is off and the gesture degenerates into a wave. She sinks back onto the bath towel, locates her cotton pads, moistens them again, and shuts out the light.

There is a great deal of fidgeting and fumbling on the bath towel next to hers, the sand shifts under her every time he moves. His grunting makes her think of sea lions. When Malte comes home she will take him to the zoo—there are so many things they have never done. But now they can afford them.

Her Svend Aage leaves her in peace until lunchtime. Then he is all over her—his shoulders twitch and his stomach rumbles.

"Odette, it's half past one!"

The situation is desperate, she can tell by his agonized tone. She sits up, spreads the cloth. Several sandwiches have already been robbed of their fillings, the mayonnaise bowl is empty. There is sand in the wrapping paper and the white wine is warm and tastes flat. She herself makes do with a peeled cucumber and a hard-boiled egg. After lunch they pack up. Svend Aage needs to get back to the room for a nap.

Late in the afternoon a hansom, ordered from town, drives up to the guest house. Odette, dressed now, and her beau are standing in the driveway with their suitcases at their feet. Her cheeks and throat are red with sunburn, her eyes circled in white like a raccoon's.

Malte comes panting up to say goodbye. He is still in his bathing trunks. His mother is given a hug; Ottosen is dismissed with his stiffest bow. Visiting hours are over. The couple climb into the hansom; the boy is gone before it rounds the first bend on Beach Road.

Beneath the bandage and the broken rib, Oda's baby is growing. She is now certain that it is a boy. Every time she nods off she has that dream again: the father ages, the boy grows to be a man, acquires black whiskers and gold in his ears and at his throat.

She is up and about. For the first time she does not feel like going back to bed. The sun streams in through the west-facing windows, low and dazzling; irregularities in the glass split the light into red and green transparencies on the walls behind her.

She bends forward and drags the floor-length nightgown over her head, backs out of the bed fug. She washes herself with lavender water from the washbasin, dabs the area around the bandage with a sponge, and weighs her breasts in her hands. They have grown heavier. Another bloodstream has linked up with hers and it branches out under the skin; its hidden springs burst forth and fill her with joy. She opens the window and lets the birdsong pour in.

Oda dries herself and slips on the dress that has been hanging over the back of the chair the whole time she has been confined to bed. She sits in front of the mirror, brushes her hair and braids it. Her personal toilet completed, she runs an eye over the room. The bed is in disarray; on the tray sits some cold tea and a plate of cheese sandwiches, the ends of which are curling in the heat. No one has thought to empty the chamber pot, the sheets and towels could do with a change.

She sets to work. Carries things out, washes and rinses until fresh lavender is once more floating in the washbasin. It feels good to turn her hand again to something other than knitting. She sweeps the room and strips the bed. The dirty linen lands in a heap in the corridor; she fetches a fresh batch from the linen cupboard. Only once the room has been aired, the bed made up with freshly ironed sheets and eiderdown cover is everything as it should be—ready for the next guest to move in.

She has cleared every trace of herself. She registers this fact with relief. Her days of lying in the count's bed are over and before the sun sinks into the sea she will be back in her own little room. Oda is well again.

The door handle dips and Malte pops his head around the door.

"The parson's wife's here. She wants to talk to Santos."

"Malte! Weren't you supposed to be leaving?"

"I've been allowed to stay," he says, beaming. "My mother sold me for some cheese and salami. So the doctor says."

"Oh, the doctor says a lot of things. He also said that I had to stay in bed until my bandage could come off. Come on, let's go find Santos. I haven't seen hide nor hair of him all day."

19

IN WHICH
CROW TOWERS
GOES UNDER

The good weep . . .

As Saint Lawrence's tears streak, blazing, across the night sky, Monsieur Charles is appointed the parish's new choir master. The old organist resigns in protest. Just as well: he plays that organ with ten thumbs and two left feet. The count, the chicken thief, the kitchen boy rises out of the ashes on the wings of music; the phoenix is a rooster and once again he crows over the church down.

Monsieur Charles demands the room with the sea view back, and Mrs. Swan seethes over the soup pots as he covers sheet after sheet of staff paper with music the choir rehearses daily. He is working miracles with lumps of clay. The choir members, most of whom are preparing for confirmation or are schoolchildren, are raised up into a crystalline sphere from the moment he gives them their key and lifts his baton. It is as though the notes he writes have a mind of their own, and what he achieved with Oda he now achieves with them all.

Even Oda is bewildered; her beloved is two people, one of

whom she knows and one of whom she quails before. The god
in the bride of Saint Lucia's mirror is Night and Day—one
minute a Santos Linares with the face of an angel, who can get
her to lift up her voice to the Lord, the next a man possessed, a
drillmaster armed with ruler and pen who makes the congregation dance to his tune.

Some of the members of the parish council sit in on the first
rehearsals. Afterwards they nod to one another. The music
flows solemnly down the nave. All eyes are on the conductor.
When his hands form themselves into a tulip, icily pure and
plangent strains stream from the choir's mouths, and in the
pause between movements the air stands still under the vaulted
ceiling. The slightest cough would seem a profanity and Monsieur Charles raps the music stand sternly with his baton at the
first hint of giggling in the ranks. The representatives of the
parish council leave the church feeling satisfied.

For his own part, he is never satisfied. Inch by inch the work
progresses across the annotated sheets; there are days when he
knocks down the whole house of cards and starts from scratch.
Then he sits in his room with a battered copy of the psalms
provided by the parson, endlessly going over a chord, repeating
the same passage again and again until the note is struck that
changes everything. His heart is in his work, that much is certain. As for the pay, it is essentially symbolic.

But no one now objects to his being provided with room
and board at Sea View, and Mrs. Swan has no intention of being out of pocket for the bill left unpaid while the gentleman
was still playing the count. That will be settled when the estate
is wound up and the legacy realized.

He has begun with a classic requiem and with the established Latin text: Kyrie, Dies Irae, the Offertory, Agnus Dei,
and Sanctus . . . that is how it has been sung for centuries. Santos taps the music stand with his pen. Inside him he carries

another rhythm, a language that is his own, songs he grew up with, the throb of the drums and harps and bamboo flutes of his childhood home.

He starts over again. The Mass is resurrected in his Creole blood; he dispenses with the Latin, frames the passages in Spanish. He shakes the dry and dusty parts from the shelf, alters the phrasing, and links the cadences in an undulating thread that causes the binding to fall off the psalmbook.

In the evenings there is no getting through to him; he gazes vacantly at other skies, whips pieces of paper out of his breast pocket, and scribbles down notes. Gone is Monsieur Charles's courteousness, the elegant conversation in French, and much that is worse. Oda catches herself missing her seducer—there are times when their bodies barely seem to exist for him; other times he thrusts and thrusts, finding release in her, with no thought for anything else.

He has entitled the work "Lucifero"—Bringer of Light.

The first flood tide sweeps in on the fishing village as the last days of summer are shedding their light over field and meadow. It comes without warning after an oppressive day in which the swallows have swooped and dived through the coach-house archway. The poplars are struck by gusts of wind that flay their boughs to switches. A stiff northwester churns up the waves, eating away at the beaches first and showering the dike with foam. The fishermen drag their boats all the way up to the farmland adjoining the beach, batten and lash down all their gear. The wharf has completely disappeared under the mass of water, the live-boxes are afloat, and the stake from the winch is suddenly nowhere to be seen.

Then the storm is over them, raging all day long. Heavy and

monotonous, the breakers roll toward the shore. Out at Crow
Towers, the sea smashes over the dike and the first foaming
white waves wash up against the main house. Swirls and eddies
froth down into the ground, bringing new ones in their wake;
scattering puddles as reflections of what is to come. The
mounds of moss on the lawn are underwater.

It keeps up through the night. The rollers burst with greenly
arched tongues behind their teeth, splatter against the windowpanes. First tasting their quarry, licking at the foundations. The
water continues to rise and the waves to pound. Like a persistent, nudging shoulder, the pressure on the house grows. The
timbers creak, the first boards start to yield, tongue and groove
to part company.

Inside, the wallpaper splits, the pattern exudes droplets that
begin to trickle. The water seeps in the windowsills. The floorboards grow darker, then shiny with moisture as the cataract
breaks through. The rolling body outside presses all its weight
against the building; the windowpanes shatter, streams of water
pour into the room. An hour or so later and the aquarium is
filled to table height. Then the kayak is set afloat and starts to
spin on its own axis.

Next is the grandfather clock, listing strangely from the
dead weight of its pendulums. The furniture twirls after; the
seabirds and the stuffed death's-head monkey plunge into
the torrent when the shelf collapses. The polar-bear skin that
lay in front of the hearth comes to life and strikes out with its
head and forepaws. The piano still stands, but ripples now play
over its ivory and ebony.

The stream presses on into the hallway, out to the narwhal
tusks forming an archway of honor over the door. The bottom
steps of the stairway to the north tower are underwater. The
joints in the brackets of the bay windows utter a loud groan.

Far out to sea a swell begins to build. Arches its back in the light of the half-moon, runs toward the shore flecked with starlight and inky reflections. The wave grows in thunder and power; the flood tide drives it forward and the wind rises with it into a sound that could be the baying of hounds. When it hits Crow Towers it bursts like a barrel that has long been straining at its hoops.

Everything is hurled out. Beneath the glass prisms the towers cave in and crash down into the sea, the collections of fossils and amber and sea horses, of seashells, turtle shells, and swordfish beaks are sluiced out, only to be carried back—in the corkscrew of the maelstrom—whence they came. Board by board, the wooden framework is ripped apart, walls give way, doors and windows drift among the household effects. A cat flap floats beside the worm-eaten leaves of the kitchen table. A chunk of the spiral stairway. A corner of the parlor with buckled nails, the rocking chair, rockers up, and a couple of wooden ladles—looking as though they are invisibly linked to the cutting board.

And before the cock crows again, Crow Towers has been reduced to driftwood. The barn, a stone building of later date, is left among the dunes. The whitened walls are gray with dampness when the flood tide at long last pulls back. On the crest of the hill, where the wind blusters, the frames hung with the dried fish are standing still. It is here that the animals gathered, bleating fearfully, when their pens were blown down, and by dawn the goats are already munching on what remains of the old woman's inheritance.

Malte is at the lighthouse. He has commandeered Olesen's chair in the watch room; a ring binder, taken down from the shelf, lies open in front of him. Dimly, through the whitewashed walls, he can hear the sea settling down, its roar growing more and more muted. Like a conch-shell tower, the lighthouse stands on the edge of the world, the echoes of the havoc wrought by the flood tide ringing in its whispering chambers, a babel of voices and cries from ships that went down in the night.

Malte has inched forward so that he is sitting on the edge of the seat as he deciphers the report that the lighthouse keeper has circled in red and left out on the desk for him.

It is what is known as a protest, and it has been submitted by a Captain Joseph Tanner, from a freighter whose name he cannot pronounce. The freighter was making its way down the Norwegian coast when, off Bergen Fjord, it ran into something drifting in the water. Each stage of the incident is logged with a precise note of the time at which it occurred. Fascinated, Malte runs his finger down the page as he reads, entry by entry:

13:01 GMT. North Sea. Second mate calls me to the bridge. He has sighted something in the water, to port on the lee half a nautical mile ahead, probably wreckage. He asks whether we should reduce speed. We are heading south-southwest, doing 14 knots. I turn the engine-room telegraph down to 9 knots. Visibility is good.

13:04 GMT. Good telescope observation, showing what is obviously wreckage, fanning out approximately one and a half cables ahead. Order further alteration in course and bear southwest to steer clear of the wreckage.

13:10 GMT. Collision with wreckage. Something scraping against the starboard bow. Reverse engines immediately. A ship's hull and parts of the rigging show between the waves. An old-style wooden schooner, a three-master. Most of the hull is underwater, the two masts farthest forward are broken, and, as far as we can see, no lifeboats have been launched. It is impossible to make out the ship's name or its home port, nor is there any trace of the crew.

13:13 GMT. Send second mate forward to the fo'c'sle to inspect the damage.

13:15 GMT. We are clear of the wreck. Put the engine-room telegraph on "Stop."

13:17 GMT. Second mate back on the bridge. Reports that the fore is intact, no leaks, some scratches in the paintwork, a dent under the hawse. Otherwise nothing. As far as he can tell, we have collided with the main mast.

13:23 GMT. More wreckage coming adrift from the sinking hull. Pass the word to the second mate to stand by. Spars and ropes float to the surface. Air escapes with a peculiar, almost plaintive sound. Pass the word to the mate again. Telescope observation shows a mahogany casket has risen to the surface and is floating among the flotsam.

13:25 GMT. Discuss with the second mate whether we ought to salvage. He feels that the dead should be left to rest in peace. Consider salvaging it and taking a closer look in the interest of the completeness of this report. Debris from the masts and rigging comes adrift, thus settling the matter. A salvage operation is now out of the question, owing to imminent risk of collision.

13:27 GMT. Full speed ahead. We are clear of the wreck. The air escapes from the last air pockets in the sinking hulk, which is no longer visible underwater.

13:30 GMT. Holding a steady course again. Leave the bridge to write report.

CONCLUSION

The wreck must be recent. All the damage seemed to be fresh and no moss or mildew could be detected. The wreck sank quickly. The circumstances must therefore be said to be mysterious. The schooner, whose name and port of origin are still unknown, showed signs of having been hit by a storm. But there has been no word of any storm in that area in the past 14 days. Calm weather, with full visibility and hardly any swell. After telegraphic contact with the coastguard at Bergen, the following can be confirmed: no shipwreck has been reported over the period in question, no SOS received. The schooner appeared to have been abandoned by its crew under circumstances that cannot be explained. We saw no drowned bodies among the wreckage. Nor is there any reef at the spot in question on which the wreck might have been caught until washed off by the tide, and the depth of the ocean at that point is considerable. This report signed and witnessed by the second mate.

J. Tanner, Captain

The boy hears a noise behind him and looks up from the ring binder. He turns his head. It is the lighthouse keeper; he has been standing there for some time, while Malte has been engrossed in his reading. Now he empties his pipe into the ashtray, clears his throat. The report dates from the beginning of the summer, around the time when the coffin was washed ashore at the fishing village.

"You see, Malte, there's an explanation for everything."

"What does GMT mean?"

"It's the time that all ships on the sea go by. The time at the observatory at Greenwich—that's in England."

Malte is all aglow. He is used to adventure stories, but this is different. It stirs him more than anything he has read—in either *The Children of Captain Grant* or *Twenty Thousand Leagues under the Sea*. Though the words are dry as dust, his heart has beaten in every one of them, minute for minute, and launched the ghost ship in his head.

"It's like *The Flying Dutchman*," he says, once the words have been digested, bit by bit. He has left his finger on the last entry and now he lifts it. Carefully brushes the protest with his hand, to make sure that he has left no marks.

"What Dutchman? None of the Dutchmen I've known could fly!"

"It's a ship," Malte explains patiently. "In a book I've read." And he adds thoughtfully, "Maybe the captain blasphemed against God!"

"Who? Captain Tanner?"

"No, the one in the coffin."

Sirius grunts. "You and your ghosts. Who's to say he was a captain? No, no, it's like I say, there's an explanation for everything. So don't you come here pulling everything to pieces with your talk. You've turned into a real scatterbrain since you started reading them books."

But Malte is lost to the world. His chin has dropped to his chest, he does not hear a word the lighthouse keeper is saying. He hears only the echo of his own, resounding still inside his head. He is back at the beginning of the summer, burying his treasure in the backyard. The photograph and the cap in the shoebox! It was a captain's cap, he's sure of it. He'd forgotten. Just like the shoe in the sand, the sock in the rock pool, the elf and the amber and the fox that howls in the night. Well, he'll show them. There was a name printed inside; he remembers now, but back then—a hundred years and a summer ago—he couldn't read.

He jumps up from the wing chair.

"Can I borrow a magnifying glass?"

Malte Alexander, detective. He is in such a state that his hands are trembling. Once he has dug up the treasure, he will write a report and sign it.

The lighthouse keeper nods. You can never tell what bees

that boy has in his bonnet. One minute he's hanging on your every word, asking questions and being given answers. The next, he's off in a world of his own with whatever it is he knows. And yet—it does stick. Sirius cannot help but smile. Malte picked up the Morse alphabet in an afternoon. They made a couple of carbide lamps with panels that slide down over the glass, so they could send messages to each other. As soon as darkness has fallen, the light travels, in short flashes and long, between the attic room and the lighthouse. It is something they share. For him, it is like having a son at this late stage in his life, when so much else seems unimportant.

Resigning himself, he sifts through sea charts and sets of compasses. Unearths the magnifying glass and slides it out of its leather case. Malte grabs at it.

"Oh no you don't. The lantern glass needs cleaning, the panes have to be polished. All part and parcel of minding the light." He holds the magnifying glass under Malte's nose, pops it into its case. Then he slips it into the boy's pocket. As soon as Malte has run upstairs, he puts the report back in the ring binder and returns it to the shelf.

Once Malte has worked his way around and polished the last large lantern with the sort of ammonia solution he once took a slug of, he stands for a moment out on the gallery, waves a hand under his nose, and takes a deep breath, filling his lungs with fresh air. The noonday sun hangs high over the sea, which billows like a long flying carpet spangled with silver, gently rising and falling. The storm that subsided around daybreak is still sending waves rolling toward the shore. Every seventh or ninth one crashes against it, to make the stones of the dike froth.

The wharf is open for use again; the fishermen have put out to sea—the weather promises to be fair—their boats disappearing from view somewhere out on the horizon, obscured by the glare off the sea. He scans the waves, his eyes straining in the bright light. He squints to see better, and an outline bobs between the crests of the waves, a darker shape. It is almost as if J. Tanner's report has come true when an unmanned craft drifts into sight. He has to pinch himself in the arm.

It looks like the kayak that he last saw hanging over the dining table at Crow Towers. He cups his hands into binoculars. It *is* the kayak. It is floating upside down, the tawny-colored keel jutting out of the water like a knife blade, rocked gently by wind and current. It is heading for the point.

He thunders down the spiral stairway, calling out to Sirius as he goes. They run out to the jetty, hop into the dinghy, and cast off. Sirius rows. Malte stands in the bow, pointing the way. When they draw level with the kayak, he leans out and catches hold of the pointed end with its bony tip. He makes fast the line that Sirius throws to him, hauls it back toward the stern, where he sits down, glorying in his prize. He is forever looking back to check that the kayak is still there. The lighthouse keeper winks at him and says that it is wreckage and therefore belongs to whoever salvages it. That's the law of the sea.

They tie up at the jetty. Malte has not let go of the line once; very carefully he steers the kayak clear of the posts. Little waves wash over the keel as they are pulling it ashore. They just make it before the seventh wave breaks and comes rushing in to take back their find. Once they are on the beach, they turn the kayak over and empty out the water. Malte is surprised at how light it is; he is carrying one end of a boat, and the boat is his! A fine craft, the type used by the hunters when they harpoon the biggest whales and row them ashore, with only a couple of inflated sealskin bladders to keep their catch afloat. What powerful forces there are in the sea, and how neatly they can be outmaneuvered . . .

The next hour or two is spent fixing up the kayak and making it seaworthy. Sirius gives him a hand. They wipe the saltwater off the skin, rub it with lamp oil to make it supple; there are no tears in it, but the framework is buckled. For Sirius, who is used to working with miniature hulls, it is the easiest thing in the world to stretch and pull the skin until it is taut once more.

The paddle is missing. Malte is dispatched to the beach to find a piece of driftwood the right size. That's the way to do it: to the Inuits, wood was so precious and so rare that they tipped the ends of their paddles with ivory, to keep them from being cut on the sharp rim of the ice. All of this is racing through Malte's mind, and the light is turning somersaults between the stones, until his eye falls on a scoured white pole that looks familiar.

It is the one from the winch down at the wharf, but that has already been fixed. The fishermen have replaced it with an oar whose blade had snapped off. The sea giveth and the sea taketh away. Today is Malte's day and he has all but forgotten his other major project until he feels the magnifying glass slapping against his thigh.

When he comes back with the pole he is twice as keyed up. Sirius yawns. It is way past his bedtime.

"Tomorrow's another day, Malte. Tomorrow we'll cut your paddle and I'll teach you how to handle it. By tomorrow the water's bound to have settled down, and that's just what I'm going to do."

Sirius pats Malte on the back of the head and goes off to his bunk. He has lifted the kayak up onto a couple of trestles. There it sits, with its long sweep from tip to tip and the patterns of bloodstreams long since spent showing through the skin, which stretches, glossy and transparent with oil, over the fragile skeleton. With the backs of his nails Malte calls up the roll of the drum, follows the lines of the kayak up to the bow. It has the look of a caress. There is a lump in the boy's throat. It is all the kites that he ever lost to the sky.

20

IN WHICH
THE SKIN IS SHED

Malte takes a short cut across the fields. The stubble scores his ankles, but he ignores it. The wind generated by his own race toward the sun fills him up. He paddles his arms, zigzags down the rows of wheat, fingertips grazing the stalks without knocking down a single sheaf. High over his head a pair of buzzards circle; shadows pass over the ground. Two short and one long.

His heels clod with earth, jacking him up and tipping him over on his ankle; he stops to clean them, finding a stick to scrape the muck off the soles. He kneads the ankle he has twisted, sets off again with a limp that soon goes away. But he has run out of steam; he saunters down the furrows of the ploughed section, then plunges into the hedgerow.

The hazel bushes are hung with green nuts, there is a chirping in the grass, and the thistles spread out in clumps that he avoids. He has forgotten to put on socks, and now he feels a stone digging into the ball of his foot. As he straightens up after shaking it out, he freezes.

First he sees the hunter, then the fox. The hunter raising the gun and the fox flattening itself into the furrow, its whole being ready to spring. He is about to shout, but before he can, the shot is fired. He feels the pellets whiz by him; they slice the tops off a bunch of thistles. Then the second barrel booms, discharging its whistling lead. The fox makes a lame attempt at a spring and falls back to the spot where it had lain. A shudder runs through it, ending at its tail. Its pelt quivers—far too long—and blood wells up among blasted tufts of fur. Its upper lip curls back over its teeth in a streak of black and pink.

Already, the light has gone from its eyes.

The shout in Malte's throat turns to a scream. At one fell swoop all the joy inside him has come crashing down. A cloud of black crows fly up from their fence posts to fill the sky with hoarseness.

His shoe flops about his foot, shoelaces trailing, as he hurtles forward and kicks the hunter on the shin. The kick glances off a rubber boot, and the shoe flies off, leaving him barefoot.

"Murderer!" he shrieks, out of his mind. "Murderer!"

He feels something brush the nape of his neck, long arms locking him in an iron grip against the gun barrel, the sight grazing his chin when the rifle slides downward and falls to the ground. Everything falls: the light on the plowed field, the crows in a vortex around them fall and are sucked into the blackness. The man has squeezed the breath out of him.

He lets go of Malte. Draws the back of his hand across his jaw, steps back, and plants the sole of his boot on the neck of the bundle that has collapsed at his feet. The small body jerks and Malte takes in a mouthful of earth.

"Ah'll give 'im murderer," he says in a low growl and grinds down with the rubber boot, as you would crush an insect. Then he lifts his foot, checks that the boy is still breathing. It is the hired hand from the farm, the one they call Hans. This is the

second time he has collared Malte. He has been in a foul mood
ever since those two wastrels got away from him and the fox
bit his hand. He picks up his shotgun, breaks it, and slings it
over the crook of his arm. He kicks the fox into the bushes:
bloody pelt's no damned use now, anyway.

He walks off without looking back.

Malte comes to enveloped in the reek of piss. Nausea forces
the earth back over his lips; he doubles up and a stream of
vomit spews out over his shirt and pants. Afterwards, he
slumps in the grass, strings of mucus hanging from his nose and
mouth. He sits there, turned to stone, until the sun descends to
eye level and drives its shards into his skull.

When at long last he pulls himself to his feet and heads for
home, the shadow at his feet has split in two, one dark and one
lighter. Silently I rise out of my animal skin and follow him.

When choir practice is over for the day, Oda and Santos stay
on in the church. He has made her soprano the center of the
piece; of the original Latin Mass, only the scaffolding remains,
concealing the walls until the day when it is torn down and the
transfigured structure stands revealed. Rather than drum the
language into the other members of the choir, he has given
them the job of singing vowel harmonies to accompany the solo
part with a polyphony of sound.

He shows her on the sheet music the places where she has to
soar and hover above the choir; he builds upon an underlying
chord, strikes out another, loses himself in the few male voices
he has to work with. She leans over his tensed shoulders as he
sits on the organ bench.

"Bam, bam, bam!" he all but shouts, his voice transformed
into a metronome; his hands strike the keyboard and he spins

his face around to catch her with an eye for which everything is self-evident. A pearly strand of sweat breaks out at the roots of his hair. Oda keeps up as best she can, flustered occasionally by a pause she does not manage to anticipate, a fermata that causes her to stumble over the text.

"It would be easier if I understood what I was singing," she grumbles. The words tie her tongue in knots. Only on his lips do they become a flamenco again. He writes the sounds down phonetically on her copy of the score, he chants the piece for her, slowly and deliberately, emphasizing the purity of the vowel sounds and steering clear of others that jut up like rocks in the stream and impede her singing. They try again—forget the pronunciation as long as it flows.

She thinks of the child growing inside her, with the prospect of two mother tongues and a cinnamon-colored father. She makes the sort of effort she never made in school. Oda has a voice like no one else's in the parish, pure and simple and with the magic heard in folk songs. She is the child of fishermen, of seafarers, and God only knows where she has the music from. The fairies who stood around her cradle must have been sirens.

He goes over the prelude one more time and this time it works. He pulls out the stop, a porcelain knob with the word *Choir* engraved on it in baroque lettering. He exploits the organ's shortcomings rather than try to get around them. The pipes fill with ghostly voices from the world of men, spirits released from the organ's innards to accompany her singing with airy echoes of the sound to be heard on the day.

The requiem will be performed by choir and organ alone. A visit to the town music society has persuaded him to give up any thought of orchestral accompaniment. He will conduct from the pulpit, confining himself to a prelude and an interlude to fill the gaps between the movements.

He builds a bridge from the Sanctus to the Agnus Dei, modulates from minor to major, and she moves with him across the bridge, casts a rune that makes the lines of music slip away; her eyes are veiled in mist and she follows him, blinded, into a world where swallows weave effortlessly between grace notes and treble clefs. In the hymn of rejoicing, Lux Aeterna, it is just the two of them, as in the early days of their love, and afterwards he jumps up and throws his arms around her, blinded by tears himself. She has brought his work to life, is still gasping for the breath that suddenly filled her and made the church disappear.

It returns as the sound of a shuffling tread under the vaulted ceiling, as coughing and the rattling of keys. The sexton has come to lock up. They pull apart. Santos gathers up the sheet music and slaps his hat on his head, Oda slips into a shawl. The one with hectic cheeks, the other fighting to subdue the heat that has risen in her. On their way out, they say goodbye.

"Goodbye, Choir Master, sir," says the sexton, and then— perhaps a shade more coolly—"Goodbye, Miss Oda."

She turns pink between her freckles, looking as if she has come straight from Bible class. No sooner has the door slammed shut behind them and the key turned in the lock than she leans toward Santos and whispers: "We're going to have to see about getting married!"

"*Sí, mi amor,*" he replies with the dignity derived from his new position, "after the requiem."

The sun, as they walk down the hill from the church, is low in the sky. The long shadows of the thuja trees fall across the landscape like the pointers of sundials. Santos and Oda crane their necks to see over the hedge, behind which marble doves have been turned to robin redbreasts, resting in eternity with their olive branches in their beaks. She shows him the sailor's grave and tells him the story. He crosses himself at the thought of that soul which, he has been taught, will have to burn in the cleansing fires of Purgatory, to find peace only when the last notes of the requiem ring out through the church.

Inside her shawl, Oda shudders, a chill running down her spine: the shadow of the thought falls heavily on the grave. She, too, could have been lying there, two lives in one, like the skeleton she once saw in the museum in town, in whose pelvis a fetus with a bird skull and spindly bones lay curled. She tugs at Santos's arm, urging him to come along. They hurry away from the hedge.

Once on the road she takes his hand and gives it a squeeze. As they leave the church farther behind, a softer wind plays about them and she swings hands with him like a schoolgirl.

The evening breeze blows in, with its scent of sea and sweetbrier. Almost a whole day has gone by without her seeing any sign of Monsieur Charles.

As they near Sea View they catch sight of Malte's dirty and bedraggled figure on the road ahead of them. A great bird of ill omen hangs over him. "Malte," cries Oda, but he does not hear a thing. She runs up to him, takes him gently by the arm. He throws himself against her; beneath the caked mud on his cheek she can see what looks like a scrape.

It is impossible to figure out what has happened, the tears strangle the words in his throat. She catches only the beginning, interrupted by sobs and sniffing: "I got a kayak, and then . . . then . . ." He gulps for air, racked by spasms that go on and on.

When at last he has breath enough to talk and the whole story has been blurted out in the last rays of the setting sun, Santos has murder in his eyes. He kneels in front of the boy. "*Maldito*," he says, "*mi pobre indio! Le vamos a matar, te juro, un día le vamos a matar.*"

These last words are uttered with a wolfish growl deep in his throat. Oda looks in amazement from one to the other.

Malte seems to understand him and to take comfort in his words at a moment when her caresses are not enough. And then, in the midst of his tears, Malte wipes off flakes of caked mud.

"Remember when the fox tricked the dogs and the dogs got hell from the police? Just as they were about to catch us? Boy, did they look dumb!"

"Who? The dogs?"

"No, the police."

And as they race to see who will tell Oda first, they both talk at once and she has to interrupt several times to try to make sense of their story. All the while she picks at the boy, plucking leaves and twigs from his pullover, brushing the dirt off him, dabbing his scrapes and scratches with spit without his noticing. She wrinkles her nose; she'll have to get these clothes washed before Mrs. Swan notices. He has cut his foot on a stone in the road and lost yet another shoe. That will have to wait until tomorrow, it's already getting dark.

"Come on," she says, addressing both of them, "we'd better be heading home."

She motions to Santos. The cut on Malte's foot has opened and started bleeding again. They cross their arms and clasp their wrists, making their hands into a chair—he is too big to ride on Santos's shoulders. They lift him up. He drapes one arm around her neck and she nuzzles it with her nose.

"Why do I have to sit in a golden chair?" he is mumbling soon afterwards, from the twilight throne.

"Because you're a prince, Malte. A real prince!"

After they have made love—in the secrecy of the midnight hour, in Oda's room—Santos lies for a while with his head on her pillow, looking up at the ceiling. He is counting beats, find-ing strains of gold in the darkness. A candle burns on her bed-side table, the sheets of music are within reach. In the beams of light, the notes hang in clusters or stand apart, pennants flying; the candle flame makes them dance along the lines, in quadrilles and constant fresh combinations. There is no end to the music.

Naked, Oda has jumped out of bed; she has snatched up the score and is memorizing the rise and fall of the words for the voice of the melody, that voice which he has made hers and hers alone. She comes to one part in the text, points at it, and frowns: "Now, what does it say there? Read it out loud, so I can understand it."

Santos props himself on his elbows, picks up the candle, and holds it over the page. "It says: 'And when he is come to the gates of hell, a choir of devils dance. And flames lick about his legs as they wave their tails and prance . . .' It's from the Dies Irae," he adds, unnecessarily.

He runs through the melody woven around the words again, dips his pen in the ink, and makes a correction. The score will soon be so covered in notes that she will have to have a new one.

"Who came to the gates of hell?"

"The Flame. That's what I call him. He came to the gates of hell. And like the man who spun his bed around every time Death stood at the foot of it, he tricked the devil himself."

"What story is that?"

"Oh, at home everyone knows the story. There was a man who had his love returned to him from Death. They made a deal: only if Death was standing at the head of the bed would he be allowed to keep his woman or his mother. If, the next time El Peladito showed himself, he was standing at the foot of the bed, they were his sure prey. So it was agreed."

"And what happened?"

"He cheated Death. The next time the King of Terrors showed his face, it was at the foot of the man's mother's bed and—woosh!—he spun the bed around. But the third time it all went wrong. No one can cheat Death when their time has come. He saved his woman as before but lost her again when—woosh!—the bony hand grabbed hold of him and threw him into the bottomless pit. And there his soul burns to this day."

"Tell me about the Flame . . ."

"The Flame was a poor Indian boy who had been brought up on an estate among day laborers and peons. He had a voice like yours and he sang in the choir. One day a friend of the landowner, the count with the pale eyes, attended Mass there and heard him sing. He bought him from the landowner. At night he visited the boy, calling him angel and stroking the back of his neck. He gave him fine clothes, took him to the town, where he had a house with many windows and lights in all of them. The boy was given the best music and singing masters, was enrolled at the conservatory. Other masters taught him to write and to read. But there was no woman in the big house, and the count used the boy."

Santos breaks off. The cat slits of his eyes throw back the candlelight as a double flame. Then he picks up the thread: "He was like the Pistacco, who kills the Indians to steal the fat from their dead bodies. As the Flame grew older he realized that the count was the devil in disguise and that he had been lured into selling his soul. His voice deserted him, a beard sprouted on his chin, and—woosh!—he was out on the street. Another boy took up residence in the house. But the Flame had acquired a taste for fine clothes, as well as some expensive habits; he did with men and older women what the count had done to him."

Oda interrupts: "Gracious! It's a good thing they don't understand the words."

Santos nods automatically. He pays no attention to her outburst. "Since his soul was lost anyway, he killed the count and traveled to another land. Like a lamb of God he is sold, and in the Dies Irae he comes to the gates of hell and demands to speak to the devil. His wrath makes the sparks fly from his flesh like a thousand fireflies. He flares up, and his light is so formidable that the devil himself is forced to yield. The Flame chokes him. Then he tears up his pact and sets fire to all the others in an infernal firework display. The little pistaccos screech and sputter and frantically try to save them. In the final movement he rises again as Lucifero . . ."

Santos has worked himself into an ecstasy. Gone is the stuttering, the struggle for words. He sounds odd without it.

But Oda is not satisfied. "I don't like it."

"But that's what happens. The requiem will free his soul."

Oda's mind is made up. Her body blocks the light; the shadows trace deep furrows in his face. She turns away. "You're not getting me to sing that."

It is her back that speaks to him.

Santos says nothing. He gets out of bed, naked as she. Lays a hand on her shoulder and tries to turn her to face him. She knocks his hand away.

"You'll have to rewrite it."

"Oda, *mi amor*—all you have to do is think about the music, the rest doesn't matter. It's just words. *Palabras, nada mas que* . . ."

"I won't do it!"

There is silence between them. He makes another move toward her, almost begging this time: "*Amor* . . ."

She turns to him, fiery as he has never seen her before. "Love! Oh yes, love will free the soul. Well, you can forget your damn Monsieur Charles. Without me there'll be no hymn of rejoicing and you know it."

"Without the Sanctus, Benedictus, and Lux Aeterna the requiem is like . . . like a candle in the church that is never lit."

"Then rewrite it. The music is wonderful, you don't need to change that, just the words. Light a candle to love, it endureth everything."

His face is set and closed. She regards him with suddenly sharpened perception, then she gets down on her knees and takes both his hands in hers. "It's not for my sake, not even for the baby's sake, but for your own. Believe me, Santos, please believe me. There is no music in my words, but what do you think I learned when you left me and Death stood at the foot of my bed?"

He falters in his silence, his jaw quivers, and his chest heaves as he tries to catch his breath. She stands up and draws him close to her, feels the grinding of his teeth against her cheek. Against her bare skin, his body trembles as if racked with fever. He sinks down and puts his ear to her navel. Now he is listening.

She says the words that tell him that she has understood. She says them very quietly. "It wasn't your soul you sold back then, just your body. The wicked count is dead. It's just us two now."

He raises his head up abruptly and she sees his pupils expanding, black on black. She pulls him up from the floor and over to the bed, holds him as he beats his head against the pillow. He draws up his knees, curls himself into a ball, starts to shake.

When at last he calms down and the paroxysm has loosened its grip on him, he is beyond the reach of words. She blows out the candle, curls herself against his back, spoonlike, and whispers into his troubled dream: "You'll get your childhood back when the baby is born, and your youth if we live long enough to see him grow up."

Malte is digging. The shovel cuts into the earth, scraping against stones and roots. The network of nettle, willow, and poplar roots forms a wall against the blade; he breaks up the sods, shakes them loose, thrusts his fingers into the hole and gropes about. Now and again he takes a break, leaning on the handle of the shovel. He leaves little hills all across the backyard in his attempt to locate the spot where he buried his treasure.

The magnifying glass is laid out in the den, together with an exercise book in which to write his report. He has borrowed the pharmacist's watch so that he can keep a minute-by-minute record of the search as it progresses.

The first entry has already been made: *8:33* GMT. *Start digging at the entrance to the den, three paces to the right of stump, seven paces from the stone wall.*

No luck there. He shifts his coordinates, making notes on the paper as he goes, to be written up later. Goutweed and burdock are thick on the ground, the couch grass has spread, and suddenly he can no longer remember whether he marked the spot when he buried the captain's cap and the picture of the young girl. The result is that every time his eye lights on two or more stones that seem to form a pattern, that is where he digs. He stands, thinking, chin resting on the handle of the shovel, as his eyes dart from bushes to nettles. Details leap out at him from the maze of patchy light filtering through the treetops.

A stick standing upright in the ground. He digs in the shovel, stamps up and down on it as hard as he can; clods of earth fly over his shoulder. He only half believes it: this stick reminds him of something else, and when the lid comes to light it is the lid of a cigar box.

Inside is a sparrow that he and Ida buried. The stick was part of a cross, but sometime over the course of the summer the cross piece has fallen off. He scrapes the soil back over the box, in a hurry to cover it up. It could be that the shoebox has fallen apart; he should have chosen a sturdier container for his treasures.

He digs the blade in again. His notes will have to wait. He is far too worked up now to think clearly; the nettles sting at his arms and legs and make his brain boil.

I hear you above my head, boy. My seed leaf aims its sharp dart at the crust as I sprout in the darkness of the earth, looking forward to the moment when once more the chlorophyll will rearrange my parts and I will become green as I was in the spring of my youth. The seasons change, gales are replaced by gentler winds, everything moves in cycles. You do a lot of worrying up there, have no idea that the Prince of Darkness and the Prince of Light are one and the same. Unlike those of most other tribes on this earth, your beliefs are primitive.

It is not dragons who guard the gold, nor is it dwarves who dig it up. Stillness broods here, stillness and growth.

There are those who live on light and those who tear at flesh. That part of me which hunts at night is my legacy from the Prince of Darkness. I know when that rat is up to his old tricks, for then I lust for human blood again! I know it—my time inside the creature's body is still sweet on my tongue. The fox's earth is thick with the carcasses of rats and mice; it never used to eat our furry little friends. That is why I left it, for that and no other reason. Soon you will see me in my full regalia;

the scraps that you are digging for now are only the smallest pieces of the puzzle that a sailor has put together in his isolation.

Above, his legs are working away like pistons now, shaking me up a bit. He fetches a hoe from the garden shed. Sets to again, hacking away with a new and more sustained stroke . . .

No, Malte, that's not how it goes. No one has ever taken a short cut to Aladdin's cave through hard work.

21

IN WHICH
THE SAILOR PUTS ON
HIS SUNDAY BEST

I have become consummate in my solitude, consummately free
of everything other than phantom pains. Outside the flesh, the
energy still burns its light in the ether. So it is with the fires of
Purgatory, and here I seethe—in every detail of my former sur-
roundings—enveloped by flames with forking tongues. I am the
tread on the stairs that creaked, the sea chest in the attic, the
moment of tenderness in the nursemaid's eye. I am your first
all-consuming love, my father's pride and joy, then his wrath,
and finally his blind spot.

Like everyone else I bear the pattern of paths taken long
ago, paths that link the houses in which I have lived with places
where I never found peace: childhood haunts and rooms where
fans of light played across the walls, hiding places and cubby-
holes where time did not exist, a whole bouquet of scents and
people, a succession of faces and voices that as yet are only part
of the music and cannot convey the sense of the words. The
weightlessness of being carried and rocked, fed and wheeled
about—until the first faltering steps over the grass and the fall

into a pair of ever-present arms. A garden in summer. The rope thwacking against the flagpole. The gold knob against the fading blue of the sky. The clouds and swans sailing by.

Another century, a world before Malte was born, but boyhood is boyhood. A rumbling over the boards of the jetty, on the lookout for ships, standing with eyes boring into the sails on the horizon while out there the world turns to water. Other foxes on the cliff side, the same lairs. And in the churchyard the same names, because here the writing is chiseled in stone—only the time between the two dates is as nothing now.

Call me damned—you don't know what that entails anyway. The fires of Purgatory are like the northern lights, ripples across a frosty sky, an organ that spews forth colors instead of sound. The phantom that takes the place of the body vibrates in spectrums of colored lights. Spasms and no release. Nothing is forgotten; only the warmth of the flesh is out of reach. God knows I am no saint; I am guilty of pride, murder, and rage. I have spent mornings committing sodomy with blacks and nights in utter abstinence. This last was the greatest sin.

The time has come for me to step back into character and show myself as I once was. I have found my going-ashore clothes and taken a lot of trouble over my final encore before the curtain comes down. Polished the brass buttons and buttoned the jacket around the ghost that used to be me. I wear gold braid on my sleeves and shoulders again and a cap over the white dome of the skull. A pair of leather gloves prevents my fingers from falling off.

I have brushed my trousers and fastened my tie with a pearl pin and monogram. I am blue and gilded and regal from top to toe, with shirt and cufflinks and hand-sewn shoes. It's always the same: full dress and flying colors each time I land on the world's shore.

In my fossil heart I carry light-years, a little petrified sun-

shine, and a memory of happiness encapsulated in amber. I
have burned my bridges, been a coffin-ship and a flying Dutchman rather than give anyone satisfaction. I have returned, and I
cover my tracks—from Crow Towers, wiped out by the sea,
back up to the end of the jetty, where everything shatters and
even memory has to give way to what is carved in runes on the
inside of the skull.

I have retained the features of the seducer, the gold ring and
the whiskers; my heart is still made of stone but my spine is a
ginkgo tree that will once more put out leafy wings and blow
its seeds across the earth. The limp wrists I inherited from the
elf, but don't let anyone be fooled by them—I'm a man to my
fingertips, a thief in a fur mask and every bit as unpredictable
as my last host, the fox. As a prince I have lived a thousand
lives and had as many faces.

For a while yet I hover over the water.

Then I dive. It all comes back to me now. I am here to make
time stand still—the boy will never live to be older than twelve!
I am merely a messenger, but believe me, I have my reasons.
Everyone has the right to an angel. The last face I wear is that
of Death.

The lighthouse keeper stoops over the workbench. Shaving for
shaving he fashions the piece of driftwood into a paddle, filling
the plane with curls of mermaid hair that froth up around his
hands, then tumble in ringlets to the ground. Malte looks on,
his anticipation growing. Bit by bit the oar takes shape. Sirius
rounds off the pole with the plane and flattens out the ends.
From beneath the gray surface the grain of the wood shows
through, aromatic and with a silken sheen where the plane has
just passed. The knots form whorls; one looks like a sea horse.

Malte is just about to touch when Sirius unscrews the pole, swings it around in an arc, and secures it again. Then he sets to work on the blade; on the block in front of him lie the knives he uses, the chisels and gouges with handles he has tailored to his big hands.

Sirius is one of those people who keep their tools neatly in place. Left on the wall are the outlines of drill, hammer, and spirit level. Malte is fascinated by the bubble in the green glass tube; there are days when he goes around checking whether everything is level, waving the tool about enough to make one's head spin.

The lighthouse keeper calls to him. Hands him a piece of cork and some sandpaper. They bend over the paddle, one at either end, sanding and buffing from the blades back, until they meet in the middle, then they look up. Malte has Eskimo eyes, from concentrating so hard, Olesen's are sunk in laughter lines.

The paddle is finished. It is put into Malte's hands as soon as it is unclamped from the workbench, and he checks the balance. It has a good feel to it. He scoops at the air, leaning forward with his whole body as he rows. Fine raspings fall from the newly sanded shaft; it feels dry and floury in his hands. The action works its way out to his shoulder blades and for a moment it feels as though he has sprouted wings.

He is out of breath when he puts down the paddle. Suddenly remembers the magnifying glass, delves into his pocket, and returns it with a quiet "Thanks."

The dead look in his eye says his search has been fruitless. The keeper takes it and does not pry into what it has been used for.

They step outside to the kayak. The skin has tautened on the frame, the long sweep of it rests on the trestles, gleaming like a lampshade. The oiling has left the skin supple and the dry whiff of museum is gone. Malte is there, smoothing the skin down; he ducks under the hull, tenses his shoulders, and raises the front end. Then gently lowers it back onto the trestles.

Morning has broken with sunshine and calm seas, not a breath of wind; close to the shore there is not so much as a ripple on the water. The perfect day for what they have in mind. Sirius takes the paddle, sits on the ground, and shows how it's done: at rest, paddle, backwater, and turn. Malte sits down next to him, his eyes drinking in the keeper's every move and imitating with a broom handle. The great hunter and his son, making their way across the waters of the fjord, while between the icebergs—slashes of turquoise underwater—glide the shadows of the sea creatures.

They lift the kayak off the trestles and set it in the water. The keeper has rolled up his trouser legs. With some difficulty he squeezes himself down through the manhole, using Malte's shoulder as a brace. The boy is kneeling, the kayak lying so low that it touches the sandy bottom. Then it is afloat again and the man buoyed up. He sends Malte back up the beach to fetch the paddle, which they have forgotten, and while the boy is pulling off his clothes, the kayak starts to drift. Only with a bit of careful swaying does the keeper manage to keep the flimsy craft upright.

Malte wades out in his underpants and hands the paddle to Sirius, who goes over the basics with him. He reads the admiration in the boy's eyes and pulls his shoulders back.

He reaches for the paddle. No sooner has he done so than he flips right over and is left hanging head down in the water, which comes up to the boy's waist. Malte veers between hooting with laughter and wrestling with the kayak to bring the keeper right side up again. He also manages to rescue Olesen's cap, which is bobbing off on its own. Then he takes hold of the bone tip and pulls him in over the reef, into the shallows, where the keeper squeezes himself out of the manhole and hands Malte the paddle, still with his dignity intact.

"Now, that just shows you! The idea is to take it nice and easy, keep your weight down in the seat, and no sudden moves."

He is soaking wet. The only things not dripping with seawater are the clogs he left on the shore. Water runs from his anorak, shirt, and trousers, dribbles from his pipe, which has been clamped firmly in the corner of his mouth since they left the workshop. He taps it out on the palm of his hand and blows into the mouthpiece. Squints and tries to peer down the stem from the tip.

He steadies the kayak for Malte as they switch places. The boy's heart pounds as he slides down into the hole, his arm muscles tense, and he stretches out his legs, carefully, so as not to scrape the skin. The strain shows in his face, in the narrowing of his eyes and lips. His backside is wet; there is water in the kayak from its capsizing. He pushes back with his rear end. Brings the paddle up over his knees, takes a deep breath, and gives Sirius the nod.

The keeper lets go and raises his hands into the air. This is it, sink or swim. And swim it is. Right away Malte is aware of the jitteriness in the hull, as it dodges about underneath him, making great, exaggerated movements for every slightest one of his. Everything is magnified by the agitation. He stills himself from within, from his tongue to the tip of his toes, ventures to dip the blade of the paddle in the water. He keeps his own weight centered. The tip of his tongue is between his lips as he tilts the paddle and dips the other blade.

The kayak skims across the water. He repeats the action. Effortlessly. Elbows and wrists swivel, the rest of his body he holds steady. He crouches a little, picks up speed, and the lighthouse keeper watches in amazement. Where did he learn that?

He almost comes to grief when he turns his head to call back to Sirius. A wave off the bow nudges him and he has to

take one hand off the paddle to regain his balance. He picks up
the thread again; curving and flashing with silver, the line runs
from earth to heaven, the route kites follow into the clouds. He
is scudding along, a cautious smile on his lips.

A trail of crescents fans out from the line of his wake. He
backwaters and brings himself parallel with the shoreline, picks
up the rhythm from before, and starts paddling; overturns and
comes up right as rain. Paddles away from the cliff and out toward the rows of fishing stakes. The tide is out and the weeds
that cling to them glisten, dripping green.

The stakes loom large in his field of vision; first cormorants,
then gulls take off, long before he gets to them. He eases his
strokes and holds his breath as the birds fly up and light again
farther out. The stakes are deserted. At time lags of a second or
so the birds take to the air.

He thinks of the spirit level, feeling like the bubble in the
green tube. He maneuvers the kayak with greater and greater
confidence. Notes how it is steered from the tail of the spine
and down the arms, constantly on edge, restless and alert. It is
a hunter's tool. Even without the fishing tackle and lines. You
don't sit and gaze about you in a kayak, you have the heart and
shining eyes of the seal.

He slips through the water, drawing behind him a line that
splits around the stakes, and out into open sea. The skin is
blood-warm against his thigh, with a hint of coolness from the
sea. The seagulls' cries sound different out here, there is another sort of magic. Sirius has shrunk to a dwarf on the shingle;
Malte sees him making a megaphone of his hands, the sound
reaching him a moment or so later. Onshore the houses have
sunk into the dunes; of Sea View only the thatched roof is still
visible and the jetty at the foot of the lighthouse is now a
domino.

The pull of the current travels outwards with the gentle

swell that licks at his new skin. The water is livelier here than close to shore, where it is like a millpond. He feels the crests of the waves beneath him, a constant, niggling challenge. Out on the horizon lies the seal island, and beyond it a land of rocks and mountains, beyond the mountains other forests, and beyond the forests, where the sun never sets, the ice sings.

He hears the lighthouse keeper's cries growing sharper. He must not sail any farther out. Next time he looks up, Sirius has moved, with a seven-league stride, out onto the jetty and is making as if to get into the dinghy. Malte backwaters and swings the bow toward the shore. Only once he is close enough to make out the details of the dike does the keeper let go of the hawser and wave to him.

Again Malte brings himself parallel with the shoreline and feels the paddle turn to wings flaring from his back, where the action is transmitted to a notch between his shoulder blades. He tilts forward from the waist and begins to paddle again.

The dawn light falls on the church grounds, lengthening the shadows of the thuja trees. A gate stands open. There are signs of activity among the graves, where the gravedigger—humpbacked from his work and with a thatch of hair like mole fur on his crown—is up and about. His wheelbarrow is parked by the unknown seaman's headstone, hoe and crowbar protruding from it, and he is busy loosening the earth around the stone with a shovel. Next to the wheelbarrow sits a sled, with a rope running up to a harness. On the sled a freshly hewn block of granite lies covered by sacking.

He digs the shovel in and rams the plinth with a sound that jars him to the marrow. He pauses, spitting out a small stream of tobacco juice, scratching the back of his hand, and resting on the shovel for a moment. He has great open pores, skin in which the soil has become embedded. A small man but wiry. He begins again. After a while, he has a go with the crowbar, to see if the plinth can be pried loose. He uses a paving stone for leverage.

The paving stone gives first. He tips the stone away from the grave. It lands with the inscription facedown and crushes a flower holder containing some withered poppies. He heaves it back a little, pulls the sled closer.

He has built up a little mound where the new stone, round as a mill wheel, is to sit. He removes the sacking, gets his hands around the granite, tilts it, and rolls it into place.

Then he starts to hack out a hole at the foot of the mound, a square hole, the sort for interring an urn. He digs until he strikes a coffin lid: here lies the drowned seaman, as unknown as ever, but now minus his headstone. Fair enough—he's had the whole summer to himself under his own monument. The gravedigger shrugs, rolls the plug of tobacco in its tar, and adds a bit of spit. He is the gardener of the dead, not their shepherd.

"Not long now till you've got company," he mutters with a nod to the coffin lid.

He finishes digging the hole, ready for the day's funeral. He gets the toppled gravestone loaded onto the sled, then puts his tools back into the wheelbarrow. He is just about to walk away when the sound of falling earth makes him turn around. And even though he is a man of much the same stamp as Olesen, the sight that meets his eyes is enough to startle him. For all at once it looks as though someone has trod on the edge of the grave, leaving his mark in the form of a heel print.

22

IN WHICH
TIME IS
TURNED BACK

Sunday in the parish—the church bells swing high and clash in the heavens above the farmsteads, the fishermen's cottages, and the boats that have crossed from the other side of the point, bound for the village with the wind in their sails. The dinghies are rigged with russet sails and steered by tillers in their sterns that draw the wake. Potbellied and heavy-laden they wallow in the water; the women are on board, along with the children and men, all in their Sunday best, with hats, ties and—in the case of the boys—sailor collars.

Those who, on every other day, are fishermen feel like guests on their own vessels, and those who, on every other day, are farmers feel like monarchs of the sea with their children around them.

The boats land on the beach. Prow after prow runs up onto the sand. Sheets are let out and sailcloth flaps loose. The sea is calm and the tide high; the passengers jump off the rower's seat and land with dry feet. The women are handed down, the smallest children lifted off, and a few of the little ones are even

whirled around before their feet touch the ground and the sand
gets into their shoes. Only when the dinghies are empty do
weather-beaten hands haul them farther up toward the dike.
The sails are furled around the masts with sprit and sheets;
then, with one quick tug, all the rigging is hoisted up and over,
and laid across the thwarts. It looks like the nets and buoys
that jut from the boats on every other day.

In little groups the families begin to make their way up the
slope. The women have taken the lead; their hat ribbons flutter
amid the lyme grass and sunshine. The dark suits have fallen
behind, sweating under the crowns of their hats. The families
climb the winding path, between heaps of gravel and stones,
squinting up at the grassy crest that breaks over their heads in a
petrified green breaker. There is a fair bit of puffing and blowing; first one and then another has to pause on the way up and
stand with head bowed and hand on knee until the dizziness
passes.

As soon as they reach the top, where the grass spreads wide
and the heather blooms in untamed swaths across the hillsides,
the sound swells. The bells peal out across the countryside and
faces turn toward the tower. From near and far the congregation gathers and converges on the churchyard.

The guest-house residents arrive in a body, with Mrs. Swan
at their head. Horse-drawn rigs roll up, both wagons and gigs,
and farther out on Beach Road, over toward town, the backfiring of an engine heralds the arrival of the doctor.

Hansen hits the horn. Groups of people on foot scatter out
of the path of the Model T, which, when it drives up to the
church, the gravel crunching beneath its wheels, proves to be
jam-packed with sisters from Saint Joseph's Infirmary, sitting
bolt upright and nodding behind the windows in their starched
headgear. The sight of the nuns makes people draw back into
the hedgerow, where they stand, hat in hand, and gape at these

outlandish birds. It is a Sunday unlike any other Sunday; word of the requiem has spread far beyond the bounds of the parish.

As soon as the car has pulled up in front of the chapel, Hansen hops out, runs around to the other side, and opens the passenger door. He assists the first of the nuns, Sister Johanne, out onto the running board and down. To the spectators, the nuns—all looking alike—seem to keep piling out of the doctor's car. Until they move as one—crowned by four strutting swans—into the church.

From the veranda at Sea View all the way out to the horizon the ocean spreads its silken sheet. I stand at the rail and send my thoughts winging far across the sea. The deck chairs are empty, the cushions already taken in. Over the summer the wood has faded, bleached by wind and weather, and the teak has taken on the same color as the hatchway on the ship that took me away from here, at the beginning of time.

I used to come here as a child. I spent my best summers here—in dimly lit rooms filled with wicker furniture, under the piano, where I sat hunched during my mother's concerts, both frightened and fascinated by the clangor produced by her dainty shoe on the pedal. That was long before Sigurd Swan's time. On the dunes I, too, have flown the kites of my childhood to victory or followed their plunge downward with sinking heart.

One moment in the light, one day of happiness—can that cancel out one hundred years of solitude? Fleeting summers, days that never end, nights of dark-blue glass—but nothing lasts. At summer's end waits a sun that shrivels to darkness in the middle of the day. We are born to the awareness of mayflies, glow for a moment in the darkness and are gone. I am thinking of a boy. His days, too, are numbered; soon time will eliminate him as it does all others.

I set out on my travels, intent on rekindling the excitement that we normally outgrow. One cannot die curious. The world was a treasure-house, a bottomless cask of experiences. I drank and never succeeded in draining it. Nor was it nonchalance that finally overtook me, or my innate tendency to melancholia: I died out of spite, at the zenith of my course.

They say that those whom the gods love die young. Nonsense! The gods love no one, they tend to themselves. I died, foreign and free as a bird, surrounded on all sides by beauty, inflamed by loss, with hair trailing and eyes bathed in crystal-clear water. At the moment of liberation, as my limbs turned to ice and my ears rang, I heard the very chime that sounded in the church a little before, when the bells fell silent: the whales gliding out of the sea's muted thunder. I exploded from within, in an echo chamber of profound happiness, for that is the way of it.

Even so, my torment was prolonged, which is why I am still here. Body and echo part company, the cause of the echo remains. There is an aching in the shoulder blades, which gleam white, six feet under. Restlessly I pace the veranda, crane my neck over the rail . . .

He comes paddling around the point, my little prince. Far out to sea I spot the kayak, now his. Silver drips from his paddle; balancing on a knife-edge, he slices through the silk. He shows up black against the golden ribbon. Dazzled, he comes into his kingdom of sea and sparkling sunlight.

The day the kayak arrived flies like a pennant from the mast of my memory. I had been a guest on earth for twelve years—like

Malte—twelve happy years with no guardian angels other than my parents. We were down at the harbor in town, waiting for a ship. The Amber King in silhouette, his stovepipe hat and silver-topped cane side by side with my mother's tailored elegance. She held me by the hand and her net gloves scratched my skin with their little bird's feet every time she gave it a squeeze.

Call me Orbit. There was a time when I went by another name; my course has brought me back to the anonymity of Captain Nemo. I stood with my head tilted back, spellbound by the forest of masts rearing up from the ships at anchor. Flags and pennants snapped; I opened myself to the wind and the sounds. From the sigh of the wind harp at the very top to the rattle of flapping tackle and the long creak of boards and timbers with every lapping wave that rocked the ships in the harbor. My gaze scrambled aloft on rope ladders and disintegrated into pinpoints of light in a tapestry of sun and sky.

The breeze swept in across the breakwater, lifted my sailor collar, and ruffled my white blouse. I had pushed my straw hat with its fluttering ribbons to the back of my head. It was held in place under my chin by a string that stretched and strained in the blustering wind.

Papa took a step closer to the quay, his hand shading his eyes under the brim of his hat. Inch by inch he scanned the horizon. Until his eyes started to water and he lowered his hand to dry his cheek on the sleeve of his frock coat. He turned in the direction of one of the warehouses he had purchased to accommodate his shipments and made a sign. An unloading cradle descended, rocking on its rope swing, the lifting gear crying out for greasing. One of his men appeared in the hatchway and yelled something that was drowned out by the racket from the bearings. From his lofty perch the man pointed out to sea, and hope turned to certainty.

White sails rounded the point, flying jib and jib first. They billowed out against the blue; and as the ship grew bigger and acquired more sails and masts, Papa grew, too, under the shoulders of his frock coat. He lifted his hat and waved it in great, wide arcs. I tugged at my mother's hand, trying to pull free.

She drew the fur trim of her coat close under her chin. Her fingers fiddled nervously with a button and her eyes flitted across me with a sadness that I did not understand.

A three-masted schooner drew into the harbor; men ran to the quay to catch the hawsers and secure them. On the bridge stood the captain, with a megaphone in his hand, and so accurate and well timed was the letting out of sheets and halyards that the slack brought the ship gliding into dock with canvas flapping and a lumbering creak around the fenders. The *Narwhal* had landed.

I broke free of the hand, ran forward, and grabbed one of the hawsers. As soon as I had worked it into place around the bollard—ignoring my mother's protests and with my white blouse smudged by the rope—I made a sign to the sailor on the deck and watched the line rise in a dripping bow. My senses reeling, I followed it, climbing aboard as soon as the gangplank landed at my feet. I was the Amber King's son; bursting with pride, I stepped onto the bridge and positioned myself next to the captain.

The *Narwhal* was his pride and joy, fitted out for long voyages, reinforced from stem to stern. Her copper sheathing enabled her to cross both tropical oceans and ice-packed arctic seas. Captain Ejnarsen—a man whose bowlegs seemed to have been made for a rolling deck—was a sailor in the service of the Lord, a ship's master by the grace of God, and the men loved him.

The only thing he could not keep track of was the paperwork, and that the shipowner attended to himself. On this last voyage he had grown a full beard and it bristled about his cheeks like a thorny thicket. He greeted me with teeth that were dark from the tobacco he sent flying over the rail at regular intervals in a long, spouting jet.

He shouted an order to the crew and they opened the hatchway amidships. A stupefying stench came pouring out, the smell of wares from foreign lands, of skins and spices and sacks, of tar, bilgewater, and slops—all the things that lay fermenting in the belly of the ship. A boom was released from the mainmast and swung out over the hold with a hook hanging from it. One sailor jumped down into the darkness, another paid out the hook.

The next thing I remember is Papa's excited shout from the quay. The hook had come up again, a harness straining beneath it, and in the harness hung the kayak, translucent in the sunlight, new and glossy-skinned, with the bony knobs at its tips, its line rest and harpoons held down by cross straps. It dangled over the mouth of the hold; slowly the ivory knob twirled around and pointed at me.

It was as if I were witnessing a birth. The *Narwhal*'s belly had opened up and brought an infant into the world, still with the moisture of living skin on the fragile skeleton.

A couple of the crew caught hold of the straps and lifted the boat free. Papa almost danced up the gangplank and onto the deck, the spring in his step reflecting his eagerness. "Easy now!" he fretted as the crewmen set it down on the deck. Their hands seemed so clumsy compared with the parchment-like texture of the skin.

Papa could not resist going up to the boat and feeling the drum roll travel up through the ring on his finger. This would be the jewel in his Eskimo collection. He took possession of it with hands that trembled with desire. "Anne Sophie," he bawled across the breakwater, "this is going to be hung up, you'll see, over the dining table . . ."

But she had turned her back on us. With a mouth that was small and set.

This I would forget, for there was no end to the wonders. The hatches opened onto a treasure house: A bale of hides was hoisted out and fell apart on the deck as soon as it was cut loose. Whole polar-bear skins, sealskin worked up into boots, trousers, and anoraks—all that was missing was the man, the nut-brown hands peeking from the ends of the sleeves and the face above the empty neck hole. Layer upon layer was turned over. After the rough work came the fine: at the very heart of the bale, pearl-embroidered costumes, shaman drums, and tupilaks.

Papa came over to join us. I felt an arm steal around my shoulders and his speechlessness left him in an awed whisper. The sight made his eyes shine and filled him with a reverence that radiated like static from his hands to me. We had cherished a common dream for so long that seeing it come true was almost too much to bear.

The devil had got into Ejnarsen. He waddled on his bow-legs, over to the heap of skins, picked up one of the anoraks, and pulled it over his head. I saw the neck cowl around his short neck, then the man took hold of it with both hands and yanked the collar upward into a chimney down which his head disappeared. The chimney bent in the middle to become a hood edged with fur; the captain's sparkling blue eyes had gone dark and it was an Eskimo who peered out at us.

I clapped my hands; the paler patches on the sealskin glistened gold in the sunlight, and the dark spots had acquired a silvery sheen. The fur had come to life, a heart beat beneath the tanned hide. The stiffness and the acrid smell were gone. Like a breath of air in the darkness, Captain Ejnarsen's laughter rolled out, ready to take up the fight against howling beasts and winds that stir in the arctic night.

We looked at each other, buoyed by his laughter. And even

as we did, it dawned on us that this was the hide that makes man and kayak one flesh. Our happiness was complete. I remember, because it would never be the same again.

The following year, when the *Narwhal* returned from her second Greenland expedition, the performance was repeated, but by then everything had changed and I was living alone with my mother.

It was not the kayak and its banishment to the summer house on Crow Point that was to blame for the breakup of their marriage, I know that now. Although for a while I thought it was, since that was what they argued about. My mother was a lady, he had started out as a day laborer. They never met on equal terms. On the surface, my father was a flamboyant man with swarthy features and black eyes. A passionate romance blossomed out of a young girl's protest against her family.

She fell for the Amber King while he was on his way up. She did not see the dull dog lurking beneath the gypsy complexion. Anne Sophie Winther—head over heels—became Anne Sophie Bertelsen, and just four months later I stepped out of Orbit and saw the light of day for God only knows which time.

In appearance she was as cool as he was fiery, but in their temperaments, which ran deep, they were like two babies switched at birth. Young Bertelsen may well have had the soul of an artist and been fascinated by beauty, but he was merely its mirror, and when it passed so deftly out of his hands it brought nothing but riches—a curse he shared with Midas, the mythical king whose Greek island kingdom he had never visited. Neither had he traveled to Greenland or drunk in with his own eyes the gold and the flaming gables of the temples of Siam. Bertelsen had become a shipowner; he accumulated objects and went nowhere.

From the start he made the mistake of trying to win her with an affluence that at all costs had to outdo what she had grown up with. And he paid the price. His business flourished, everything he touched turned to gold. He worshiped her, pampered her, gave her everything. But she had never asked for anything except love. Placed on a pedestal and elevated to a goddess, she felt like an ornament in rooms of pointless luxury. He did not understand why she was so distant.

She converted her abiding passion to the Catholic faith, in which I was raised. She assuaged her temperament with piano lessons—music had been a part of her life since childhood and it permeated her being; to her, everything came down to striking the right note. She developed into a brilliant pianist and celebrated her first triumphs in the capital before my fifth birthday.

As a child I loved the smell of the workshops, and I would trail after my father like a little shadow. The smell of wood shavings and glue, of varnish and imported woods. The crackle in the air from polished amber and the humming of the pedal-driven machines. To me he was the wizard of fairy tale, commanding the transformation of raw material into objects. On the shelves lay mother-of-pearl, ivory, and unicorn's horn.

He showed me the narwhal's tusk. I had never seen anything like it, a twisting spire many times my height, plucked from the world's finest sand castle. The surface was smooth as a billiard ball, but if one looked closely, a pattern was discernible in the ivory, a network of tiny cracks, and one's finger ran in perpetual loops around the inner side of the coils, sleek with pale pink tallow.

I marveled at his hands when he worked—as I marveled at my mother's when she played the big concert grand, whirling over the keys, tossing the notes in the air, and transforming them into cascades. Instinctively I understood that without his ivory and ebony there would have been no pianos either.

It was with a sense of loss that I stood on the pier the second time the ship docked and heard Captain Ejnarsen issuing orders to his crew through the brass megaphone. That was the first winter of my discontent. I had spent the dark months alone with my mother in the merchant's mansion down by the harbor, which seemed a frustrating place to me without the extension to workshops and warehouses.

Again it was early spring, with brisk breezes and scudding clouds. I had not seen much of my father; he had a wild-eyed look about him and spent most of his time at Crow Towers, which he had had built around the family's summer house and with which he stifled memories that would never again give him peace.

From my hiding place in the gloom of the warehouse I saw him. He walked across and lifted a tarpaulin. On the pallet underneath, turtle shells lay side by side with the raw materials of his business. Conch shells and abalone shells—once he had carved the ornaments himself, now he had others to do that sort of thing. And the number of products kept growing: lampshades, ashtrays, combs, bookends. Things once borne by creatures of legend—over the ice cap, through colonnades of light, and across coral seas—were turned to use in people's parlors, and he surveyed his booty with satisfaction. I had just turned thirteen; my birthday fell on April Fool's Day and for the rest of my life I was to hate that day above all others.

Like a thief in the night I watched the cargo being unloaded. The barrels behind which I had concealed myself stank of herring brine. No one had any idea that I had sneaked in there. After all, I no longer had any business on my father's ships. There was a feeling in my throat like fish scales; I swallowed and fought down my rising gorge. The transition from light to dark sliced across my eyeballs and strained my sight.

The *Narwhal* creaked and groaned against the quay. She was riding high in the water, lightened of her load, and the waterline was visible, with its garlands of green weed. On the bridge stood Captain Ejnarsen, the brass megaphone tucked under his arm, and on the quay the Amber King commanded his people as they struggled with the cargo. The space was much too big. I could hear myself breathe. The chill crept up my legs and my skin rose in goose bumps on my arms, so abruptly had I run from sunlight to shadow.

Ejnarsen leaned over and beckoned to my father. Then he disappeared into the fo'c'sle and a moment later my father was heading up the gangplank. Three great bounds brought him on board the ship. I watched in disbelief as his hat flew off his head and rolled into the water without his seeming to notice. Meanwhile the captain had appeared at the opening to the hatch; he handed a bundle, totally swathed in furs, up to my father, who took it and hugged it to his chest. A squawk issued from the bundle, stubby arms and legs stabbed at the air and flailed like drumsticks. He let go of the child, who took a couple of steps across the deck before sitting down on her behind with a jolt of surprise in her dark seal-pup eyes.

That was the first time I saw Aviaja.

I dashed out of the warehouse and down to the drying ground, where I clung to the fishing nets and banners of seaweed as the vomit poured out of me in one great shoal.

23

IN WHICH
THE HEIR
IS INSTALLED

I am an angel, I am a prisoner of the instant. Anyone who thinks we have our place in eternity is mistaken. None of us breathe in the absolute zero of space or flourish in crystal formations. There are reasons for our being here, ties that bind; to each his own. When I was alive I collected stellar moments, freedom was all I asked. It has been said that the gods punish us by granting our wishes. Right now I find that insight rather painful.

From infancy I was a slave to the beauty on which the Amber King's realm was built. And I inherited my mother's feel for music and her total attunement to life. I breathed from one high point to the next, *had* to be happy every hour of the day. Would not stand for anything less and descended into gloom with the darkness at summer's end. If so much as a scratch appeared in the paint on a toy, the object died in my hands that very instant. One wrong note and everything lay in pieces at my feet. I call it—in my present incarnation—the glass gene. Because it is fragile, refracts the light, and fills me with visions and sleeplessness.

To be let loose in the wonderland of childhood—that is what it means to be born a prince. Whatever else passed between my parents took place among the clouds. From their Olympus they shone their rays over my ocean, where no beggars ever showed their faces and no one ever grew old and ugly. Through my twelfth year I was the apple of their eye, the only child, and I stored up sunbeams for the rest of my life.

I was a devout child. Devoutness was something I shared with my mother. I loved ritual, incense, and holy water. Was even allowed to swing the censer myself as a choir boy. We were different, we did not attend the same church as the others. On Sundays I saw the fisherfolk and the villagers walking about the town with shuttered faces. In their church there was no Holy Mother, no boy playing with golden rays on her lap, and no tapers burning behind red lamp glass.

She took me to church concerts, showed me the trail of notes across the page. The first time I heard the choir intone the Ave Maria to her organ accompaniment, the dove in the ceiling painting exploded with light and the angels soared.

It is *that* sort of instant I am talking about.

Every summer we spent the last two weeks of June as guests at Sea View. I recall the dancing at midsummer, the bonfires on the beach, the firelight leaping from faces to wave crests, and the heat crackling in our clothes. The flames tinged her dress, continued on out over the water, and her voice when she sang turned everyone else into halfhearted, mealymouthed also-rans. She did everything her way and she was the most courageous woman of her day.

Papa's admiration knew no bounds. Tears would well up in his eyes when he looked at her, and he would hug me so close that I could feel my shoulder blades meet in the middle.

In the evening, after dinner at the guest house, Mother would give concerts in the parlor for the other guests. First chance I got, I would crawl under the piano and lose myself in the reverberation. Once she had been playing long enough, the notes collided in my head and sounded like church bells chiming underwater.

One summer she taught me to swim. I was delighted. Here was something Papa could not do—and never learned. He sank to the bottom while I sped like a porpoise over the waves.

We built kites and sand castles, went for walks along the water's edge, and combed the rockweed for amber. He always found the biggest pieces. He said himself that his luck stemmed from the days when he wandered the highways and byways with the gypsies. He called them kings of Egypt because they came from the land to which the storks flew in winter. Other than that, he never spoke about where he came from, wore a strange amulet around his neck, an iron coin on a leather thong that he never took off. When he put me to bed, he told me stories of princes changing places with swineherds and maidens turned into swans.

That day on the drying ground, when I puked over a fishing net, what I was throwing up was an icon, pieces of a holy image drenched in bile. The moment my father took another woman, the divorce became final. It fell like a blow, lopping the branch off the main stem. He made a changeling of me. In the mesh of the net hung the vestiges of that flesh that would no longer be mine. I had crossed a threshold. I was no longer invulnerable, merely a mortal like everyone else.

The church bells fall silent over the down, the doors are closed, and the requiem can begin. Outside the church sits the gravedigger's wheelbarrow, with a shovel and gravel for the burial. There is no one left at Sea View. I have the sun terrace to myself and stand with my gloves draped limply over the rail. A dash on the skyline catches my attention, a droplet in the midday sun. Malte has paddled farther out over a sea that is dead calm—I alone hear the hum of doomsday on the horizon. Everything is going according to plan and nothing takes place without my knowing.

I have angel vision. It pierces matter, flits from near to far in no time. I see the world as in a crystal ball, in which everything runs together and the surrounding space arches into a dome. The thujas in the churchyard are like grotesque Christmas trees, the wheelbarrow is a vehicle for giants, with the shovel handle rearing skywards as the tower bends back on itself and the red tiles of the roof swell into onion domes.

I need only blink and the scene shifts.

Every seat in the church is taken, even the pews at the very front are filled. Whispers, a bit of shuffling, the odd cough are still permitted to ring out. Cravats chafe and a musty smell emanates from the dark clothing.

The parson kneels in front of the altar with his back to the congregation, wearing the white chasuble he puts on for the Easter service. Above him rises the crucifix—an ancient Christ, darkly patinaed, the wood chipped and worm-eaten. There is even a niche for the Virgin and Child, a thing to warm the heart; the vestiges of frescoes can be seen—an Annunciation in faded blues and reds and, on the wall of the transept, a kneeling Saint Olaf surrounded by armored henchmen.

The church dates from the days of chivalry. Set in the floor are tombstones bearing the contours of former bishops and marked with well-trodden names. On the wall a tablet depicting the king's man and lady who directed the building of the church. Beneath the plaster gleams another and more colorful century.

On a chain from the ceiling hangs the naval frigate donated

by the parish fishermen. The figurehead is a mermaid blowing on a conch and the gun ports are overlaid with gold leaf. To everything there is a season.

The parson rests, head bowed, in his prayer. His back radiates introspection. There is some tut-tutting among his flock—this is not how it's usually done. The catafalque is there all right, covered by the black pall, but the place of the coffin itself is taken by an arrangement of roses, lilies of the valley, and evergreens, which, during the requiem, is to represent my mortal remains.

Next to the floral arrangement sits Aviaja's urn.

I blink again. For a moment my eye waters. Inside the crystal ball, time telescopes, the spark leaps and sets me down early one summer morning at the gate to Crow Towers.

I had driven out from town in a horse-drawn wagon, I was in my late twenties, newly graduated from the naval academy. My uniform was freshly pressed, my gloves buttoned with mother-of-pearl. My cap cover pipe-clayed and not a crack in the patent brim.

In the doorway stood my father. He had aged. The black hair was white as embers and thin on his skull; his scalp shone through. The muttonchop whiskers were neatly brushed and he had acquired prominent cheekbones. I was a little taken aback, though he seemed to be well cared for, wearing dress trousers with satiny stripes down the side and a frock coat of green velvet with stock and gold pin.

When he put his arms around me, he smelled of shaving soap and cologne. This was a very special day for the Amber King. The day on which—according to the pact we had made years before—I was to be installed as prince and heir to his empire.

He had never remarried; instead he lived, an eccentric, among his glass towers. Had no interest in anything but his collections, never went out among people, and ignored their gossip. He lived with his adopted daughter—the only person he owned body and soul. He was a visionary and a dreamer—and dreams, once conceived, tend to be self-perpetuating. He had been running his business and the shipping company through front men.

All that was over now. This was a fateful day for us. On both sides, long-standing hopes were about to be fulfilled. Soon I would be handed the keys to the kingdom, with unlimited access to his treasures. That is why I had turned out.

Seven lean years and seven fat years had had to pass before that meeting. My mother had pursued the career of pianist as a single woman, but it was not easy to get people to pay for concerts that they had swooned over when she was younger and played for free. She was out of step with the times and eventually she gave up. We moved from the merchant's mansion to a poorer part of town.

From being a nice, well-behaved boy I turned into a monster. I tormented the nuns at the Catholic school with lizards, snakes, and toads that I would swallow, then regurgitate. I did not know why, but the feeling in my throat was familiar. The holy image I had vomited on another occasion trailed the others in its wake.

I played hooky and went my own wild way, changed schools, and got kicked out again. With my hot temper I was a demon in a fight. I became leader of a gang, roamed around with the other alley cats. We were at war with the shanties across the street. One boy had an ear ripped off, another was left a vegetable by a blow on the back of the head with a fence post.

I turned to stealing because we never had enough to eat. That was the last straw. Finally my mother swallowed her pride and wrote to the man who, like a wounded animal, had never stopped loving her. But the Amber King had not lost the knack for trading. It was at this point that the pact was drawn up and she renounced custody of me.

One burning desire I still held intact: to be a sea captain like Ejnarsen and sail a ship to the ends of the earth. For that I needed an education and it was this that she persuaded him to finance.

"He'll never let you go now. He's bought you back for his collection," she sighed, and took the veil. Spiritually speaking. In fact, the only difference between her and the other nuns was her dress. Her wings were clipped. The wine she drank was altar wine, and the bread she ate, thin wafers.

Those were the lean years. After them came the fat.

I entered the naval academy. Board and lodging—with a room of my own—all paid for. I passed my exams with flying colors. It was my own dreams I was chasing. I had swapped the marriage between heaven and hell for Newton's compasses. The rule of three: map reading, celestial navigation, mathematics, and weapons training. Ranked first on the shooting range, outmatched as a swordsman only by a dragoon from Schleswig.

Once a year—every April 1—I met my father at the Post House Inn, where he handed me the brown envelope. It was only right that I should know where the money came from. Afterwards we would go off and celebrate my birthday. He would ask me how I was getting on at the academy and I would present my results with pride. Aviaja's name was never mentioned. On the subject of their life together at Crow Towers he was silent as the grave.

The rest of the year was my own, to do with as I pleased. I

had acquired a taste for the good life and helped myself to all the delights offered. Aladdin with an annual allowance and his own personal genie. As a boy I had been the terror of the ladies, now I was their darling. I was welcomed into a circle of young cadets, all the children of good families; we frequented the saloons as well as the bordellos.

To please my mother I still went to confession now and then. When I confessed my sins, there was silence behind the curtain—then I was given a list of prayers a mile long for my penance.

The day I turned twenty-one I took for myself the motto *Non serviam*, because I did not wish to serve, because I wished to be my own master. When this came up in confession, the curtain was wrenched aside. With appalled blue eyes, the Catholic priest stared at me through the grille, a captive of his faith. I had chosen Lucifer's axiom. I chuckled to myself as I left. The world was before me, ripe for the plucking.

Not long afterwards, my mother left my life forever. Her health had been failing for some time and she had found peace in a retreat in Italy, where, at long last, she was received into the angelic order.

After a couple of years at sea I had risen to the rank of lieutenant. I had visited warmer climes, voyaged to the slave coast, and lain with its women, whose skins smelled of nutmeg. I had dived with the dolphins off Zanzibar and become a blueback myself from the sunshine and the sea. It was a man of the world and a conquering hero who set foot once more on his father's land.

It is one hundred years and a summer since I walked through the door of Crow Towers. From the moment we entered the house I had the impression of walking on glass. Smiled at the sight of the kayak. Such a dusty old thing over the dining table. Not only that, but it stank—like an old whale-oil lamp. We passed quickly through the parlor and out into the hall, from which a stairway led up to the north tower.

I had been expecting to be dragged from one glass case to the next. From the world of minerals to the display cabinets, from the larval stage to frames full of butterflies. I knew the elements by heart and was prepared to add to my knowledge, but the shells I had seen on the world's shores I had left where they lay. I loved their colors and their rainbow sheen, but even then I had realized that you cannot take it with you. It is like packing bubbles in a suitcase: when you open it again they have turned to slush. I would rather have gone back one day and found everything as it was.

Great was my amazement, then, when we walked into the turret room and I found that it was empty. Freshly painted walls, gleaming windowpanes. There was not a fly speck on the glass, not a stick of furniture in the room. The skylight streamed through the prisms of the roof and cast spectrums onto the walls and floorboards. Otherwise nothing.

I turned to my maker with a question in my eyes. Was this another bit of April Foolery? Did he have something up his sleeve? But in his eyes I detected only celebration and the anticipation of watching a child unwrap presents. Then lightning struck. It was a gift from him, the finest he could give me. I was free to do with the place as I saw fit.

My suspicion was confirmed when he cleared his throat and said, "Anything you need, just say the word."

A shiver ran down my spine. I had never had any intention of coming to live here. If anything, my idea had been to keep him at arm's length. Ours was a business relationship, pure and simple; all that remained was for me to put my signature to the contract he was waving about and the pact was sealed. That tower would be my display case. Here I would sit behind glass and be my father's pride.

I bit my lip. So there was a price to be paid after all, although it was still not too late to pull out. I had carved out my own career, there was a slave uprising on Saint Croix, and the navy had need of men like me.

Seeing that I had reservations, he tempted me with a crystalline little note that wrapped itself around the words: "I have been thinking of giving you command of the *Narwhal* . . ."

There was someone on the stairs. I never had a chance to reply, because just then the Amber King's daughter entered the turret room. And took my breath away. The last time I had seen her, she had been little more than a snot-encrusted turned-up nose. Here stood a young woman, lovelier than any I had ever seen in all the lands I had visited as a ravenous sailor.

The light played across her cheekbones, her eyes showed no transition from iris to pupil, only a blue-black cast. Her hair was drawn into a knot on the top of her head, bound with a leather thong. From the thong, strings of colored beads fell to form a headdress that stopped just above her eyes.

Aviaja approached with faltering step, extended her hand. Her eyes widened the instant they met mine and I felt something give way in me. I had planned only a nod, but now I felt my arm lifting, and as I touched her cheek the spark leapt and our skins conjoined. We awoke to the same wonder.

From then on I had no idea what I was doing. I signed the contract.

24

IN WHICH
A BENEDICTION IS
SUNG FOR THE
SUMMER'S DEAD

From that day on I was a captive in the Amber King's palace, held spellbound. I moved into the turret room with my sea chest, made a bunk with drawers underneath for the bedding, set myself up with garden chairs and a writing desk that faced out to sea. I wanted to live with the lightness of the summer intact, under scudding clouds and with the sun, moon, and stars constantly revolving above my head. From the tower I had a view of the jetty my father had had extended beyond the third reef, so that our ships could tie up at the end of it.

In the beginning he sought to endear himself to me. Treated me like someone sent from heaven to sweeten his old age. He brightened up, ventured out of the den where he had his workshop. He denied me nothing, would talk animatedly throughout the meals for which we presented ourselves, he in smoking jacket, I in full-dress uniform complete with saber. His pride in me knew no bounds.

I was allocated an office in the old warehouse in which the shipping company had its headquarters. The first thing I did was ask to be made familiar with the accounts. The bookkeeper and I went through the columns of figures in the ledgers that he took down from the shelves, ledgers covering years and years of the company's activity. I was thoroughly bored, but never let it show. He reminded me of my old arithmetic teacher—wing collar, ruler and inkwell, debit and credit and once more from the top. I asked the inventory man to come and see me: gross and net, invoices and stock. I had meetings with the chief clerk: register tonnage, cargoes, payrolls, and insurance policies. In my father's absence it was this troika that had been running the business.

I found everything in perfect order, fired all three of them, and put myself in charge. The rest of the staff loved me. I organized company parties and Sunday outings. I was the prodigal son returned, and then, too, I was—so they said—the spitting image of my father.

He never interfered in what I did.

I made the odd foray onto my old hunting grounds, brought down my prey, but rose again from the seducer's couch, covered in shame. Aviaja had got under my skin. I experienced only the aftertaste of a former lust; it ebbed away of its own accord. All day long my thoughts revolved around Aviaja, growing to an obsession that rendered me distant and distracted in all other situations.

Not least because she was taboo.

She loved him as a daughter. There was not a shadow of doubt in her heart when it came to this man who had taken her in and given her everything. She had never set foot inside a school: he could not stand the thought of her mixing with other people. He taught her to read and write himself, but she never opened a book. Her every hour was spoken for; she looked after the livestock, cooked his meals, and did his washing. She mucked out the barn, set nets, and caught fish, all with the same ease. I refuse to call her a slave, because it was she who controlled the course of her day.

She was deft in her dealings with the elements—lit fires, fetched water from the well, dug in the vegetable plot, and sniffed the wind before she hung the fish up to dry. Otherwise they'll rot, she would say. She smoked mackerel and trout in her earthen oven, added juniper berries and herbs to wood shavings and spread the mixture across the charcoal.

When we went out in the dinghy to tend the nets and she grabbed the catch with a flick of the wrist and broke the neck of a salmon with her teeth, all I wanted was to kiss those lips that spit out the scales. Love had reduced me to a fool. In the navy we said that bathing in the sea was for children and summer visitors—now I swam with her in all weather merely to catch a glimpse of the wet skin that glistened through the shift that clung to her body when we climbed out of the water.

I was besotted, bewitched by the sense of her. All the other women I had known faded into hazy images and drifted off in perfumed reflections. How often had I fallen for a queen—and made do with the chambermaid? Because she was younger, because her curves were plumper.

This time it would be different. Aviaja alone was real. I caught myself wishing that we had been playmates forever. I could not sleep, sat up all night in my turret room. Suffered from shortness of breath and palpitations, turned hot, then cold. Above my head, the daytime light never went out; instead it turned blue and gave birth to a star that shone down on the glass. She was an elf maiden, and as time passed I pursued her, dancing, across the meadows of the summer night.

But still I restrained myself.

That is the alpha and omega of all things in the towers of the Amber King.

As the summer flew by, Aviaja's disquiet also grew. There were two of us playing this game. She showed me, by sign and deed, that she felt the same longing. She had awakened from a trance. The day the prince kissed her she would rise up from her glass coffin and throw her arms about his neck. I told her that when our ship came in we would leave that place and run away together to the world's end. I kept my tone light, allowing room for laughter, never overstepped the mark. We went for walks along the dunes, wandered into the enchanted forest where dwarf pines and dog roses grew. If our hands touched or our eyes met, the blood would rush to her cheeks and she would grow as short of breath as I.

The daily ritual of the dinner table became torture. He guarded her jealously, like an old dragon sitting on his gold. I had to restrain myself from yelling out loud and drawing my sword. Aviaja cleared the table; the china rattled and the sound of knife and fork dominated the room. I jumped every time the grandfather clock struck the quarter.

He did not stint when he poured from the wine decanter. Crystal with a silver lip to cut off the stream. Every time she turned her back he would fix burning eyes on her and forget the glass in his hand. Search for signs of change in her. Drop his gaze to hip level and let it linger there. I felt the nausea from my childhood rising and I looked away. Aviaja disappeared into the kitchen, came back with the main course, and sat down to eat with us.

She was at her wit's end. She had spent her whole life in captivity and she did not even know it. Every beat of her heart split her body in two. At the head of the table sat her adoptive father, who loved her more than anything else in all the world. If she were to leave him he could neither live nor die. This we both knew. We never spoke of it. We waited for the blow that would sever the Gordian knot—what is known as the hand of fate. But one could have waited till one was old and gray.

I told her that love was right. She replied, What love? Is love a piece of knitting with a right side and a wrong? I had no answer to that. I had pushed my plate away, unable to eat. And I sat there, lost to the world, gazing at the neckline of her dress.

He cleared his throat.

"Pour your sister some wine," he said, and sent me a look.

Only once did we have a visitor. It was Ejnarsen, come to submit his resignation. He was an old man by then, with a wooden leg—frostbite had claimed the original—and our hearts were overflowing when we embraced. We were delighted to see each other again. Once he was settled and his glass filled, Aviaja placed herself on his lap and snuggled against his sealskin coat. As she sat, the wooden leg jerked up, sticking straight out in the air. She buried her nose in the fur, sniffing her way to a bliss that harked back to her infancy.

First chance I got I took him aside and quizzed him about Aviaja's background. She was from the deep fjords on the east coast; it was from there that she derived her cheekbones and the dark sheen of her skin. He did not know much. She had been discovered on the foredeck one morning, wrapped in a sort of fur sling, an *amaad*. No one had heard or seen anything. The *Narwhal* had been at anchor and the crew were asleep.

In more than one place the fishing had been poor. The villages had been hit first by famine, then by outbreaks of measles. Then, suddenly, there she lay with her seal-pup eyes, gurgling and stretching her paws into the air to be lifted. In no time the crew were fighting over who should feed her oatmeal and hard-tack soaked in lukewarm water. She must have been two or three years old, because she chattered away in Greenlandic and started toddling about the minute they extricated her from the fur.

Ejnarson had named her after a woman from Kulusuk he had known in his younger days; he winked at me, waggling his wooden leg gleefully. Each time he tapped the leg with the base of his glass it was a sign for me to fill it up again from the bottle.

"Yep, it's a good thing Bertelsen took the little thing in. Me, I was always at sea. And this I will say; she couldn't have done any better!"

He looked at me, eyes sharp under his brows. He was the only person to come near the place in all those years. With a pang I realized that Aviaja had had two fathers. I could have done with one of them myself.

The Amber King had fallen to reminiscing. When the conversation touched on Aviaja, his voice softened, as it always did, and the clouds over Crow Towers dispersed. We drained our glasses and filled them again. The *Narwhal* was in dry dock. As soon as she was seaworthy again I would be given command of her.

It was late before the captain left. The light still lingered on the horizon and the dunes were aglow. Aviaja offered to drive him home and went to hitch up the gig. We gathered in the yard to say goodbye. The old sea dog was a bit tipsy, and so was the Amber King, who had behaved like an angel all afternoon. He helped the captain up and raised his hand in salute. Aviaja flicked the reins. But when, at the last minute, I, too, sprang up onto the seat, he turned his back and staggered off into the house without a word of farewell.

Aviaja protested. I did not waste words. "It's getting dark

and I don't want you driving back through the forest by yourself."

Behind us the captain had sunk back against the upholstered
seat, his head lolling to the side, his mouth hanging open, giving his snores free vent. We trotted along for a while in silence.
I stole a glance at her; she sensed it and returned it out of the
corner of her eye as the leafy shadows played across our bodies.
Each time the gig swayed we bumped shoulders. I was the one
who was suddenly shy, she who eventually gathered the reins in
one hand and placed the other on my knee. Before long she was
smiling like Sleeping Beauty awakening from her enchanted
slumber.

Only when we pulled up outside the seamen's mission in
town did the captain stir, woken by the silence the minute the
cobbles ceased to rumble under the wheels. Gas lights were
burning in the alley. I hopped down, helped him descend, and
propped him up on his crutch. The old aroma of tobacco and
tar trailed after him as he said good night and hobbled off to
his lodgings.

On the way back to Crow Towers, we moved closer in our
seats. We drove along the dike. When we passed Sea View there
were lights in the parlor and curtains billowed out of the windows in the warm evening air. By the brier hedge stood a
woman in a crocheted shawl, Sigurd Swan's mother. She was
young still, and it would be some years before Sigurd would be
born.

Just before the enchanted forest, we swapped places and I
took the reins. There was magic in the night and she wrapped
her arms around my waist and laid her head on my shoulder.
We trundled along the lane, ducking to avoid overhanging
branches; one body, two breaths, daring everything except the
forbidden words. On the last bit of the way across the meadows we saw the clouds of mist shining in the summer night. I

dropped the reins and left the horses to find their own way home. Before we drove back into the courtyard, I had kissed her for the first time.

In the parlor the kerosene lamps were still burning. We found him slumped in the armchair, his head on his chest, his arms dangling limp. It looked like a stroke. Aviaja went rigid, curling in on herself, biting her knuckles to dull the pain. Then I noticed the cognac glass in his hand, and our eyes met across the empty carafe on the table. The look of fright on her face gave way to resignation. It was not the first time she had had to deal with this. Together we helped him to bed, his body heavy as an old hulk. We removed his slippers, loosened his collar, and covered him with a blanket. His breath rattled in his throat. It smelled of the formalin he used for his specimens.

Then we were back in the parlor. Aviaja slept in the room next to his. The door was open; a band of light fell across the wallpaper and I caught the scent of lavender from her bed-clothes. She was crying. She had covered her face, not wanting me to see, but her shoulders gave her away. When I reached out to lay a hand on her arm she turned away and hurried into the room. The door slammed behind her.

I dug out a bottle from the liquor cabinet, uncorked it. I poured myself a cognac and swirled it around in the glass as my thoughts churned and the clock chimed. I unbuttoned my jacket, slid down between the arms of the chair, and stared blankly at the floor. From its corner the death's-head monkey had seized possession of the room; the stuffed birds and his whole damn bestiary cast their shadows over walls and ceiling when the wick of one of the lamps started to gutter. Before the light went out, my mind was made up. I was leaving, and the sooner the better!

A floorboard creaked and the door to Aviaja's room opened again. She stood there in the room. Hair hanging loose, naked as the seals who had created her. She put a finger to her lips and I followed. Silently and with thudding hearts, we climbed up to the tower. Step by step we left the stairway behind us; she opened the door to my room and led me across to the bunk. The deluge burst forth in us both, all the dikes were washed away.

Not until the night was almost over did we lie still in each other's arms and gaze up at the crystal heavens, while the music of the spheres stilled in our limbs and the nightingale's song died away. Before we parted, she promised to follow me to the world's end.

In fairy tales, long stories are cut short and the characters re-worked into dragons and princesses. I have looked deep into the crystal ball. Father was not a dragon, merely an old man with a lifelong disappointment behind him. The divorce was not his fault. But those facts did not stop me from dubbing him in the face, and no one ever came by a knighthood that way. But I do not regret it. *Non serviam.* On the day when all sins are confessed we are neither men nor women, virgins nor uni-corns. Only eunuchs. Which is why all saints smell of the crypt.

I blink. Until the moment when the parson gets to his feet before the altar and turns to face the congregation, not a note has sounded in the church. Now he begins to chant.

And I miss the sound of the Kyrie Eleison, in which the whole choir echoes his words, in the ritual intended to send the soul on its way. The miracle of the transformation. If you had eyes like mine, you would see beyond the clay's form and the gilded ties that bind the floral wreaths. You would see far be-yond the vale of tears—you would see the lieutenant, royal-blue and ramrod-straight, lead his bride to the altar.

At length the choir files out of the vestry, schoolchildren and white-clad confirmation students; their long robes whisper as they walk and they look self-conscious, the men especially, as they take their places, stepping on one another's toes. One boy and one girl, each carrying a palm branch, stand on either side of Oda, whose eyes are fixed on the organ. She looks like the bride of Saint Lucia she once was.

Santos has appeared in the organ loft. The old choirmaster's morning suit is baggy on his frame. With a toss of his head he sits down at the keyboard. Kneads his fingers to warm them, then leans over, scans the stops, and adjusts one setting. The organ pipes tower, like staircases rising and falling, above his head.

A hush descends. He closes his eyes, pitches forward from the waist, and starts to play. At the very first notes of the adagio, the church fills with sails.

IN WHICH
THE MUSIC PLAYS

The canvas sagged, then puffed out again as the ship heeled in the swell and headed toward us. It was autumn, golden October. We stood on the jetty, squeezing each other's hands. Aviaja's dress fluttered beneath her cape and the waves slapped against the jetty posts. We stepped back a bit when a shower of spray flew up, but I felt the cold water seep through my boot leather. At sea this was what we called a rogue wave. Aviaja laughed at the way I said it.

Our love was at its height. We pursued it where no one could find us—took the dinghy out, lay in the bottom, and left the boat to the wind and weather. We took each other in rough sea and calm, as the terns screeched and our skins ran with salt. Afterwards we would jump into the water and continue our romping there.

Either that or we would row ashore, pull the dinghy up onto the beach, and find a hollow in the dunes where the sun had burned before us. A hunter's hide in the forest had screened our embraces. We spent nights on mounds of moss and woke to the munching of the deer, because we are as naked as they. Still we hid our faces from him. We lived in a glass house and balked at throwing the first stone.

I proposed to her and she said yes. Unsure what the law had to say, I had been into the office and searched the files for her adoption papers. Someone had removed them. So we conducted our own ceremony, tied the knot before the Virgin and Child and the Mother of All the Oceans, and I said the words "till death do us part" and placed the ring on her finger.

She made a vow that held fast. If I died first, she—when she, too, felt that death was at hand—would order a Mass to be sung for my soul, that we might be reunited on the other side. In return I promised to be faithful to her till Judgment Day. A rosary had changed hands and sealed the vow.

I shivered inside my pea jacket. The wind was blowing offshore. Out on the water the sailors trimmed the sails aback, and the *Narwhal* careened and came about. Each tack brought her nearer the jetty. It was Ejnarsen's last trip. I had a suspicion that he was dragging it out, making the leg as long as possible on each tack. Fresh water and provisions had been taken on board. Everything was ready for the voyage; one sailor was going ashore, another was all set to board.

Aviaja shuffled her feet, gnawed at her knuckles. It was now or never, if she was to get away from here. We had made up our minds to tell him. But he had locked himself in his room and refused to see a living soul. For every step we took out into the open he pulled back two.

It was as if there were a tide inside him, draining him of strength. His back was no longer straight, his hair was disheveled, and the white had taken over completely. He shuffled round and round on himself—hear no evil, see no evil. The third monkey, though, cried out when he had one of his fits, afterwards to sink back immediately into apathy and self-propagating ruin. Or he would take to the bottle and force his anguish to the very brink.

Aviaja, who had cared for him as if for a difficult child, was no longer able to satisfy his whims. I had come to an agreement with a housekeeper who was willing to come and live out there; a hired hand could see to the rest. It wouldn't be so bad. That, at least, is what I tried to tell Aviaja. She was not convinced, and deep down I understood her. I wished I felt the same about him.

The ship was now close enough for us to wave to it. Ejnarsen grabbed hold of the shroud and stuck his crutch in the air. The *Narwhal* swung around again and the maneuver took our breath away; she took the last tack with the bow slicing through the foam. She turned into the eye of the wind, and as the sails cracked and flapped, the crew scrambled aloft to restrain the ratlines and yardarms; they slung lashes around the buffeting canvas as she lost speed. All the while, Ejnarsen bellowed in true captain's fashion. The fenders were hung over the side; one by one I caught the lines thrown ashore and made them fast at the head of the jetty. The lines were drawn tight and with a sighing of her timbers she came alongside.

That was the third time the ship came into my life.

The *Narwhal* lay rocking in the little cove in the lee of Crow Isle. The captain went ashore, leaving his ship with not a single backward glance. Under his arm he carried the tubes with the charts, and in his hand a mahogany box containing the sextant.

A little later we were seated in the parlor. He unrolled one chart after another, we put our heads together, and he went over all the main sailing routes with me. The doldrums, sea currents, hurricane depressions. We worked our way down to the roaring forties, south around Cape Horn. Soon we were in the Sunda Strait, then on to Shanghai, Siam, and Ceylon, where the tea clippers sailed back and forth. I lost myself in the infinitude of voyages.

Suddenly he looked up, caught Aviaja with a golden glint in his eye. "What've you done with Bertelsen?"

She cocked her head in the direction of the closed door. "He's asleep. He isn't feeling well."

I came to her aid. Aviaja was incapable of lying. "He asked me to pass on his thanks for all your years with him. And to give you this."

I handed him a manila envelope. Inside was a generous sum of money that I had taken from the cash box and made up into bundles for him. He did not count it, just tucked it inside his jacket and grunted his thanks. His eyes rested on me long enough for the blood to rush to my cheeks. I cleared my throat, fiddled with the twine around the last roll.

"What have we here?"

He dropped his gaze and undid the knot. When he unrolled the chart, half the dining table was covered by Greenland. He beckoned Aviaja to him.

"Somewhere up there you were born, under the midnight sun, where the dogs howl night and day." He pointed to the ceiling. "That's where the kayak comes from, too. They call it the Land of the Real People . . ."

The captain placed his finger on Kulusuk and Ammasalik. With one horny nail he traced a line down the coast to Nanortalik, traveled west and up the other side to Nuuk, Sisimiut, and all the way to Thule. She repeated the names after Ejnarsen as he rattled them off. He told her about the wildlife and she raised her eyes.

"There are seals here," she said wonderingly. "Sometimes they take my fish. I've seen them from the boat, sticking their heads out of the water. When I was little I used to think I could hear them talking to me in a language I had forgotten."

Her voice grew distant. At that moment I loved them both with all my heart. He had stirred a longing in her that ran even deeper. The battle was half won. Now she would *have* to leave, her kin were calling her. It began as a whisper underneath the pack ice and soon it would be trumpeting from one end of the ocean to the other . . . .

Her whole face changed shape. Aviaja embodied echoes of the world she had left as a baby. There are no sirens but these. I do not hear them myself, for the traveler has plugged his ears and seeks his Ithaca only in order to settle the score with something that he does not want anyway. And the voyage continues. He is doomed to leave his homeland and burn his candle at both ends.

Ejnarsen was calling for glasses and Aviaja awakened from her trance. She brought out the aquavit that had been sitting since last season with walnuts steeping in it. The captain got to his feet, tucked his crutch in at his armpit. Then he picked up the box containing the sextant, held it out to me without a word. I realized that the command had just changed hands. I lifted the lid. There the instrument lay, gleaming brass. I ran a finger along the ornamental silver chasing of the graduated arc.

We drank to one another and the aquavit burned a hole in my throat where the lump had been. I had dreamed of this moment for as long as I could remember.

Ejnarsen made to leave. He was not a man for prolonging the agony. A whole lifetime was held in that box, and we respected it. We did not urge him to stay. Aviaja went out to hitch up the gig. This time she was allowed to drive him to town herself; they had plenty to talk about. He turned back one last time on the threshold.

"Take good care of her!" he said.

And I was left with the feeling that he suspected more than we thought. At the time I was not sure whether he was referring to the ship.

Some hours passed before I heard the gig roll up in front of the house. Still no sound from behind his door. Invested with my new rank, I sat with my cap on the table in front of me and noted down the things Ejnarsen had told me about the sailing routes. Where water and provisions could be taken on, which harbors were safe, the best places to dock for repairs. Anyone can sail a ship—good seamanship is in the details.

She came into the room and pointed questioningly at the door. I shook my head. I sensed a change in her—something, perhaps, that had passed between her and the captain in private. The map of Greenland was still spread out on the table. I dipped the nib of my pen in ink, hovered for a moment over the fjords before drawing a circle round Kulusuk.

"Aviaja, say the word and that's where the ship will sail. The rest of the world can wait."

That was the second time I saw her cry.

Who it was who compromised, she or I, does not matter now. Word and deed interlace, creating new labyrinths in which the living lose their way. But by the time one starts to unravel the threads it is already too late and the ship has sailed.

Over the next day or two I got to know the crew, furnished the captain's cabin to my own taste, took the *Narwhal* for a trial run. At Crow Towers madness reigned. She set his meals outside his door, but he would not touch them until we went away. Only by the plates that reappeared empty could we tell that he was alive.

I took Aviaja to the island where the seals lived. We set off in the morning. It was twelve nautical miles away, so we had the whole day. We dropped anchor by the lighthouse, swam ashore. We made love one last time among the seals baking on

the rocks. Afterwards I lay for a while tickling her under the
nose with a blade of grass. She sneezed, propped herself up on
her elbow. My impatient heart demanded an answer from her.
She sighed and looked away.

Then she said it, in a whisper that was barely audible: "I
can't go with you."

"Aviaja . . ."

"Papa won't hear of it."

"Have you told him?"

She nodded.

"Why didn't you say anything before? I can't keep the crew
hanging around here."

"I want so much to come. But I need time."

"What did he say?"

"That I would have to wait a few years."

"Aviaja, he's going to kill us, the way he goes on. We're going to have to wait till he's dead . . ."

"He loves you!"

I flew into a rage, leaping to my feet and kicking a piece of
driftwood. "He's crazy!"

She looked at the ground. Said nothing for a long time. I
tried again. Turned my back to her. She must not see my anger.
Anger had been my faithful companion ever since the split.
When it was around, there was nothing else.

"Come with me. For love's sake, for your own . . ."

"I can't. Papa says no."

I exploded. "Of course he says no. We always knew he
would, didn't we?"

Silence. I turned to look at her. Defiant. I motioned with my
hand, urging her to go on.

"You don't understand any of it. I'm not talking about your
father—he still won't see me. It's Ejnarsen."

She was right, I didn't understand a thing. She paused. Then out it came. Slowly, her eyes opened mine. "Ejnarsen is my father . . ."

I was thunderstruck, stared at her, open-mouthed. In that instant, everything fell into place. I swallowed.

She reached for my hand, stroked it. "It's not so bad, Jonah. Papa only wants the best for us. He's the only friend the Amber King has. He says we'll only regret it if we go off together now. *You* go, and when you come back everything will be fine. He swears it will."

"How long have you known?"

"Since the day before yesterday."

I nodded. Nodded and nodded like the Mandarin in the fairy tale. All the nightingales had been silenced. I could neither say "P" nor beat a drum.

"So be it," was all I said, and saw her astonished look before I dived off the rocks and started swimming out to the ship. She caught up with me before I reached it. No sooner had I climbed aboard than I showed myself on the bridge.

"Weigh anchor," I yelled into the megaphone, "tomorrow we sail!"

In the church, Santos rises from the organ bench after the last chord of the overture dies out. He positions himself in front of a music stand, facing Oda and the choir, his hands drift upward until they are level with his head. He turns a page, slashes downward, and the first vocal harmonies ring out.

The choir sounds shaky. The composer is hard put to conceal his annoyance. He drops his right hand, cueing Oda's part; molds her voice with his fingers and draws it out to the front of the choir. She can carry the song; it swells and provides a breathing space for the others.

He smiles down on her blissfully and her relief is tangible. Her gaze ceases to wander; she casts sidelong glances at the boy and girl holding the palm branches, cocks an eyebrow at them, and passes on a smile. Then she throws her head back and sings for the sheer joy of it.

Santos conducts with hair and hands flying. Oda's soprano climbs like a lone bird over the mountains, then circles beneath a gap in the clouds through which the light pours. I prick up my ears. The images called up by the music engulf me in memories of the rain forest I once journeyed through on a river steamer. The choir is the river, its whirlpools and cascades, the long stretch under the canopy of leaves from which the vines fell in a thick curtain. Oda is the siren, a sudden scream soaring above the trees. The voices of the river dolphins are resurrected as a piping in the church.

It is a sound never heard in this part of the world before, not even in the church of my childhood. My respect for Santos, the master of this gay requiem, increases.

Little by little, the warbling cicada landscape alters, underpinned by male voices. The pastoral idyll is invaded by a menacing note. All at once, Santos spins around to face the organ, where—hunched over the keys but without sitting down—he strikes a doomsday chord. It descends on the church like a peal of thunder that makes the farmers and fishermen jump out of their pews.

A booming bass note fills the organ pipes. Not until this chord has faded does Santos turn back to face the choir. Among the living, only Oda knows why he slams the doors of Hell, but the passion that drives the work makes itself felt.

With a flaming red lash, he whips up devils. The soul rejoices. I have to restrain myself from swooping inside Santos. He stands writhing at the music stand as he relives his story. The shame that turned to the Day of Wrath. The hate that turned to the flame.

Outside, the sky has been like cold blue varnish, a fresco of the fires of Purgatory. Now it changes. I see the first clouds come swirling in and gather into an ever-deepening darkness that engulfs the church windows. It is felt as a chill off the walls, and more than one congregant turns to look at the door at the other end of the nave. The wind has risen. That persistent knocking must come from a branch banging against the door.

26

IN WHICH
THE SHIP SETS SAIL

Aviaja was knocking on my door. I knew it was her, but I did not let her in. She begged me, calling my name, but I did not let her in. I had spent my first night on board the ship, lying awake in the captain's bunk and waiting for the dawn. The bunk was only just wide enough for my shoulders. It reminded me—when the curtain was drawn—of a coffin.

Only when I heard her footsteps retreating up the ladder did I tear back the curtain and get up. I waited a while before unlocking the cabin door, then climbed the ladder and poked my nose out the hatch. She was gone, had stepped ashore again. I jumped onto the deck in time to see her figure moving away between the dunes. She had drawn her cape tight around her shoulders and walked with her head lowered against the blast.

The sun was up and a stiff offshore wind was blowing. The tide was ebbing. Farther out, the swell turned to waves topped with foam. I mustered the crew and gave the order: Make ready to sail. No sooner said than done—they were good men, who knew the ship better than I did and could have sailed her in their sleep. I wasted no time, hopped ashore myself to cast off, and was back on board as fast as the *Narwhal* could move the first few feet from the jetty. Most of the crew had climbed into the rigging to set the sails.

The foresails snapped and were hauled taut. The flying jib lifted the prow, and as the sails filled with wind, she lunged forward. I stood on the bridge and gazed at the shore. Up among the dunes I spied the solitary figure of Aviaja. The wind had changed direction. I watched her without blinking. The corner of her shawl whipped out from her head along with her hair. It drew a line abaft the beam, running away from the shore.

Next to the helmsman a hole had been bored in the planks for Ejnarsen's wooden leg. The shrouds on both sides had been fitted with rings for him to hang onto during his watch. Here he could hold himself steady even when it was blowing a gale and mountainous waves were breaking over the deck.

We had just built up steerageway when I saw the Amber King come stomping down the jetty. He knew the whole story; I could tell by the way he moved—suddenly so agile. His stick pounded the boards. When he reached the end of the jetty he raised the stick, waved it in the air, and started to shout, cursing me to hell and back, disowning me, and heaven knows what else. And I saw red. That is the best explanation I can give for what I then did.

The *Narwhal* was built to sail through pack ice, with extra reinforcement around the bow. I shoved the helmsman aside, brought the wheel around hard, and turned the vessel about. I steered straight for the jetty, did not heave to until the last minute, felt the crunch and the boards being shredded by the copper sheathing. I saw him slip down between splintered timbers, clutch at a post, and cling there, splashing and spluttering in the chilly water. Then I veered onto the opposite bow, pulling away from the shore.

I looked back one last time. In time to see Aviaja run up and jump into the water.

The helmsman was white as a sheet, shaken to the core like the rest of the men. But no one said a thing. That crazy maneuver would have to speak for itself. Besides being their captain I was the owner's son. The miserable milksop at my side kept his mouth shut, but he was trembling from top to toe. I let him have the wheel, went below to the chart room to plot a course. My anger was still cold, I was still in control of my actions and I had no regrets.

Then I saw the photograph. It was sitting on the chart table. Aviaja behind glass, framed in silver, regarding me with unfathomable seriousness. She had left a last message for me; it was written in india ink, in slanting script, across the pasteboard. It was like a blow: so few words, so fiendishly true that they left me breathless. I turned the photograph over and laid it face down.

Anger burns bridges, but shame crushes spirits. I collapsed over the chart, sobbed like a man possessed. It was done. I ran up my death mask and sailed away. After that day I could never go home.

More and more heads turn toward the banging. There is some fidgeting in the pews as the choir falters through the Offertory, struggling to keep time. The vocal harmonies disintegrate into discord. Only Oda still keeps her voice steady; several of the others have dried up completely and stand gaping at the score like tongue-tied fish. Santos goes on conducting, an indignant crease between his brows his only response to the din.

The parish clerk gives the parson a baffled look and the nuns cross themselves, while the fisherfolk from the evangelical mission bare their heads and clasp their hands in prayer, having first exchanged eloquent looks. The guest of honor has arrived—what do you expect when the parson opens his church doors to Beelzebub?

The windows rattle, as if struck by huge hailstones, and the light has taken on the coppery cast that usually heralds a thunderstorm. Outside, gusts of wind can be heard working up into a wail. At the foot of the nave the sound has altered to an insistent drumming. Several people are now on their feet, facing the church door.

A shock runs through the congregation when the door bursts open and the moan of the wind fills the village church. Something clatters up the aisle and Oda's voice falls silent. It is the gravedigger's wheelbarrow, rolling in with the sea fog, shovel handle first. Sheets of music fly up from the stand in the organ loft, spiraling upwards into a whirlwind with fallen leaves and twigs.

Santos gropes after the white wings that are suddenly swarming round about him. The frigate twirls once on its chain. The wheelbarrow topples and the tornado proceeds alone up to the altar. Incredulous eyes watch as Aviaja's urn hovers for a moment above the catafalque before smashing to the floor. Roses, lilies of the valley, and evergreens are swept from the centerpiece and take to the air. The wailing now sounds both inside and out; the flowers swirl, everything swirls.

Openmouthed and deathly pale, the churchgoers see the ashes lift off the floor. In a gray veil they unite with the flowers, linger for a second before the altar, where the pastor stands with hair and chasuble flying. Into the teeth of the tempest he shouts, "Shut the door!" But the sexton has been turned to a pillar of salt. No one makes a move; some have buried their faces in their hands, others rock to and fro in ecstasy.

Ashes and roses rise in a cone toward the vaulted ceiling, spin with the tornado for a few seconds. Together they form a figure—half spinning top, half ballerina—that tilts forward on its point, leaning toward the exit. Thus joined, after one final pirouette we take our leave of the congregation and vanish with the tornado out to sea.

There is a lull in the church after the storm. The squall has passed over, as abruptly as it came. It rumbles still on the horizon with the sound of distant thunder. Sea fog still drifts around the chancel dome. The catafalque has been stripped clean, the urn lies in pieces on the floor. A stem of lily of the valley lying on the soil from the wheelbarrow makes it look as if a potted plant had fallen over.

One by one the pillars of salt come to life. The sexton shuts the door. Light bursts through the clouds and falls through the windows in the apse, streaming in again under the crossties of the vaulting and reflecting off the women's hats and the men's bared heads. There has been a transfiguration, it is whispered from pew to pew. Deprived, that is what the parish has been until this day, deprived of miracles.

For a while yet the parson seems at a loss. Then he raises his arms, nods to Santos, who sits down at the organ. This time the parson sounds as if he might burst into song himself.

"Holy, holy, holy is God, Lord of the heavenly hosts. Blessed are thee that cometh in the name of the Lord. Hosanna in the highest!"

The Sanctus splits the air like a fanfare. Oda sings and the organ answers her. The choir members are silent, their music scattered to the four winds. They have no need of anyone but each other. The remainder of the requiem becomes a duet between these two. Rhythmically he plies the stops, switching from strings to flügelhorn and flutes, coaxing out notes that fall like vibrant curtains of northern lights from the pipes.

Now and then, Santos turns his head and catches her eye, or he takes his hands off the keys and uses the pedals alone, twisting his body around to her to spur her on. Flushed with the triumph of the melody, they forget all else. Standing on tiptoe, she hurls out the song. A fountain of power builds inside her. She feels herself lifting, rendered weightless by the jubilation they unleash between them. She makes no gestures, stands with her arms at her sides, in her white gown. She seems to have risen above the music itself, simply opens her lips and lets it pour out.

Then the organ, too, falls silent and she sings on—solo— with Santos conducting her from the bench. They have abandoned the score. She stands between the palm branches, places her hands on the heads of the boy and girl. With the skill of a trumpeter circling around the arabesques of her voice, she picks up the thread and sings the Agnus Dei through to the end.

In the closing sequence, Santos brings in the choir and organ, all the while holding Oda's soprano aloft. The polyphony of the voices weaves around the peal of the organ, undulating upward from the bedrock of the bass. And all the time, the soprano hangs at the very top, swooping in ever-decreasing circles—like the dove in the ceiling painting, whose outspread wings at last become one, once more, with the sun.

When the requiem is over and the last resounding note has been absorbed by the chancel dome, Santos looks down at her and laughs with relief. With a long, slow aftertouch, silence descends on the church. The members of the congregation sit bolt upright, weather-beaten faces above stocks and collars, pasty-faced matrons and rosy-cheeked young girls. They cannot bring themselves to look at one another. The paint on the picture created by the music is still wet.

Santos has not moved from his music stand. He catches the parson's eye and receives a nod in reply. He clears his throat and the choir automatically falls into line, as if expecting a coda.

"I asked Oda to marry me," he begins, and his voice sounds a little hoarse after Oda's bell-like tones. Then the words come rushing out, almost without a trace of an accent, now that the

music has gone to his head: ". . . and she said yes! The proclamation of marriage has to be made before this congregation
and the parson has promised to give us his blessing. The wedding will take place in September—if no one has any objection."

Oda shudders at the very thought. When the parson has
given his blessing and no one has raised an objection, she seems
relieved, looks up at Santos. Their eyes meet and they beam at
each other. And then the inconceivable happens. One or two
members of the congregation stand up. Suddenly everyone is on
their feet, applauding. Oda blushes from the roots of her hair
to the tips of her toes, where they peek out from under her
gown.

It is enough to make one cringe with embarrassment. Luck-
ily the applause dies away; someone has thought better of it—
one doesn't clap in church.

The sexton throws open the door. Pew by pew the congre-
gants meet in the aisle and start to file out. The four swans at
the foot of the nave are the first to leave; nodding under their
snowy wimples, they talk to one another in Latin, eagerly dis-
secting the ritual of the holy transfiguration. Behind them
comes the congregation. Gradually the church empties. No one
says a word, but in their silence they harbor a wonder that will
be remembered in these parts for as long as memory lives.

Outside stands the gravedigger, cap in hand, looking agi-
tated. He points from the hilltop toward the horizon, where the
tornado can still be seen. Like a gyrating column, out where the
sky and the sea become one.

Ashes and roses, what a tango for angels! The bride leads as
we speed like the wind across the sea, lunging at one another as

we did when our love was new. The wave crests dance: first we are up, then we are down. She dips my feet in the foam and vibrates the skin of the shaman drum—how it thrills! She keeps a tight rein on me in her amulet harness—Aviaja, who tames the elements, tames her lover with the same power.

My backbone is her rattle; she washes me in rogue waves and my gnashers chatter: *castanets* is the word. Ethereal spirits have no place in this world—only the flesh dances the flamenco. Soon I have crept under the skin, where the body is drained of all juices, and you crawl out the other side, a powerless skeleton, stripped of everything. They say that the tears of the living bind us to the earth—in which case, no one should be allowed to get away with bewailing their dead.

I do not know how long we go on like this, forming a tupilak together, before the tornado starts to disintegrate and the ashes fall. The vortex stops spinning, we are no longer whirling but drifting—in long sweeps—down over the waves. Yet again I find myself reaching out vainly and feel a beloved woman slip through my fingers.

It is as I am on my way down that I see the kayak.

High in my clear sky I freeze: the flimsy craft has capsized and is floating bottom up. Malte is nowhere to be seen. The squall caught him unawares. I have the feeling that I am to blame—because I wanted him to stay in the sparkling sunlight and to make time stand still, so that he would never grow any older than the boy I was back then, when my happiness overturned and sent me to the bottom. Under the laws by which we are governed, interfering in the fate of human beings is forbidden.

Clouds drift between him and me. They break up into wisps as I glide farther down. I can see an arm now. He is struggling to right the kayak as he has been taught. But he is struggling in vain, his strength is failing. His nails score the hide, his hand gives a last twitch as it loses its grip and his arm sinks into the sea.

The kayak revolves in the current and the waves wash over it. Soon he will be tape grass and seaweed, and eels nibbling at an eyelid, picking at his frontal lobe. One of these days he will float ashore, bloated, tinged blue, and stippled with cold from head to toe. A dog will sniff at him, the foxes tug at his hand.

I disrupt the pattern, gainsay my own motto; for the first time during this visitation I take the liberty of spreading my wings. Like the elf from a long time ago, I dive to rescue my only friend. On impact I fold my wings and slice through the splash in a galaxy of bubbles. I can see his form on the bottom, eyes wide open, hair trailing as he bobs, limp-limbed, over stones and fluted sand.

Malte is drowned. It is already too late, the boy's heart no longer beats and a deathly hush rises from his hair roots with the bubbles.

It is then that I overstep the mark. I grab hold of his ankles. I push off from the bottom, dragging him backwards out of the sea with saltwater and mucus gushing from his mouth. I shake him, thump him between the shoulder blades, and blow the breath of life into him, fill his lungs with air and press him flat again. I turn him upside down and pound and pound. It feels like an eternity before he starts to wheeze and throw up of his own accord. I tuck him under my arm and fly toward land with steady beats of my wings.

Beneath us, a wreath of flowers floats around the kayak.

When we land on the veranda the boy is still unconscious, but he is breathing. The air with which I have filled him ripples between us in an iridescent haze, and if we were not before, then we are now luminous beings. I lug out the cushions, wrap him in rugs, and gently lower him into the deck chair. Finally, I pull a corner of rug over his head so that he looks like a sleeping monk. Then I stand for a minute, shaking my head.

Our hours together are almost over. No one can stop the passage of time. I see that now. Soon he will be returning to the town and I dread to think what will happen to him. Oh, Malte, you cannot stay a summer boy forever.

He moans in his sleep. I reach out and stroke his hand. It is cold as water. He squirms restlessly in the deck chair, his head falls to one side. He is coming out of the nightmare, but it has left its mark. It is no big thing to save a life; most lives are frittered away afterwards anyway, through everyday neglect. For a long time after this, he will wake, his sheets soaked with sweat, each time the water closes over his head and his lungs start to strain. I mop his brow with my sleeve.

As his angel, I watch over Malte until he opens his eyes. Then—presto!—I'm in my chair, cap tipped to the back of my head, eyes fixed on my feet, and toes waggling. As I settle back, the feathers rustle around my shoulders, then merge with the pattern on the cushion cover, and I look like any other summer visitor.

He gazes at me in bewilderment, eyes darting back and forth. He has no recollection of what happened. I have erased any trace from his memory.

"Who are you?" he asks.

27

IN WHICH
THE JOURNEY
CONTINUES

He looks me up and down, a bit green about the gills. He has had a fit of shivering while he was out for the count; I have stripped him and hung his wet clothes to dry over the rail. He is naked underneath the rugs. He sneezes with the beginnings of a fever, cheeks and eyes already burning. His teeth chatter. I place a hand on his brow. Not, as he thinks, to feel how hot he is. A hefty sneeze dislodges my hand. I rap my ring against the arm of the chair.

"Did you know that passengers sit all day long in just this sort of chair on the sun-decks of the big liners as they plow across the Atlantic?"

He nods. His brow is still furrowed, as if there is something he has forgotten. He eyes me suspiciously.

"Are you staying here?"

There he has me stumped. All the rooms at Sea View are already taken. But we're not about to let a petty detail like that come between us. Soon I have him where I had him before. This boy is insatiable. A glutton for stories.

We revisit the white town in the jungle where the huts stand on stilts on the mud flats that run down to the river. In contrast, the mansions of the wealthy surround the square, where the walls dazzle the eyes and bells ring out from open-sided towers. There are cathedrals here from colonial times, an opera house built by the rubber barons that has stood empty since its grand opening. I tell him how they laid rubber under the paving stones to muffle the sound of the carriages when the stars of the Vienna Opera came to sing. They were so rich that for a while it was the fashion among the ladies of the town to dispatch their laundry to Paris by oceangoing steamer and horse-drawn cab.

A snap of the fingers and we are there. In the square at Iquitos, where a platoon of soldiers has trooped out of the garrison at sunset to lower the national flag. The bugler sounds the fanfare. The officer stands with lowered saber while a couple of privates in high-crowned caps trimmed with gold braid fold the flag. Afterwards we saunter up and down among the rugs on which the Indians have set out every imaginable sort of herb, as well as dried llama embryos and an enormous lizard that has had its front legs tied together and its mouth sewn shut to keep it from snapping at the hand that puts it in the pot.

There are women in bowler hats and men who look like butterflies. We stop beside a blind harpist. Standing next to him, beating on a leather drum, is an Indian wearing a poncho adorned with the designs of his village in the mountains. The blind man sings in a cracked voice and the strings sound like steel wire strung across a box of nails.

The song is simple and deep. We drop some money into his upturned hat. A hummingbird flies out of the crown, in which it has built its nest—that is how long it has been since anyone tossed a few coins after his song. The bird hangs whirring in the last rays of the sun, just level with Malte's nose, and he sneezes pollen and gets nectar up his nose.

I buy him a flute carved from the thighbone of a condor, and a drum that looks like an ant's egg. We put up at an inn with no rooms. The beds are hammocks slung up in the open courtyard under the stars, because the night is warm. The next day we travel on.

I make him thrill by killing a man, a half-breed scoundrel with a hawk nose who draws a knife on me on the next stage of the steamer trip and who is tipped over the side to join the piranhas, after scarring my face.

I lift my chin and point to the scar.

"Did you shoot him?" he asks hopefully. I shrug my shoulders, which only serves to increase his awe. Malte will never know what I did, but it was a bloody business, that's all I'll say. Afterwards, my hands stank of raw meat and the smell would not wash off.

The boy tugs at my sleeve; I have fallen into the pot. The cannibals of Borneo boil my skull and place it in the niche dedicated to their forefathers.

"What's your name?"

"Wouldn't you like to know!"

I chuck him under the chin; he pulls his head back.

"Stop that!"

Rhymes and riddles drive children crazy. I tease him a little more. "My name is Riddle-me-ree, dig down deep and you will see . . ."

"That doesn't make sense," he points out dryly.

He looks me up and down. Same suspicious look as before. "Can I see your pistol?"

I give him my knife. Show him the catch to press to make the stiletto spring out. He masters the trick to perfection. The sun is coming back into its own again; it sends flashes of light glancing off the double-edged knife.

"Keep it," I say when he hands it back to me with an odd

elasticity in his arm. And we are friends again. Children are easy—you just have to handle them right.

"Is it true that you've sailed all the way around the world?"

"You bet I have."

"Do you know the doctor?"

"Well, somewhat . . ."

"He has a Model T. He's promised to take me for a ride in it."

He shaves a sliver off the arm of the chair. The knife slips and he cuts his thumb and sticks it in his mouth. We pass the next half hour very pleasantly in each other's company while he sucks the blood. Coffee and cake are being served at the parsonage and the guest-house contingent has not yet returned. We have the whole place to ourselves.

He hears about the lighthouse on Dundra Head, about Krakatoa, which blew sky-high with a bang that could be heard as far away as Alice Springs in the center of Australia. The Strait was shrouded in darkness for days while the volcanic ash drifted down, turning day to night and summer to winter as the cloud hid both sun and moon. The tidal wave that followed hurled the hulls of ships and dolphins, boiled pink, deep into the Sumatra hinterland, and the natives in the villages danced torch dances and walked over glowing coals because at long last they had been granted a share of the cargo pickings.

Malte yawns. He has stopped shaking and is drowsy with fever. While the drums rage on through the tropical night, he takes a nap and I lapse into memories that dance barefoot on a basket of coals . . .

We had passed through the roaring forties, rounded Cape Horn, and swept up the coast of Chile without once going ashore. Not until Callao did I leave the ship to travel alone into the heart of Peru. When I returned from my trip along the rivers of the Amazon basin, a letter was waiting for me at the agent's office. It was from the company at home; forwarded from one port to another, it had taken six months to reach me.

I learned that the Amber King had been a cripple since the ramming of the jetty and his plunge into the cold water. Confined to a wheelchair, he was being looked after by Aviaja. I found a suitable dive in the alley, chucked the letter into the toilet—to hell with it—and drowned its words in piss. I rejoined the crew and the *Narwhal* sailed on its way. We departed Callao, bound for the Galapagos Islands, where turtle shells and sea lions are swept along in the cool Humboldt Stream and, from the deck, billions of anchovies can be seen turning in a single flash that lights up the waves.

I am left to cross the Pacific Ocean alone.

The shimmering coral reefs were one thing, the ship—which ran low on provisions and fresh water several times along the way—was something else again. In Siam I visited a whorehouse—everybody did—but the girls' moon faces only reminded me of Aviaja and I left the place with my tail between my legs. How can I put it: the overture was interesting, but not the performance.

Malte does not wake until we reach Shanghai. After we have visited the fakir, I take him to see the square where row upon row of executioners lift the pigtails of the condemned and bring the sword swishing down. As if on command, they let go of the plaits and only then do the heads roll. Earthenware pots are set out to collect the blood; fragments of discarded craniums and shards of pottery have built up into a charnel mound. The condemned are carried to this spot, bound hand and foot in baskets. Around their necks hang signs proclaiming their crimes.

He comes with me to India, where the pyres blaze along the Ganges, the dead sizzle in butter and evaporate, while the smoke of immolated widows spirals upwards and the professional mourners keen. Now he has seen as much of the world as I have—and is ready to take even worse.

"How do you like your blue-eyed boy, Mister Death?" I hum when he has dozed off once more.

He came aboard at Cape Town, where we had called to take on provisions—the man with the skin that had been seared off in great white continents and islands, making him look like a fabulous sea chart himself. A whaler, he had been swallowed by a sperm whale, and when his mates hacked off the blubber and cut up the whale, they found him in the digestive tract, still alive but scarred for life by his dip in acid.

With him he brought on board a macabre piece of luggage, a coffin of crafted mahogany; the minute he set foot on deck the men started muttering under their breath. But he had promised to pay well and I was glad of the company, isolated as I had been since the start of the voyage. I had not one friend on board; they all avoided me like the plague.

Elton Jones, he called himself. Each evening he joined me as my guest in the aft cabin and we took our meals together. He told me his story, one that had made him a legend. He bore the proof of it on his skin: he unbuttoned his shirt and showed me the quarter of the tattoo of a full-rigger that was left on his chest. The rest had been eaten away. Snow-white blotches marked his face.

Word had spread around the ship that he slept in the coffin during the day and only came out after sunset. Superstitious hogwash. Granted, he kept his door locked during the day, but I had heard him moving around in his cabin, which had no porthole. The truth of the matter was that he could not stand the sun's brand on his skin. But rumor is a stubborn bastard once it gets its teeth into something. And in any case, he helped himself to whatever was served up, the wine had never turned to blood in his glass, and there were no fewer rats in the hold.

One evening—between the sauterne and the cognac—he warned me against my own crew. There was mutiny in the air. Old salt that he was, he knew what he was talking about. I made light of it, took his word for it—and so what? He struck me as a gentleman, driven by the same death wish as I.

That day he had spent in the gullet of the whale had been enough to provide him with a glimpse of another world. Why else did he carry his coffin about with him? He was no undertaker, that was certain, and I greatly enjoyed our talks. As the Eskimos say, "Hang a man by his neck and cut him down when his face turns blue—then ask him if he had a vision!" That is the sort of thing we had a good laugh over.

We sailed on with Africa to starboard. On the Gold Coast we went ashore and loaded up with ivory. We took on fresh water at the Canary Isles and filled the storeroom with barrels and sacks, smoked hams and sauerkraut. For the third year running, I had sailed the oceans and found no peace. And perhaps it was dawning on me that this was no way to grow old— I would be thirty soon. I considered my next move. Then I set course for Iceland. The crew members were up in arms. They had been hoping to be home for Christmas.

For a man born with four seasons in his blood it was a relief to be back in the Northern Hemisphere. The choppy seas, the changes in the weather. The sky is never as blue as after a cloudburst. Once again I stood on the bridge in sou'wester and gum boots. The winds were kind to me, carrying me to Aviaja's land, the land of the real people. The old whaler was the only one who knew my secret. The fjord where she had been born had begun to shine in my dreams at night as the ultimate goal of the voyage.

At Reykjavik Mr. Jones disappeared like the morning dew. One day he was simply no longer there. Not a word of farewell, not a red cent paid. The cabin had been cleaned and put to rights. As a last gesture, he had left the coffin behind. When I lifted the lid I found the payment for his passage scattered across the upholstered lining in good English pounds. At the foot lay a letter.

"I, Elton Jones, indigestible to the bone, hereby consign myself to the devil, also known as Lucifer, on the following condition: if he is able to share my uncommonly hard bed, then let the pact be sealed. If he is not, then I request that I be made his second in command when we rise up together to overthrow God and all his gang."

I tipped my finger to my cap, already missing the old joker. The crew was horrified and demanded that the coffin be jettisoned. I kept my souvenir; you have to look death in the eye— that is something we had often talked about. Some of the crew jumped ship. The hard nuts stayed on.

We headed into the Denmark Strait. The *Narwhal* was bound for Kulusuk. We were traveling with the current; it was as if the ship were finding her own way. When I unrolled the chart, the first thing I saw was the ring I had once drawn around the village. At the time my intention had been to make Aviaja's dream come true—now the dream was all I had. It was bitterly cold sailing, and it was not long before the first icebergs appeared on the horizon.

The mutiny was on me before I knew it.

28

IN WHICH
THE SPIRIT TAKES
HIS REVENGE

At midsummer, after the long famine of winter, we lay at anchor in Ammassalik Fjord. The waters of the fjord and the hills conspired to create a fantastic archipelago, with Kulusuk as one of the smaller islands. When I ran across the legend of the orphan girl I knew right away that I had traced Aviaja's origins. She came from a place that was later known as Death Camp, because the survivors there had eaten the bodies of the dead. Several years running, winter followed winter, the summer never showed its face, and the animals disappeared. The sun never gained ascendancy, the pale spring moon took on the color of yellowed blubber. They ate the dogs, then they gnawed the hide of the kayaks. And only then did they turn to the dead.

According to the legend, there was a woman named Naligateq, also known as Lung Eater. She had a bad reputation, chased other women's men. Even the most powerful shamans feared her; she led them on with dancing and drumming and monkeying around, and if they so much as smiled she threw herself at them, ripping their chests open to eat their lungs and intestines raw—only the man in the moon had the power to put them back. Woe betide the man who happened to cross her path, for it was hard not to laugh. When she danced, the witch showed her crotch, and between her legs she had what looked like a dog's—or was it a sea dog's?—head. If you drank from her whale-oil lamp the face of the moon would grow dark and you would never see the new sun.

When she gave birth to a daughter at Death Camp no one knew who the man was and muck was heaped on the fatherless child. One winter passed, then two more, before the witch rose up to the spirit world.

But among her toys the little girl had a tupilak, a seal-pup skull tied to the ribcage of the bird they call the sea king. She sucked on the ribcage, drew strength from it, and did not notice the screaming in her gut. The time came when she could stand and walk, and one day the man in the moon came and carried her to the bottom of the sea in a kayak pulled by swimming birds: sea kings and fulmars, the wind's helpers. After that she was known as Crookmouth, sister to the wind and the moon, and gained a reputation for being a witch herself.

Now, it so happened that all the filth that the people had thrown into the sea piled up on top of the Mother of All the Oceans—as head lice, as vermin. So she kept the animals away and the villages were stricken by famine. Not until the day when they stopped what they were doing or a shaman cleaned out her house would the seas run clear again and muck and vermin stream from her and turn back into animals for the people to hunt.

It took me two seconds to decipher the myth: Lung Eater was Aviaja's mother and the sea dog between her legs was an old friend: Ejnarsen.

I went to my crew and demanded that we up anchor right then and there. They had got themselves women on shore. They complained, but I had my will, and mine was stronger than theirs. When legend and landscape speak the same language, it is the man with the ear for it who listens. I fly across the mountains: farther north, up to the midnight sun, it sings inside me.

For the first time on the voyage, the venture began to make sense. Everything that lay hidden inside Aviaja was to be found here. I pursued this thought like one possessed, could not rest until I had found the village where she had been born. I had been told to look for places where the hunters had pitched tents, for a grass hut on the hillside, well disguised by its own turf, for a couple of flints used to build a fireplace and blackened with soot, for graves covered with rocks to stop bears and wolves from getting at them.

It was no use showing these people maps. They laughed at our flat planes and squares, longitude and latitude. They carried the landscape inside them, written into stories by which they could always find their way. If I inquired as to compass bearings I was given the color of moss and lichen. A mountain that swelled upward in curves that were the cause of much hilarity was as good as a lighthouse at sea. Depending on the season, the fjords were either passable or not, the game alone dictated whether there was any point in moving on. And only fools set out on expeditions that were but an end in themselves.

After the first day and night at sea I spotted narwhals. They swam off the bow of their namesake, two big males with tusks that curled counterclockwise. I tucked this sign away in my heart. With the first mate's assistance, I navigated according to a chart I had found in Ejnarsen's drawer. I knew that the *Narwhal* had been here before and all the routes ended in a fjord on the Blosseville coast. I aimed for there. In places the inland ice stood several hundred meters high; below it the landscape had been laid bare by summer, plains dotted with yellow poppies, saxifrage, and pole stars. Nunataks reared up, and farther in we could see herds of musk ox, like brown wisps galloping across the plain, or gleaming white ribcages and skulls where the snow had melted. In the twilight the ice was edged with blue and transformed by the fog.

We sailed north of the north, as they say up here, crossed the polar circle. Icebergs came floating toward us, their peaks listing, gilded by the midnight sun. Glaciers calved and started to drift, the sound of cracking rang out across the smooth waters of the fjords, and night and day the light never faded. Everything I had ever dreamed of. I stood on the bridge, my heel wedged in Ejnarsen's hole, and contemplated the ice. But the crew sat and smoldered below decks, up forward of the hawsehole and in their quarters.

We came to a steep and stormy coastline. Fuzzy lichen and animal tracks covered the slopes, the earth was reddish brown where the snow had melted. In a hollow, crowberries and wild flowers grew. White tufts of cotton grass and mountain poppies. I found Death Camp deserted; the people had gone south to find food. The fjords froze over and the waterway gradually began to close up again. The summer was short, the light did not linger long here. Still I refused to turn back.

The men were fed sauerkraut morning, noon, and evening; it prevented them from catching scurvy, but I almost regretted that. When you sail with mad dogs in the hold there is no point letting them keep their teeth. We topped up the water supply by melting lumps of ice in the big copper kettle on the foredeck. The galley consisted of a wood-burning stove and a rack for pots and pans. I dreaded to think what would happen when the firewood ran out.

The first sign of life we came across in the wasteland, during one of our forays ashore, was a cairn. When we removed the stones, we found a cache of meat left by hunters. Whole seals—both the hooded and the bearded variety—and a solitary wal-

rus, looking, with its great sad eyes, like a slumbering Saint
Bernard with tusks. The meat was fresh, it might have been
caught yesterday, but it was impossible to tell how long it had
lain there. The arctic air is wonderfully devoid of the corrup-
tion of time. We pulled away a hide to find a bundle of blood
sausages packed in intestines and studded with angelica and
dewberries.

We gloated over the stony grave, a gaunt and wasted band.
Stomachs rumbled, more than one mouth watered. The men
were seized by euphoria; for once here was something they
could get a grip on. The coxswain was the first to drop to his
knees, pulling out his sheath knife. But I stayed his arm before
he could cut himself a slice of the sausage.

I appealed to them, thinking of Aviaja: this cache had been
left as a safeguard against a future famine; we would have to
leave it untouched and manage with what we had on board. It
was true that we could have done with a bit of variation in our
diet, but our need was not that pressing. They grumbled, but
they did as I said. Captain's orders. I stood with one hand on
the butt of my pistol and faced the hate in their eyes.

When we rowed out to the ship in the longboat, the crew
was straining at the leash. I sat on my thwart and held my
peace. Had I bared my throat at that moment they would have
been on me like a flash. Safely back on board, I had the stopper
knocked out of a keg of rum, the last one, and poured alcohol
on troubled minds. What greater challenge could I have given
them? What the hell—let them drink themselves senseless and
beat my brains in! But they merely got drunk as skunks and
carried on, muttering and grumbling in their quarters—until
they fell flat on their faces in pools of vomit.

We had given up keeping track of the nights and days; they
revolved in a circle with the midnight sun, which was starting
to sink, drawing noticeably closer to the horizon. The *Narwhal*

rode at anchor in an inlet, off a glacier shot through with
gashes that gave the ice the look of a tarnished mirror. Crags
reared up around us, providing shelter. The rim of the ice jutted
out over them. Only in the ship's log did I keep a record of the
days. In August the night returned to us. I kept a round-the-
clock watch in my cabin, slept with my pistol under my pillow.
The first snow began to drift off the hills.

Suddenly there they were, Aviaja's kin. They were standing on
the shore, pointing at the ship while the dogs yelped in their
traces. I had the longboat lowered and rowed in to them.
Shortly afterwards I rowed out again—with an invitation for
the crew. Though we did not speak the same language there
was no mistaking their gestures. A finger was bored into my
stomach, tongues were stuck out at me and tips turned upward.
They waved to the men, encompassing the ship with a sweep
of the hand. The meaning was clear enough, that we should
eat until our bellies were bursting and our tongues standing
straight up in our mouths.

By the time we presented ourselves on the ice they had
pitched their tents and darkness had fallen. We sat in the glow
of the whale-oil lamps; chunks of meat were handed around—
narwhal, I think. They ate the skin, prepared as *mattak,* rich in
oil and with a nutty taste to it. Their faces glistened and I saw
the living image of Aviaja—for the first time in ages.

I gulped the meat down for the sustenance it offered, but the
men gagged and spat it out. No nasty looks from our hosts—
they were more than happy to eat it themselves. All in all, the
things we did made the people laugh. The coxswain took his
knife and held a chunk of meat over the oil lamp to roast it. It
filled the tent with smoke and smelled of burnt goat hooves. We

were served roots pickled in blubber and marvelously fermented auk packed into intestines that were tied off at the ends.

I looked at my own people in disgust. One choice morsel after another passed in front of their long faces; they complained loudly about the food, called the East Greenlanders cranky old crones, turned surly themselves, and got it into their heads that someone was trying to poison them. Idiots!

But the feast continued. The food had gone to our hosts' heads; soon they were dancing and beating on drums, sticking bones in their mouths, and pushing out their cheeks. Then they toppled back onto the hides and groped at one another's bare backsides. I had made a friend in the great hunter Kivfak and was beginning to feel like one of the family. Kivfak kept stuffing things into my mouth.

When Aviaja's kin tied his hands behind his back and started to beat their seal-gut drums, I was given my first experience of a shamanic journey. They dragged the bearskin trousers off him and tipped him over so one could see right up his asshole. And as the drumsticks beat and the song did its conjuring, the hole expanded before my eyes, until it had become like a telescope tube. I could see all the way up to the heart; the red muscle throbbed away merrily at the end of the tube while Kivfak ululated wildly. I fell back, laughing, onto the pile of hides.

The festivities were at their height. I had crawled out of the tent to relieve myself. In the polar night, the northern lights stretched in an iridescent span from east to west. The sky rippled with an array of different-colored bands. The sight was breathtaking in itself, but the sound . . . One sensed more than one heard: a deep thrum that seemed to emanate from this backdrop. I pictured the restless souls fluttering about up there. Their lighting effects were extraordinary.

I stood there for a long time, snug and warm inside the fur

anorak I had borrowed from Kivfak. Out of the night a decision was born in my mind. This meeting with Aviaja's kin had
tipped the scales.

When I went back inside and the gut tent flap fell behind
me, I saw that trouble had broken out. The orgy of eating had
given way to drinking—unbeknownst to me, the men had filled
a couple of bottles with rum and brought them ashore. The Eskimos were already out of their skulls, staggering in a daze.

My men were calling the tune now and a new note had been
struck. Their laughter filled the tent like the stench of raw meat.
Kivfak had taken a snuffbox from one of the crew members, I
did not know which, nor did I care. He had smeared his face
with soot and was playing the clown. The sight made my heart
bleed. The gift bestowed by this feast was no longer soaring
spirits but firewater.

One of the women had taken off her anorak. The sight of
her small form in little fur trousers must have inflamed the
coxswain, because he began to paw at her uncontrollably. She
turned her head away, trying to escape his bristly beard and the
liquor on his breath. She was about the same age as Aviaja, and
there was terror in her eyes. Furious, I grabbed him by the collar, pulled him off her, and shook him.

He lashed out at me. I shoved him away. No sooner was he
on his feet again than out sprang the knife. He took a flying
leap at me, locked his arm around my windpipe. Turning his
own weight against him, I tipped him over my head. He landed
on top of Kivfak, who had collapsed into the ashes in the fireplace. Rage turned a somersault in his thick skull, and with
bloodshot eyes he wheeled around and slit Kivfak's stomach
open.

I made quick work of him: a shot to the head and he was
gone, the lead ball boring straight to the bone and embedding
itself there like a blue carbuncle beneath the skin. Next I sent

the cabin boy for the medical kit. I disinfected Kivfak's wound.
It was not as bad as I had first feared. For the second time that
night the shaman was bound up—by the book this time—and
when I was done he opened his eyes. He complained of the pain
and begged for more firewater.

It had gone very quiet in the tent. One by one, my men
walked away from me. They put on their hats and their thick
wool coats, dragged the coxswain out. I heard the sound of the
body being dumped in the boat, heavy as a sack. Alone
with the hunters and their women, I ran my eyes over the
group. There was not a smile on their faces, no one thanked
me. And I realized why. They were party now to an unavenged
killing.

The following day I rowed out to the ship myself, in one
of their kayaks. Tippa, Kivfak's twelve-year-old son, came
with me. As soon as I had climbed aboard he took my kayak
in tow and paddled away—without looking back and without responding to my farewell. He disappeared around the
point.

On the shore I could see that the tents were down and the
dogsleds had already left. The land of the people lay deserted.

The men had gone below deck; their absence hung like a
pall over the ship. The coxswain dangled from the mainmast,
sewn up in canvas. They had taken down the flag and wrapped
him in it, attached weights to his feet. Had it not been for the
red and white Danish colors, he would have looked like an
Egyptian mummy. I wondered for a moment whether we could
have become friends.

Then I took myself off to my cabin and sat down at the
chart table. For the first time in three damned years I turned

over the photograph of Aviaja, propped it up in front of me, and dipped my pen in the ink. At long last I wrote the letter I had carried inside me for so long.

It was an appeal for mercy, banal as love. All I wanted was for us to be together for the rest of our lives; I would even tolerate the Amber King. If she could, so could I. I had seen the northern lights flare and drained the last dregs of meaning from the greatest adventures. Now I was ready. This very day I would turn my kayak around and head for home. The pen exulted in my hand. I did not want to die. I wanted to live, love, bring children into the world . . .

When the letter was finished, I slipped it into an envelope, sealed it with a kiss. I had unburdened my heart. I addressed the envelope in the painstaking script of a schoolboy. Now all I had to do was to muster the crew—it was time to set sail.

The best way to put your enemies to shame is by being big-hearted—that much I had learned in this part of the world. They would be home for Christmas!

Here is how the day ended. I stuck my head out the hatch to summon the men and was hit on the back of the head with a spar. There were shooting flames as the blow struck. I never saw the hand that dealt the blow, nor did I hear the sound as my skull was crushed—my senses were gone before then. I sped down the telescope tube, past the red heart, which was still beating, and out the other side, east of the sun and west of the moon. The kaleidoscope spun in a riot of crystal stars as my body sank into water. A chill crept over the fluid warmth in my veins; in a blinding flash the last and innermost breath escaped from my skull through the hole at the top.

It was not the blow that killed me, it was the icy water into which they heaved me. But before the day was done I showed myself to them again: adrift on an ice floe, crucified to the cold. I lay with arms outstretched, bobbing just short of the cable, my face coated with frost, my eyeballs ruptured. I was a daunting sight for the men on board. They would have preferred to leave me to drift south with the ice field.

The first mate, the most levelheaded of the lot, persuaded the rest to think better of that plan. Bodies that wash ashore with their heads caved in tell tales. The men had the goodness to fish me out again and place me in the coffin. That way they could keep the shipping company off their backs and give me a Christian burial. There would be no protest or inquest.

But it would have taken more than fifteen men had armed with ice axes to bury me in the ground. That would have to wait until they reached warmer climes. The first mate took a last look around, found the letter on the chart table. He had enough brains to burn it. He saw the picture in its frame and was reminded of his sweetheart at home. Sailors are sentimental folk. He picked up the photograph and laid it on my breast along with a posy of flowers. He read a hymn from the book, then they put the lid on and stowed the coffin in the hold, where it sat lashed to the foot of the mast. They made the ship ready and raised the anchor to put out to sea.

Fools! You don't bring a dead seal into a house until three days have passed and the soul has adapted to its new state. Do so and it will take its revenge. Everyone in these parts knows that. And the same goes for humans. Nor do you sail with a corpse in the hold—talk about skeletons in closets! Had they only waited, my soul would have been over the heavenly hills and far away.

So I proceeded to haunt them then and there. Blotted out the sun and whipped up a gale. It swept, howling, down from the north, bringing thick banners of snow, sliced the tops off the waves, and dashed over man and ship in pounding breakers. The coxswain was the first to go. Soon the Danish flag was waving over the seabed.

They had no chance to take in sail—the masts snapped like matchsticks. Only the spanker was left standing. With the men no longer able to maneuver her, the *Narwhal* was soon stuck fast in the ice. And the wind departed as abruptly as it had come. They launched the longboat, evacuated the ship, and carried the provisions ashore.

They made tents out of the sailcloth. Prepared to sit out the winter there. Month after month went by. When the fjords became ice-bound and the men's supplies had been gnawed right down to the last biscuit, they made an attempt at hunting. With no great success. The winter set in from the north and ripped the tents to shreds. They turned the longboat over and sought refuge in the darkness. They collected wood from the ship and warmed themselves by a fire. The matches ran out before the firewood.

The mate was the first to go. He had never been that strong. He was followed by a couple more. Those still alive ran their eyes over their companions, watched for signs of fever and frostbite, woke raving from their sleep. When they grew thirsty they crammed snow and chunks of ice into their mouths—and sucked their way to blisters and sores. They were God-fearing people: they did not violate the taboo of the flesh, they piled rocks on top of their dead. They dug down to the soil and chewed on the grass and roots at the bottom of the holes.

They headed farther inland, all suffering from gangrene, and found the cache untouched.

The final scenes were played out in snow and moonlight. It was almost Christmas. The sun never showed itself above the horizon; darkness reigned. Of the crew, only five were left, the real hard nuts. With rime on their beards and eyebrows and their breath steaming, they threw themselves on the meat cache. Scurvy had loosened their teeth, they were missing fingers and toes—taken by the cold.

With bandaged hands they pushed the rocks aside. They dropped to their knees and roared with joy when they saw the blood sausages tucked in among the animal carcasses. But the meat was iced over, it tinkled like glass. They found themselves staring straight into Paradise; powerless to help themselves, they collapsed in a huddle and cried out to their maker. I did not hear them.

A curse on those who bound me to my last wish. It froze into an awl in the medulla as the glacier rocked the hull and an avalanche buried the ship from stem to stern. I felt the ribs and planks creak, a cold hitherto unknown settled over my resting place, and the wreck was wedged in place.

Frozen deep, I lay there, stiff in my mantle of time and ice.

Late in the summer the hunters returned. They were looking for the ship, with its great wealth of iron. They had held onto the memory: four times a bird dart had to be thrown to measure the length; the bowsprit alone was as long as a kayak. With the bony tip of the paddle and one's body half out of the manhole, one could just reach up and touch the rail.

Kivfak hopped off the sled and strutted about like a gentleman in the boatswain's high hat. The whole place was quiet and deserted, with only the waves swelling up and rolling in toward the ice, their crests sparkling. He sniffed the air and shot a glance at his dogs, which were straining at their harness and whining, tails in the air.

They found the longboat and the mounded graves at the head of the little inlet. The ship was gone, but the glacier had grown, and it lay there with rosy sunlight playing over its crevices.

Kivfak, who had the power to invoke the mountain spirits,

began to throw stones in the water. The scar on his belly con-
tracted. He fell to the ground, yelling and screaming, his limbs
seized by cramp. His son leapt to his side and performed a
dance of celebration. From this day on, no one would starve,
because his father had found a new and more powerful helper.

29

IN WHICH
CRACKS APPEAR
IN THE ICE

The balmy August evening has descended on the veranda. The
sun hangs on the horizon and never sets; the twilight is a long
time coming. Down on the shoreline the pebbles rattle with the
water's movement and the swallows are flying high once more
over the thatched roof. Malte is sunk in feverish slumber and
tosses restlessly in the deck chair when Oda comes out to take
in the cushions. They should have been taken in before
church—she must have forgotten. She shakes her head at herself.

She has been picking wild asters in the meadow. Her stomach has grown noticeably rounder. She does not bustle about
the way she used to, but takes her time as the summer wanes.
Soon the season will be over, the guest house will close, and
everyone will go their separate ways. What is to become of
Malte then?

She brushes the thought away with a fly. Every time she
thinks of the proclamation in the church she hears a wedding
waltz in her ears. They have one secret left to them—no, not

that, the baby is there for everyone to see, and she is never going to hear the last of it. But she has given notice! They are
leaving for Peru! They have secured berths on a cargo steamer
sailing across the Atlantic. Paid for out of her savings. Of
course, Santos will be working in the galley, but they will also
need something to live on once they get there.

She catches sight of the boy's clothes draped over the rail,
goes over to feel them. They are still wet. Then she sees him,
half buried in rugs. She puts out a hand and strokes his cheek
with her finger. He is burning hot. She wakes him gently as she
can; even so, he starts up and looks about him in bewilderment.
The knife slides from his lap onto the veranda floor.

"What have you been up to this time?"

Malte picks up the knife. She notices that he is naked. He
does not and is quick to answer: "Nothing!"

But he is not himself at all. His eyes wander and his cheeks
are aflame. Well, she is pretty much used to that by now. She
merely sighs, while Malte looks this way and that, his eye coming to rest on the empty chair.

"Where's the man?"

"What man?"

"The doctor."

"The doctor's at the parsonage with everybody else."

"He put his hand on my forehead."

"Who are you talking about, Malte?"

"The man. The one who we all dressed up."

"You must have dreamt it. There's nobody here. Oh, you
should have been in church. It went just fine, thank heavens
for that. The parson called me a songbird for the Lord and
people said such nice things about Santos's music. They
were quite carried away. And now there's going to be a dinner
in the village hall and—guess what, Malte—I'm not going
to wait at the table, I'm to sit down with everyone else! I have

to get changed. You need to help me, I don't know what I'm going to wear."

She smooths the white gown. Giggles.

"You look fine as you are. Like an angel."

"You'd better see about getting into some clothes yourself. Before you catch your death. You're running a temperature, that much I can see."

"Can I lie on the sofa?"

Oda nods. Malte wraps himself in one of the rugs. So tightly that he has to hop. They are about to make their way downstairs when Oda stops. Malte is tripping over himself in his attempts to hold the rug closed and keep his treasure clenched in his fist.

"What have you got there?"

Malte shows her the knife, flicking out the blade and making her start. He looks almost radiant.

"That man gave me it."

"Oh, sure, Malte."

Before they leave the veranda, Oda stops to gather up the cushions, gives Malte's a shake; its floral-print cover has been faded by the summer sun. The light falls through the balustrade, creating a pattern of brightly colored prisms on the other cushion. She holds them both out, frowns.

"Did we get new cushions?"

They disappear from view. The treads reverberate with every hop that Malte takes. I pray that he reaches the bottom before he takes a tumble. In no time a bed has been made up for him on the sofa in the captain's saloon; he will have rosehip soup and velvety gruel for supper, and Oda will show off her dress, like Cinderella going to the ball at the prince's palace.

I am left alone with the flotsam of my thoughts. It is not true that angels have white wings. Our feathers are all the colors of the rainbow, a fact that was known to the icon painters

of the Middle Ages, although this knowledge has since been
lost.

I have landed on a shelf containing naphthalene bags, a
thing we cannot abide. I climb out of the cupboard, rustle the
plumage at my back—it sounds like a swan—and return to the
deck chair to enjoy the last rays of the evening sun. When I
open my eyes again it is dark, I am somewhere off the Newfoundland coast, the stars shine bright over the Atlantic, and I
can hear the propellers of a ship murmuring its way through
the night.

The transatlantic liner is on its maiden voyage. It is a bitterly
cold April night, just before midnight. The sea is like a mirror,
the darkness arching high above, clear and starry. There is a
new moon—the slenderest sickle of light in the heavens and not
a cloud in sight.

The floating palace forges ahead at a speed of twenty-two
knots; holding steady on her course, she slices through the
waves. Directly ahead, the skyline is suddenly broken by an iceberg gliding through the night, a blue light on its jagged edges
and dripping hollows, and a darker outline at the heart, where
cracks are appearing in the ice.

In the smoking saloon, with its mirrors and stained glass
and roomy armchairs, the gentlemen are playing cards. In the
palm court the tables have been cleared; the murals on the
walls are art nouveau. This colossus is fitted out with staircases,
marble pillars, and bronze figurines holding luminous globes. It
has Turkish baths, a gymnasium, and tennis courts. Plaster ceiling roses and heavy velvet curtains.

The dinner menu was first-class. Most of the passengers
have turned in for the night. Very few feel the bump; it runs

through the hull below the waterline. A little plaster sifts down from the ballroom ceiling, and only in the engine room, a couple of meters above the keelson, does a siren sound and the red lights come on as the water starts to pour in.

Most of the passengers are woken by the silence when the propellers stop turning.

I did not wake when the glacier calved, nor did I wake to the hooting of the foghorn. I woke to the sound of marbles running over the iron hull of a ship. A collision that ran like an almighty tremor through the ice and shook me to the depths of my crystal structure. A hundred years had flown by; I woke in a fairy-tale palace and saw that time had slipped some way into the next century.

I was born in 1812, spent the last seventy years encased in the ice, young and well-preserved, while Aviaja grew old. I am one hundred years and fifteen days old, no age at all for an angel. They always talk about the ship that sank, never about the myriad of crystalline forms that shattered and hailed down on the deck like broken glass.

A hissing sound spreads throughout the vessel: the boilers, releasing steam. It is like locomotives being driven into platforms in the bowels of the ship. I think of a whale I once saw spouting, shot in the heart by a harpoon. The jet shot out of the blowhole in a bloody fountain.

As yet I lie stiff as a board on the padded lining. But above my head things are moving fast and cracks are appearing all over the crystal palace.

At a quarter past midnight the first distress signal clicks out of the wireless room.

On the boat deck the crew get ready to man the lifeboats,

remove the tarpaulins, hammer away the chocks, and swing the boats out on the davits. They are lowered from the starboard side, women and children first. There is no great panic. Most of the boats enter the water with far too few people in them. No one ever thinks it is serious when disaster strikes them.

The dance band is roused. The French cellist drags his instrument up from the cabin decks, across the upper deck, the end pin of the cello tapping over the planks, and into the saloon, where the band members take their positions, every last one of them. They play in their life jackets, which is awkward, particularly for the strings, who keep missing the beat. They play ragtime. A few couples dance—nearer to God than to each other.

All the lamps are lit, lights blaze in the resplendent rows of portholes, in the saloons, and in the promenade room with its panorama windows. The engineers keep the generators running to save the power from cutting out. The stokers are wading up to their knees in water. Then at last that enervating hiss stops: the boilers have run out of steam. A new hush descends. A distress rocket shoots into the air from the foredeck and showers the ship with a rain of stars. The party is only just beginning. There are some hours yet to go before the end.

A little before two o'clock the ship lists ominously. Her nose is starting to dip. Tableware slides out of cupboards and off shelves, tidal waves of porcelain and silverware, glass and champagne bottles spill onto the deck. Furniture bobs about in the cabins. Deck chairs and barrels from the sundeck tumble down over the heads of the seamen. The engine-room telegraph clickety-clicks for the last time: "Signing off." The crew have done their duty, the crew are at liberty to leave.

Only fifteen minutes later the ship groans from a blow that sends a tremor through the hull. It spins on its axis. The forebody vanishes into the depths, the stern thrusts upwards. The three propellers are exposed to the night as the water streams off them in cascades of phosphorus. The great shift triggers a wave that washes the first passengers overboard. The water is terrifyingly cold and pierces their skin like awls of ice. The electric bulbs shine more faintly and take on a reddish glow that turns to green as the light slips below the waves and is transformed into pillars of phosphorescence.

Minutes later the stern is standing straight up, 150 feet in the air, and its momentum is not to be checked. Those on board—and most still are—cling to the flagpole on the afterdeck, hang onto the frames of hatchways and to portholes, see floors become walls—or decks become bulkheads, as they say at sea.

They dangle by their fingernails and toes, are shaken off or are sucked into the vacuum that has formed inside the ship. By the dozens and scores they plunge into the water, dragging others with them in their fall. The funnels, tall as eight-story buildings, topple when the backstays snap. The standing rigging is wrenched loose, massive chunks of metal come crashing through the hull, smashing the bulkheads. "Like a ton weight being hurled into the depths of a vault," as survivors were later to describe it.

Inside the ship, one group is hit by the grand piano when the floor of the smoking saloon tips and the piano slides toward a stained-glass panel showing a sailing ship. The panel explodes in a shower of glass and sends brightly colored fragments raining down on the lid as the piano is brought up short by the wood paneling. The lights do not go out until the boilers and engines come adrift, to be followed by an exhalation of hot air.

Over two thousand souls are on board, including crew. Of these, more than fifteen hundred are crushed like eggshells in the galley. Talk about fireworks!

From my time as an elf I remember how the smallest fliers'

brains shine like fireflies in the dark. I saw it for myself when I hung suspended and dead in the lump of resin. But that is nothing compared with the souls that shoot into the air that night. Wailing and whistling all around me—with life preservers as launching pads.

Never—neither before nor since—have I seen such a burst of angels. Auras explode in the heavens, in delicate pink, venomous green, delft blue, tourmaline, and topaz. They stream down over the firmament, hang in clusters of smoke after their ascension. Some thinned down to watercolors, others mixed with oil or egg, all according to the substance of the soul.

The entire spectrum bursts asunder. From raucous red and ice blue to the red-gold of the Buddha. Each and every one with its own luster. Following straight paths and crooked paths, each ascent unique, soaring upwards on the tails of the others' sparks. There is also the occasional dud, but only among the sanctimonious. Give me firecrackers, Roman candles, and sparklers any day.

It is death's greatest night in my new life. I am utterly at the mercy of the solar wind, flitting about the atmosphere on magnetic waves to greet my brothers and sisters in light. At the time I knew no better . . .

All secrets are now mine; I hear the music of a thousand sunken grand pianos, I see a ship with a hundred masts, fifty cathedrals have drifted past, their stained-glass windows shattered. I wake to the white day on the mountain that is loftier than ever before. What do you want with the name of God? Does the sea remember the names of its drowned?

The ice is long gone by the time the terrified screams of the dying begin.

I have not yet used my last wish. I sail inside my crystal, rocked under towers of glass whose windows catch the sun's fire. The winds guide me; the heart of the stream, which lies deep in the Mexican Gulf, puts me into orbit. I have left the Denmark Strait, taken my leave of Cape Farewell, passed Newfoundland, where the collision occurred, and drifted with the current until I am north of the Shetlands.

Meanwhile, the ice melts, growing clearer and clearer, and the ship comes to light once more. I live through it, reflection by reflection. Not until the North Sea, just out from Bergen Fjord, does the iceberg dissolve and set the wreck free. I hear a propeller in the water—a coaster driven by the steam engine of a new age—and feel my last vessel loose itself from the heel of the mast.

The wood is dark with age, but no one sees it, because the fractures are still fresh. Nails work their way out, ribs and planks part company. For a few seconds, the hulk remains in one piece, then it is nothing but flotsam and jetsam dancing on the waves. The nameboard floats off, flanked by pennants. Shaving brushes, bowls, and the contents of drawers bob to the surface; the compass, the telescope, and the mirror sink to the bottom.

Last of all, my wish melts. Like a sea butterfly, the icicle sits in the medulla. In the end it thaws and sweeps me and my longing for Aviaja farther into Skagerrak. It is here that I hear the foghorn and wash up one day on the shore, where I am seen by a boy.

30

IN WHICH
IT SNOWS

Now you know more than you did at the start.

I see a boy. The day before the day when the guest house closes. I see Malte. He is walking into the backyard with Ida. Ida is talking—she has been doing that for a while, but only when they are alone. They are all dressed up because they have just been to a wedding at the church. The grown-ups are celebrating at Sea View. Half the parish seems to be there.

Clear September air blows over the poplars; where the elderflower umbrellas hung in the spring, looking like wedding bouquets, there are now red berries. In the hazel bushes the nuts have ripened, and spotted woodpeckers flock in the willow hedge. The ground is colored by the first clumps of mushrooms. Malte and Ida have seen the cranes fly south and the swifts soaring high in the sky.

They are about to crawl into the den when Malte spots the shoot of a tree for which he has no name. It has broken through the topsoil, still green. The seed leaf's dart is starting to unfold. He stops. Ida stumbles into his heel, he turns and shushes her, while the images from the summer pass in review. Something is beginning to dawn on him.

He wastes no time digging, tugs the shoot out, root and all. He clears the earth away and calls Ida to come. The shoebox lid gleams up at them brightly. Both get down on their knees. When they take an end each and try to pry the box up, the cardboard crumbles away in soggy flakes. Ida wipes her fingers on her princess dress and Malte scolds her.

Then he dips his hand into the cotton with which he lined the box before burying it. The first thing he brings up is the cap. He knocks it against his thigh to get the dirt off, rubs the anchor with his cuff, spits on the gold braid, and polishes it until it shines again. Then he turns the cap over and stares at the inside of the crown. His thoughts drift.

His name wasn't Riddle-me-ree at all. Because it's here, written on a tag sewn into the sweatband. For a moment he is lost in thought. His eyes mist over. Then the light dawns and spreads across his face. He hooks a fingernail under the tag and reads to Ida, with no great surprise: *Jonathan Bertelsen.* Everything comes to light, the photograph in its frame last of all. They brush the earth off my darling's picture. Ida sounds out the words written across it, her tongue still a bit stiff:

"Yours forever, Avi-aja."

I doze off for a moment in the chair; when I wake, Oda is halfway across the Atlantic. The first stars of the evening have appeared in the night air that has grown warmer day by day. Just think, at home the October storms are blowing now, and here she stands on the quarterdeck, wearing only a coat, no shawl, and a cloche hat around whose brim her hair curls. She has had it cut. She draws her coat across her stomach, leans

over the rail. The line of the wake churns up phosphorescence
from the water and trails a luminous comet tail of green sparks
behind the steamer.

With every mile they put behind them her expectations of
the New World grow. Santos has been the soul of attentiveness,
supporting her when the ship rolls, patting her brow when sea-
sickness occasionally gets the better of her. Every free moment
he has he babbles on about the white town in the jungle where
he was born—and where she, if all goes well, will give birth.
There are a good two months of her pregnancy left to go, but it
is as if the fetus did not have a soul until after the wedding. A
silly thought and she has not dared to voice it.

Santos does the washing up in the ship's galley, where he has
been given the job of cook's mate. She, on the other hand, does
not have to lift a finger; she whiles away the days on the sundeck, eats well, and tends to her big belly. The baby kicks like a
grumpy little foot soldier!

I blink. The summer night's dream is over.

It is winter in Kikhavn. Sea fog drifts over the dunes, frost
has settled on sand and field. The meadow has turned to glass;
not a breath stirs and the lyme grass is still. The thatched roof
is decked with lace. Sea View is dark and silent. Curtains are
drawn across the windows and the door is boarded up.

I go downstairs. In the dining room a sheet has been draped
over the piano, the chairs are stacked in a corner, and the windowsills are bare of potted plants. The frost gathers in swags in
the corners of the windowpanes. A screen has been placed in
front of the fireplace and the log basket is empty. Were I to
breathe, you would see the cloud in front of my mouth. I shiver
and pass into the captain's saloon, where everything is as it

was—except that the desk has been cleared and there are no bills on Mrs. Swan's spike.

I place my hand on the iron crown on the stove. A unicorn leaps across the lid and the ashes have grown cold. I look around the room. The grandfather clock has been stopped, the pendulum hangs straight down. Then I hear a click from the barometer. It has fallen a couple of notches and darkness closes in on the windowpanes.

It is snowing. The air hangs still in the room, doors and windows are closed, no draft from the sills. The snow sifts down, straight out of the ceiling's plaster sky. Settles over desk and stove, falls onto chairs and sofa, mantles the clipper's rigging, and hides the jar of tobacco under an overhang. One by one the tiles disappear; the Dutch windmills and ships blanked out. The room can no longer be seen for snowflakes. A bucket of coal turns from black to white.

Slowly the snow fills the room. It freezes my bare head, forms a coronet around my brow, and adorns me with crystal pendants. The walls accumulate drifts that build into towers around me. The sextant on the windowsill has frosted over, the foliage and the leaping stags on the rugs are erased by snow; a moment later and it is up to the wainscoting. Out of the mountains of nothingness it comes swirling, while time slips away.

I turn up my palms and accept everything that falls.